The SKILL *of* OUR HANDS

ALSO BY STEVEN BRUST AND SKYLER WHITE

The Incrementalists

The SKILL *of* OUR HANDS

Steven Brust
and
Skyler White

A TOM DOHERTY ASSOCIATES BOOK
NEW YORK

THE SKILL OF OUR HANDS

A Tor Book
Published by Tom Doherty Associates
175 Fifth Avenue
New York, NY 10010

www.tor-forge.com

Tor® is a registered trademark of Macmillan Publishing Group, LLC.

The Library of Congress Cataloging-in-Publication Data is available upon request.

ISBN 978-0-7653-8288-7 (hardcover)
ISBN 978-1-4668-8973-6 (e-book)

Our books may be purchased in bulk for promotional, educational, or business use. Please contact your local bookseller or the Macmillan Corporate and Premium Sales Department at 1-800-221-7945, extension 5442, or by e-mail at MacmillanSpecialMarkets@macmillan.com.

First Edition: January 2017

Printed in the United States of America

0 9 8 7 6 5 4 3 2 1

This one is for Jeff and Jen

ACKNOWLEDGMENTS

Our thanks for much helpful criticism to Emma Bull, Pamela Dean, Will Shetterly, and Adam Stemple. Also thanks to Andy Krell and the Lawrence, Kansas, Historical Society for help with research, Corwin Brust for website support, Teresa Nielsen Hayden for a thorough line edit, Ed Chapman for a splendid copyedit, Irene Gallo and her whole team for making us look good, and Anita Okoye for saintlike patience. Our thanks, also, to the Incrementalists, especially Ethan, John, Jesse, and Alexander for taking the time to meddle with our book.

The SKILL *of* OUR HANDS

Look, I'm not going to tell you we didn't ask for our power. We did. Each one of us opted in, and risked our lives to do so. I'm not going to tell you we don't deserve it either. Most of us do. But we don't deserve, and I certainly didn't ask for, secrecy—even privacy—around it.

We tried going public in 2014 with The Incrementalists. It was a big step. Or a big gesture, anyway. Big steps that cover no distance are just jumping up and down.

So what am I doing now? Jumping plus waving? Maybe. Maybe I'm meddling with you. Maybe I'm outing my friends—taking their seeded memories of the events of April 2014 and putting them honestly, and in all their complexity, into words to put in your memories.

Why? Three reasons. One, because our collective memory already holds yours, and we mine it for data, and you have a right to know. Two, because we don't always do well. Or good. We get shot for idiot reasons. We manipulate with sex. We hold ourselves apart geographically and emotionally. We out our friends. And Phil, Irina, Kate, and I aren't the only ones who need to be held up for your scrutiny. Even Jimmy got things wrong this time. And three, I believe we all would have done better if you'd been watching. So watch now. After the fact. And then do something about it.

Do what, you ask? If I get this right, you'll know.

—Oskar

Milwaukee, Wisconsin, USA

"It is becoming quite common to under-rate the heroism that saved Kansas for freedom. The cold-blooded historian goes mousing among old letters and he finds that these early heroes were men and women, of like frailties with ourselves. But the glory of heroism is not that angels come down to mingle in the affairs of men, but that common men and women, when the occasion demands, can rise to such sublime heights of heroism and self sacrifice."

I'm going to try not to interrupt much, but Phil insisted I include this quotation from the Rev. Richard Cordley (1895). Sam showed it to Phil after it was all over. I think it's a little overblown, but since it was Phil's only request, I agreed. You'll see why.

—Oskar

ONE

What's Your Involvement?

Phil's first thought when the bullet hit him was, *Oh, come on.*

Some of his deaths had been easy and peaceful—in his sleep, just drifting off. He knew that was true. He was sure that was true. But those were never the ones he remembered. He remembered the times he was in horrible pain from some disease, or had been executed for heresy, or had died violently in some war, or someone had just killed him on the conviction he was "up to something." Meddlework used to be much more dangerous on several levels for several reasons, one of them being how much clumsier he—they all—used to be.

But the thing that got him about so many of his violent deaths was how *casual* they were. Like, whoever killed him didn't think it was a big deal. He wasn't a person, he was just, you know, the guy who was there.

He found that offensive.

He had only rarely, in his two thousand years, had reason to take a life. And even back when society considered life less valuable than it did now, he hadn't committed murder without thought, without soul-searching. And more often than not, he still came to regret it. He had never taken a human life casually.

At least this time there wasn't any pain—there was a thump, like something smacked him with a solid thud in the back of the neck, and he'd thought someone had hit him. But then he heard the report—the distinctive crack of the 9 mm—and then another hit him in the back, and another, and he was disgusted. He tried to turn around to see who'd shot him, but ended up falling onto his face. His last thought before he blacked out was, "This is so not what Ren needs to deal with right now. Fuck."

Then the lights went out for a while.

★   ★   ★

Ren figured yoga class was an hour long for the same reason there were a hundred pages in a self-help book, even if the author's big idea could be restated twice in half that. Twenty minutes of stretching was great, just what her body needed, but hardly worth the trip halfway across Tucson and the cost. The class was just more than she wanted. She'd get a DVD, or go back to her preferred sedentary lifestyle, except this was the best way to meet girls.

Specifically, yoga was the only way to meet Jane Astarte, whom Ren didn't even really want to know. She wanted to know her husband. But she liked Jane. They had smiled at each other last week, after Ren's first class, and she'd made a note of Jane's shoes—red floral Toms. Today, Ren had arrived late. After class, Jane helped her find her oh-so-mysteriously missing moccasin. It had gotten into Jane's cubby somehow, and they had chatted all the way to the parking lot. They said good-bye at Ren's car.

And that's where Ren was still, with her head between her legs, when Jane circled back around and found her.

"Ren?" she called. "Are you okay?"

The parking lot asphalt burned Ren's ass through her yoga pants but she was shivering. She needed to swallow, but there was no spit in her mouth. She closed her eyes and tried to taste root beer, or smell the brackish funk of her quiet, mental Garden, but someone was calling to her.

"Ren? Are you okay?" Jane clambered out of her car, leaving it running, and the bing-binging of its open door made as much sense to Ren as words did.

"I need to go to the hospital," she told Jane. "UMC."

"Okay." Jane threw Ren's yoga bag in the back of her car. She picked up the phone Ren had dropped when she stood up, and put it in Ren's lap. Ren stared at the screen. Six missed calls and a string of texts. The amount of activity had been her first alarm. The dangerous calm of Jimmy's voice mail had been the second: "Ren, I'm booking a flight to Tucson, but I won't leave Paris until I hear from you that I'm not needed in the Garden."

Jane pulled out of the parking lot. "Did you faint?" she asked. "Do you need some water?"

Ren shook her head. She still couldn't swallow, but Jane deserved some explanation, so Ren put her phone on speaker and replayed the voice mail message—the first one. It had come in halfway through yoga, but Ren had heard it only after scrolling through texts from Ramon and Oskar, who said they were on their way, but didn't say why.

"This is Amy Schiller at University Medical Center calling for Renee Mathers," said the voice mail. "I'm sorry, but we have Charles Purcell here in surgery. He had your phone number on an information card in his pocket. You can call me back at this number or just come in through Emergency and ask at the triage desk for Amy or the social worker on call."

"Oh, sweetie!" Jane reached out and squeezed Ren's knee. "Is Charles your . . ."

"We live together."

"I'm so sorry," Jane said.

Some insulated bureaucratic part of Ren's brain noted this fit the meddlework profile she and Phil had been compiling on Jane.

This. It's exactly this kind of casual attitude to profile compilation— the sifting of your e-mails and diaries, doodles and rituals—that demands greater transparency from us. People are encoding more in symbol than ever before, so we see more of you, and must show you more of us.

—Oskar

Ren knew Jane was deeply compassionate, taught high school English, and practiced Wicca. She was also the reason Ren was taking yoga halfway across town.

"I'm sure Charles is going to be fine," Jane said. "UMC is very good."

"Phil," Ren said. "He goes by Phil."

"Okay."

"He—" Ren started, but couldn't. "I always thought I'd know if something happened to him," she said. "But I don't know anything right now."

Jane squeezed her knee again. "You don't have to."

"Thank you," Ren said, wondering whether it was a mole or a zit on Jane's chin. Either way, it helped her look the witch part—that, and the size of her nose. It was too big and out of place in the pretty, suburban rest of her. It was also the least reasonable thing for Ren to be pondering with Phil possibly dead or probably dying and Ramon, Jimmy, and Oskar already on their way to Tucson.

"I'll park and come find you," Jane said, pulling up to the emergency room doors behind a Lexus convertible.

Ren couldn't tell her not to bother, that she'd be fine. "Thank you," she said again. She wasn't fine. She got out of Jane's car and went inside to ask about Chuck Purcell, even though what she needed to know wasn't anything a nurse or social worker could tell her. She needed the Garden, and a mind calm enough to reach it. She needed Phil, and even though she knew it shouldn't matter, she needed him in the body she loved, the lanky, forty-two-year-old body with the one crooked toe and the mustache-cloaked dimples—Chuck's body, the one dying just beyond the information desk.

★　　★　　★

The Garden was a strange place when you were dying.

It was a strange place anyway, what with being a product of your subconscious, blended with everyone else's at the edges. But when you were dying, things got really weird there.

Phil was in his atrium, and then he was outside in the olive grove, and then he was on the other side, where his imaginary Garden bordered Ren's. To him, her Garden appeared as a lush green valley dotted with windmills—put whatever Freudian spin on that you care to.

Phil stood above it looking down, and then he was back in his villa, flat on his back, staring up at a chandelier he didn't have.

Confused? Yeah, so was he.

He fought to control it; to stay in one place. There was something he wanted to do, and he knew it was important even though he couldn't think what it was.

He stood up, tried to walk, and stumbled over a tall vase filled with cattails. He cursed it for being in his way, and remembered that it was the seed of, of something.

That was it; he needed to seed the shooting.

Did he have anything useful to record and share with the others? He had been shot. Not a lot of details in that. He wanted to talk to Ren about it, but she wasn't there. He was alone—where? His Garden, right. Seed the shooting.

He was still alive, anyway. You can't get to the Garden while you're dead, you're just planted in it. Something about that struck him as funny, and he laughed, but then couldn't remember what he was laughing about.

He wondered, if he went into Ren's Garden—her Garden as represented in his Garden—if he'd feel closer to her. He picked up the vase, trying to remember what seed it contained, and wondering if maybe it had something to do with getting shot. He felt like it probably did, but couldn't think why. Why—?

Oh, right.

Why had he been shot?

Now there was a question worth exploring.

Consciousness in the real world and awareness in the Garden don't strictly go together, but neither are they entirely separate. As you fade in the real world, your Garden starts to waver, and at some point you go so far down that you can't hold the image. Phil didn't understand how deep you had to go under to be unable to walk the Garden, but he'd only had a couple of thousand years to look at the question.

Phil considered asking Ray about it. But Ray was dead. Then again, Phil was dead too, or dying. Wait, no, Ray was alive again, spiked into a woman's body this time. He'd come to visit them when—

The light faded, then came back brighter than ever; something to do with dying in the real world, or waking up, or maybe even surgical lights in his semiconscious eyes.

Phil made a pen and paper appear in his hand. He wrote, "This isn't leaving. I'm coming back," and folded it into a paper airplane and sent it to Ren's Garden.

Then he blacked out or went under or died or something.

★   ★   ★

Ren spoke to a redheaded nurse named Jenny who said Charles Purcell had been shot three times and was still in surgery. Ren spoke to a plain-clothes police officer who asked if she knew what a law-abiding guy was doing on the Southside. Ren thought she'd never seen a flattop that bristle-flat, and the cop said he'd never seen a woman who really knew what her man did away from home. He kept asking questions, and she answered them until his phone rang. He answered, listened, and after that, he was done with Ren.

She called Jimmy in Paris, who very gently told her that the fish pool in his Garden was nearly transparent—dangerously more air than water—which told Ren more about the fragility of Phil's condition than any medical information could have. Ren thanked him and closed her eyes. In the blank sky over her Garden mudflats, a tiny puff of cloud un-folded, like corn popping in slow motion, "I'll be back" scrawled across its belly.

It gusted away, but Ren brought it back, and made it swell, darker and fatter, until it thundered and rained, drenching her in him. "We'll call Dr. Freud for a consult on that one," Phil would have said, if he were there.

Which he wasn't.

"Hi." Jane touched Ren's arm. "How're you doing?"

"We were going to get married in the fall," Ren said. "If he dies, I'm telling everyone he got cold feet."

Jane looked at Ren before she laughed, sitting down beside her. "He'll never live it down," she said with a credibly straight face.

"The nurse said it could go either way," Ren said. "I think it's weird that there are only two options for something that important, but you're dead or you're not. Married or not." Ren sagged into the waiting room vinyl.

Jane nodded slowly, hiding a smile. "They're only mostly the same thing," she said.

Ren elbowed her, glad to have been yanked back. "Don't feel like you need to stay with me, Jane."

"It's fine," she said. "I wasn't really ready to go home anyway."

"Oh? Too quiet?" Ren probed.

"Too small. My husband and I both teach high school. Every summer our house shrinks."

"What do you teach?"

"English."

"And your husband?"

"History. Civics."

"At the same school?"

Jane shook her head with a hint of a blush. "No. I'm at Howenstine, just around the corner. He's at Southside."

"Is that how you met?" Ren asked, and just like that, she was working again, gathering the information she'd started taking yoga to try and collect. She focused on each moment, paying close attention to the way Jane covered her mouth with her hand when she laughed, and to what made her sit forward in the uncomfortable chair. Ren wished she'd prepared even one of Jane's switches before class—maybe the cedar whiff of her best friend's deep-closet clubhouse—to trigger trust so Jane would open up about her husband. "It must be tough to be young liberal teachers in a state that's still trying to get anti-evolution legislation on the books," she guessed.

Jane sat back and crossed her leg away from Ren. "It is hard," she said.

Ren noted the withdrawal. She would need to sidle up to politics more subtly next time.

Every time.

—O

"You have to learn to separate personal and professional." Jane made a guillotine of her pinky finger against her open palm. Her voice had the tightness of a mother saying to be a big girl and not cry. "But what are we doing talking about me when you're the one with a *Major Life Event* unfolding right now?" she asked Ren.

"We're keeping me from cycling obsessively through the text, mail, and voice apps on my phone, or through worse things in my head," Ren said, mentally filing Jane's chopped separation of person and politics to seed later when she got back to her Garden. "Without you, I'd be sitting here trying to conjure a smiling surgeon through that door or attempting to keep Phil's heart beating with the sheer force of my will."

Ren knew Jane was a Wiccan, but right now, if Jane told her about creating her own reality, Ren was going to have trouble forgiving her enough to do good meddlework. "Do you believe we can do that?" she asked anyway.

"You mean do I think there's anything you can do from here to help Phil in there?"

Ren didn't trust her voice; she nodded.

"No," Jane said.

"Me either."

"You could pray."

Ren untwisted her hands and looked at Jane. "It wouldn't help."

"Not him," Jane agreed. "Maybe you."

"He helps me."

"I know." Jane squeezed Ren's knee, and didn't tell her that things work out in the end, or that everything happens for a reason.

Ren closed her eyes, and let it rain.

TWO

Powerfully Reasoned and Passionate

It's not like dying would be the end of the world or anything. Phil had died before. How many times? Um. Many. It was hard to think.

He made a stuffed chair appear in his peristylium, and he sat there, trying to focus, trying to figure out what to do. There was a chair opposite him, and he wasn't sure how it got there. There was someone in it, and it took him a moment to realize that it was real—as real as things get in the Garden. He knew—though he couldn't remember exactly how he knew—that Oskar could break into his Garden and actually be there.

Sorry for the intrusion, but it's a confusing concept, and Phil was confused here, so it has to be hard for you to make sense of it. The short version is this: the Garden is a mental state. We create it collectively—a shared hallucination that brains make, but only minds can access. The Garden's reality is distributed through all our brains, but each mind navigates it with an individual map—a unique analogy. No brain, no mind, no metaphor. That's how we had known Celeste wasn't dead, even after Phil had spiked her stub into Ren—we could still get into her Garden. Now we can't. Think about it like this: if the Garden were a real house, instead of a collective memory palace, it would be as if we had recently found a way to open each other's private bedroom doors. So I was on a plane, and I was there, in Phil's personal section of our shared mental construct, and able to talk to him. But like I said, it was something we'd only recently learned, and Phil's been around for two thousand years, so I guess his poor, befuddled, dying brain was having trouble grasping it. I hope the explanation helps. It's important later.

—*Oskar*

So, Phil decided, that meant that maybe Oskar was real—using the relatively loose definition of "real" that applied in the Garden. He decided to test it. "Hello, Oskar."

"Hey, Phil. I just heard. Other than dying, how are you?"

"Fair enough. Any idea how things are with my body?"

"Sorry, no. I'm on a plane on the way to Tucson. You're almost certainly in surgery. Be grateful you can't feel it."

"How are things going in Milwaukee?"

"You've been reading the boards."

"I know. I was just asking to irritate you."

"I've been thinking about giving up and going back to Munich. Your unions in this country aren't significantly better than no unions at all."

"Wasn't like that forty years ago."

"I know."

Oskar was trying to sound casual, and trying to look relaxed in his big stuffed chair, but tension, even fear, radiated from him.

"Do you know why you were shot? Was it meddlework?"

"I don't know. I think so."

"What were you working on?"

Phil gestured toward the atrium. "There's a vase in there, with cattails in it. The seed is there."

"Seed of?"

"I don't remember."

Oskar really did look worried. "I'll check. Don't go anywhere."

Phil chuckled, then forgot what he was chuckling about, then remembered. Dying was really annoying. Maybe not as annoying as having someone hit a two-outer that costs you all the chips you've built up for the last six hours, but almost.

Oskar came back after Phil had forgotten he was there, and Phil wasn't sure how long he'd been gone in real or subjective time. Oskar sat down.

"You fucking idiot," he said kindly.

★   ★   ★

What do you do when there's nothing you can do? When something agonizingly important to you is entirely beyond your ability to control or even affect? When all your future joy is in someone else's hands, or fate's, or floating free on the winds of "shit happens"? Maybe it was always the case, and choice and planning were illusions that only clothed Ren's helplessness like Eve's itchy fig leaf. She had no idea. Maybe all her suffering came from not accepting things as they were, from her deluded attempt to force her will on an indifferent universe, to demand that reality be different, better—just a little bit. "Fuck it," she said.

"Okay." Jane was good at acceptance.

"I know there's nothing I can do to make things go the way I want them to in there, and I don't know how to pray without it feeling like a letter to Santa."

Jane nodded and didn't offer to teach her.

Grateful, Ren went on, "But I do know how to do something else, something that might actually help Phil. It's kind of like meditating. Or taking a nap."

"Do you want to go to the chapel where it's quiet?" Jane asked. "I can stay here and call you if anyone comes out with news."

"No, it's okay. We can stay here, I just wanted you to know I was going."

Ren closed her eyes and felt the air moving over the sensitive skin at the edge of her nostrils. For a minute, she just felt that, concentrating on her body in the moment, in her slightly clammy yoga top on the creaky plastic waiting room chair.

She tasted brown and fizzy, mostly sweet, but with a little bite on the back of the tongue—root beer—the first of her two body-anchored triggers that opened her Garden. She always came into it from away and above, gliding like a kite—usually at a gradual, slender angle, with the occasional tight spiral. She was sloping gently when a weird blade of fire slashed her trajectory, and she fell.

The soupy sponge of her Garden mud absorbed the impact, but the plunge frightened Ren. Things didn't just appear in her Garden—certainly not flaming things—and she lay still, watching the radiating waves diminish in size. When she sat up, mud clung to her hair and dripped from her fingers, but that was how memories worked for her. Ren's memories weren't discrete things neatly correlated one-to-one, but a morass she could filter and sieve. But that wasn't helpful right now. Right now what Ren wanted was a way to reach Phil—not his memories or his Garden—but Phil as the surgeons in the next room knew him, the meat and teeth of him.

Three years ago, Phil had given Ren a symbolic suitcase. In it, he had packed all his switches—every emotion-associated smell or memory-linked taste, the power to trigger any of a lexicon of emotions in him. If she had kept it, maybe Ren could have cooked up a "stay alive" combo for him now, but she had let it compost into her Garden mud. She never wanted to meddle with him like Celeste had.

Ren scooped up a handful of Garden, weighed it on her palm. She remembered her glimpse of Phil as a union man, with his wife-made apron and stone-tasting kiss, and knew he would stand and fight if he could. He didn't need her to stoke his will. He'd come back to her if he could. But what if he couldn't? What if Phil left?

Ren squeezed her hand into a goopy fist, and thought about poker, the Civil War, and Celeste. But Phil was a person who chose toward rather than against. Ren thought about Susi, their sweet dog, and the new house they were finally all moved into. She thought about their sex, and Phil's unshakeable optimism, and the meddlework they were involved in together, but couldn't think what she might make out of mud that would keep him or return him to life. Not something in his own image like God or Prometheus.

Something inevitable.

Ren imagined a square around her feet with a matching empty one next to it for Phil. Beneath them, she made a new square twice their size, and next to all three, another as big as the one-alone plus the one-alone, plus the two they made together. She added the new square standing on the base of all that had come before it, and she started walking diagonally, one box after the next, in an urgent, infinite, opening logarithmic spiral.

★   ★   ★

Several things all happened at once, or so close to at once that they seemed simultaneous to Oskar. What looked like a bolt of fire streaked across the length of Phil's villa, starting in the atrium and continuing through to where Phil sat. Phil reached for it and caught it, two-handed. A look of bewilderment crossed his features and he shook his head. He stared at whatever was in his hands. It blurred, and they were empty, useless. But it changed form again, and Phil tossed it to Oskar.

"Tell Ren," Phil said, and his Garden dissolved.

Probably because of how he'd entered, Oskar found himself, instead of back in the real world, in his own Garden, on the Rue Victor near Rue des Noyers. The Seine stank of human waste and dead animals and rotting vegetables, and he made a strong wind come up and blow the stench away.

> *It's always the first thing I do, and I do it without thinking about it. It's harder than I expected not to annotate my own seeds. I'll try to show more restraint.*
>
> *—O*

The first thing he saw, right at his feet, was an old-fashioned stylus just lying on the road; he didn't need to touch it in order to recognize Phil's stub. So Phil was really dead. Well, all right, then.

> *Sorry, but this bears explaining. When one of us dies, our memories and personality go into stub, inactive and inert (as far as we know), until a Second is found and recruited. We're always on the*

lookout for potential Seconds, but it's a subtle operation. A person who'd be a great Second for Phil wouldn't necessarily be a good fit for me, so it usually takes us a few months.

—O

Oskar took a long, slow breath, and gripped the thing Phil had thrown him too tightly before it occurred to him to look at it.

He didn't know what Phil had tossed, but in Oskar's hand, it manifested as a wicked-looking dagger of the type once called an Arkansas Toothpick in what was then still the New World. It was an awfully violent image for Phil, and not the kind of shape Oskar's thoughts usually took either. He played with the knife for a bit, wondering what strange combination of their identities had produced it. Then he figured out how to use it.

"Asshole," he muttered, convinced that Phil had done it on purpose. Oskar cut his palm. It hurt, and the memories entered him.

The knife was an index—a pointer to all the memories Phil had seeded related to the same meddlework as the vase in his atrium: an effort to get the Arizona immigration law overturned.

Idiot, as well as asshole.

Yeah, let's appeal to the wolves to be kinder, gentler wolves. That always works out well. But then, Phil must have hit a nerve somewhere, somehow, because someone had killed him for it. Phil's failure was proof of his success. Phil would have made a sarcastic comment about it being dialectical, as if he had a clue what that meant.

Oskar let 1790 Paris go back to where it came from and opened his eyes. He checked his watch. They were still forty-five minutes out from Tucson. He'd meddled his way into first class because he didn't fit in coach, and to be closer to the door. When they landed, he'd meddle his way into the fastest transportation he could find and, with luck, be at the hospital in under ninety minutes. He opened up the *Milwaukee Journal Sentinel* and wondered if World War III would break out in Ukraine before he arrived in Tucson, or if the diplomats would postpone it a little longer. He scowled and thought of all the problems he could be working on if that idiot Phil hadn't gotten himself shot. Then he tried to put it out of his head. It was time to concentrate on what he needed to do, not what he couldn't do.

Ninety minutes. It was going to be a long, long ninety minutes for Ren whether or not she knew Phil was already in stub.

★ ★ ★

Ren followed Mike from the trauma center through a tiled labyrinth to a tidy consultation room where she waited again, politely. It seemed important to behave, as if by doing so she could earn good news.

"Renee Mathers?" There were two of them—the surgeon and another woman.

Ren stood. They sat. For a second Ren thought maybe, if she didn't sit back down, they'd be afraid she might faint and not tell her, and it wouldn't be true.

"I'm Renee," she said and sat. Eye-level with her, Ren thought the surgeon's elegant, sloped, kohl-lined eyes seemed caught between the traces of gold shimmer above, and the purple shadow of exhaustion below.

"I'm Doctor Henedi."

She was the pivot Ren's life would turn on, and Ren knew she'd never see her again.

"I'm sorry," the doctor said. "We did everything we could."

But her "sorry" had turned a vacuum cleaner on that roared in Ren's ears, and set an icy suction under her scalp and against the soles of her feet.

"The damage was too severe. We couldn't control the bleeding. He went into cardiac arrest and we couldn't revive him."

The empty, strategically placed trash can was for Ren to vomit in, but she was scoured out.

"We did everything we could."

Ren didn't know where the sound came from. Voids don't sob.

"Tina is here to help you, but I can answer any questions about the surgery for you before I go."

Or maybe the universe was full of howling, with no air to carry the sound—like Phil now—a wave without water.

"Do you have any questions?"

"No," Ren told the doctor. "Thank you."

29

*   *   *

Jimmy calculated that if British Airways flight 333 left Paris at 9:00 A.M., and he changed planes in London, and again in Dallas, that by the time he landed in Tucson, nearly a full day would have elapsed—and he'd arrive exhausted. He considered it for less than half a minute before having his personal assistant, Etienne, call his travel agent to arrange a charter.

Financially, with the amount of travel he did, he knew he should long ago have just bought shares in a damned jet, but he couldn't bring himself to do it. He'd grown accustomed to indulging himself up to a point, now that he could afford it, but there were some boundaries he just couldn't cross. He bought a new BMW every year, but wouldn't buy a Bentley. He treated himself to vacations in Marseille when he could get away, staying at Le Petit Nice Passedat, but he wouldn't buy a home there. He ate in the best restaurants in Paris, but wouldn't hire a private cook. He had a comfortable house in Samois-sur-Seine, but not a mansion. He also knew that these distinctions made no sense, but he didn't care.

Etienne, *le joli garçon qui ne doit pas être touché*, confirmed when the limousine would arrive, hung up, and began helping Jimmy pack. Etienne knew when Jimmy didn't feel like talking.

Phil was in stub.

Phil was always uncomfortable around Jimmy's wealth—a reflection of Jimmy's own discomfort. Oddly, the only one in Salt who wasn't uncomfortable, was Oskar.

Accidental wealth is merely an asset for the group's work, which I feel not the least qualm in calling upon. It's also a massive inconvenience if you're going to be responsible about it. If Jimmy uses some of it to indulge his pleasures, that's just compensation for the time and energy it demands. Better him than me.

—O

Phil always seemed a little hesitant, a little uncertain, as if he were imposing; which made Jimmy uncomfortable too. On reflection, though,

Phil spent much of his time unsure, hesitant, second-guessing himself. Which made it all the more surprising when he would suddenly commit himself to something, throw himself into it without looking back, *push in all his chips,* as he would say. As he had, most recently, thrown himself into life with Ren.

Poor Ren. Jimmy had a pretty good idea how much this was tearing her up. Even if she were as certain as he was that Phil's personality would emerge dominant in his next Second, it had to be brutal for her. She'd told Jimmy once before that she needed Phil to stay, not just come back. There were some occasions where Jimmy knew he could help, and this was one. His presence would not ease Ren's pain or fear; he wouldn't presume to try. But he would weep and wait with her.

A limousine to Charles De Gaulle Airport, a chartered flight: Etienne was arranging the details.

Jimmy remembered Violette, his first great love, and how much it had hurt when she'd been taken from him. He had vowed never to love again outside of the group—a vow that had lasted almost thirty years, until he'd met Jacque.

But Jimmy could no more control his love than any of his other passions.

No more than Ren could help feeling her pain.

Jimmy had a long flight ahead of him, and he didn't know what he would find when he got there, but it wouldn't be pleasant.

These memories of Phil's—or, as he was then known, Carter—from the nineteenth century are seeds within seeds (that will make more sense later). I'd omit them entirely, but they're part of the story, and without them you might miss my point. I can't seem to get them out of first person though, leaving me no choice but to let Carter speak for himself.

—Oskar

We had agreed to meet in the library of Northwestern University at Chicago, where she was doing some research. Outside it was bitter cold, and wet, and refuse from the New Year's celebration still mixed with the mud and the snow, but inside it was warm and pleasant. She was easy enough to identify from Oskar's description, and because she was the only woman there. I took off my hat and approached her. She stood and said, "Mr. Carter?"

I nodded. "Just Carter. You must be Miss Voight."

"Susan, please," she said, and shook my hand like a man. I must have looked a little startled at the offer of familiarity, because she said,

"As a courtesy to your friend Oskar, who has never even told me his patro-nymic. I think it's a small form of rebellion for him."

It's more complicated than that, but I don't want to go into it.

—O

I nodded and suppressed a smile.

"Have you found accommodations?" Her British accent was unmis-takable, but some of its precision had been worn away by her stay in America.

"Yes," I said. "The Briggs House. There are finer hotels here than I'd thought there would be. I imagine in the East we think of the West as more universally rustic than it is."

"But not more muddy," she said with a quirk of her lips and a glance at my boots. "Please sit."

I did, matching her body language and expression. She relaxed a little.

"I admire your work," I told her. "I've been reading your articles. Powerfully reasoned and passionate."

She nodded. "What is your involvement?"

"Less than yours. My work often brings me south of Mason-Dixon, especially to New Orleans. I do what I can to convince the overseers to be a bit less brutal. When I'm in the north, I interfere with the slave-catchers."

She shook her head. "As long as the institution itself survives, such measures are quite nearly pointless."

"I agree," I said. I was a lot more effective in my meddling than she had any way of knowing, but she was still right. "The question is, can we succeed?"

"In ending slavery? Not peacefully, I'm afraid. The slave power won't surrender without a fight."

"So, you're gathering armies? If there's to be violence—"

"No."

"What then?"

"You've read my articles." She reminded me a little of Oskar: always convinced that Great Events were just around the corner, in spite of all evidence to the contrary. Yet that comparison somehow made me like her.

"You think John Fremont has a chance?" I asked.

"I don't know. But he's worth supporting. He's more easily elected than Seward or Chase, and wresting control of the Federal Government from the slave power is the next step."

I nodded. Oskar had convinced me of that much, anyway. "Free soil, free labor, free men, Fremont. If he wins the nomination, it'll make a good campaign slogan."

"You left out 'free speech.' In the deep south, and in Kansas, it is illegal to suggest human beings ought not to be chattel. They can imprison you for saying it."

"If he's elected, they'll never let him take office."

"If they try to stop him, they'll rouse the whole North. Even more if they attempt to secede."

I had severe doubts about the North's willingness to be roused—too many of them were happy and satisfied. There had been no '48 on this side of the ocean because we Yankees didn't go in for that sort of thing. "The South will never secede," I said. "They'll just threaten until the North caves in again."

"Mr. Carter, in your letter, you said you wanted my advice. About what?"

"Where?"

Her brows came together. "Where what?"

"Where can I do the most good?"

She hesitated. I could see what she saw: a frail-looking old man who might not survive anything rigorous. Then she almost nodded to herself, and apparently decided that I had to make that decision myself. "Kansas," she said.

"I was afraid you'd say that."

"It isn't merely Kansas by itself, and whether it's free soil. Right now the fight for Kansas is the key to everything else. We can lose the battle and win the war, or win the battle and lose the war. Right there, in Kansas."

"Which means how we fight is as important as the result?"

"More important."

"All right then, I'll go."

"Good. The thing to remember is that it may take guns to protect yourselves, but guns aren't how we need to win this. We need to win the heart of the North."

"I know."

"Do you think you can convince the settlers of that?"

"We'll see," I said. "I can be very convincing."

THREE

What Brings You to Town?

At a desk in the Toronto Public Library, Research and Reference Division, Takamatsu Toshitsugu stopped reading the Incrementalists forum, controlled his breathing, and let calm wash over him.

Phil was in stub.

It wasn't the first time Phil had died, nor was it likely to be the last. But effectively, for now, there was no Phil. The Incrementalists were an unevenly weighted three-dimensional pendulum with no pivot. *We have halted, our own weight straining against us.*

He felt himself frowning. *Why did I just think that?*

What was happening now that made Phil's death especially troublesome for the group? There must be something, because when such thoughts formed in his head, Takamatsu had learned to trust them. So what was it? What pattern had his subconscious mind detected?

Takamatsu considered what he knew.

There were many things the Incrementalists didn't understand about the process of death, stub, and Second, but they knew this much: while in stub, there is no "you." You exist as potential. Not a person, not a being, but something that could become one. Sometimes it could feel like you had consciousness in stub, but that's because the process of entering stub—dying—and the process of coming out of stub—spiking—bring with them floods of disorganized memories. It is as if you are incapable of dreaming, but your thoughts before falling asleep and just upon waking combine to convince you you have dreamed.

Takamatsu reconsidered. Yes, Celeste had shaded, but she had still managed to secrete some of her memories away from Ren, who had gotten her stub. Takamatsu did not believe any remnant of Celeste—not her pattern nor agenda nor even her metaphorical thread—remained in the Garden as a threat to Phil, his stub, or the larger organization. Only perhaps her absolute conviction had any power to outlive her in their collective, distributed imagination.

Takamatsu turned his attention to what he did not know.

Jimmy would be flying to the support of Ren as quickly as he could, Takamatsu was certain. But Oskar? Irina? Ramon? He didn't know. And how had Phil died, for that matter? He was young and in good health. Something must have happened.

Ren was the key. An Incrementalist for only three years, one of their newest in love with their oldest, untested but central. Axial, but thought herself a tangent. She could crumble and trigger a collapse, or she could bear up under the strain and become something new, a pivot, and that was where a touch—gentle, embrocating—might be needed.

Takamatsu prepared to enter his Garden to look for patterns.

★　　★　　★

Oskar made it to the hospital in under ninety minutes, no meddling re quired until he reached the ER waiting room.

He considered how many of the dozen or so people waiting there would be bankrupt in a year because of what happened today, then he mentally shook his head. Not now. Ren wasn't in the waiting room, and the nurse at the triage desk had the withdrawn look that indicated someone hard to meddle with without switches. Oskar could be very convincing, but it would take more time than he wanted to spend to get the nurse to tell him where Ren was.

He studied the people waiting again. One, an attractive, dark-haired soccer mom, was reading from her phone. Her hands were still and relaxed, and she was absorbed in her reading, so it wasn't her children, her parents, or a sibling she was waiting for; and if it was her husband they should have split up years ago. There was a little tension in her back, so it was actually someone she cared about, and it was something serious, a big "yes" or "no" she was waiting for. And when she looked up, her eyes went toward the doors that obviously went toward the consultation rooms. Clearly, she wasn't with a patient, she was with someone who was with a patient.

Oskar approached her. "Pardon me," he said. "I'm looking for Renee Mathers. Do you know her?"

The woman jumped a little, nodded, then frowned. "How did you know?"

"I was going to ask everyone in the room; just got lucky and asked you first."

"Some guy came and got her about twenty minutes ago."

"Has he come back out?"

"I think so. I wasn't watching closely. I don't really know her. We just met—"

"Thank you."

Oskar ducked into his Garden long enough to check the hospital architecture and learn that the consulting rooms were labeled by number rather than letter—about ten seconds. Then he went up to the triage nurse, pitched his low voice lower, added a light overlay of boredom, and said, "Mathers, Renee. Consulting two. Grief Counseling. Buzz me in."

The nurse gave him a quick glance, then did.

Oskar found Ren in Consulting three. She looked at him, her freckles too stark against her normally dark skin. She stood up, and he put his arms around her. "We'll get him back," he said. "I promise, we'll get him back."

"You can't know that," she said into his shirt.

"I know," he said. "As sure as I've ever known anything."

Ren's shoulders shook as she cried.

★   ★   ★

Irina pulled into the parking lot on the far side of Sir Vezas's Taco Garage and popped the Miata's trunk. From the tackle box labeled FACE AND HAIR she selected an iridescent butterfly clip, and from the SMELLS

AND TASTES box she took a piece of blue Juicy Fruit gum and popped it into her mouth. She chewed it, working the taste of Jack Harris's first girlfriend's kisses into her mouth, wishing she knew why the assistant police chief had summoned her. His texts had been urgent but vague. He needed to see her. He had bad news.

Irina chewed the Juicy Fruit and fretted over whether to smell like Bisquick or sweat. She had no way of knowing whether Jack would need maternal comfort or simple friendship. Either way, he was a highly trained police detective, adroit as any Incrementalist at reading people, and Irina knew she was visibly nervous. It was okay, she reminded herself, she had good reason to be. She was worried about him.

She was worried about what his bad news was too—it could be very bad. But even that worry would be okay for Jack to notice. What he mustn't pick up on was any indication that Irina was recording it. She adjusted the butterfly, its cylindrical body battery-warm and heavy, and decided against an olfactory switch. She opened another button on her blouse instead. Breasts were marvelously multipurpose.

On the other side of the restaurant, beyond the Dumpster, Jack Harris was waiting for her in the stingy shade of a single scrubby tree. "Hi yo, Kimo Sabe!" he greeted her without taking his bandy shoulders or his booted foot off the trunk he leaned against.

Irina gave the Juicy Fruit a final chomp, and swallowed the gum. "Hi yo, Silver!" she responded, leaning in to kiss the blue taste of innocence onto his lips.

Assistant Police Chief Harris had almost no upper lip and hair that had retreated dramatically and in a uniform line across the top of his head, leaving him with a shining knife blade of close-cropped silver haloing his elongating forehead. He rarely lied, never swore, and he only cheated on his wife to spare her their badly matched libidos. He gripped Irina's hips in squat, capable hands and pulled her closer. "Thanks for coming all the way out here, baby." He contracted his eyebrows into a deliberate frown, but displeasure didn't reach as far as his eyes. Something strange was going on.

"Anything for you." Irina hadn't intended to care for this blunt man with his clean hands and monochrome morality. But by the time she knew enough about anyone to meddle well, she was almost half in love. Jack Harris was a cop, and a brutal one, and exposing him would break her heart, and she would have to let it be broken. "What's the bad news?" she asked.

Jack chuckled and kissed her Juicy Fruit mouth. He kissed her slowly, without artifice or nuance, but Irina couldn't relax. "What happened, Jack?"

Jack's crooked grin split his face. "Aw, I was just having a little fun with you. There's nothing wrong. Matter of fact, today's turned out top shelf."

"Yeah?" Adrenaline surged through Irina's body, but she forced herself to stay pliant in the chief's strong hand, her hair clip close to his chin. "Are you going to tell me about it now since I've come all the way out here?" Irina slid her hands under Jack's coat, and around his waist where he sagged and pooched a little over his belt. She loved the places his skin felt thin where the muscle under it had cured and hardened from meat into wood, deliciously tested and enduring, but something kept her from reaching his hard, bare shoulders under his shirt. Irina realized what she'd touched and recoiled several steps. "Jack!"

He shrugged. "I'm here with the guys. I couldn't take my coat and holster off just to go out for a smoke." He held out his hands to her again. "Come here."

Irina shook her head, remembering her old .38 in Phil's hand, the impact and cold pain of being shot. Guns were a switch for her now. Go figure.

"Ah, come on, my wild Indian," he coaxed. "I'll tell you my news."

Vanessa Surya, whose body Irina had gotten after Phil shot her, had been born in Jakarta, but Jack wasn't the sort to know Indian from Indonesian. His crooked grin crinkled one cheek. "They got him."

Irina froze. "Who? Who got who?"

"That guy I've been telling you about, the one making trouble for my rangers, someone shot him."

Irina managed to morph the starting sound of Phil's name into a low "Fuck."

"Yup." Jack beamed. "Chopped the head clean off that damn snake."

"Is he . . ."

"Don't know yet. They've got him at UMC." Jack shrugged his hard shoulders. "I say let him die. I would have shot him myself, if I'd got the chance."

"You could have done that? Looked an innocent man in the eyes and pulled the trigger?"

"For the good of my country? Hell yeah, I could have. And this guy wasn't innocent, not by a long sight. He's been stirring up all kinds of shit. I was saving it for a secret, but we had a raid planned for Sunday." Jack grinned and pulled Irina against him. "I promised you baby, I always get my man. And weren't you the one always telling me about sins of omission and all that?"

"I was talking about having him arrested." Irina reeled with shock and not wanting to touch him. "Do you know who shot him?"

The sapphire barrel of Jack's blue eyes contracted around their pupils' black bore. "Probably a rival vigilante group," he said. His eyes dropped to Irina's chest. "One of Tanton's guys, or Taylor's," he told her breasts. "That's how it goes. Some liberal dropping off water in the desert, running a frickin' underground railroad, slashing the tires of enforcement vehicles. Another crazy shoots him. I say good riddance." Irina nodded. The only flicker of guilt Irina had seen came when Jack had named his suspects. "Arrest anyone yet?" she asked.

"Nah."

"Are you going to?"

"Come here." Jack's thin lips brushed Irina's throat like spider feet. "God, you smell good enough to eat. We'll run a watered-down version of our sting op on Sunday just to mop up."

"But not to catch whoever shot Ph— Fucking Snake Head Guy."

Jack grunted and his lips crawled up Irina's neck. She turned her mouth to his, wishing she'd gone with music instead of kissing. Irina always went with touch. It was more effective than any of the senses except maybe smell, and it cut both ways. It made it seem fairer, less manipulative, somehow, to let the people she worked on work on her.

Still, right at the moment, Irina wished to God she had gone with music. Toy Caldwell wailing "Can't You See" would make her assistant police chief wistful as easily as Juicy Fruit kisses would. Jack wasn't a man to stand for anything less than a girl's full attention, but it was Ren, who'd need food for the hordes descending to help her, that Irina kept thinking about. But there was so much Irina needed to take care of. She'd need to meddle Menzie into breaking the story on his blog soon enough to cancel Jack's mop-up raid, which meant picking a place to meet him and hiring a couple of extras. And she had to find a way to warn the kids and immigrants who comprised the sinuous vertebrae of Phil's subversive snake.

Beheaded.

The thought of Phil dead sent a shudder through Irina, and Jack chuckled, flattering himself. Phil was going to be so pissed about this. Not to mention Oskar. Phil's face materialized before Irina's closed eyes as he'd looked the last time she'd seen him—angry and cold and pointing a gun right at her. It didn't seem possible he could be dead.

"You're sure they shot the right guy?" Irina asked her chief. "Your guy?"

"Absolutely. Chuck Purcell, the meddling son of a bitch."

★   ★   ★

Kate was late to pick up the kids again, darn it all, and traffic wasn't co-operating. It was ten minutes from her house to the school if she timed the lights right. Half hour should have been plenty of time to just pop onto the forum and see why Oskar needed her to send a scrip for sleeping pills in to Ren's pharmacy, but gracious, what a mess!

Phil was dead and in stub in the Garden. It wasn't like they didn't know what to do about that, but everyone was posting and leaving comments, even the folk with nothing to say. Well, Phil was a pivot at the best of times, which these weren't. He was also the oldest and the most incremental of them all. Some might argue Celeste had been even more incremental; and sure, if she could have, she would have stopped them meddling entirely just on principle, but wasn't that the definition of an extremist? It was the opposite of Oskar, anyway, and he was radical as surely as Kate was late, and Kate was late before she left the house.

Besides, when Celeste died, and Phil spiked her into Ren, her stub had gone AWOL and hidden or unlooped or whatever. Ren had gotten some of it, enough to become an Incrementalist anyway, and Oskar and Phil and the rest of Salt with their "no real power" and their secrets had turned the rest into a pattern or a book or something. Pretty dang radical, if you wanted Kate's opinion. Not that anyone did.

Which was fine. She didn't actually have much of an opinion on most of what the rest of them got so worked up about. But now Phil was dead and in the Garden, and everyone else was on the forum handing out opinions like condoms at a Pride parade. Even Ramon sounded emotional, if you could imagine. He and Jimmy both wrote long posts, Ramon giving background, Jimmy offering perspective. Oskar posted that he was in the Garden when Phil died, and was going to Tucson to support Ren. Ren, bless her, hadn't written or seeded a thing. She was more like Kate that way, didn't like to get herself so involved with the whole group dynamic. Well, she was in it now for sure and certain with Phil dead, poor dear.

Kate called Legal One as she drove, but it went straight to his voice mail, and there was no point in calling Homewrecker. He was four hundred miles away with his mother and couldn't have picked up the kids anyway because he was grieving, even if he didn't know it yet. Kate wasn't sure he knew his mom was dying. But he'd driven the six hours to see her when Kate had told him to.

By the time she pulled into the school parking lot, Kate was happy to get out of the car and hug the kids. They were not quite two years apart, and before anyone could make the joke about a doctor not knowing how that happened, Kate would tell them she did know. She'd done it on purpose, thank you, because she also knew what kids do to a woman's body and career, and she wanted that acute, not chronic.

And they were cute.

They were cute and messy and funny and selfish as hell. Like kids should be.

Kate hugged them both and bundled them into the minivan. She sang along with them to the *Frozen* soundtrack the whole way to Chuck E. Cheese, where she gave them bad pizza and a plastic cupful of tokens. They dove into the ball pit, and Kate put on her tinted glasses, opened the latest edition of *The Lancet,* and double-checked it was right side up. She closed her eyes to have a good, long look through Oskar's.

I didn't know until I started collecting seeds for this narrative that Kate had been grazing mine so thoroughly. It surprised me. Like she says, Kate doesn't usually get involved in issues not related to children's health, but she had more to do with how things finally played out for Ren and Phil, and thus for the entire organization (not to mention Matsu) than almost anyone else.

—Oskar

JUNE, 1856

"MY NAME IS CARTER. WHAT HAPPENED TO ME?"

I admit to being a little tickled at having traveled through the South taking money over a card table from slave-owners to finance a trip to Kansas so I could work for abolition. Having the money helped a great deal; I was able to supply myself well for the trip, even adding a Sharp's carbine and a shotgun in case of the worst. I collected a good supply of clothing, including two pairs of over-alls, winter gear, a nice suit for Sundays, and plenty of socks and drawers. I had a sack of flour, a sack of dried beans, jerky, sugar, and tobacco as well as top-grade shovels, rakes, hammers, saws, and a hoe, all purchased from Elwood Adams Hardware. I splurged to the extent of $400, plus more for shipping, for a house from Kansas and Nebraska Portable Cottages that would be waiting for me, complete if not assembled, when I arrived at Lawrence. When I'd finished my purchases, I still had more money than I wanted to be carrying around, so I sent some to the Emigrant Aid Company in Massachusetts, imagining the look on some of the faces of some of my card-playing opponents if they knew.

I spent a good deal of time with maps of Nebraska, Iowa, Missouri, and Kansas, and determined to go through Nebraska. I arranged for hotel stays where I could, and for rail and steamboat travel when possible, which turned out to be a lot more of the journey than I'd have thought.

And then I started hearing horror stories about the winter, and I deci-ded someone who'd been gallivanting through the deep South lately had no business in Kansas in February. I resolved to wait for spring or sum-mer. That's how I missed the raid on Lawrence.

FOUR

Complete If Not Assembled

Ren started to pull away but Oskar only held her closer. "What do we need to do before we leave?" he asked over her head.

"Renee may need to speak with the police again." Tina's chair scraped back from her desk.

"I'll do that," Oskar said. "Phil will be cremated—we called him Phil."

"I gathered. His middle name, I guess?"

"Probably." Oskar shifted Ren into his left arm. "We'll make funeral arrangements privately. Phil would have signed an organ donor card, so whatever needs to happen there . . ." Oskar extracted a piece of paper from his back pocket, and the muscles in his chest flexed against Ren's cheek as he held his arm extended. "Here's everything I think you'll need."

Incrementalists were all so organized, so experienced with death. They all had wills, info cards, and contact lists in a shared directory on the website. Ren did too, but she'd never felt less like one of the tribe. It was all new to her. Oskar finished with Tina and deposited Ren at a bathroom door.

"I made a Fibonacci spiral for Phil in my Garden," she told Oskar. "It was the only thing I could think of to reel him back."

"Go wash your face," he said.

"It didn't work."

"Ren." Oskar bent to her eyes like a man to a gun sight. His hands on her arms were the first thing Ren had felt since the parking lot asphalt. "We'll get him back," he said.

"I know." Ren nodded. "We will. Our Phil. But I won't. Not mine."

"Bodies don't matter." Oskar straightened. "What's the name of the woman in the waiting room?"

"Jane."

"Use the bathroom. Don't look in the mirror."

Ren wondered how bad she must look. She hadn't worn any makeup to yoga or gelled her short hair, but Oskar wasn't the type to notice. Still, she went obediently into a stall and sat on the toilet. Her feet looked distant and strange against the clinical tile. How could she own teal moccasins? Those weren't the shoes of a widow. She just couldn't see herself wearing them. Her feet were bad mirrors, and Oskar had said not to look. Ren stood up and blew her nose. At the sink, she cupped cold water to her face, and dried it with brown paper towels that melted like lunch bags in her hands.

Oskar had retrieved Jane from the waiting room, and was consulting with her outside the bathroom door. Jane startled and put some space between their bodies when Ren approached. Oskar stayed where he was, one shoulder leaning against the hallway wall, his blond head bending over Jane's. He opened one arm and drew Ren against his side.

Jane reached out and squeezed Ren's wrist. "How are you doing?" she asked.

"I don't know," Ren said. She was made of prickling cold and hollow bones, mummified in ice, but wide awake, blinking through the miles of white. "I can't go home," she said.

"You have to," Oskar said. His hand took almost all the space between Ren's shoulder and elbow.

"You could come to my place," Jane offered.

"No." Oskar tightened his arm around Ren. "We should get the worst things over while you're still a little shocky." He bowed his head to Ren's. "Grief is a trauma to memory," he said, "an amputation of what was to be. What you dread is what will fester."

"Ren?" Jane asked.

Ren drew a deep breath and met Jane's eyes. "It's okay," she said. "I trust him."

Jane nodded. "Which CVS?" she asked Oskar.

"Corner of Thornydale and Ina."

"She's that far north?"

"Yeah. Ren, Jane is going to drive to the yoga studio, pick up your car and bring it to us. Where are your keys?"

"In my bag. I don't know where my bag is."

"You left it in the waiting room." Jane slipped it off her shoulder and handed it to Ren.

Ren dug her car keys out and gave them to Jane. "Thank you," she said again.

"Oskar told me you have a large family and an extended support network, but if there's any way I can help . . ." Jane glanced up at Oskar.

"You've already helped so much," Ren said. "I don't know what I would have done if you hadn't seen me in the parking lot. Other than burn my butt."

"We'll see you in about an hour, Jane," Oskar said.

Ren stayed still under his arm watching Jane walk away. She knew Oskar was right about dread, but she wasn't ready. "Celeste was in my Garden," she told Oskar. "This is all her fault."

"It isn't."

"There was a fire in my Garden, Oskar."

"That wasn't Celeste, Ren, I promise. She shaded. This isn't about her. This is about meddlework."

"And Jane?"

"I didn't meddle with her much."

Ren almost rolled her eyes. "*You* didn't meddle with her at all; you're just six foot six and ridiculously good-looking. *I* was meddling with her. Before you got here, before Phil . . ." Ren's brief focus evaporated.

Oskar's never wavered. "This is about the meddlework Phil was doing."

"He was helping me," Ren told him. "Jane's husband teaches at a high school where there's something weird about the boys."

Oskar snorted derisively. "Everything's weird about high school boys everywhere. That's not what I'm talking about. I was in the Garden with Phil when he was dying. He showed me all the anti-immigration switches. SB 1070, Brewer, Pearce, Arpaio. Ren, he had some for John Tanton and Jared Taylor. What the hell did he think he was playing at? Why hadn't he posted anything to the forum?"

Clear as a seeded memory, Ren's mind delivered a snapshot of her once future husband floating on his back in their pool one late night. Phil's big toes stuck out of the water, and he splashed her occasionally with a lazy finger flick. He'd tried to talk her into taking off her clothes and joining him, but she had stayed sitting on the edge in a tank top and her underwear. She was dangling her feet in the cool water, enjoying the night, the distance of the stars and the nearness of her man. He'd been humming softly for a while before he rolled onto his belly and frog-kicked over to her. "What do you think about SB 1070?"

"You know what I think."

"Want to do something about it?"

"I kinda thought that was why we moved to Arizona."

"I moved here for you." He kissed both Ren's knees.

"Funny," she said. "I moved here because you didn't want to move to Phoenix."

"You said you preferred Tucson to Phoenix." He shrugged. "I've been reading up on it, the DREAM Act and immigration in general." Phil ran his hands over Ren's thighs, sliding water and goose bumps up them. "Did you know high school officials are reporting not just a decrease in enrollment and parent involvement, but an increase in student stress-related illness and marriage?"

"It's all part of the same constellation, isn't it?"

"What?" Phil dimpled under his wet mustache. "Illness and marriage?"

Ren brushed her thumb over the wiry hairs of his eyebrows, and his hands slipped up over her hips. "Does marriage sicken you, my love?" His voice was playful, but the dimple was gone.

"No, but I don't think it's healthy for high school kids," she said.

"How about for us?" He was standing between her legs, and Ren leaned in to kiss him, wrapping her arms around his shoulders. His hands ran over her hips and rear.

"Sure, but probably not for our work. At least not in the short run, and this is important."

He groaned and lifted her, drawing her to him into the water. "You are important."

The pool water wicked up Ren's T-shirt to her breasts, and her nipples tightened with the chill. Phil held her close to his body and kissed her.

"Mmm," she said.

"What?" Oskar's arm tightened around her in the hospital corridor. "Are you dizzy? Do you need to sit down?"

"No." Ren's tears ran like pool water. "I don't know why he hadn't posted anything about it. But it's not like him to keep anything secret."

"True," Oskar said darkly.

"I don't think it was a conscious decision not to," Ren added. "It seemed very personal to him."

Oskar grunted, brooding. Ren closed her eyes and rested against him.

He straightened with such force she staggered. "Let's go," he said.

"I thought you needed to talk to the police."

"Fuck the police," Oskar said. "They're part of the problem. They aren't going to solve this, we are."

⋏　⋆　⋆

Oskar thought he had walked out of the hospital without his luggage and almost went back for it before he remembered that it was in his rental. The momentary confusion suggested to him that maybe he wasn't handling things as well as he'd thought he was. But he needed to fake it. Falling apart would not help Ren.

He considered stopping for groceries, but the plane flight and car rental had left him fairly broke. He could still manage a few supplies if needed. Jimmy would help. Jimmy could afford to, and he always came through.

Oskar guided Ren into his rental, and almost buckled her seat belt for her, but she shook her head. He put her address into his GPS and headed out. He didn't try to talk. Ren stared straight ahead, not sobbing, but there was a steady flow of tears as Oskar drove.

He exited the freeway and turned into a compact neighborhood of houses mostly dating from the '50s, when the postwar boom plus a wave of strikes produced a massive increase in the number of working-class families who could afford to buy their own homes. Most of those homes now showed the kind of neglect of the yard, roof, and trim that indicated they were rentals. There were a lot of toys in the yards, but most of them looked pretty cheap. In contrast, there were bright designs on many of the retaining walls—attractive, if abstract; lots of turquoise. The art was in good condition. Even allowing for the preservative effects of the desert, it was being maintained.

Oskar pulled into the driveway behind Phil's Prius. No, the Prius wasn't Phil's, it belonged to Charles Purcell, and Charles Purcell was dead.

Oskar helped Ren out of the car and into the house, and the first thing he saw was the horrid painting. Ren saw it too and started sobbing.

"Ren," Oskar said. "Look at the painting. That wasn't Chuck, that was Phil. That's a piece of what will be back. Do you understand?"

She nodded, but she needed to be held so he held her.

After a while, she went to the patio door, let the dog in and fed it—usually Phil's job, Oskar guessed from the way Ren had to look for the scoop. Then she sat on the sofa petting the creature while Oskar put water on for tea and checked his phone. Jimmy was en route. Good. For consoling someone who was hurting, for providing support, and for helping to choose a path amid a morass of morally ambiguous choices, Jimmy was the best.

Oskar returned to Ren, squatting next to her where she sat. "Jimmy is—"

The doorbell rang.

Ren started to get up in an automatic gesture, but Oskar took her shoulders until she stopped. He answered the door and found a tall, young Asian woman, with the most startling and lovely blue eyes set off by utterly black hair, smiling almost shyly.

Oskar managed to keep his voice low. "Get the fuck out of here," he said.

★   ★   ★

Ren knew Oskar rarely used his size to make a point or to get his way, but she couldn't see around him. She quit trying. She didn't really care who he was filling up her doorway to shield her from anyway. It wasn't Phil. She closed her eyes, tasted root beer and smelled salt mud, and her desolate Garden unspooled under her. Vast and empty as always, it seemed newly interior and claustrophobic, and she opened her eyes. Oskar was still growling at a shrill woman in a muffled audio negative of her parents' fights heard from under the blankets. She walked out the back door, through the side gate and around the crispy front yard. Neither she nor Phil cared about landscaping.

Oskar had one elbow on the doorframe, his hand shielding his eyes from the setting sun. The gesture accentuated the span of his shoulders, as did the slender build of the woman arguing with him.

"You have no talent for delicacy, Oskar. No subtlety!" she exploded, tossing back waves of sleek black hair. "Did you even ask Ren if she wanted you here? Have you asked her anything at all? Or did you just march into her life at its most painful pivot, trample over her choices, and take charge? Ren needs a woman's touch right now. She needs me."

Ren was pretty sure she didn't. Whoever that was.

"Ren needs pampering and listening to," the woman went on. "She needs beauty and nature, flowers and silk sheets."

Irina. So that was what she looked like now. Oskar was right to keep her on the doorstep. Ren walked back through the side fence and stared into the pool. She wished it were a lake. Phil loved having a pool but Ren didn't like swimming in water she could see through. "Phil, can you hear me?" she whispered, knowing he couldn't. "I don't know what to do. Oskar's in charge and Irina's here. Ramon and Jimmy are coming, almost full Salt. These are your people, Phil. Not mine. I don't know what to do. Phil—"

Phil—his memories and personality, his habits, abilities, and preferences—were waiting in stub in the Garden. Almost everything she loved about him was stored and safe, but inaccessible, waiting for some Incrementalist somewhere, but probably Oskar, to recruit someone willing to let his body become Phil's. Ren was lucky, she reminded herself, compared to any other grieving person. It was a kind of decadence to ache this much over Phil's lost hands and eyebrows. She knew that, she just couldn't make herself stop.

"Ren?" Oskar came across the deck on silent bare feet. "I couldn't find you."

If it hadn't been Oskar, Ren would have said he looked frightened.

"I'm sorry," he added. And he looked that too.

"If you get any less Oskar-like, I'm going to stop believing in you," she told him.

He shrugged and added "embarrassed" to the day's list of uncharacteristic expressions. "Jane's here," he said.

"And she found you and Irina on the front porch yelling at each other," Ren guessed. "And gave you hell for leaving me alone."

"Yeah," Oskar said. "How did you know it was Irina?"

"I peeked."

"She has a new Second—Vanessa Surya. Sally recruited and titaned."

"I read the forum posts."

"Oh right. Of course. Do you want to meet her?"

"No."

"I didn't think you would."

"Wasn't she in Florida? How'd she get here so fast?"

"Apparently Vanessa had a condo south of Tucson." Oskar scowled. "I can make her leave."

"It's okay."

"Kate called in a prescription for Ambien for you. Jane picked it up. You should take one now. I can bring it out here to you, if you want, and avoid Irina."

"God, you left Jane in there alone with her?" Ren followed Oskar inside feeling like a guest in his house. Or Irina's.

Irina was rummaging in the kitchen, pretending not to see Jane, who sat sentry at the kitchen table. "Ren!" Irina cried, dropping a cookie sheet with a clatter. "You poor girl!"

"Go away, Irina."

Irina stopped like a butterfly frozen in the air. "I'll make bruschetta."

"Don't."

"Irina," Oskar began.

Ren cut him off. "I'll do the bruschetta," she told Irina. "You make drinks."

Neither Irina or Oskar moved.

"Great!" Jane said.

"Ren?" Oskar's face stayed expressionless.

"Mojitos?" Irina suggested.

The last time Irina had made drinks, she'd poisoned Ren's. Ren had mostly blamed Celeste, but hadn't been ready to forgive Irina until now. "Let's have gin and tonics," she decided.

"Great!" Jane said again.

Irina had been an Incrementalist for longer than anyone alive except Ramon, and if Phil needed that kind of deep expertise, Ren wasn't going to let her own shallow past get in the way. Besides, Irina would fight Oskar just on principle, and Ren knew the one thing that Phil distrusted most was having any one Incrementalist in charge.

It galls me to say it, but Ren was right about Irina. I ended up glad to have her there. And not just because we started seeing each other in the aftermath.

—O

JUNE, 1856

"THE SECOND'S NAME WAS, AH, JIMMY?"

I arrived in June, and they were already rebuilding from the attack of May. They'd cleared the rubble from what had been the hotel, and new printing presses had arrived to replace the ones the border ruffians had destroyed. I pitched in, because Lawrence, Kansas, had no good way for a card player to make a living. It was a dusty town, and everything felt temporary—the buildings, the streets, the people. The one brick building had been the hotel. When the wind came up, it seemed like everything might blow away—and, in fact, the roofs of some of the older, grass-thatched huts did just that, though they were quickly re-thatched.

We hauled wood and stone, sometimes a long way. After hours of sweat, stopping for a drink of water felt like complete self-indulgence. The Emigrant Aid Company sent us hammers and nails from back East; that helped.

At night I'd take a turn at guard duty. I had my Sharp's. Most of them had poor muskets that reminded me of the one I could hardly shoot during the Revolutionary War. I've been a soldier—a bad one—several times, but this was one of the few times I felt like, if I had to, I could aim and shoot—we were protecting our town, and we didn't know if or when the ruffians would be back to burn us out, or worse. I thought about going back to Massachusetts and meddling with Thayer and Lawrence to send us more arms and ammunition, but it turned out I didn't need to.

I did a bit of meddling here and there around the town; I made sure our version of the truth was printed in the newspapers. To be fair, the editors, particularly George Brown of the *Herald of Freedom,* probably didn't need much meddling.

They didn't attack again, though. And we rebuilt Lawrence.

FIVE

Gallivanting through the Deep

Kate knew her Garden smelled of new felt, but every blessed time she thought, "wet dog."

Wet dog and fleas.

Felting is nicer than it smells, but the fleas were smallpox, actually, and itched like the dickens until she scratched them. Then they burned. Kate didn't much care for her sense triggers.

But she loved her Garden cottage. She opened her eyes, and walked through its cozy sitting room, touching chair backs, passing rows and rows of yarn. Oskar had seeded his memory of Phil's death as a curl of orange rind left in the drained café glass of a heavy drinker on the Rue de Guerre. Kate opened her bead box and found it as a polished but asymmetric undrilled chunk of amber. She fashioned a simple wire wrap, and put it on.

Unlike her own memories, which she could put on and relive, Oskar's she could only wear and remember. Donning the amber, she knew the heat of Tucson, but didn't feel its warmth. She knew there were three women in Ren's house, and that Oskar was livid about something. The police, most likely. That wouldn't create problems for Ren, so Kate dilated on the other women, and knew Ren was in shock, and Irina—beautiful and young again in her latest Second—was still a pain in the behind, and there, getting in Oskar's way. Good. She recognized Jane from Ren's in-progress meddlework posts, and knew from Oskar's seed that the pretty Wiccan had been good with Ren, and that Oskar thought Jane would be a good recruit for Phil's Second.

That would never do.

Kate took off the bead, and held it up to the sunshine streaming through her big bay window. The stone caught the light and knifed an orange glint of fire across her cozy studio. Oskar, bless him, was ferocious and smart and pathologically farsighted. He could never see a person, only people. He'd thought to wonder how Irina got to Ren's so quickly, but not why she'd want to. He'd noticed Jane's altruism, but not how attracted she was to him. Kate made a note on an index card and filed the bead with the rest of her amber, satisfied she'd done the right thing in writing the Ambien scrip. Oskar would try to do right by Ren, but he'd only make a muddle of it. Jimmy and Ramon and Irina—all of Salt—would get involved but not one of them, old and experienced as they were, knew half what Kate did about love. And Ren would have enough to deal with, what with the grief and the politics of Phil's death.

Since everybody's been talking about Salt, I should explain. It's an informal group that consists of the five longest-enduring personalities—in other words, the five oldest of us. We have no power, no authority, except that we tend to be listened to by those who are newer at this whole immortality thing. I don't know where the term "Salt" came from. It goes back so many thousands of years that it would take days or probably weeks in the Garden sifting through old memories to find out, and I just don't care enough to bother.

—Oskar

Kate opened her eyes and blinked at the ball pit. Her kids were invisible, buried under plastic balls, but Kate knew her babies were in there with the germs and lost socks the same way she knew what Ren needed.

She stood up, yawned, and collected her magazine, the stuffed bunny, and an extra shoe. Kate had two husbands because she couldn't lie. When she was seven, she had stolen a Wilbur's candy bar from her sister's

Christmas stocking, and chocolate hadn't tasted good to her since. But she would lie on the forum and steal from the Garden to get Ren the right Second for Phil. Kate had risked her life, taken the spike, and become an Incrementalist because she loved people—not in groups or factions or tribes, but one by one. She cared about Ren, not Salt, and if that got her in trouble, well, let it.

★　★　★

In the bathroom, Ren picked up the ancient bathrobe of Phil's that he had long since ceded to her and put it on over her clothes. It made her feel like she'd swallowed a hole and wrapped herself in its packaging paper. She took it off and folded the faded, aged-fragile cotton into a warm little rectangle too small to staunch the emptiness. She hid it behind the spare towels on a shelf and braced herself to be around people.

Ren went back into the living room, and dutifully swallowed the pill Jane gave her. "Oskar's on the phone with Alexander," Irina told her. "He's finding out what the police know, and asking questions about tradecraft."

It was an instructive conversation. Alexander is our intel expert and talking to him convinced me that I'd been right about the police being part of the problem. They almost always are, but this time more so than even I or Alexander could have known.

—O

"Okay," Ren said. "What else needs to be done?"

"You don't have to do anything," Jane said.

"I want to."

"Good." Irina squinted at Jane, evaluating her, although Ren wasn't sure for what. "We have things that need doing." Irina stood up. "How kind of you to drive Ren's car back," she told Jane. "Did you say your husband was on his way to get you?"

"No. I said he drove our car home."

Irina sucked at her gin and tonic, and Ren marveled that she'd thought to bring not just limes, but straws. "How very kind of you," Irina said. "I'll call you a cab."

"Oskar said he'd run me home once Ren went to bed."

"No, I'll take you." Irina and Jane eyed each other like chess players. "Oskar is staying with Ren, and your house is on my way."

Jane opened her mouth, but Oskar walked into the living room, moving too quickly for a space its size. "There is no more unimaginative breed of reactionary rule-followers than police detectives. They see what they want to and treat any attempt to widen their perspective as an assault on their eyesight. They defend property from the property-less and can't imagine a world in which a kid growing up on the Southside with a working mom and no dad, lousy food and a worse education might be the victim rather than the perp." He glared at Irina. "They're saying Phil got caught in the crossfire of a gang shooting. It was a couple of high school kids. Exactly the demographic Jared Taylor recruits."

"Oskar?" Jane stood up. "Why don't you come help me rustle us up a drink?"

"Oh god, Jane," Ren said. "I'm sorry. I thought you didn't want one."

"I didn't offer," Irina said. "I thought she was leaving. We have things to discuss among ourselves."

"Phil's an idiot," Oskar said. "But nobody gets shot three times by accident. I grazed the police report. The shooting was surgical. No way Phil was some innocent bystander."

"Oskar." The steel in Jane's voice got his attention.

"Irina, for god's sake, would you please have the decency to get Jane a drink?" Oskar growled.

"I'll take a beer, thanks, Irina," Jane said sweetly.

Irina didn't move, which Jane ignored and Oskar failed to notice. "See if Phil has any scotch, would you?" he added.

"We do," Ren said. "I'll get it."

Ren went into the kitchen. Being around people was starting to feel like doing stupid planks in stupid yoga. Irina had left the tonic out, so Ren put it back in the fridge and wiped up the juice where Irina had sliced limes on the counter.

"You can't ask her about that now!" Jane scolded Oskar in the other room.

Ren managed not to cry over the empty six-pack carton and the memory of eating pizza, watching *Argo,* and sharing the last beer with Phil because he wanted one more slice, and she was already a little tipsy.

The front door slammed.

Ren poured scotch and carried the drinks back into the living room. She handed Jane a bottle. "It's hard cider," she said. "We're out of beer."

"Oskar stepped outside," Irina explained.

"I'll go get him." Jane put her cider by Oskar's scotch glass and went out.

"Eager little thing, isn't she?" Irina's habitual tartness sounded somehow more acid coming out of her new Second's sweet face.

"You're jealous of Jane?" Ren asked. Irina had been nearly seventy when they first met, and Ren wasn't sure youth suited her. She wondered if it would be that way with Phil.

"She's in the way," Irina said. "We have work to do: Phil's dust ritual, Chuck's funeral, who to have recruit and titan Phil's new Second."

"Me," Ren said. "I want to titan."

Irina sucked on her straw.

"Oskar won't want me to."

Irina squinted owlishly at Ren. "Oskar is not in charge. Also, we need to find out who really shot Phil, in case the rest of us—and you particularly—are in danger."

Ren yawned. "Why would we be? Celeste was right about Phil. He leaves. But he comes back. He has to. I made a spiral. Without him—"

"A spiral?" Irina said, but the Ambien was creeping over Ren like the thunder blanket they'd bought for Susi.

"Where's the wolf?" she asked Irina. "My dog."

"I put it in the guest room."

"Get him?"

"Why don't you go on to bed, Ren dear?"

"Why don't you fuck off, Irina love?"

"Or you can just curl up here on the sofa."

Ren nodded. She wasn't sure she had a choice about sleeping on the sofa. But Oskar came in and scooped her up. He carried her out of the living room in arms that were alive and encompassing. Her head fell against his chest and her eyes focused precisely on a single blond hair at the base of his throat. He smelled masculine and competent and safe. Nothing about Oskar was safe.

Ren wanted to ask him to stay holding on to her, but her breathing was already too deep and rhythmic to disrupt by talking. Susi barked and whined, jostling Ren's dangling foot with his head. Ren understood Oskar had carried her into the guest bedroom, not the one she and Phil shared, and a deeper breath, almost a sigh, sank through her. Oskar sat on the bed and eased her onto it.

"I'll undress her." Irina always had the most terrible voices.

"She's wearing yoga pants," Jane said. "They're practically pajamas."

Ren nodded her agreement, grateful again for Jane's practical calm to offset the Incrementalists' intensity. Ren wondered how Jane managed it, staying level amid upheaval.

The moment Oskar let her go, Ren wanted him back. He was principled enough to sleep next to her and not let it complicate anything, but she was principled enough not to ask it of him. Not that she could talk. Susi jumped up on the mattress next to her, his weight making the bed jiggle and Ren tremble. She gave the dog a bleary whistle and he nuzzled her face in that "let's play!" way he did when Phil came home.

"That dog will disrupt her sleep," Irina said. "She needs to rest."

"Go away, Irina," Oskar said, and they all left. Or Ren did.

*   *   *

They left Ren sleeping, and Oskar followed Irina and Jane down the hall and through the kitchen He stopped to look for something to eat and wondered how long it would take to find Ren's seeds for Jane. Had she put pointers to them in the forum? He didn't think so. Oskar didn't actually want to meddle with Jane—at least not yet—but it would be nice to know something about her.

Of course, they could have a conversation, and he could learn about her that way, just like normal people. Oskar got himself some bruschetta and walked into the living room to see that Irina had apparently come to the same conclusion, and was acting on it. She was talking, and Jane was nodding, but looking wary. Her body language said she wasn't at all certain about this Irina person. Irina was mirroring, and breath-matching, using her eyes and mouth and every other trick there is to gain the trust of a Focus when you have no switches.

"Irina," Oskar said, "let's talk." He took her arm to let her know that he *would* fucking drag her with him if he had to. He could see her considering it, weighing the effect it would have on Jane's trust in her, and in him; then she got to her feet.

"Of course," she said. "I'll be back in a moment, Jane."

Jane didn't answer.

Oskar led Irina out the front door.

"What's on your mind?" she said.

"You need to leave."

"That 'go away' thing is going to get boring fast," she said. "Maybe it would be more productive to concentrate on how we can work together to help Ren."

"She doesn't want your help. And I don't want to work together. Why do you get to make the decisions without caring what anyone else thinks?"

She laughed. "Is that really coming from your mouth, Oskar? From *yours*?"

"Please go fuck yourself. Do you really think Ren wants you around right now?"

"Why wouldn't she?"

"You almost killed her."

"So? Phil actually killed me. Am I bearing a grudge?"

"Probably."

"I am not. I'm here for Ren. It's not where I'd choose to be. I didn't want to drop everything I was doing and go shopping, but has anybody else thought to stop for supplies? I didn't particularly want everyone knowing I have a place in Tucson. It's awkward. And no one likes being hated, Oskar. But none of that matters right now. Ren does."

"She doesn't need your help, Irina. She needs Phil back."

"She does or you do?"

"We all do. We need to find a new Second for him, which your presence here is preventing. Is it deliberate, or are you just—"

"Please go fuck yourself. There's no rush. I'll make us a drink." Irina started for the house. "Ren wants to titan."

Oskar remained where he was, between Irina and the door. Her new Second's lithe, plump body ran into his, and she didn't move back from the contact. She flipped her long hair over her shoulder, and Oskar thought it smelled like something he should recognize. "You don't want a drink?" she asked him, and Oskar realized he very much did.

"Ren's blaming Celeste," he told her.

That made Irina put some space between their bodies. She crossed her arms over her chest, frowning. "She said something similar to me. But it's irrational to think Celeste had anything to do with Phil's death."

"There's not a lot rationality going around," Oskar remarked dryly. "Phil's level of emotional involvement in the SB 1070 issue was irrational. The official story of his death is insultingly so. And yes, I'll concede my sense of urgency to find a Second and get Phil back doesn't make complete logical sense either, even to me. But Celeste is the first place Ren's mind went. So even though it's impossible, and on some level she knows that, we have to acknowledge the reality of Ren's pattern of fear. When Phil gets hurt, Ren blames Celeste. When Ren's life is endangered, she blames you."

"She's forgiven me."

"Forgiven you, maybe. But she won't trust you yet."

"If that's true," said Irina acidly, "and I'm not agreeing it is, then now's the perfect time for her to learn. Whether she likes it or not, we're family. We have to trust each other. Not my choice, or hers, and God knows not yours, but we're all part of the Garden. We're all any of us have. The sooner Ren faces that, and gets past it, the sooner—"

"Jesus Fucking Christ, Irina. I can't believe I'm hearing this. Celeste inhabited your body and controlled your mind. You tried to poison Ren, and you taunted Phil about it until he shot you. And now you think *you* can be the one who gets to insist—"

Jane was there, and Oskar suddenly wished he'd thought to take Irina further away from the front door for their conversation.

"All right," said Jane, in a voice low and quiet and emitting intensity like an acetylene torch. "Just who are you people, anyway?"

JULY, 1856

Is it safe to give him that much?

Robinson greeted me with the words, "Good morning, old man. What brings you to town?"

"I think you know," I told him. "Are they going to do it?"

It was Independence Day, and I'd just completed the hot, dusty trip from Lawrence to Topeka. We stood outside of Constitution Hall next to where someone had made a crude drawing and written something even more crude about Jones. We dripped sweat, and watched the horsemen not two hundred yards away. Robinson didn't have to ask what I was talking about.

"They have five companies of cavalry, and a couple of field pieces. I think they will."

"Who's the commander?"

"Sumner."

Sumner. I had no switches for him, and no time to gather any. "Has anyone spoken to him?"

Robinson nodded. "He isn't budging. He's under orders to—"

"Under orders from a fraudulent Territorial government, or from a President who's a whore to the slave power?"

"You're preaching to the choir, old man." Then he added, "Jim Lane wants to fight."

"Jim Lane always wants to fight, especially when it gets his name in the papers. What about you?"

"I'm thinking about it," he said.

I reached into my pocket and crushed some pine needles, then rubbed my hand over my shirt. I found a piece of rock candy in my pocket, popped some in my mouth, and held out the rest of the waxed paper packet to Robinson. He took a chunk and smiled. One of the local children, a girl I didn't recognize, spotted it, and gave me a wide-eyed look of polite begging. I handed what was left to her, and she ran off. Robinson and I spent a few seconds looking like little kids ourselves, sucking on our candy. To him, it felt like Christmas morning, and he'd always loved Christmas morning.

"Difficult decision," I said after a moment. "I remember you saying, in Lawrence, that we'd win this with public opinion, not bullets. But it's hard to let them break up the legislature. I don't think I could do it."

"Branson," he said.

"I know."

Half a year before I'd arrived in Kansas, a ruffian named Coleman shot and killed an unarmed Free State man named Dow. A little later, Sheriff Jones—the same man who'd overseen the raid on Lawrence—had arrested a guy named Jacob Branson for daring to suggest that Coleman should be arrested. We were still furious about it.

"But," I added, "it's about how to win the war. Like I said, I'm glad it isn't my decision."

"Going to come in and listen to the speeches?"

"Why? I've already made up my mind."

I had also, as it turned out, made up Robinson's.

Sumner dispersed the legislature without resistance—and our printing presses went to work.

And that, my friends, is how meddlework is done right.

—O

SIX

Everything Might Blow Away

Oskar saw that Jane had her feet firmly planted, her eyes going from one of them to the other, slowly, steadily. She was going to get an answer.

"Go ahead, Irina," Oskar said. "Why don't you get this one."

Irina gave a sort of low-key snort. "Nice," she said, and walked past Jane into the house.

Oskar shrugged. "We might as well be comfortable." He managed to step past Jane without making contact, and went from the heat of Tucson into the coolness of the living room. He sat down in the only chair he could comfortably fit in. Jane followed him in and sat, all business, on the sofa opposite, her eyes narrowed, her body focused. Irina came in from the kitchen carrying a long, thin, green bottle of wine and three glasses. She poured, smiling, looking at each of them like she was trying to decide who'd taste nicer with a vinho verde.

"Jane, have you ever risked or sacrificed something important for a stranger?" Oskar asked.

Jane's nostrils flared. "I asked you a question."

Oskar nodded. "And you answering that one is the best way to answer you. I can find out for myself, but it's liable to take awhile. So tell me, have you?"

"I don't know. What are you talking about?"

Oskar was trying to figure out how to put it when he noticed Irina had her eyes closed, and her lashes were twitching, so he just waited and drank a little wine.

Jane opened her mouth, but he held a finger up. "One moment."

A minute went by. Then another. Jane shifted, her eyes narrowed, and she didn't touch her glass.

Irina stirred. She opened her eyes. "Yes," she said.

"Yeah?" Oskar put his wine down.

Irina nodded. "Lowest fruit on the plum tree, right in front."

"That was fast."

"Thank you. If you bothered to read the boards, you'd know where Ren has her switches. The history was right next to it."

Oskar ignored her jibe and said, "All right, Jane. Just another moment, and I'll be able to tell you something."

He reached out for the sound of cannon fire echoing from stone walls, and the sight of the rosemary bush, and stood once more near the Seine. In three steps he covered several miles to the Rue de Grenelle, which is where Irina's Garden began within his. He held the image of a plum tree in his mind, imagining the lowest fruit, and found a piece of torn leather that looked like it had once been part of a boot. He folded it, unfolded it, and it gave up its secrets.

Oskar opened his eyes.

"High school, senior year," he told Jane. "You missed your prom."

Jane turned red. "How did you know—"

"We know pretty much everything, about everyone. Or we can with a little work."

"That's—"

"Your cat's name was Satha because when you got her you couldn't pronounce Samantha. Your big brother has a small white scar over his left eye where you pushed him into the edge of the piano when he wouldn't stop poking you. Your favorite dessert is blueberries with sugar and half and half. You became a Wiccan in college because you liked the people, the community, and the attitude, but you're not sure you really believe it all. You kept your last name when you married because you had it legally changed from 'Rossi' to 'Astarte' two years before, and you didn't want to look fickle."

Jane was staring at Oskar, her eyes widening. When he stopped speaking, she stood up abruptly, and stepped back a little. "Okay," she said. "This is creepy."

"Yeah," he said. "I know. Sorry."

"Way to be reassuring, Oskar," said Irina.

"Go fuck yourself," Oskar appeased, and turned back to Jane. "We *are* kind of creepy," he admitted. "But our intentions are good."

"Who's *we*?"

"That's a difficult question to answer. We're a small group of people who try to make things better."

"Is Ren one of you?"

Oskar nodded. "So was Phil."

Jane swallowed some wine. "I hang around with people who use incense and incantations to manifest abundance, sometimes instead of getting an actual job, and let me tell you, you people are weird."

"I know," he said.

"Do you know why Phil was killed?"

Oskar nodded. "He tried to make things better in a stupid way without telling anyone else about it, and he pissed off someone he shouldn't have."

"Make *what* better?"

"He was trying to reverse SB 1070. By himself."

Jane stared. "He could do that?"

"Evidently not," said Oskar.

"Oskar, dear heart," Irina said. "You are *so* not helping."

"I guess it's been too long since I told you to go away," he said.

"Go fuck yourself," she appeased.

"Do you all get along this well?" asked Jane.

"Sometimes it's worse," said Irina.

"Phil and Ren got along," Oskar said.

Jane frowned. "I think you're nuts."

"Reasonable," Oskar agreed. "I won't argue with you. I mean, if someone told me what I just told you, I wouldn't believe him."

"If you didn't expect me to believe you, why did you tell me?"

Irina said, "You asked," before Oskar could, which annoyed him a little.

Jane shook her head. "This is— I don't know what this is."

"Crazy," Oskar suggested. "Unbelievable. Weird. Also creepy. And you haven't even heard the strange parts yet."

"But you're overwhelmed," Irina said. "And you've had an exhausting day. It's too much to take in all at once."

Jane nodded, taking the suggestion. "I want to go home. But I want to be here for Ren when she wakes up."

Oskar pointed to the sofa. "Sleep there. I'll find you a blanket."

"What about you?"

"I can sleep in this chair."

"What about you?" Jane asked Irina.

"She's leaving," Oskar said before Irina could answer, which he hoped annoyed her a little.

"Play the gentleman, at least, won't you darling, and walk me to my car?" Irina asked him.

"Go to hell."

Irina left and Jane went out onto the patio to call her husband about her plans to stay the night at Ren's. Oskar was curious about how that conversation would go, but he didn't try to listen. He found a blanket for Jane in Ren and Phil's bedroom, and put it and a pillow on the couch. He thought about Ren alone in the guest room, then he sat down and closed his eyes.

★   ★   ★

Irina opened her car door, slammed it, and waited, listening. Two years in her new body, and she still got a thrill from young eyes, and ears that could hear the patio door at the back of the house slide open and shut. Irina knew it wouldn't be Oskar out on the deck with its tiny pool and lack of hot tub. He wouldn't leave Jane inside alone, or abandon Ren to go outside with Jane.

Jane, Irina concluded, must be outside on her own.

Irina picked her stealthy way around the house and through the side gate. Jane half sat, squatting on the edge of a cheap, plastic chaise, talking on the phone. Her shoulders had a guilty droop but her free hand was fidgety. So, she was aware of her attraction to Oskar then, and jumpy about spending the night near him, away from her husband. Jane stood and paced, getting frustrated, working up distance and justification. Whatever was wrong in her marriage, being alone with Oskar wasn't going to help it.

Irina picked a moment on the outswing of Jane's pacing, and retreated around to the front of the house. Oskar hadn't locked the door, so she just walked back in, expecting to find him seeding what they'd learned, and what they'd told Jane. She nearly slammed the door to make a point about not being shooed away when Ren had clearly forgiven her, but Oskar's stillness caught her eye. His beauty stopped her.

Hoping Jane felt guilty enough to keep her on the phone a while longer, Irina closed the door without a sound. She knew the pretty little witch wanted Oskar, and thought Ren did too, although in some fuzzy "being close to the person who was close to Phil when he died" kind of way. Oskar wouldn't pursue either of them. He never wooed women, but he didn't always turn them away. Incrementalists regularly underestimated the persuasive power of sex. Irina did not. She and Celeste had had that much in common anyway.

Let them say she was overly sexualized, maybe she was, but Irina knew it would damage Jane to sleep with Oskar. And while it wouldn't hurt Ren directly, if she and Oskar had even one night together, it might turn him into the buffer between Ren and the rest of the Incrementalists that Phil had always been. And that would be worse. It would be best if Oskar had sex with Irina instead. A public service, almost. Also, she was lonely, and Phil's death had been a blow, and Ren's forgiveness had touched her.

Irina was beginning to suspect Phil hadn't told Ren about the underground immigrant-aiding, cop-antagonizing group he'd been running out of the Southside and which had gotten him killed. Oskar clearly didn't know, or he'd be crowing. Add secrecy as another new and out-of-character aspect of Phil's life since the Incrementalists went public.

Irina would keep his secret for him. It was the least she could do. But feeling overwhelmed by it all, Irina crept closer to Oskar. Oskar was over-focused on finding Phil's Second, but Irina was beginning to believe he was right about the urgency of getting Phil re-spiked because they weren't doing well without him.

Irina was wrong about almost everything here. She was wrong about what Phil had been doing, wrong about my interest in either Jane or Ren, or her, and most important, wrong about the reason we were all starting to want Phil back in the quickest rather than the best possible way.

—Oskar

★　　★　　★

Physical, mental, spiritual. So often treated as three distinct things, but Takamatsu knew they were not. Extend your arm at a ninety-degree angle, ask someone to push it back to your shoulder while you fight against it. Now try it again, but this time, instead of fighting, simply close your eyes and imagine a line extending from your shoulder out of your fingers to infinity, and tell yourself that the arm is not moving. You will find that, the second way, the arm is much harder to move.

Why does it work that way? Is it because, when fighting directly against the pressure, you bring muscles into play along the biceps that actually work against holding the arm in place? Is it because you have made the decision that your arm will not move, and the mind is a powerful instrument? Is it because you have spiritually connected yourself to the universe? Of course it is all of these.

No it isn't. It's because of the muscles.

—()

As Takamatsu prepared to explore his Garden, he felt that losing Phil right now, even for a while, was dangerous for the group, but he didn't know why, and so he didn't know how to address it. But the feeling wouldn't go away—that this was as critical a time for the group as when they were caught flat-footed by the outbreak of war in 1914 and were afraid half of them would be sent off to fight each other. As when too many of them were all in London at the same time and plague had broken out. As when so many of them were caught in the fall of Constantinople. The danger was more subtle, perhaps, and certainly more mysterious; but it was real.

Takamatsu would need to be at his best to decide what to do, even if that ended up being nothing.

So he stood, and stretched. Each arm over his head, shoulders around, head around, back and forth, up and down. Hips, legs. A good, long, careful stretch that left his body loose and relaxed and ready, which left his mind loose and relaxed and ready, which left his spirit loose and relaxed and ready.

He closed his eyes and entered his Garden.

*   *   *

Irina leaned over Oskar. No tension haunted his long bones. No intention animated his closed eyes—he wasn't grazing. He sprawled—his arms on the armrests, his feet on the same line, but way in front of the chair's. His broad chest rose and fell hypnotically and Irina matched her breathing to his, her smaller lungs barely able to sustain the luxuriating, long inhalations.

The perpetual crease between his eyebrows was smoothed by sleep, and without it, his Nordic cheekbones and soft lips gave his face an angelic beauty. Irina wanted to unbutton his shirt and touch the tiny brass pendant on its red thread. She wanted to trace the gorgeous ridges of his abdomen, and stroke the furrow between them down and down. Irina had always admired Oskar's beauty, but it had taken seeing him asleep to get over her innate distaste for white men.

He must have been exhausted to be this deeply asleep so quickly. Irina knelt and took his large, limp hand in both her own. Watching his face, still matching his breath, she worked her way over the shiatsu points in his fingers down into the meat of his palm. She rubbed in small circles, feeling for the telltale grains under the skin that revealed stress or illness. The whole structure of him was taut, and Irina worked gently, but with strength, breathing with him. She pressed her thumb hard into the base of his palm until he turned his head and groaned. She shifted to his other hand, massaging between the bones, easing tension away. He was carrying too much. They all were.

Oskar's eyes slid open, but he made no move to retract his hand. "Fuck off," he mumbled.

Irina went on working.

"What are you playing at, Irina?"

"What makes you think I'm playing?" She worked her fingers up the sleeve of Oskar's shirt, kneading the hard muscles of his forearms to his elbow and then down the whole arm to his fingertips again.

Oskar sighed, but kept his eyes open, wary. "You never do anything but."

Irina switched her hands to his other beautifully muscled arm. "I'm just having fun."

Oskar's body stayed pliant in her hands, but he chuckled, deep in his chest. "Oh, I don't doubt that." His eyelids flickered, wanting to close. "I want to know why."

Irina widened her eyes. "Why am I enjoying this? Oskar, you're a magnificent specimen."

Well, this is awkward.

—*O*

"Surely someone has told you as much?" Irina teased. "I know you're dedicated and disciplined, but you've had lovers in this lifetime haven't you? With this body?"

Oskar opened his mouth to say something, but Irina stood, moving behind him, and slid her strong fingers into his hair to work the small muscles of his scalp. "How selfish of you," she chided, "to have such natural resources, and not share."

"I share." His voice was gruff.

Her hunger for him bordered on greed, but in the way Oskar surrendered the weight of his head to her ministering hands, Irina felt how long it had been since he'd been touched. He needed this more.

This whole seed is embarrassing. I hope you appreciate what I'm sacrificing here in the name of transparency.

—O

Irina wanted to put her lips to the spots her fingers worked, to know what Oskar's hair smelled like, but she slid her hands down the proud column of his neck instead, fanning her fingers over his hard shoulders.

"Why were you in Tucson?" His voice was level with grim determination.

She dug into his shoulders, and he groaned.

"I told you," she said, pressing her thumbs hard into taut muscle. "My newest Second—"

Oskar grunted at the pressure, but Irina didn't ease up and felt the tension start to lessen. "That answers how," he said. "Not why."

"Florida is too muggy. I can't make my hair behave there. Sit forward."

Oskar sat forward, allowing Irina access to the wide field of his back. "And?" he said.

"I wanted to be close to Ren and Phil in case anything went wrong," she told him, perhaps more truthfully than she should.

"Why would anything go wrong?"

"Doesn't it always?" She kept her voice casual, but her thumb had found a pocket of pain between Oskar's spine and shoulder blade that was years older than the muscles it torqued.

"What do you know about who shot him?" Oskar exhaled unsteadily with the increased pressure of Irina's thumbs.

"Nothing you don't," Irina told him, which was, distressingly, entirely true. She tugged at Oskar's shirt; he yanked it over his head. Irina ran her hands over the warm skin of his shoulders, surveying his back—strong, beautifully sculpted, and haunted as a graveyard. She tracked his spine with her thumbs, and visualized the knot under his skin breaking up and letting go. She drew the tension up through her hands and arms, and breathed it out her mouth. Oskar sighed and stopped her, reaching back to encircle her wrist in one of his large paws. He drew her around to standing in front of him, rising slowly to tower over her.

No one could meet Oskar and not notice his size—tall, with most of his height in his torso, and big too, muscled in the carved, lean way of swimmers. Still, what you noticed most about Oskar was his grace. The feline ease of his movements, even when he moved quickly, almost eclipsed his height; you could forget he was big. Then he looked down into your eyes. "What do you want from me, Irina?"

She wanted to feel close to him, to minister to him and make him her ally, but she could scarcely say that. The beauty of his bare torso humbled her, and the delicate corona of hair around his nipples and beneath his navel stirred a tenderness in her that ached. The corded muscles of his belly made her greedy.

I'm leaving this as it stands, not redacting or hiding anything to prove I'm serious about full disclosure, even when it's unpleasant.

—O

"I'll ask you again, Irina." Oskar touched her, tender fingertips running along her jaw to turn her face up to his. "Tell me what you're playing at or fuck off."

"Don't recruit Jane," she whispered.

"Why not?" His fingers wove into her hair, his thumb rested under her chin.

"It's not right for Phil, not now. And it won't work for Ren."

"It might," Oskar said. "We can ask her." He turned her face, exposing her throat, and bowed his head over it.

Desire, heavy and too long a stranger, dusted Irina's skin. She'd had this body for two years already, but she'd had the last one for fifty by the time Phil shot it. Maybe it was grief, maybe it was hope, but Irina hadn't been this rattled by lust since 1979.

"No," Irina said. "Ren's need to have Phil back will blind her to the problems with Jane. You have no business cowboying off on your own with this one, Oskar. You have got to play well with others this time."

Oskar's lips brushed the delicate skin behind Irina's ear and whispered down the length of her neck. "I'm playing well with you."

"You are," she told him, stepping against his motionless body. "Let's work together on this one."

"There's not much more work to be done. Jane's well vetted."

Irina slid her hands around Oskar's narrow waist and up the bare skin of his back. "I miss him too," she whispered. "But there's no rush. Let's take the time to recruit the right Second for Phil. We owe him that much."

Oskar opened his mouth to say something, but Irina ran her hands over his delicious biceps to his chest and down, slowly, allowing herself an appreciative sigh that silenced him.

So that was what it took.

"I've been looking into Phil's meddlework, Irina." Oskar's eyes held to hers with grim determination, but his hands stayed gentle on her face and in her hair. "This was a terrible time for him to die."

"There's never a good one," Irina quipped, but her insides washed cold. Oskar had no idea how right he was.

If Oskar noticed, he didn't say anything. His fingers stroked her cheek. He brought his face to hers and touched their temples together.

All the air in Irina's lungs left in a whoosh and she clung to Oskar's broad body for support as his filthy Paris and Phil's atrium crowded out her vision. She felt the stiff leather of an armchair against her thighs and the gouge of a knife blade over her palm. She held a vase of cattails in her lap, tickling her nose with details of SB 1070's tiny pollen. She sneezed. Oskar held her closer against his warmth and courage, and Irina smelled Ren's salt marsh garden on his skin, and saw her own footprints spiraling out behind them as they walked through the mud.

A sob shook Irina, and Oskar held her against his chest. He tangled the fingers of one hand into her hair and ran the other open-palmed down her back. Irina took a slower, shuddering breath, desire replacing desperation. Oskar repeated the caress more slowly, with his fingertips instead of his palm, tracing the bones of her spine, trailing along the last rib.

So pleasure was not only where Oskar was silent, it was the one place he listened. His fingers and—god help her—now his mouth were more than simply skillful. They were astute, learning from her body even more than she knew about what most aroused her. Irina wanted him, but how could she trust the body she was in? She didn't know it yet, but she knew her mind. She knew she'd kissed a boy she loved before they married and had come just from the touch of his mouth, so earnest and enthralled.

Oskar tipped her face up to his again. His velvet blue eyes were vulnerable and strong, and Irina knew if he kissed her, she would come and he would win. She couldn't allow that, but how she wanted his mouth on her lips one more time. She'd been alone too long and Phil's death frightened her, coming months too soon and from god-knows-where. She desperately needed this strength and pleasure. Oskar lowered his blond head to her mouth, but Irina couldn't risk it. Oskar had asked her what she was playing at, but he was playing her. Like a fiddle. Like a goddamn sudoku grid.

To be fair, I thought I was just returning fire.

—*O*

"I'm going home to seed everything we need to consider in recruiting Phil's Second," she informed him. "Maybe you could put your considerable energy into figuring out who shot him and why."

"I know why."

"I'm fairly certain you don't."

"What do you know that you're not saying, Irina?" His voice was clean as a knife blade and as uncluttered with love.

Irina leaned into him. "If I asked you the same question, would our answers be the same?"

His mouth was inches above hers. Now, she wanted him to kiss her.

"Fuck off, Irina," he said, and for the first time, Irina thought perhaps he meant it.

★   ★   ★

Kate bustled into Daniel Whitman's room with her clipboard in one hand and a plastic travel mug in the other. He gave her such a warm smile, she got flustered and checked her clipboard for no reason.

"Daniel Whitman?" she said. "I'm Dr. Donnally. It looks like you're doing better. I'm ordering one last set of tests."

"Well," the young man gave a deep sigh of mock resignation, "at least you're pretty. That's nice. If a doctor is going to kill me, it's a blessing if she's cute."

Kate felt her cheeks flame. She wasn't cute. Not in this Second. She was a pink-cheeked, blond, Midwestern farmwife with no makeup and a white lab coat, but gracious, if she didn't like the way this young man talked! "We'll have you out of here tomorrow," she said, peering at her empty clipboard again. "And we won't be poking you any more. I mean there's no more bloodwork. I've ordered one last breathing test."

"All right," he said, and Kate set her travel mug down on the hospital tray with a bump. She studied Daniel's monitor, noting a heart rate likely lower than her own, settling herself, and letting the mug waft the scent of mint Daniel-ward. It would remind him of his first crush, a girl named Peggy, when they were both eight, but he'd said Kate was pretty before he smelled it.

"Mr. Whitman—" she said.

"Call me Daniel."

"I will." Kate gave Daniel a smile, feeling calmer now the meddle was underway. She might not even visit the two other potential recruits she'd identified in her late-night comb of local hospitals. "Call me Kate," she said. "I want to let you know how sorry we are for all the complications since you've been here."

"Not your fault," he said. "Hospitals."

Kate nodded and queued up a distant rumble of trains, barely audible, on her pocketed iPhone. "I still feel bad," she said. "You're something of a hero, you know."

Daniel's lips compressed. He had a beautiful shape to his mouth, but Kate noted this only in her working capacity. She was over the surprise of his flirtation. Ren would find him attractive, Kate was sure.

"I know you don't feel like a hero," she said, settling her broad hips on the edge of his bed. "You can't get the faces out of your mind—the ones you didn't save. I understand that." Kate slid her hand to her lab coat pocket, turning up the trains. "We both know what matters is the lives you saved, not the ones you couldn't, and we both know it'll never feel that way."

Daniel looked up at her, and she put her well-scrubbed hand on his shoulder in a precisely calibrated gesture of professional tenderness. If her meddle was going to plan, Daniel would be remembering the backstairs now. He'd almost be back there, in the apartment where he and Josh had grown up with their dad and the rumble of trains and the glare of the streetlights at night. Daniel and Josh would sit on those stairs for hours sometimes while Dad was off at his second job. They'd talk sports, then girls, then music, then girls. It was hitting him. Kate could practically see the tears form.

"I think you're the first person I've met who understands that," he said.

He'd endured so much since the fire and not yet cried. Kate wished she could give him the catharsis, and let him off the hook, but she wasn't just meddling, here. She was recruiting. "How you feel about it doesn't matter," she told him, maternal hand on his shoulder. "You made things better."

Daniel nodded, bundling his pain away. "For a few of them, yeah."

"Do you want to do more?"

"It's too late."

"What if it isn't?"

He blinked and asked her what she meant.

AUGUST, 1856

"I KNEW A GUY ONCE . . . FELLOW NAMED JOHN BROWN."

It was the end of August, and Kansas gave us a clear sky and a hot day, and Governor Woodson had declared Kansas to be in a state of insurrection. I wasn't sure exactly what that meant, under the circumstances, but it was a safe bet that the ruffians would use it as an excuse for more killing. The pretext for the declaration had probably been the dust-up at Fort Titus, where we'd freed some slaves. I say "we" although I hadn't been there, and if I'd had the chance, I'd have tried to stop it. But I couldn't be unhappy with the result.

I was feeling generally optimistic. While I'd so far failed to find switches for Captain Brown, I'd had better luck with his son, Frederick. One of Fred's brothers had written a letter home in which he mentioned how much Fred loved horses (there were, it seems, a lot of them in Springfield), and on another occasion he mentioned fishing on the Westfield River. These things, since they'd been written down, made it into the Garden, and led to a few others.

We used to know the letters we wrote would be handed around from person to person. There was not the assumption of privacy then that we have now, and I never felt bad about grazing such documents, even diaries. There's something about the immateriality of words typed on a screen and never printed out that's changed the way people think about the permanence and accessibility of what they commit to writing.

—Oskar

I felt good about my chances with Fred, and I had hopes that he could exert some influence on his father. I will admit I felt a little uncomfortable meddling with Fred. He was pretty simple at the best of times, and since the massacre at Dutch Henry's Crossing, he'd been about halfway out of his head—sometimes more than halfway, to be honest. But it was the best chance I had.

It was early afternoon when I picked up the Big Osage, which brought me into Osawatomie. I heard later that I'd passed only a few miles from the older Brown on my way in. Maybe so, but I never saw where he was camped.

My first stop was Reverend Adair. The Reverend always knew who was where among the local Abolitionists, at least better than anyone else did. He had no trouble pointing me to Fred Brown: he was lying in Adair's cabin, shot to death.

"Found him when I came home," said Adair. "Practically on my doorstep."

There was a lump in my throat, and I had to look away. You get to know someone pretty well when you're preparing to meddle with him, and gunshot wounds are wretched things.

Phil's absolutely right here. On both counts.

—O

I turned to Adair. "Does his father know?"

He shook his head. "I sent my boy to tell him, and warn him."

"Ruffians?"

"Maybe five, six hundred of them. I thank God my wife and children weren't home when they came by."

I cursed, then apologized.

"Where are you going?" he asked my back.

I didn't answer him; I didn't know myself.

SEVEN

A Small Form of Rebellion

Ren rolled herself to standing, swaying a little with the residual Ambien. Her eyes were gummy, her mouth was crusty, and her skin was stuck to her yoga top. She staggered across the hall to the bathroom and turned on the shower.

"Ren?" Jane tapped gently on the door. "Good morning. Do you need anything?"

"I'm okay," Ren said. "Thanks." She put one palm flat on the cupboard door to steady herself, and could almost feel Phil's bathrobe folded away inside it. He was in stub. They would get him back. They had to. Soon.

In the shower, Ren stood under the water. It was cleansing, but not clean. Transitional. Like she was, like Phil was. Ren put her face to the water, then her back, then the top of her head, wishing she could wash worry down the drain. What if Phil didn't come back? She cycled face, back, crown, face again, but Oskar would need hot water. Jane too, since it seemed she'd stayed the night, which was interesting. Had Irina?

Ren got out, wrapped herself up in a towel, and brushed her teeth. She looked no different as a widow than she had yesterday morning as a fiancée, but she understood why Oskar had counseled against mirrors. It was going to be a day full of things she wasn't ready to face, and didn't want to see, and the unreality of how unchanged she looked didn't help.

Dressed and ready for her next chore, she marched herself into the kitchen to find it full of flowers. "Fucking Irina," she muttered.

"What?" Jane appeared from behind the refrigerator door.

"Nothing," Ren said. "The flowers."

"They came yesterday, after you were asleep," Jane told her. "I signed for them. They're from someone named Liam."

"My boss." Ren pushed tears away.

"You should eat something," Jane said. "I know you don't want to, but you know it will help."

Ren put water on for tea and poured Frosted Flakes into a bowl. When she dumped unsweetened yogurt on top, Jane raised her eyebrows. She didn't say anything though, and Ren didn't feel like explaining her compromises with adulthood and with Phil, so she just carried her bowl to the kitchen table. She ate dutifully for several bites. Jane was right, it did help. "You were so great yesterday," Ren told her. "Thank you."

"Of course." Jane took the kettle off the burner and shrugged, but something in the hitch of her shoulders caught Ren's attention.

"I promise I'm okay now, Jane. Jimmy will have gotten in overnight, and I already have more help than I can use. I'll run you home after breakfast."

Jane's eyes darted toward the living room where Oskar lay like a collapsed tent over Phil's favorite chair. She opened a cabinet.

"I fell asleep and left you in the company of some very intense people," Ren said, choosing her words carefully. "I hope it wasn't unpleasant."

Jane's eyes drifted toward Oskar again. "Not unpleasant," she said. "No."

Ren went back to her breakfast. If Jane and Oskar had started something last night, Ren couldn't blame Jane. But she couldn't help her either.

"What do you know about my husband?" Jane was in front of the pantry, holding its door open, and Ren couldn't see her face.

"You told me yesterday he taught high school."

"Do you know about his high school prom?"

"No," Ren said with great care.

"But you know about mine."

"Jane?"

"You know I didn't go. And why I didn't, don't you?"

Ren stood up and walked into the kitchen.

"You know what my favorite dessert is, and about Satha."

Ren took Jane's hand off the pantry doorknob and closed the door. "Satha?"

"My cat!"

"Right. Jane—"

"How the fuck do you know about my dead fucking cat?" Jane looked about as willing to be touched as a cornered hedgehog.

Ren kept her distance, but she held her ground. "Come sit down and tell me what happened last night. I'll explain."

Jane glanced Oskar's direction again. "He explained."

"I'll do better."

"Is that a joke?"

Ren didn't smile. "No."

Jane looked around the kitchen like she'd lost something. "What about your tea?"

"It'll wait." Ren risked a gentle tug on Jane's wrist, and Jane seated herself across the table from Ren's breakfast. "You need to finish this mess," she decreed, then her shoulders collapsed. "Is he in trouble?"

"Oskar?"

Jane delivered a withering glare. "Sam."

"I don't know," Ren said. If Jane didn't look so ready to either cry or punch her, Ren would have walked into the other room and wakened Oskar to find out what the hell he'd said. Oskar called the Garden "the original commons" and believed it should be as available as the Incrementalists could make it to as many non-Incrementalists as possible, but Ren didn't think he walked around spontaneously telling every nemone he met about it. If he did, they were going to have words.

I don't, and we didn't. Although maybe here I am, and we will.

—Oskar

"He's not a bad guy," Jane mumbled.

Unwilling to guess guys again, Ren stayed quiet.

"He's just frustrated. You have to understand the pressure he's under. Well over half his students are minorities, he's underpaid and overqualified, and the kids who aren't already inured to it all, or dropping out to have babies, or only coming to school to mule drugs, are asking questions he'd be fired for answering honestly. He teaches civics and current events, for god's sake! What's he supposed to tell them?"

"I don't know."

"Then why are you trying to get him in trouble?"

"We're not. Wait. What do you mean 'you'? What did Oskar say?"

"That you are all part of some secret spy organization. And your boyfriend was shot in the line of duty."

"Oskar said 'spy'?"

"Has my husband gotten involved in something dangerous? Some militia or something? I know he's been upset recently. Angry. But he's not a bad guy, I swear, Ren. I'll talk to him. I can get him to stop."

"Hang on." Ren pushed her pulverized breakfast away. "Oskar said we were spies?"

Jane's eyes went sideways, re-playing the conversation in her mind. "He said you were a small, secret organization trying to make things better, that Phil was shot because he was working on SB 1070, and that you knew pretty much everything about everyone. Or could find it out."

"Did he say how?"

"It's all NSA stuff, right? Honestly, Sam doesn't know anything important."

"Jane." Ren waited until Jane looked at her. "That's not who we are. We're more like secret whistleblowers. If Sam were one, we'd be helping him."

Jane shook her head vigorously. "He's not."

"Okay," Ren said. "We aren't spies, and we aren't trying to get Sam in trouble. We have no idea what he's up to."

"But he's up to something?"

"I have no idea," Ren repeated, but she was watching Jane closely, and saw Jane knew Sam was, in fact, up to something. Ren filed that tidbit away and went back to being reassuring. "We know almost nothing about your husband," she said truthfully. Sam didn't seem to write much down.

Jane blanched. "Is it me? It's me, isn't it? You're investigating me. I'm the one Oskar had all the information about. Oh my god. It's because I'm Wiccan, isn't it?"

"Jane."

"You're going to get me fired."

"No, we're not. We're . . ." Ren reached around for something that wouldn't keep making things worse. "We're closer to witches ourselves than anything else."

"What do you mean?" Jane looked leery, which was a step better than panicked.

"Remember at the hospital I said I could do something that was like praying?"

Jane nodded.

"We call it grazing. That's how we learn about people. We close our eyes and look inside ourselves."

"I saw them do that, but I thought it was like Tony Stark's suit."

"No, it's not a technology. Or it is, but more like the wheel than a computer," Ren said. "It's made out of symbols and rituals and imagination. And we're on your side anyway. We're trying to make things better. Not report anyone, or get anyone in trouble."

"Unless they're doing things you don't like."

"Not even then."

Jane looked right at Ren.

"Okay," Ren said. "Look. If, for example, we thought it was bad for a Wiccan to teach school—and please understand we don't, this is just an example because I'm too tired to come up with a better one—if we thought it was bad, we wouldn't report you. We'd suggest, very gently, and only to you, that maybe there's a better way to do things and nudge you in that direction."

"What better way?"

Ren sighed and got ready to try again, but Jane put it together on her own. "Oh, right." She nodded. "That was an example."

"Thank you."

"So it's magic?"

"Not really."

"But there are symbols and rituals."

The weight of Jane's anxiety and relief, and of all the truth Ren had told and hidden, settled over her like a granny's shawl. "Yeah." Ren dragged her smashed breakfast back and forced in a mouthful.

"Tell me about one of them," Jane said.

"Well, there's the dust ritual we do when one of us dies. Someone, usually the living Incrementalist closest to the dead one, picks a seed— that's what we called a saved memory—from the dead guy's life, and we all graze it. It's the only time we can actually relive another person's memory."

"Can nonmembers attend?"

"Yeah, actually. Sometimes Incrementalists marry nemones, er, nonmembers. But if they know about us and they're willing to sign up for a nasty hangover, we can share the ritual with them. Very occasionally, especially if the person goes into—" Ren stopped herself. She wasn't sure why she wasn't able to tell Jane about the coming back out of stub, but she wasn't. "If the person dies very shortly after joining us and they were still very close to family members from before, we get those people drunk on purpose and include them without their really knowing."

"Will you have one for Phil?"

Ren had to force herself to swallow again.

"No." Oskar's voice came from behind her, and Ren nearly toppled her chair, turning around. Oskar walked through the kitchen toward the bathroom, shucking out of his shirt, and even Ren, hungry, tea-less, and grief-riddled, had to take a moment to appreciate the sight. "The dust ritual is a formality, not a requirement," Oskar said. "It doesn't have actual utility, and we don't have time."

"Bullshit." Ren was on her feet. "We are not cutting any corners with Phil's transition, Oskar. We're going to follow every tradition, meet every criterion, double-check our work, and get second opinions on every last detail until Phil's out of stub and integrated in his new Second."

Oskar stopped in the doorway, looking as surprised as Ren felt by her own certainty and determination.

"We'll do all that, Oskar, and wear our goddamn lucky socks too until Phil's back here to make fun of them."

Oskar turned and walked into the bathroom.

★   ★   ★

Irina left her condo with only an untraceable, prepaid cell phone, a single car key, and the small folded emergency contact sheet no Incrementalist went anywhere without. You don't die without one more than once to get good about keeping it about.

Irina had had lifetimes of practice facing facts, and on the drive downtown, she faced the truth that she might have really fucked up. It had been known to happen. You can't run with the big dogs if you don't leave the yard, and God knows Irina had done her share of jumping fences. Well, she'd mend any she could. The only fuckup worse than the mistake she wasn't yet sure she'd made would be not finding out, and leaving Ren to suffer for it.

Irina drove down to the hospital, and left her car in the parking lot, slamming the door too hard, and took a bus to the south side. The first thing was to learn the territory, start wide and zoom in. Arizona's shitty economy, distrust in the feds' ability to secure the national border, and ancient, simple racism had colluded to give the state the broadest and most brutal anti-immigration law in the nation, Senate Bill 1070, and cops all too happy to enforce it. It was a gaping sore of a human rights breach, and closely tied to the increasing militarization of the civilian police, which was the biggest threat any of them had seen in a long time. It made sense for Phil to have gotten involved. It was only his methods that had surprised Irina. And impressed her, if she were being honest.

The bus smelled like ammonia—either pee or the stuff they used to clean it—and the driver felt obliged to mash either the brake or gas pedal at all times, but it was more pleasant than going back to Ren's. Irina couldn't face Oskar just yet. She should have kissed him. She could survive—hell, flourish—fed only on the kisses of men and women who wanted her. And Oskar did. Just not how Irina wanted him to.

She wanted him on her side. She wanted all the Incrementalists on the same side. She wanted Ren and Phil over their obsessions with Celeste, and she wanted Ren integrated with the group and relying on Incrementalists beyond Phil. Phil's wrongful arrest might have accomplished all that and more.

And that was the countermeddle. That's what started the whole mess.

—Oskar

Tucson wasn't Phoenix, where the oppressive law was most abusively enforced, but here it had sparked something that reminded Irina of the forests of Hispaniola. She saw it in how kids watched the bus going by, in the alertness of the old man at the taco truck, in the tense shoulders of the mother and daughter carrying their groceries home. Most of them wouldn't know what was going on, exactly, or even that it had anything to do with what was happening in Phoenix. But there was a righteous, subversive violence waiting at the margins, and the people felt its promise. Phil's arrest, as reported by Menzie Pulu with help from unnamed sources named Irina, could have brought it out on the streets.

She had to find a way to make his death do the same.

I hate to say it, but Irina was right on every point here. I hate countermeddling like Louis hated Robespierre, but if I'd had known what she was up to, I might have helped her. But people can't do any better than their circumstance allows, and Irina's lives have left her with a tendency toward secrecy I'm still—and here—trying to remedy.

—Oskar

Irina got off the bus a block before the corner where Phil had died and zipped her sunglasses into the same inside pocket of her coat that held her car key, info card, and disposable phone. The danger she was walking into felt like stepping waist deep into a very cold ocean. But Irina had lifetimes of putting her body on the line. She very much preferred its pleasures, but she had learned to endure pain if she had to.

AUGUST, 1856

"DON'T WASTE YOUR BREATH."

I left the Reverend Adair's cabin and walked for half an hour, not paying much attention to where I was going except that it was vaguely in the direction of Lawrence. I found a reasonably sized tree on the riverbank, and sat down with my back against it. I closed my eyes and imagined the smell of cherry blossoms and the taste of chive. I checked the message wall of my Garden first. Rishabh reported mounting tensions, and asked for ideas on how to diffuse the situation; I knew nothing of conditions in India, so I stayed out of that one. Julianna reported that there'd still been no contact with Qing, but doubted he'd returned to China. I'd last run into him in South America and the memory still rankled, so I didn't much care. Here in the U.S., Rosemary reported on some of the after-effects of the Philadelphia Convention, and suggested a few bits of med-dlework to help cement the new Party without giving in to the odious Know-Nothings who hung around it like flies after a honey pot. All of her ideas made sense, so I wrote back with my agreement and tacked the note to the door of the barn at the edge of her Garden.

Then I seeded Fred's death and set it as a silver bowl on the table in the triclinium. I put a marker to it on my wall and opened my eyes.

John Brown, the father: he was the key. He was charismatic, deter-mined, and had a following like Lane, without the limits that Lane's egoism imposed. Winning Brown over to the cause of peaceful change would alter the entire political landscape of Kansas for the better.

Had I tried hard enough to find Brown's switches? The trouble was, he never wrote about himself in such a way that details like the ones I needed would find their way into the Garden. It was frustrating. And he was not the sort of man who could be swayed without switches.

But now one of his sons was dead, and, I don't know, maybe I could have prevented it if I'd done a more thorough search. I shook my head. I'd tried, dammit. And I wasn't bad at grazing, even if I wasn't as good as—

Jimmy.

I went back into the Garden. I conjured pencil and paper and wrote, "Jimmy, I'm unable to find switches for John Brown—the stack of plates next to the sink in my cucina. Can you help? Thanks—Carter." I turned the note into a plum and set it on a glass pedestal in what my Garden saw as Jimmy's.

Then I left the Garden and sat against the tree and remembered Frederick. I sat there, unmoving, for a long time. I fell asleep there, and woke up with the sun, and just continued leaning against that tree for most of the day. Not all that far away, just out of earshot, there was shooting and yelling and what would become known as the Battle of Osawatomie, but I knew nothing about it.

EIGHT

Something to Work With

Ren didn't want to do yoga and Jane wasn't ready to leave, so Ren sat on the ground while Jane folded and unbent herself. They made small talk until Oskar—showered and dressed for battle—emerged from the bathroom. He came into the living room and reinstalled himself in Phil's chair, where he'd slept the night.

Ren only managed a low, "Oskar," before he raised his hand to quiet her.

"I'm sorry, Ren," he said, fishing his laptop out of a bag. "I was abrupt. My point was, we need to get Phil back, not mourn him. But I can understand your position, even if I don't agree, and it's your call. We can hold the dust ritual. I'll put a post on the forum."

"I'll do it," she said and sat down.

"What does that mean?" said Jane. "Get Phil back, not mourn him?"

Oskar looked at Ren, surprise on his beautiful face. "You haven't told Jane about stubs and the Garden?"

"Why would I have?"

Oskar dove in. "We—Incrementalists—have access to externally stored memory. That's how we learned what we know about you. We call it the Garden. When one of us dies, his memories and personality go into storage there until they can be recovered and restored."

Oskar had Jane's whole attention, but Ren wished he'd shut up. Jane didn't need to know any of this, and every weirdness Oskar revealed would make it harder for Ren to learn what she had wanted to about Jane's husband and the bizarre spike in the number of guns confiscated from the school where he taught. Oskar wasn't helping.

"Restored?" Jane repeated. "You mean, like warehoused or recorded somehow?"

"No. Put back into a living body."

Jane sat down. "You put the someone who died—*into* someone who's alive?"

"Their memories and personality," Oskar said. "Yes."

Ren tried to catch Oskar's eye, but he was focused on Jane, doing everything he could with tone and body language to be matter-of-fact, not-crazy, that's-just-how-it-is convincing. Jane looked dizzy. "You mean, like, downloading a new file over an old one?" she asked.

"Not over, next to," Oskar explained. "So there are two files."

"That's . . ." Her voice trailed off.

"Crazy? Yeah. Only it's true, and I don't have time right now to be gentle about it. We need you—"

Ren was on her feet before she fully realized what she'd understood. "For Christ's sake, Oskar!" she shouted. "Is *that* what this is about? You want to recruit Jane? For Phil's stub?"

Oskar blinked. "I'm sorry, I thought it was obvious. You clearly get along."

Ren kept her voice low, under rigid control. "We get along?"

Oskar's mouth opened and closed. "We need—" he said.

"I know," Ren cut him off. "I know we do. Without Phil, there's no us. But without the right Phil, there's no me."

"I don't understand," he said.

He didn't, poor gorgeous darling.

"What?" he demanded.

Ren's anger slid away before Oskar's utter griplessness. How could he care so much and understand so little?

"What does that mean?" Jane was very pale. "Recruit me for Phil's stub?"

"Don't worry about it," Ren told her. "It's not going to happen."

"Give me one good reason—" Oskar started, looked at Ren, and stopped.

"I'll give you two." Ren sat forward on the sofa. "Because I don't want to lose Jane, and because Phil needs to be a man."

"That's absurd. Ren, you haven't been through stub-and-Second yet, but believe me—"

"No, Oskar." Ren cut him off. "You believe me. I know Phil, and I don't know why, but something he started in Chuck's body, not anything to do with me, SB 1070 maybe . . ." Ren faltered. "It's not just that I . . ."

"Ren—" Oskar started.

"What does it mean, 'lose Jane'?" Jane's body was rigid inside an aura of pivotal stress. "Explain it."

Ren looked at Jane. She needed help.

"May I?" Oskar asked. Ren nodded, and Oskar's stomach gave a thunderous growl.

"Go make yourself something to eat," Ren suggested. "We can talk in the kitchen."

Oskar stood, then squatted before Jane holding his hands out, palms up for her to take. She looked from them to his face and blood started moving behind her skin again. Oskar helped Jane stand, and Ren climbed to her feet feeling the empty air on her shoulders where Oskar's hands settled on Jane's.

Ren didn't want to watch Oskar in Phil's kitchen, so she sat at the kitchen table with her back to him facing Jane, and explained how Phil had lived for two thousand years by transferring his memories and personality from body to body. She told Jane how, three years ago, Phil had recruited her for Celeste's Second, and things had gotten very strange. Jane focused her questions on the death or sublimation of the Second's soul, and Ren tried to answer honestly even though she didn't really believe in souls and couldn't see the point of Jane's questions since they'd clearly ruled out recruiting her.

Oskar used all the eggs in the fridge, and came to the table bearing three enormous omelets. "Celeste had suspected her personality might not survive another stub-and-Second, and she had taken some precautions that made for an unusual transition when Phil spiked her stub into Ren," he explained. "But Ramon and Irina have both gotten new Seconds since, and those spikes went smoothly."

"Irina," Jane said. "I didn't much like her."

"No one does," Ren agreed.

"No one likes me either," Oskar observed.

"But everyone likes Jimmy." Ren hated how negative and fractious Incrementalists sounded when they tried to explain themselves to others. It didn't feel that way from the inside. "You'll meet him soon," she told Jane. "He's on his way."

Jane cut into her omelet. "But you still have all the magic the rest of them do, right?" she asked Ren. "Ren can work the possession magic for Phil, right?" she asked Oskar.

"Jane—" Ren started.

Oskar talked over her. "It isn't magic."

"Sure it is."

"No. It's not," Oskar said. "Magic isn't a thing."

"You can't prove that."

"The more deeply we've understood the world, the more we've been able to change it, and nothing magical has ever been part of that understanding or that change." Oskar forked eggs into his mouth.

Jane watched him. "And not being part of how you've explained stuff makes it not a thing?"

Oskar held Jane's eyes for a moment, chewing. "Yes," he said around the eggs. "One of the things we've come to understand, is why people believe in magic. And how much smaller the domain of magic becomes as we've understood the processes of nature."

"Sure sounds like magic to me," Jane said. "And you've said you can't explain how it works."

Oskar swallowed. "The existence of the unexplained, does not imply the inexplicable. All of human history has demonstrated—"

"It's practically the definition of magic," Jane interrupted. " You can't explain it, but you know what gestures to make and the words to say. That's a spell. You use all sorts of bizarre constructions to keep from saying 'soul' or 'spirit' but that's exactly what you're talking about retaining in stub after the body's death. You have mystical powers of persuasion and glamour, no matter what neurochemical language you wrap them in. And your 'Garden' is obviously just a higher vibrational plane."

Oskar choked on his eggs.

"Jane—" Ren tried again.

"Do you ever just take people who don't want to do it?"

"We can't," said Ren. "They have to cooperate with the ritual. If they don't—" She shivered in spite of herself, remembering Celeste's final moment. "If they don't, it goes badly for everyone."

"Why would anyone agree to let you do that?"

"You know," said Oskar, "I've heard that question before, and never understood it. How could you not? I mean, it isn't just a chance at immortality—die now, or go on indefinitely. That by itself seems like a pretty good deal. But it's more. It's a chance to make things better. To actually improve the world. You know how long it took me to make up my mind when I was recruited for Gerard's stub? About a week to convince me it was real, then two seconds to decide."

"That's you, Oskar," said Ren. "Not everyone is like you."

"You should use Sam," Jane said.

Oskar had his mouth open to say something to Ren, and just left it that way as he looked at Jane.

"What?" said Ren.

"My husband." Jane didn't look up from her plate. "Sam. He's not religious, but he's a very spiritual person. And he's good. Deeply, permanently, in his soul, good. It's killing him that he can't do anything to make things better at Southside. He feels so helpless." Jane didn't look up, but tears slipped from under her lashes. "This would allow him to make a difference. A real difference." She took a slow, uneven breath. "I know he wouldn't survive the spike. Sam wouldn't. That's what you want, right? His soul wouldn't stand up to Phil's. It's already broken." Jane met Ren's eyes, and Ren knew what a widow looked like. "It's what he wants."

"We'll have to hear that from him," Oskar said, watching Jane intently.

Ren reached a hand across the table and Jane took it. "What about you?" she asked. "Is that what you want?"

Jane's breath caught with a little sob. She nodded, and Ren got up and walked around the table to her. Jane was on her feet by the time Ren reached her, and in her arms. Oskar started to stand, but Jane and Ren held on to just each other, and he sat back down. They stood and hugged and cried and Oskar ate all the omelets.

★   ★   ★

Irina found the intersection where Phil had been shot empty of crime scene suits investigating, or even police tape. She knew the ground wouldn't talk to her, nor Phil's blood whisper from it, but Irina walked each of the four corners anyway, trying to feel where Phil had died. She didn't get a thing but overheated.

The promise of convenience store air conditioning beckoned from behind burglar bars and layers of Spanish-language ads, so Irina went in and began her research. Someone around here must know something worth discovering. The official police line was, "another innocent victim of gangland crossfire," but no Incrementalist was buying that. Oskar was thinking professional hit designed to protect the anti-immigration bill. Irina was keeping her mind open.

She had slept in her makeup and scrubbed her eyes to smear it, but her new body was too fit to pass for much of a junkie. And it drew more attention. She shambled the aisles, gaping at the refrigerated cases until she had an audience of two. She selected a forty, dug in her coat pocket and produced a five-dollar bill. Clutching it fiercely, she headed for the register, careful to shed another five and a wadded single on the way.

A gratifying scuffle erupted behind her as she paid, just enough to stress the cashier. Irina watched, but nothing in the way he shouted at the kids, or unwadded her crumpled five, or slid her beer into a paper bag indicated anything more than poverty weighed on him. God knows, that can be enough. Irina dropped another bill on her way out the door, and the kids followed her that far. They hung back as she wove across the street to roost on the bus bench.

Irina sat in the middle, like a good little hen, leaving room for both kids, one on either side. They watched her drink beer. Masked by the wrinkled brown paper, she read in their wary young bellies and preposterous shoes that they were not friends, although they knew each other's names and siblings. The younger boy was darker, an ethnic collage, beautiful and taut. The older was pure *cholo,* and particularly pleased with himself just now. He sank back into the store's cooler shadows to spend the five she had dropped. The other stayed in the sun wearing something he couldn't shrug off his shoulders. Guilt, maybe. He ambled over.

"Yo, *gabacha.*"

Irina squinted at him and belched.

"Hell." He dragged the word out into a caramel of vowels. "What are you doing out here? You looking for something?"

Irina drank beer, and put her hand in her pocket.

"You waiting for the bus? They not going to let you take that beer on the bus. Give it here."

Across the street, a short, muscular, redheaded man in high performance sportswear emerged from the mouth of an unpaved alley. Score one for the rival vigilante theory. The man was clean-cut for militia, but Irina could shake off her preconceptions quick as anyone who'd been around a few hundred years.

"Fuck off." She waved the kid from her field of vision.

"Nah, I'll hold it for you."

Irina couldn't see over the kid's shoulder, skinny as it was, and stood up, but he was too close. She tripped on his shoes, and sat back hard on the bench. "You little fucker," she said. "You made me spill my beer." She sloshed some at him. The kid swore and backed up, then came straight for her.

But Irina had gotten a good long look at the middle-aged man with the professional haircut and haunted shoulders. She needed to talk to that guy. He had as much business on the south side of Tucson as a leather daddy at a *quinceañera.* And stuck out more. This kid was just in her way.

She tottered up again. "Take it." Irina shoved the beer at the kid, but he batted it out of her hand, crouched and bristling. All the markers she hadn't seen in him before were coiled in his hands and racked on his shoulders. He was balancing, but only just. And he was between her and someone who either knew something about Phil's death, or was up to something else big and dangerous in the same bad block.

"Fuck yourself, bitch!" The kid's voice cracked on the "f," snapping the authority of outrage into its component fear and shame. "Fuck off outta here!"

The man turned at the boy's strangled shout, caught Irina's eye, and vanished—maybe into the bar, maybe the neighboring Laundromat. It irritated Irina that she hadn't seen which. The second, older kid emerged from the store across the street with a packet of Oreos and a bag of cat food. The littler one pushed Irina again. She yawned and sat back on the bench. She squinted up at him. "That you, Misha?"

"What the fuck?"

"Go get granny a beer, okay, baby?"

"You fucking crazy, bitch. You not old enough to be my mama."

Damn. Irina had forgotten. Good as it felt, you'd think she'd remember how young her new body was.

"A need a beer," she said to no one, and shed a couple more bills from her pocket as she stood. She'd try the bar first.

"S'up?" Oreo-boy had crossed the street, and his presence puffed up the little man. Shit. Irina started to shamble away from the money and the beer.

"Pick up that beer," the older kid demanded.

The light at the intersection turned red and a car stopped, blocking Irina's most direct route out.

"Misha?" she tried again, but she kept her eyes down, watching the boys' feet moving—or not—and feeling her morning's coffee again at the root of her tongue. She sidled street-ward. The woman in the car looked resolutely forward.

"Hey! What else you got in that coat?" The older boy's big feet were spaced wide and they didn't shuffle. "What you got under it?"

Well, damn.

The light turned green and the car pulled away hard from the corner. The convenience store was closer than the bar. The kids wouldn't follow her back there.

"Yeah," the littler one said. "Show us your tits."

"Shut up." One of the larger shoes pivoted. Irina took off running for the store.

She heard the blow land, felt bad for the little guy, glanced back, and slammed into the solid, lean musculature of a man's body.

"Fuck." He staggered a little and shifted his body to her side.

"I'm sorry." Irina suddenly wished she didn't smell like beer. He was coiled and hard as rebar.

"Get outta the street." He had Irina's shoulders, and hauled her back toward the little shits at the bus stop.

"Look," she started, but he jerked his chin, and the two boys loped off. "I'm okay now," Irina said, just as it occurred to her that maybe a man who scared those boys wasn't really here to help her. "So yeah, thanks. I got it from here."

His skin was the warm brown of bricks, and as tender. He dumped Irina back on the bench and sat next to her, elbows on knees, hunched forward. He smelled of engine grease and cumin. "We're gonna wait for the bus," he informed her.

He had a very active way of waiting. Someone had dispatched him to get rid of her.

Irina slipped her sunglasses out of their hiding place and put them on. They were cheap plastic, but made an adequate screen. "Thank you," she said low and sweet. "What's your name?"

"Santi."

The words tattooed across Santi's arms and up his neck were so embroidered with curlicues and flourishes that Irina couldn't make out the letters.

"I'm Irina," she told him.

He scowled at her, a hint of gold between his pirate's lips. "That Russian, or something?" His inflection was Hispanic, cinnamon and cactus, and when he looked away from her, his lashes fringed their lids like fallen feathers. But he rubbed the first knuckle of one thumb with the ball of the other, a man not as calm as he sounded.

"Yeah," Irina said. But she was watching the thumb too closely, and let the conversation falter. She elbowed him gently, just to put their skins together. "Russian," she agreed. "How'd you know?"

He lifted his shoulders in feigned ignorance, but a pivotal hitch shadowed the shrug. "History channel," he lied.

"Did you know Chuck Purcell?" Irina asked. "White guy in his forties, maybe called himself Phil?"

It was instinct, a blind guess, but a knifepoint nudged Irina's bottom rib before she'd even seen Santi flinch. "Get on the bus." His sweat stunk of adrenaline.

"Okay," Irina promised.

Santi didn't move, and they sat, breathing together, waiting and knife-ready, until the bus came.

★　　★　　★

Jimmy got out of the cab, picked up his suitcase, and strode up to the door without even a glance at Phil and Ren's new house. A worried-looking Oskar let him in and, in the time it took him to cross the living room to where Ren and someone he assumed to be Jane were standing together on the far side of the table—

The tannins on his tongue and the sounds of Concerto Number 23 in A Major and he stood in the courtyard of his castle where he leapt atop the wall, then out over the moat into the field beside the western wall, then jumped past the forest, his feet no longer hurting, because in the Garden they didn't, and they were light, and he inhaled the scent of acres of wildflowers, with a stream off to his left, asking himself only one question: what is up with Ren, and though there was no breeze, still, a few blooms, here and there, waved as if to get his attention: he plucked a wild petunia, and Queen Ann's lace, and a common daisy, and a periwinkle, and a Maryland golden aster, and studied the bouquet in his hand, admiring it as it vanished, along with the stream and sky and castle behind him—

"Jimmy."

Jimmy ignored Oskar, and folded Ren into his arms. "We'll get him back," he promised.

"If one more person tells me that, I'm going to stop believing it."

Jimmy chuckled. "Believe whatever you need to." He spared Oskar a brief "I dare you to open your mouth" look, and nodded to the woman next to Ren. "Hello, Jane. I'm Jimmy. Thank you, dear, for all you've done. This came as such a shock, I'm afraid we may not have all been on our best behavior."

"It's fine," Jane said.

"Jimmy," said Ren, her voice just above a whisper, recalling Jimmy to the real reason he'd endured hours in unforgiving chairs drinking mediocre wine. "Things are really fucked up, Jimmy. You know what Oskar was proposing?"

He glanced a warning at Oskar, then nodded to Ren.

"And you get why I don't want to do that?"

Among the possible replies were, *of course I get it because I have more empathy than a rock,* and, *yes I get it because I'm not Oskar.* Jimmy settled for nodding.

"Look, Jimmy," said Oskar. "I think we should talk about this. I don't see why there is a prob—"

"Oskar," Jimmy said. "Shut the fuck up."

Oskar stopped, looking shocked. Jimmy had never said such a thing to him before, and maybe he shouldn't have this time, but he was having a lot of trouble controlling his temper just then and, in any case, it shut Oskar up.

Jimmy took Ren's shoulders and looked into her eyes until he saw the tears start to rise in them. "Take some time, my dear, pull yourself together," Jimmy suggested gently. "Then the four of us will sit at the table and drink Phil's execrable coffee and talk about everything. The one luxury we have is time."

Jimmy's gamble paid off. Instead of bursting into tears at the *execrable coffee,* Ren smiled bravely, and nodded. Jimmy glared at Oskar, but it had finally gotten through to him that now was not the time to speak, and a few minutes later they were seated at the table, Jimmy with a cup of coffee before him that wasn't all *that* bad, really. He said, "Jane, pardon me, please. I have to tell these two something. I promise you, if you're lost and want me to, I'll fill you in shortly."

"It's okay," Jane said. "I'll finish stretching." She left her coffee on the table and went back into the living room.

Jimmy covered Ren's free hand with one of his and turned first to Oskar and then back to Ren. "Kate is recruiting for Phil's stub," he said.

Oskar frowned. "She didn't tell me."

"She didn't tell anyone," Jimmy said. "I just this instant found out.

She gave her cell number to a patient at a hospital where she does not work."

"Then you should—" Oskar began.

"Let her continue, with Ren's permission. Kate knows what she's doing," Jimmy told Ren. "And she understands love better, I think, than any of us."

Oskar shook his head. "What does that have to do with it? What we need—"

"That's fine," Ren told Jimmy. "But I want to titan," she said, not looking up from his hand over hers. "Oskar and Irina agree."

"Really?" Jimmy managed to keep most of the shock from his voice. He glanced at Oskar, who shrugged.

I can see now that Ren cleverly played Irina and me against each other to win our assent. But it wasn't such an outlandish idea anyway. Titans don't get to pick a stubbed Incrementalist's new Second, they simply conduct the ritual that spikes the stub into the Second, and then shepherd the subsequent transition. That part's mostly watching and waiting, listening and explaining. Sure, it's best to be well-rested and emotionally stable when you undertake work as intense as the spiking ritual, but none of us exactly qualified on that front, and I wouldn't have liked to be the one to keep Ren away from the newly incarnated Phil anyway, so might as well let her do the work as well as keep the vigil.

—Oskar

Ren squeezed her eyes shut and opened them again. "We need a plan," she said. "I want us to make a plan now."

"All right," Jimmy said. Planning is a kind of time travel, and he could see Ren needed to get away.

"It'd be better if Irina were here," said Oskar. "Or, rather, I wish she weren't here, but since she's here, I wish she were here."

"You sound like Phil," said Jimmy with a chuckle.

The sudden tears in Ren's eyes told him she'd noticed it too, and he gave her hand a squeeze. She blinked them back impatiently.

"Where's the rest of him?"

I went into the Garden, brought myself to the peach tree, and there was a note, just where I'd hoped it would be.

> Carter: You got lucky. It turns out that Brown is the son of Owen Brown. I don't know if you remember the name, but Clara meddled with Owen some years ago to get a couple of colleges started in Ohio. Looking at special moments, I think it's a good bet to say John Brown's switches would include coffee with chicory (smell), the hymn "All For Jesus," the hymn "Thy Bountiful Care," and poppy seed cake with honey (taste). I've taken the seeds for the two hymns, words and music, and the recipe, and made them the grotesque facing due north above my front gate. Luck with your work.
>
> —Jimmy

Good, then. I had something to work with. I opened my eyes and let the Garden dissolve, then stood, brushed myself off, and started back toward Lawrence.

NINE

A State of Insurrection

By the time Irina reached the Roy Laos Transit Center, got off one bus and onto another one back to the intersection where Phil had died, she was pissing mad. Those kids with their Oreos and her beer belonged in school. She didn't care if it was Saturday. And that kid with the knife, Santi, who'd put her back on the bus, he had to be one of Phil's foot soldiers. So, yeah. Maybe Jack had been telling the truth and Phil had been shot by some anti-immigration, nationalist wingnut. A white guy. Maybe a white guy in athletic clothes and a tight haircut. So maybe the cops weren't looking, but Irina was, and what had she seen? A white guy. She stepped off the bus into the morbid asphalt glare, and strode straight for the Crazy Horse Saloon. Fifty-fifty odds, and it would be cooler than the Laundromat, and not smell like lint.

Irina was being reckless, but I have to admire her courage. She was trying to find Phil's killer. She was working hard to understand. Her motive was guilt and her methods were bullshit, but she was out there doing something while the rest of us were still talking about what to do. Of course if she'd talked more before she started doing months ago, before she started countermeddling, trying to get Phil arrested, he might not have gotten shot in the first place. Might not have. He'd been being pretty reckless himself, and at least Irina knew she was gambling.

—Oskar

"Shit." Santi's voice was a low whistle in the bar's darkness.

Irina hesitated, waiting for her eyes to adjust.

"What you doing off your bus?"

"Miss me?" She vamped.

"Oh hell no." Santi took Irina by the arm and turned toward the door, but she leaned into him and purred his name.

"Get on the bus," he commanded.

"You knew a friend of mine," Irina said.

"Didn't. Get on the bus."

"I have money."

"Then buy a car."

"I'll pay you to talk to me."

Santi moved Irina out to the street. Knowing his eyes had been longer in the dark than hers, Irina took the momentary advantage to soften her new, slim body against his. "He was my friend, Santi. I just want to know how he died."

The sound he made was almost a grunt. "I'm not talking to you about that."

"Anything else then? Come on, baby, tell me something."

Santi scanned the intersection; and something in him shifted. "You're not supposed to be here."

"I'll leave if you come with me."

"Fuck. What is it with you?"

"I just want to talk."

"Fuck."

If Irina hadn't had half an eye on the alley already watching for the red-haired sportswear vigilante she'd seen earlier, she might have lost Santi, he rounded the corner that fast. Irina trotted after him, trying not to grin. Watching the way he kept space between all his fingers, and between his arms and his bandy chest, walking fast, his body low and compact, Irina revised her estimate of Santi's age downward to maybe seventeen. High school age. He wasn't done growing yet, but already made of gristle. He gave no indication he knew Irina was following him, but she doubted he'd ever been followed and not known.

Santi threaded the alley like his mama's kitchen and rounded the corner, stepping easily over a hole where the road and sidewalk missed each other. He swung himself between the rails and through the front door of a small branch library. Irina followed. The curvy blond librarian in tight red gingham glanced up, saw Santi—his tattoos and prison teeth—and went back to rubbing the spines of books against a metal plate. She was as familiar with him as he was with the walk between the Crazy Horse and the library.

Irina trailed Santi past the audiobooks, and the movies on DVD and VHS, and barely kept from falling into him when he turned into the reference stacks and stopped short. "Christ, you're an ignorant bitch." The knife was in his hand again and pressed against her.

"That's not a very nice thing to say."

"Why the fuck'd you come back here?"

"I told you. I want to talk."

"Well you can't."

"Well I am."

Santi's balled fist came up by his ear. "Fuck!" He took a step at Irina, and she braced for the blow.

"Santiago," she cooed.

He scrubbed his hand across the bristly top of his head in frustration. Irina kept her voice low and tried a new tack. "I know you don't want anyone to see us talking; I'm not trying to get you in trouble. I'm on your side. If Phil was your friend too, if you were involved in something . . ."

Santi glowered and shook his head, derision mixing with his anger.

"Were you working with my friend, Santi?"

"Fuck." He looked ready to climb the stacks and jump out of the skylight to get away from her.

"You're feeling trapped," she suggested.

"Fuck yeah," he exploded. "You fucking trapped me."

"How did I trap you, Santi?"

"Stop using my name, Irina."

"How did I trap you?"

"You won't fucking leave."

"Why is that your problem?"

"God damn, you're stupid."

"Okay, why is *that* your problem?"

Santi's nails scratched Irina's chest as he grabbed a wad of her coat into his fist. His lips twisted, inches from hers. "You're no cop."

"No."

His grip on her clothes loosened slightly.

"Is that what you thought?" she asked.

He shrugged, and it let some more of the anger out of his shoulders.

"I can see why you'd think that," Irina said, working the fraction of an opening she'd stumbled onto. "I show up wanting to talk to you, asking questions about Phil, or did he go by Chuck?"

Santi shrugged.

"Of course you thought that. Probably thought I was offering you a plea deal just now?"

He nodded fractionally and released her.

"But you're right, I'm not a cop, Santi." She caught herself. "Sorry." She gave him her best sheepish smile, and it earned her a half-cracked grin. "The guy who got shot yesterday was my friend, that's all."

The smile vanished with a flash of gold and a shimmer of guilt. Irina kept her smile girlish and sweet. "I have no business playing CSI, do I?"

Nothing.

"I'm no good at this detective stuff, right?"

He shook his head, but the anger was fading.

"But you really do want me out of here, don't you?"

Santi didn't smile, but he made a rueful space between Irina's kidney and his blade. "You're not safe around here."

"Why do you care if I'm safe?" The tears in her voice surprised even Irina.

"I don't. Kelly do." Santi put the knife away.

"Is Kelly the redheaded man I saw earlier?"

Santi's face softened and understanding washed over Irina. Santi wasn't a foot soldier; he was a mercenary. He obeyed.

"He had you shoot Phil."

"Fuck." Santi threw a punch, and Irina blacked out.

★   ★   ★

Jimmy knew his own eyes were close to overflowing, but he kept them steadily on Ren. "I'm very sorry, *ma chère,* but getting Phil back is the one piece of this we can take our time with. It's much more pressing that we learn what happened—who shot Phil and why—and that we take steps to protect Jane and her husband and anyone else who might be in danger."

"I don't agree," Oskar said.

"Really?" Jimmy regarded Oskar with interest.

"No." Oskar's sculptural jaw was set. "I think we're all in danger until we get Phil spiked back into a new Second."

Jimmy nodded. "Matsu thinks the same."

A hint of distaste curled Oskar's lip. "What do you know that I don't?"

"He posted on the forum," Jimmy said.

"Does he have a reason or did he just sense a great disturbance in the Force?"

"Oskar," said Jimmy.

"What does he say?"

"He says he's sensing a pattern that indicates it's urgent to get Phil back, but he doesn't understand why."

Oskar scowled. "That's pretty much how I feel."

If you had been watching, would you have noticed this? That I said "I feel" instead of "I think" or "I've observed"? It should have been our first clue. Jimmy should have noticed. Hell, I should have noticed, but he was the only one not yet affected.

—O

"I want him back as quickly as—" Ren's hand covered her mouth as soon as the words had escaped. Jimmy obliged, pretending he hadn't heard her, and was gratified to see Oskar do the same.

◞◟

"I'll speak to Matsu," Jimmy promised. "As for making plans, Kate is already working on a recruit. Irina seems to have taken point on investigating the shooting. Oskar, you might be a second set of eyes."

Oskar scowled again, but Jimmy went on unperturbed. "Murder always takes two lives. Whoever staked his soul on the belief that Phil was better dead needs to be meddled into turning himself in."

"Or taking himself out," Oskar muttered.

"I'll follow up on other avenues Phil was investigating, if Ren, you'll—"

"I know," she said. "Sam."

"Jane and Sam," Jimmy agreed. "You've already built up some trust."

Ren nodded.

"I'm sorry," Jimmy said.

"No, you're right," Ren said. "It's important that whatever happened doesn't blow back on them."

"That's what I don't get," said Oskar. "Why should it?"

"Because Phil and Ren were looking into something odd going on at Sam's high school, and now Phil is dead, and until we know who killed him, we can't rule out physical danger to Sam."

"And Jane—" Ren said, but her voice cracked.

"Jane has been given a great deal of very strange information about us that she needs to process and she's also been made aware that Sam is involved in something beyond his teaching duties," Jimmy took over smoothly. "And that puts them both in emotional danger."

"Jane said we should recruit Sam," Ren said.

Jimmy gave her knee a comforting squeeze. "They need your help, Ren."

"I know. I—" Ren started, but stopped as Jane brought herself to the middle of the kitchen and put her hands on her hips, glaring at Oskar.

"I've been thinking this over."

Oskar waited. Jimmy thought it wise of him.

"Ren says you don't do anything bad to people. But what if—" Jane stopped. "What?" she asked Jimmy.

Sometimes Jimmy wished not everything he felt manifested so obviously on his person.

⋆　　⋆　　⋆

Takamatsu felt the calm wash over him, and looked at the rocks of his Garden; each one special and unique, but working together to create beauty. He studied them, entered them, let them enter him; the pattern in which all other patterns in the Garden were reflected.

With how things ended up for Matsu, I'm going to try to put into words the way grazing works if you're what we call a Pattern Shaman, and your name is Takamatsu. I replayed this seed twenty-seven times trying to get it right, but Matsu's memories aren't verbal. He doesn't tell himself stories the way we all do. He just experiences. He sees and feels and hears, and he thinks, but he doesn't do it in words. I've done my best.

—O

It begins with abstractions, symbols, metaphors. They dance in front of you, and you watch the dance until you become aware that you are predicting the next steps. There is the Dragon ducking under the arm of War, with Wisdom moving back and forth as if to keep them from touching. Over here is Love, dancing by herself, but in time to the same music. And there is the empty space where the Pivot used to be, and everyone is dancing around it.

Once the pattern becomes apparent, the abstractions become concrete; the symbols become images; the metaphors, people: Ren is the Dragon, Oskar is War, Jimmy is Wisdom, Kate is Love. And it is only then that you realize that Irina is nowhere to be seen in the moving, shifting dance.

The process goes back and forth: metaphor to person to symbol to image to metaphor. With each transition, you learn a little more. The Dragon's dance is somewhere between traditional ballet and its modern, improvisational offspring; War almost parodies itself with a *paso doble*; Wisdom twirls in a Viennese Waltz against the four-four tempo as if the implied polyrhythm were as natural as breathing, Love contents itself with a rumba, because of course it does. And somehow, they all work together, tell a larger story.

Now you must see what is not before you, and that is harder. You must find what is missing, what is not in the pattern but should be: the missing dancer, the missing dance. And although it may seem as if they are dancing for you, they are not; they are dancing for each other, and for themselves. If you forget that, it becomes nearly impossible to—

There.

Irina is Pride, off by herself dancing Flamenco to her own tempo, her own song.

Follow her steps, see where her eyes go, wait for the empty place to fill. There is no hurry, for there is no time, any more than there is space.

Yes. Pride is dancing with her own partner, Fear. Fear guides her steps. Fear of—?

That shape is not clear yet, for it is someone who is not in the group, someone none of them know. The unknown dancer has no face, and no name; only Irina knows who it is, and even she may not be certain; see how hesitant her steps are? Her hands and arms tell of secrets kept; her feet spiral inward and away at once, because uncertainty is the hole at the center filled by Fear.

You do not know what she fears, but you fear it too, because Pride cannot stop it.

War cannot defeat it, Wisdom cannot convince it, Love cannot move it, the Dragon cannot consume it. Only the Pivot can turn it from enemy to friend; from disaster to triumph.

There is no need for abstraction anymore, because everything, even the unknown, is sharp and clear and has hard edges.

Irina was involved with someone who could destroy them—destroy them in a very real and physical way. The possibility of all of Salt, and maybe some others, being stubbed at the same time was very real, and things were moving in exactly that direction. And the one person able to transform the threat was Phil, and Phil was in stub.

Takamatsu's Garden returned to empty stillness, and vanished. He opened his eyes, sat down at his desktop, and consulted his bank account, then Hipmunk. If he were willing to make two stops and spend eleven hours in the air, he could just afford it.

He booked a flight to Tucson, called in sick to work, got up and started packing.

★   ★   ★

Irina was not cut out for detective work. She just wasn't. Spy? Sure. Bond girl? Absolutely. But she didn't like waiting around, and she wasn't exactly ace at subtlety.

"Irina?"

She opened one achy eye to find the soccer-coach-looking guy she'd seen in the alley squatting in front of her. His heavy eyebrows—dark, trimmed short, and spiked with an occasional gray wire—were drawn together in genuine concern. His hands almost glowed with urgency. "Do you need to go to the hospital?"

Irina shifted against the shelves and knocked a book to the ground.

The man, who could only be Kelly the vigilante who'd had Phil shot, picked it up and stacked it with the rest of the deadfall. "I'll reshelve these," he promised. He was considerate for a racist talking to a brown girl, but terribly on edge. His guilty shoulders were bundled like dynamite sticks and his jaw looked like the center pin of a Ferris wheel. Irina rotated her own jaw experimentally. Not broken. She ran her tongue around the inside of her mouth, but the blood seemed to be only from where she had bitten her tongue.

"Do you have somewhere you can go?" Kelly asked.

Irina had lived everywhere from Haiti to Paris to Siem Reap in her seven hundred years, thank you very much, and she had both the condo in Tucson and the house in Florida, but she was bleeding from the mouth, had mascara ground into her eyelids, and stank of cheap beer so, okay. She might look like a walking—or a collapsing—disaster. But Kelly was living at the center of one.

"I can drive you," he offered.

"Where's Santi?"

"He's making sure we don't get interrupted. Can you stand?"

115

The nice man who'd had Phil killed for helping illegal immigrants not die in the desert, offered Irina one hand, a wide, square palm, to help her up. His other clutched a modest ring of keys.

"Tell you what," she suggested, "why don't, instead, you sit down?" Irina pushed herself up a little straighter against the bookshelf. "Santi punched me," she recollected.

"I'm sorry about that."

"*You* are?"

"He is too." Kelly blushed—an incongruous cardiac blossom over his stubbled cheeks.

"He works for you?"

"We're friends."

"Really?" Irina checked again, but there was no hint he was lying. Weird. "He knocked me out," she said.

"You, er. You hit the back of your head on a shelf."

"So it's not his fault? The shelf's, then?"

Kelly had possibly the worst fake smile Irina had ever seen. "You know that's not what I mean," he said.

Irina squinted at him through a scrim of headache. "How do you know," she asked him, "what I know?"

Kelly shrugged in a way that was also squaring off. "You're not a fool."

"Okay," she said.

"And you're not a drunk or a junkie, either." He said it like a confession she'd wrung from him.

"Are you calling my bluff?"

Kelly seemed like a nice guy, soft-spoken and educated, but Irina had been reading jaws and hands and shoulders, spotting the signs of lives at pivots—where everything changes and one way of being dies and a new one staggers out into the world—too long to think this guy was anything but imminent. He must have pulled the trigger himself.

"Just let me help you get on your feet." He was almost pleading. "There's a room we can use."

"You must be feeling pretty clever."

"I'm not. Believe me."

Oddly, Irina did. Odder, she thought he might cry. Sure, all pivots are dark, you don't turn yourself around if you're headed the right direction in the kind sunshine but, "My god," she said without thinking. "What's happening to you?"

His laugh was just like Oskar's, but more hollow. "Let's just get you to the community room, okay?"

"No, seriously. What the hell is going on with you and Santi?"

Kelly's eyes flicked to his left where Santi must be stationed. "This shouldn't concern him," Kelly muttered, looking, if possible, even more hunted.

"Maybe it shouldn't," Irina finished for him. "But it does."

The man swallowed, choking back vomit or tears.

"It concerns him," Irina went on, feeling her way around the tattered edge of Kelly's psyche, "because this—whatever 'this' is—concerns you, and Santi has made your concerns his own."

Out of love or loyalty, Irina realized. Not out of fear or for money.

"You didn't kill Phil, did you?"

"Jesus." Kelly dropped Irina's eyes and stood abruptly, like he needed to get out of the space where those words hung. "Of course I didn't. I could never kill anyone."

Irina tipped up her head to see what besides guilt was in Kelly's face, but an angry white pain knifed behind her eyes, and she had to close them. Kelly knelt next to her and put a solicitous hand on her shoulder.

"Santi could," she whispered. "Maybe has, but not Phil. Still, you're friends with a killer, and you feel responsible for Phil's death." Irina cranked one eye open. "Why?"

The quiet of Kelly's not answering stretched between them, but the storm playing over his face demanded patience of her. When he met her eyes at last, his were the blue of inland oceans. "I'll explain that," he promised, "but can we please get you out of here before the same thing happens to you?"

"Were you with him—Phil—when he died?"

"No. He was alone."

Something in that sent a shiver through Irina; she felt like crying. "But you knew him."

"He'd been coming down here a while to use the reference section.

I'd spoken to him once or twice. He asked a lot of questions." Kelly's voice was low and desperate.

"What sort of questions?"

"About alien registration and border patrol mostly. I tried to warn him off. We knew he was asking the same questions up in Phoenix."

Irina added Kelly's obvious heft of secrets to the strength of Santi's loyalty and toted up a wild, improbable sum. Could this man's "we" be Jack Harris's "they"? Could a guerrilla leader be so suburban? "Kelly," she said gently. "Who's 'we'?"

He sprang to standing, too fast for Irina's headache. She swallowed hard.

"God, this is unbelievably messed up!" Kelly groaned. "Why are you here? Why wouldn't you just go home? You don't have any idea how dangerous this is."

"You're not dangerous."

"I am!"

"Not to me."

Kelly looked around like he might start tearing books from the shelves. It hurt Irina too much to turn her head to watch him pace, so she just waited for him to come back into frame.

"No," he said, not looking at her. "Not to you. Or not directly. God, now can we please get you out of here?"

"Once you explain who your 'we' is."

"No!" Kelly was back crouching in front of her. "You explain yours, Irina. You tell me what the hell you and Phil are part of, and why you keep asking questions. It got him killed. Why are you doing the same thing? And how in the name of hope and meaning did my wife get involved?"

"Your wife?"

He sank back on his heels like a deflating balloon. "She spent the night at Phil's house with his widow."

"You're married to Jane?"

"How do you know her name?" It was nearly a whimper.

"You're Sam," Irina said.

Sam Kelly stayed where he was, looking like a man who knew all the real impetus of his life had left him. He was nothing like Oskar, but Irina could see how someone who loved this man would find Oskar irresistible. Of course, it was hard to imagine a woman who wouldn't.

"And you know Jane spent last night at Phil's house?" Irina asked. "I was there, too."

"How does Phil's wife—"

"Fiancée. Her name's Ren. Short for Renee."

"How does she know Jane?"

"I don't think she does. She was just investigating her."

"She's a detective?" Anger animated Sam.

"No."

"A reporter?"

"Closer."

"What about Jane, exactly, was Renee investigating?"

"I don't know, actually. Something about kids bringing guns to school."

"Oh god." Sam slumped against the stacks. "That was us."

"Sam?"

He met her eyes.

"Sam, who's 'us'?"

SEPTEMBER, 1856

THE GRAVITY OF THE GROUP'S MORAL CORE

After Lane's tussle at Hickory Point, a bunch of us sitting around Robinson's house had another argument. Morrow was there, and Cody, and Montgomery, and a few others, including Judge Wakefield, a solid Free-Soiler, though not an abolitionist. I think Wakefield might have supported the "No Negroes In Kansas" Free-Soil constitution, so I steered us away from that whole subject. Other than that, I didn't say much, and the argument accomplished less—those like Montgomery who wanted to go after Sheriff Jones still wanted to, those like Robinson who wanted to stay within the strict letter of the law didn't budge. The move from bad coffee to decent whiskey didn't help anything either.

The whole argument was set off, of course, by the Lecompton Constitution, one of foulest pieces of chicanery ever attempted to be practiced. We'd gotten word that it had passed, by a vote of something like twice as many people as were legally in the territory. I learned a few days later that Montgomery had actually walked up to one of the ballot boxes full of fraudulent votes and smashed it, but I didn't know that then. If I had, I would have told him it was the wrong way to fight, and shaken him by the hand.

I sat, and I listened, and I knew what would happen: those who wanted to fight by creating a Free-State constitution would do that, and those who wanted to fight by killing border ruffians would go ahead and do that, and nothing anyone said would stop either faction.

And old Osawatomie Brown would be right in the middle of those wanting to fight. I needed to get to him. After the meeting, I managed to find a friend of his, a young Jew named Bondi. Oskar had known him in Austria in '48, and was able to give me his switches.

August Bondi. He was twelve years old in '48, and fought like a tiger.

—O

I used them, and we had a friendly conversation that went nowhere. As soon as I started asking about Brown, however subtle I tried to be, Bondi would change the subject. Brown had managed to surround himself with a loyal band that wasn't giving anything away, no matter what.

I had the strong feeling I was running out of time.

TEN

A Loyal Band That Wasn't Giving
Anything Away

The full weight of the last sixteen hours landed on Jimmy's shoulders with a dismal thump. Phil had been murdered. Ren teetered between devastated and determined. And somewhere out there, someone they didn't know had been driven by something they had done to the breaking point of his own humanity, and then beyond it. With Jane and Ren both staring at him, Jimmy drew a heavy breath and explained, "It's almost true, and it should be completely true, that we never do anything bad, but it isn't."

"Jimmy," said Ren, warning in her voice. "What are you talking about?"

"Countermeddling," he said. "Sometimes we call it backmeddling. If you stayed current on the boards, you'd see the arguments."

"That's why I don't stay current," said Ren, and Oskar barked an Oskar-laugh. Jane just watched Jimmy.

"Countermeddling," he explained, "is when we make something bad even worse to create a backlash that makes things better."

"We do that?" said Ren, frowning. "It seems . . . I don't know. I don't like it."

"Nor do I," said Jimmy. "I hate it. It is rarely a good idea, and never the best one. If we had the right to forbid anything, we'd forbid that. Even Oskar is against it."

Oskar scowled. "What's that supposed to mean?"

Jimmy ignored him, something he thought he should probably do more.

"Give me an example?" Jane asked.

"Watergate, I think, most recently. We countermeddled some of Nixon's advisers so they'd give him bad advice. I didn't like it then; almost no one did. But one of us—I won't name names—went ahead and did it anyway."

"Don't you people have any control?" Jane asked. "Checks and balances? Ways to make sure you're doing good?"

"No."

"That," said Oskar, "is why recruiting is so important. That's where we decide if someone is really the sort of person we can count on to want to make things better."

"Just because someone did something decent, you think that means you can depend—"

"No, no," said Oskar. Then, "Excuse me, I shouldn't have interrupted you."

"No, go ahead."

Oskar nodded "The 'doing something decent' is what gets our attention, if you will. It's the first requirement. After that, we investigate the person. Thoroughly," he added.

"How?

"We have a good chance of finding any information that anyone has ever expressed symbolically."

" 'Expressed symbolically?' "

"Written down," said Jimmy.

Oskar nodded. "For the most part, or represented with any other sort of symbol. As I recall, Ren learned about your cat because of an art project you did in the eighth grade."

Jane's mouth opened, then closed. Her eyes never left Oskar.

"Anything anyone puts into symbol can go into our Garden." Oskar continued, "Usually it's simply writing. Computers—the Internet—makes it laughably easy, but letters, diaries—"

"So then," said Jane. "You can just decide to read my diary? All the way back to college? At my most vulnerable?" She looked—no, she was—outraged. "What by Astarte's tits gives you the right?"

"Because we can, and if it can help us make things better for Sam," Ren said, her voice hard, talking over both Oskar and Jimmy's started explanations, "what gives us the right not to?"

Wordless, Jane held Ren's eyes a long time, but Ren wasn't going to apologize for their privacy violations, and Jane wasn't going to forgive them. Jimmy remembered the first time he'd seen a photo of Ren, the pixie-haired UI girl Phil wanted to recruit for Celeste's Second. He'd been afraid Phil wanted someone fragile to give Celeste a better chance. Jimmy was glad to have been proved wrong.

"So you go intruding into people's personal lives in order to find people who are good," Jane said, "by a definition of good that permits snooping like the fucking NSA."

"Yes," said Oskar. "That's about right."

"And that definition of good is the only thing that prevents a horrific abuse of power?"

"Yes," said Oskar.

"And that works?" said Jane, in a tone somewhere between skeptical and mocking.

"Yes," Jimmy said.

"Usually," corrected Ren, a touch of bitterness in her voice.

I want you to understand our complacency here is due to the fact that we know our intrusions: one, are personal and respectful, and two, make things better, but Jane's outrage is correct and admirable, and her courage in calling us on it is, I hope, inspiring.

—Oskar

"That's crazy," said Jane. "What happens if someone just, I don't know, goes off on his own, and tries to fix something in some crazy way?"

"Then," said Oskar, "that person is likely to be shot in the back three times and throw us all into a crisis and drag in a few innocent strangers, as well."

Ren was away from the table before Jimmy realized she'd stood up.

* * *

If Oskar made one more snarky comment about Phil or implied again that he'd deserved to get shot, Ren thought she might—

Or if Jimmy, for that matter, much as Ren loved him, revealed another secret idiocy of theirs that she didn't know about because she hadn't gotten all of Celeste's memories, Ren was going to—

Or if Oskar answered her door and let people in or kept them out like he lived there, Ren could—

Or if they both decided it was okay for Kate to titan without even looking at Ren, or announced Jane and Phil were the priorities, or told her to take some time to pull herself together, Ren would—

And if either of them acted one more time like Jane was the one with the big problem here, Ren was going to lose her ever-loving mind.

She picked up the omelet plates and carried them to the sink.

"But it works?" Jane asked. "Most of the time?"

"Yes."

Ren could hear Jimmy's warmest smile in his voice as she scraped the plates.

"Most of the time it works, and things get better." Jimmy's head nodded inside his folds of neck. "Just a little bit."

Oskar shifted forward, elbows on the table. "Sometimes it gets quite a lot better. There are times when we have been able to marshal our disparate resources and make a courageous move instead of a merely cosmetic one."

Jimmy said, "Do you call it 'cosmetic' when—"

Ren turned the water and the garbage disposal on and Jimmy's voice got lost in the metal grinding, but it wasn't working. For them, this was another problem to solve, another stub, another recruit, another bit of meddlework. Ren kept feeding food scraps to the drain, cramming them in with her fork. Cleaning usually made her feel better, but she was integrating about as smoothly as the disposal gears with the fork tines.

Jimmy's velvet hands wrapped her wrists, freed the fork from her fingers, and turned her away from the spinning handle. He flipped the disposal off, and folded Ren against his chest. She let her forehead drop against him, but couldn't lift her arms to hug him back. She just stood there.

"Ren." Jimmy's voice resonated in his piano-deep chest. "I know. I miss him too."

Ren nodded, and he tightened his massive arms around her.

"SB 1070 was more than just meddlework to him, Jimmy. It represented something, or stood for something, about optimism, maybe."

Jimmy nodded. "I can see how it might. Immigration and the idea that any nation or bit of land could belong to one type of people has always been problematic for him."

"It was personal to him, and it killed him."

"Ren?"

"We need to hold the dust ritual."

"Of course."

"I want you to pick the memory."

"*Bien sûr*," Jimmy said, and his voice caught. A shudder went through his massive frame, then a sob.

Ren put her arms around him. Her fingers didn't reach and she put her palms flat on the heavy silk of his shirt.

"I made a Fibonacci spiral for him in my Garden," she told Jimmy. "He has to come back."

"There is no question."

"I already told her that," Oskar said.

"Be quiet now," Jane told him, and left him at the table to put her arms around Ren and Jimmy.

"We need a recruit for Phil," Oskar muttered. "And Irina's up to something. And we have to have the dust ritual." Oskar threw himself out of his chair. "I'm going to swim," he announced. "Because here I can. It's still freezing in Milwaukee."

★   ★   ★

"Kate," Daniel said, opening the passenger door of Kate's minivan as she pulled up in front of the hospital doors, "Right on time."

Kate kept her smile friendly, but not overly so. "How are you feeling?"

"Like I just got out of prison." Daniel sat down heavily. "They made me sit in a wheelchair and they pushed me out the door, like, 'Fly, little bird! You're free now!'" Daniel gave a wry chuckle as Kate put the van in gear. "Whatever. I was starting to think I'd spend the rest of my life there. Staph infection, pneumonia—what else was I going to catch?"

"I think we got everything."

"We? You said this morning you didn't really work there."

"Right. Sorry," Kate said. "They."

"Are you doing it again? What you did before, with the mint tea, and the train sounds?" He was studying her face, but not with the aesthetic appreciation he had earlier.

"Meddling? No, now we're just talking. I'll tell you anything. What do you want to know?" Kate pulled into traffic. She drove, tracking the turmoil in the young man next to her more closely than the changing traffic lights. He'd want to know a lot of things, starting with "Are you insane?" Kate tried to figure out a way to answer that without making him ask. She said, "I said some pretty wild things this morning, and I'll be saying more this afternoon, so maybe try to treat it as a game. Pretend I'm telling you a story, and go along with it as a thought experiment. Ask yourself, what if it was all true?"

"I can do that," he said carefully. The sweet flintiness of yesterday was gone, but not the frustrated, nascent heroism.

Kate straightened her spine and swallowed the tenderness blocking her throat. "You're at loose ends," she said. "You had a defining moment where you almost died. You know you don't want to go back to working for the city, but you look forward and it's terrifying. You want to do something big, but all your options are tiny. So I'll tell you a story, and maybe we'll both learn something from it."

She took Bartlett to Panther Hollow Road, found a parking place, and they got out. She let Daniel amble in the sunlight until she guessed his leg was about to start throbbing, then led them to a bench. It was cool and cloudy, but pleasant.

"So, this group that you're a part of, are you all 'heroes?'" Daniel did that thing where you make quotation marks with your fingers.

"I'm certainly not!" Kate said. "Gracious. Look at me! I'm a *mom!*"

Daniel laughed, which gave Kate permission to be serious. "I never risked my life for anyone the way you did. The Incrementalists recruited me because I had a patient who needed an abortion—preeclampsia, it used to be called toxemia. I diagnosed her, submitted the paperwork, the court refused, I performed it, they threw me in jail for a while, and I lost my license."

"I didn't know that still happened."

"Things were different then."

"Then?"

"1961."

Daniel stared. "You can't be more than—"

"I'm ninety," she said, flirting just a little.

"That's . . . okay."

"Remember now, just pretend. It's all make-believe."

"All right." Daniel scrubbed at the new growth on his scalp. "What would I ask you if I believed you?" he mused. "All right, I'll go with the obvious: why do you look so young? Are you immortal or something?"

"Immortal? No. Or something? Yes."

"Okay. Start there. Start explaining with that."

"Right you are!" Kate patted his knee and settled herself on the bench. "A lot of this we know and understand, but there are a couple of big things we don't, so let's start with those. Imagine that forty thousand years ago . . ."

★   ★   ★

Ren watched Jimmy settle himself on the living room sofa, his body somehow more cushioned than the upholstery, his skin's warmth and depth making the gray velvet look wan by comparison. He closed his dark-lashed eyes and an indulgent smile curled his lips.

"He's going to seed what's been happening to keep everyone up to date," she told Jane. "Then he'll graze for one of Phil's memories for the dust ritual. He'll pick the right one, one that Incrementalists all over the planet can share today and not just remember, but relive, as if they were Phil."

"Okay," Jane said.

"Then this afternoon, each one of our disbanded little band will hold one broken piece, one portion of my dead and dismembered almost-husband and together, we will re-member him."

"Okay," Jane said again. "A little Osiris, but okay." She checked messages on her phone while Ren made a quick post to the Incrementalists forum announcing the time of Phil's dust ritual.

"Let's go outside," Ren suggested, and led Jane out into the heat and shade of the back patio. She knew Jane believed the earth and sky were imbued with a sentient benevolence. Even if they weren't, they couldn't hurt, and Jane looked like she needed all the help she could get.

What she got was Oskar, in Phil's entirely-too-small-for-him trunks, moving through the water like a pale shark, all cartilage and teeth. When he spotted Ren and Jane, he stood up, waist deep in the water, dripping and winded. Ren thought Jane looked a bit the same.

"Ready for me to run you home?" he asked.

"What? Oh. No," Jane said. "Actually, I've messaged Sam."

Oskar squeezed water from his hair in a way that did something lovely to his arms.

Jane gave a tiny sigh. "My husband," she clarified. "Your new recruit?"

"And?" Oskar wiped water from his face.

"He's on his way."

"Excellent!" Oskar clapped his big hands together and arced himself onto the decking in a fluid swoop that took half the pool with him. "I'll go graze for his switches. Ren, do you have anything already?" He wrapped his narrow hips in one of Ren's bath towels. "Maybe I should get Jimmy to help."

"Don't you fucking dare," Ren said.

Oskar looked at her. "Why is it," he asked with a superior sniff, "that everyone feels the need to be so fucking vulgar today?"

Jane snorted.

"Jimmy is seeding what's happening, and then he's grazing for the dust ritual," Ren explained.

"I know that," Oskar said. "How long will it take Sam to get here?"

"Twenty minutes maybe," Jane said.

"That's not a lot of time, Ren. Jimmy could—"

"No."

"But—"

"But nothing, Oskar," Ren said. "But not a solitary god damned thing."

"Ren, do you want . . ." Oskar stopped. Ren could see him trying to make his face gentle. "Look, you miss him. You want him back. We have an excellent potential recruit on the way right now. He's altruistic. He actively wants to make things better. He's not overly, narcissistically attached to his own personality. His wife is willing to let him go. Ren. We may not get a better chance. Why not get Phil back as soon as possible? Why choose to keep on grieving?"

"I don't even know what he looks like."

"So?" Oskar looked from Ren to Jane, uncomprehending.

"It matters," Jane told him.

Oskar shrugged. "Jane's pretty enough."

Jane blushed, and it was Ren's turn to look between them in confusion. "Pretty enough for what?" she asked. She had felt the tension between Oskar and Jane, but she didn't think he had, or would comment so baldly on it.

"People select partners of approximately comparable physical attractiveness," Oskar explained toweling himself. "Jane's husband should be about as good-looking as Jane is. Which should more than suffice."

Jane dusted invisible dust from her yoga pants. Ren took a slow breath. "It's not about good-looking enough."

"What then?" Oskar rounded on her drippily. "What is it Ren? Does he need to have a mustache? Does he have to fit in Phil's clothes? Why do you care? It's Phil. Or it will be. The man you love." He took her shoulders, trying to see some hint of rationality in her eyes. "Would you be this fussy if he'd lived through the shooting, but with new scars? Or missing a leg? How much of his old body would be enough for you?"

Jane hit him. Or she tried to. Oskar caught her hand and stepped back and Jane missed her footing and nearly fell into the pool.

"Stop it!" Ren said, surprised by the screaming in her very quiet voice.

"We are not going to act this way," she said. "It's sordid, and embarrassing, and you all are the closest thing I have to family, and we are not going to be like this. I do not allow it. We will be better than this, starting now. Dignified. Unified. We will hold Phil's dust ritual at three thirty our time. I've already written the group and said so. Jimmy is right now re-seeding the memory we'll all share. And it will be a memory of something noble. And not divisive. Because we do make things better, god damn it. And we will not meddle with Sam when he comes over. We will meet him like normal people and we will tell him the truth. Jane, you can go home with him afterward and talk it all over, and you can make whatever decision is best for the two of you. Together. And you, dear Oskar, will be pleasant, like a normal person. Friendly. Agreeable."

"I don't—" Oskar started, but Jimmy interrupted.

"Jane?" Jimmy's bulk filled the opening he'd made in the sliding door. "Is this your phone?" He held the buzzing thing in his hand.

"Yeah, thanks!" Jane took the phone from him, walking a few steps toward the house as Jimmy came out onto the patio, smiling into the grinding sun.

"How's everything out here?" he asked.

"Fine," Ren said.

"Oskar?"

"Normal as fuck."

"Sam's going to be a while," Jane said. "Some kind of ruckus at the library."

★   ★   ★

Jimmy returned to the sofa and closed his eyes. Having seeded highlights of their current events for the group, he prepared his mind to graze for Phil's dusting—a pleasurable prospect. Sometimes, when he wasn't in a hurry, he would just fly or jump up to his western turret and sit in the window, looking out over the rolling hills and meadows beyond the stream. His subconscious, it seemed, had a thing for beauty. He was given to understand that Matsu's Garden was also beautiful, and so were Irina's and Stacy's. Most of them weren't; most were simple and practical, and if you wanted something of beauty you made a seed of what you wanted, like

Phil did. Or you just concentrated on the purely practical, like Alexander. Or ignored it entirely, like John and Ramon.

But Jimmy felt fortunate in the natural beauty of the area surrounding the castle his subconscious provided for him, and sometimes, before grazing, he would take some time to simply sit in the turret window and enjoy it.

It could be overdone, of course. It was possible to become so used to sitting in a high place knowing one is perfectly safe, that one returns to the real world with normal caution unnaturally suppressed. Jimmy had accidentally stubbed himself that way once, about a hundred and fifty years ago, and it took a quarter of a century for his fellows to stop kidding him about it.

So after only a few minutes, he jumped down to the courtyard. The doors opened and he took himself past the entrance hall to the inner hall, and so to the withdrawing room. His first seed, of his first spiking, was a large chair, and the first seed of his most recent spiking was, as always, a footstool. Jimmy sat in the one, put his feet upon the other, and leaned back his head.

Ah, Phil.

Across the room, the fire roared into life, and Jimmy stared into it. He brought the flames into the room, engulfing himself and everything else and imagined being warmed just a little by those flames because a bit of realism gave the imagination something to latch on to.

He set the fire to searching for seeds of Phil. The first Jimmy examined was of the first time he had met Phil. Jimmy turned it into a pear. He loved pears. He made a mental note to pick up a good pear brandy back in the real world. He took a healthy bite, the juice running over his chin.

It was after the American War for Independence, and just before the Great Revolution. Jimmy had met Phil in La Havre, where his ship landed, and he was the first one off it. Phil spoke perfect French, then, with only the least trace of the accent of Picardy, and had recognized Jimmy at once and approached him. A tiny little man, balding, and missing a hand, Phil—going by Carter in those days—had hugged Jimmy saying he was glad to see him, and that if he didn't find a decent bottle of wine in the next ten minutes, he'd stub the younger man. Jimmy had laughed and found Carter the wine. They ate roast goose in roux while Carter told story after story about famous people in the past, each more ribald than the last, and it had taken Jimmy a long time to realize Carter was making them up. He decided later that Carter must have known how intimidated Jimmy had been to meet a man who had lived for eighteen centuries and wanted to put him at his ease. It had worked.

It wasn't the right memory for Phil's dust ritual: it wasn't his most recent Second, and it was too much about Jimmy, not enough about Phil, but Jimmy played out the whole seed because he wanted to. He could find things in the Garden pretty quickly when it was needed, but he took his time with this; the search felt like his own, private ritual. What could that gracious, easygoing man have done to make someone want to murder him?

He knew they'd get Phil back. He was certain of it. He was just superstitious enough not to take any comfort in that certainty for fear he might jinx it. But in truth, with Phil so deeply in love, so involved in the work, and so full of passion, how could there could be anyone whose will might overpower his? So, yes, Jimmy knew they'd get Phil back out of stub.

But the death of a Second is still the death of a Second; it affected them all. And Jimmy wouldn't run through Phil's seeds as if he were scanning his contact list for someone's phone number. He should concentrate on this Second, on Chuck, but—

Wait.

"Fuck ritual. Fuck tradition." That's what Phil had told him once, and Ren both needed and deserved to know him, to see who he was. Ren, of all of them, had never known Phil in any previous Second, and Jimmy knew she suffered the absence of her Celeste-stolen memories like a constant badge, an invisible scarlet "O" for outsider. He'd seen it again today, when she'd had to learn from him about countermeddling. So yes, traditions said you use the most recent Second to find the memory for the dust ritual. But fuck tradition and fuck ritual. Jimmy would search as long as he needed to, and if the seed he found to show Ren more of the man she loved was of an older Second, then so be it.

Jimmy spent a long time there, amid an inferno, eating pears and plums, smelling roses, watching waterfalls and mountain storms, until an ocean wave crashing into a cliff drenched him in a memory that made him go, "Oh, yes. Of course."

JULY, 1857

"OLD JOHN BROWN, WHOSE SOUL IS MARCHING ON?"

I met with Brown on one of his trips into Lawrence. We were on Massachusetts Street, just opposite the site of the old Free State Hotel, which the Eldridge brothers were in the middle of rebuilding. I studied him, his deep-set eyes, low forehead, mouth permanently set in a frown of righteous fury. In spite of my efforts to befriend him, he'd always been cool toward me—by which I mean that he was willing to talk, but not so much inclined to listen. I think he realized I didn't approve of violence, and so he figured I wasn't as committed to the cause as I should be.

It was like trying to meddle with a brick wall. He ate some of the poppyseed cake I'd made, and I hummed "Thy Bountiful Care" under my breath, and I had the coffee smeared on my flannel shirt, and I might as well not have bothered. We exchanged a few words; I spoke of the Lecompton Constitution, he spoke of the plight of the slaves. I opined that we, in Kansas, had the chance to unite the whole North behind us, and he declared that every man who owned a slave deserved to be hanged.

He wouldn't tell me what he was going to do, but he was determined to do it, and nothing I could say would change that. I tried to get at least a hint as to what he had in mind, but nothing. My best guess was more raids into Missouri to free slaves, but something about the way he held himself told me he had bigger thoughts, bigger plans.

Leaving me with the eternal question: Now what?

Phil asks that question more often than he should, but even I wouldn't have known what to do with Brown. Besides join him, that is.

—*Oskar*

ELEVEN

How We Fight Is As Important

"She shouldn't be here." A tall, attractive man appeared between the library shelves like Samson at the temple's pillars.

Irina twisted her head up for a better look at him. "Hiya," she said.

He regarded her with all the warmth he'd show Delilah. "Want me to put her outside?" he asked Sam.

"Throw me over your shoulder and I'll puke down your back," Irina promised.

"It's okay," Sam said although it was perfectly clear that nothing was okay in his world. "Irina, this is Frio. Frio, this is Irina. She's a friend of Jane's."

"I'm not, actually. I was a friend of Phil's, the guy who got shot down here yesterday," Irina said.

Frio took a step toward his boss, and stopped himself with feline balance, indifferent to Phil's death itself, deeply concerned with its effect on Sam. Inordinately so.

If Irina was right about Sam being who she thought he was and doing what she thought Phil had been doing, Officer Jack Harris had bigger problems than he knew.

Sam, still sitting on the floor, his back against a shelf, looked up at his subordinate like he expected to have to shoulder the weight of all the books behind him when he stood. He just shook his head and looked back down at his hands, limp in his lap, still holding his car keys.

"Sam, were you headed to Phil and Ren's house to see Jane?"

He nodded.

"Come on," the big guy said, reaching for Irina's arm. "Let's go."

"It's okay," Sam said again, no more convincingly, but it stopped his enforcer, who straightened, clearly uncomfortable with standing while Sam sat, but with no excuse to get on the ground, and nothing he could do about Irina except scowl.

"Could you give me a lift?" Irina gingerly touched the bruised place on her jaw, keeping her focus on Sam. "They're expecting me too."

"Sure," Sam said.

"We don't know her."

"It's okay."

"I'll drive." The big guy reached down and took the keys from Sam's unprotesting hand. "I'll bring the car around front, load you both in quick."

Sam just nodded, and Irina shifted to a more comfortable position against one of the bookcase's vertical supports. Frio turned on his heel with an almost military repressed anger, startling a homeless woman who'd been napping at a study table. She whirled to her feet like a heap of blown leaves, and Irina watched the powerfully built man, frustrated as he'd been, catch the poor thing by her shoulders and gently re-seat her.

"You're afraid that whoever killed Phil is still hunting rabble-rousers," Irina said.

Sam nodded.

"And your 'we' has roused a bit of rabble."

Sam just shrugged.

"That 'we' includes, at the very least, you—a high school civics teacher, and Santi—one of your students?"

Sam nodded.

"Who had you for Russian history?" Irina guessed. "No," she quickly corrected, reading Sam's face, "for something broader. A topics class. A unit on revolutions? No, revolt. Serfs, Slaves, and Insurgents, something like that?"

Sam's smile was bitter. Behind him, the homeless woman lurched from her table and limped toward the john.

"Interesting," Irina mused, which wasn't really the word. She'd been a serf and a slave, run revolutionary and rebel, and she doubtless would again. In fact, she'd been feeling pretty damn insurgent quite recently, but not right now. Right now, she was investigating, not inciting. "So you, Santi, and the Army guy."

"Frio?" Sam asked. "He's not Army."

"You, Santi, and Frio—any others?"

Sam nodded again, but Irina decided not to push for more names or a number. Sam was the type to protect information about his people over anything else, no matter what. Like she was.

"And you're up to something dangerous and illegal. Something anti-authoritarian." That much was obvious from what he taught and who he was working with.

The rest—that Sam was the guy who'd been giving the local police and federal enforcers such fits, who'd been behind the sabotaged immigration raids, who'd protected the water drops in the desert—surprised Irina as much as it would surprise Sam that she knew about them. All the local news outfits had been silent on the subject. All except Menzie's, anyway.

Sam was not at all what Irina had been imagining, but of course she'd been imagining Phil. Well, she'd been wrong before. For example, she thought she'd come down here hunting Phil's killer, but found his new Second instead. Frio was better than Oskar or Phil, or both put together, as far as change agents went. He reminded her of a one-armed man she'd known even before she took the spike the first time—a man she'd loved and watched burn on the public square of Cap Françaison.

"Sam," Irina asked him, "do you know what the difference is between a revolt and a revolution?"

"No."

"Nobody does," she said. "Not going into one anyway."

I do. Revolt is movement against. Revolution moves things forward, creates something new.

—Oskar

★   ★   ★

Jimmy recalled, in 1977 Phil was living in Pittsburgh. He traveled to Texas a lot for poker games in what he half-jokingly called "The Negro Poker League," and he had picked Jimmy up at the airport in a 1966 Shelby Mustang that had seen better days. Jimmy had known it was a 1966 Shelby Mustang because three years earlier, the last time he had visited the States, Phil had mentioned it five times in a five-kilometer drive.

But in 1977, neither Phil nor Jimmy spoke during the drive. In his current Second, Phil was husky and about forty, his short hair prematurely gray. His apartment building looked like it was ready to slide into the Allegheny River, but inside it was clean and spare, if hot. Phil put some Louis Armstrong on the stereo, and Jimmy listened to it with him as the others arrived. Jimmy wasn't sure if the coronet was laughing or crying or both—maybe that was the point. It reminded him of this New World he found himself in, harsh and unforgiving and vital, and always moving forward—the dynamics building incrementally. He looked at Phil, but didn't say anything.

Irina was the last to get there. Once she was seated, Phil took the record off and carefully returned the album to its spot. When everyone had something to drink, Ramon spoke. "I assume we all know by now that Sophal has been stubbed?"

There were nods from around the room.

Ramon continued, "I've been in touch with Ahn Hoang, but it will take her some time. And until we know more, and can decide what to do, we don't know if we can risk another recruit in Phnom Pehn, much less ask her to travel there."

There were more nods from around the room, and, after a moment, Ramon continued. "To be clear, we're here to decide whether there's anything we can do about this situation, and, if so, how to go about it. We aren't here to beat ourselves up about what's past."

"I think, dear Dewey," said Celeste, "that it is worth taking some time to see how the mistakes were made so they might be avoided moving forward, unless, perchance, I'm the only one here interested in the avoidance of future calamity, in which case I will let the matter drop out of courtesy if not conviction."

Jimmy adored Celeste, but he had to admit that sometimes she irritated him. He was the newest member of Salt, and still felt he should listen more than speak. But then Irina fell into Celeste's trap and went into a monologue about how, if she hadn't been in stub when the decisions were made she would have had things to say, and Ramon, contradicting himself, said it was important they get what lessons they could out of it.

Jimmy was perfectly aware of what Celeste was doing: she was saying, "I told you so," in as subtle and indirect a manner as she could. And she was right, she *had* told them to stay out of things in Cambodia; but that wasn't helpful for dealing with the guilt, or for figuring out what had gone wrong, or deciding if they could do anything useful, and before he had really decided to, Jimmy had said, "If the only available lesson, Celeste, is that next time we should listen to you and not get involved, I've had a long and tiring plane flight for nothing."

And that had done it. They were off, screaming, shouting, gesticulating, and getting nowhere. Eventually, after about two hours, there was a lull in the conversation (no pun intended, Ramon). While everyone gathered up energy to start in again, Phil cleared his throat. He hadn't said a word the entire time. "There's a place that will deliver pizza here," he said. "And they have decent pasta, Celeste. Howard wired me some money for the meeting, so I'll pick up the check."

An hour later, they had quieted down, and were munching away (the pizza was surprisingly good, Jimmy remembered, the sauce wonderfully heavy on oregano), and while they all ate, Phil talked.

"We will never get over this," he said in a voice almost too low to hear. "This will leave scars on us for at least as long as I've been alive. We were wrong, and that brings into question everything we've ever done, and makes us doubt the very value of our existence. That is as it should be. Whatever our exact role in this, each of us needs to wear those scars. Each of us," he repeated, with a sharp glance at Celeste, who had opened her mouth to speak.

"To imagine that we can proceed as we have been after this is lunacy. To imagine that our whole existence is a mistake is cynicism. Whether we want to or not, for a while we're going to be afraid to do things. We need to accept that. We need to feel this doubt. We deserve to feel this pain.

"And then we need to go on.

"Not because of how we feel, but because the amnemones still need us, and we can still help them, and at the end of the day, how we feel about it—our guilt, our terror, our hesitation—just doesn't matter. The amnemones matter. Our meddlework matters. Making things better matters.

"Ray suggests that we're here to see if we can do anything about Cambodia now, and I don't disagree. We have to talk about that, and decide. But the most important thing is simply that, first, we recognize that for a while we're going to feel like wounded animals, and second, that we recognize that we have a duty to overcome that feeling and get on with our work.

"Because that's the only way we can even begin to make up for what we did."

Phil went back to eating his pizza, but even Celeste had been cowed into silence. The meeting lasted two more days, with only minimal shouting, and it accomplished a great deal.

In his castle Garden, Jimmy's fire returned to the fireplace, and went out. Jimmy sat for just a few more minutes before returning to Ren and Phil's house in the real world, where he already knew he was crying.

★　　★　　★

Kate gave Daniel enough information to drown a weaker man, then dropped him off in front of the hotel where a grateful city had paid ahead for two weeks in a modest suite. "Now what?" he asked her.

"Now, you think about it. Then, when you're ready, maybe tomorrow, maybe next week, we get together, and I'll make you believe the make-believe. You'll come over to my house. It'll take a full day. I'll show you the Garden, what a stub looks like, and how we do what we do. We'll talk, you'll have dinner with the fam. Then you go away and think about it some more, and decide if you want to close your eyes and jump."

"Yeah," Daniel had said, no doubt trying to imagine, even if it were all real, risking his life in a fifty-fifty shot at everything Kate had told him about. She knew he couldn't imagine doing it. "Okay," he'd said. "I'll think about it."

Kate smiled at him, waving good-bye from the minivan, and pulled into traffic. Poor kid. It was a lot to sort through. Of course, he would be convinced it was crazy. He would think he'd just wasted several hours talking to a woman who was clearly certifiable. She could almost hear him talking to himself. *And she's a doctor. Healthcare is hosed.*

She'd read it all in his broad forehead and nervous hands. He'd think about it, and he'd pace—and only partially because his legs hurt. Pacing wouldn't reduce the pain, but sitting still made it worse. Kate couldn't explain it. She had given him a supply of big white pills, but he wouldn't take one. He would want his head clear.

Would he believe her? Would he take the gamble?

No. That wasn't the question. Of course he'd take the gamble. If he thought it was real. If he thought the Incrementalists really could offer a shot at immortality, or close to it, where every day he could go to bed knowing things were just a bit less messed up because of him. He wouldn't say no to that. If the odds were one in twenty, rather than fifty-fifty, he still wouldn't.

So the question was just: did he believe her?

Her phone rang. Digging it out of her bag, she nearly ran into a mail truck.

"I'm no fucking hero!" Daniel's voice, still raspy from the smoke damage, sounded choked with something harder. "A hero wouldn't have stood there, scared, while people died."

"Daniel—"

"I'm not how you see me. I'm not as good as that. I'm really selfish sometimes. I get really scared. What if I sign up with you for all the wrong reasons? What if I end up making things worse?"

Confusion and upset were a normal part of the process, but Kate hated hearing the torment in Dan's damaged voice. "I'm coming back to get you."

"Kate?"

"I'm making a U-ey."

"It's tempting enough to make a person selfish anyway. I mean, immortality? Except it isn't, exactly. It's transferring memories from one person to another, and is that even possible? Hell, I don't know enough to say it isn't. But, from a *dead* person? Well, yeah. I mean, if it can be done at all, that means that memories can be stored, and if they can be stored, it doesn't matter if the original source is dead. But the whole thing—it's nuts. You're nuts!"

"I'm almost back to you."

"You're a nut job! Except that you're a nut job who did stuff to me based on knowing things no one could know. And a nut job who has a way of making the preposterous seem mundane, and making the mundane seem magic." His breath came over the phone, then, "I'm not magic, Kate." It was an ugly scraped whisper. "I'm kind of a loser."

"Come downstairs, Daniel."

He was waiting for her when Kate rolled the minivan up to the valet station. They looked sniffy, but Dan yanked open the passenger door and stood there, looking in. "You said you'd convince me it's all real."

"Yes."

"You said the guy who died—"

"Phil."

"You said he was recruited because of helping in a fire, only it was a car fire."

"His most recent Second, yes. Daniel, the valets are showing signs of coronary stress at the state of my van. Can you get in and we'll go just around the corner?"

"You said he didn't get burned in the fire."

"That's right."

"But it was enough to show he was willing to give something up, or at least risk something, for strangers. That's what you're looking for."

"Yes."

He got into the van. "I'm ready for you to make me believe in it, Kate."

"Daniel—"

"No, fuck that. You don't have to convince me; if there's a one-in-a-hundred shot, I'll take it. I want you to make me one of you."

"Daniel—" Kate maneuvered around the valet, nosed the van into the fire lane, and put on her hazard lights.

Dan waited for her, watching her dashboard armada of bobble heads nodding him along.

"I can't forget the sounds of it, Kate," he said. "The crunching, tearing sound of the ceiling beam giving way, landing on the poor bastard I was dragging. I heard it. Then I felt like I was burning alive, then a monster in a mask came, and I almost panicked and ran until I realized he was a fireman.

"I remember people being treated by EMTs, and I realized that four of them were alive because of me, and I started to swell with pride, and then I heard the whole thing come down, and there were screams, and all I could think of were the seconds—maybe a minute, maybe two—that I stood there trying to make myself go in, and I wondered how many more I could have saved if I hadn't hesitated, and then my eyes were full of flashing lights and I wished to Christ they'd turn them off. And then I woke up and all there was was pain."

"Dan." Kate put her hand on his shoulder, but he shrugged it off.

"No," he said. "I'm ready now. If it works, good. I'll help make things better. If it fails, at least I won't have to hear how it sounds."

⋆　　⋆　　⋆

Irina hoisted herself to standing and, leaving Sam to reshelve the tumbled library books, headed for the john. She pushed open the bathroom door, and the fruit-and-filth stink of homelessness hit her like a second punch. She pressed her mouth into her shoulder and gulped the vinylled air of her raincoat. She ran water in the sink and peeked under the stall just to prove to herself she hadn't mistaken the limp. Nope. The woman's feet, at odd angles to each other and in badly duct-taped shoes, were swollen over the laces and bleeding at the heels.

"You think it's gonna rain?" Irina asked her, remembering how good you get at weather when you live outside.

"I'm using the bathroom." The woman didn't sound as old as she'd looked. She didn't sound drunk either. "It's a public bathroom." She sounded worried.

"I know," Irina said. "I'm using it too. I need to wash my socks."

A pause, then: "You can't. They throw you out for that."

"Yeah, well they'll throw me out with clean socks then."

The woman laughed.

"You think it'll rain?" Irina asked again.

"I don't think it will," the woman answered, sounding more relaxed. "It rained last week a little in the afternoon. I figure it won't now for a while to come."

With no name for the woman and not even able to see her, Irina was meddling switch-less and blind, with who-knew-how-much time before Frio came back with Sam's car. Irina had high hopes for him, but there were still entirely too many unknowns in that case. This, she knew she could help. "I can see your feet," Irina said, hoisting herself onto the counter by the sink. "But you can't see mine, can you?"

The woman didn't answer.

"I'm not crazy," Irina said.

"Okay." The woman was wary again, but Irina didn't have time to earn her trust, or any way to create a connection.

"It's just that my shoes make my feet disappear," Irina explained.

"No they don't."

"Can you see them?"

There was a pause. "No." The woman's feet twisted on the dirty tile as she tried looking around more. "But I'm in here."

Irina pulled off her shoes and slid down to standing in her socks. The floor was damp.

"I can see your feet," the woman said. "Put your shoes back on."

"No way!"

"Shoes can't make your feet invisible." The woman tried to comfort Irina. "I promise."

"They can too. You try them," Irina suggested, sticking her nearly new Nikes under the stall.

"Oh, these are nice."

Irina stepped away to check through the bathroom door that Sam was still waiting for her. The woman came out of the stall. "See?"

Irina looked, gauging the woman, trying to see through the intelligent wariness. She saw depression and signs of PTSD, but living on the street or even in shelters will do that to you even if it's not what got you there in the first place. "I'm Irina," she said.

"Lucy."

"Hi, Lucy," Irina said, noticing the same, if less trained assessment of her in Lucy's gray eyes. "Hey, my shoes don't make your feet go invisible. Can we trade?"

"I . . ." Lucy considered. She looked down at the Nikes and at Irina's sock feet. "Mine are pretty old," she said.

"Mine were too," Irina said, "until I found those in the Dumpster. But whoever threw them away must have been like me." She shrugged. "With feet that disappear."

"They don't, really," Lucy said, exhausted. "You should put these back on."

"Please?" Irina wheedled.

"It wouldn't be right for me to take them," Lucy said.

"Okay." Irina turned to go.

"No." Lucy's voice had the edge of someone who dealt with erratic behavior more than she'd like. "You have to put your shoes back on."

"Nope," Irina said. "I'm throwing those away. Back from whence they came, I say! I don't want them." She met Lucy's eyes. "Are you sure I can't wear yours? Just for a little?"

Lucy looked down at her feet in Irina's shoes, and then at her old, taped ones. "You really want to trade?"

"Please?"

"Okay." Lucy handed Irina the old pair and wriggled her toes inside the new ones. "But I feel bad taking your nice shoes."

"Invisible shoes," Irina corrected her. "Yuck. Come here, Lucy. See that man out there?"

Lucy peeked out of the bathroom door. "There're two. Which? The preacher or the cop?"

Irina looked and saw Frio was back, with his stubbled cheeks, ragged ponytail, and soldier shoulders. He'd be delighted for an excuse to whisk Sam away, and leave her behind. She didn't think Sam would let him, but she didn't have much time. "Both of them," she told Lucy, and pulled the prepaid cell phone from her pocket. "The priest one. He's my brother. And I have to go with him now. We're going back to the hospital where I take medicine and feel better, so I don't need this anymore." She put the phone in Lucy's hands. "But you can use it, right?"

Lucy nodded. A phone made a huge difference on the street.

"There's sixty minutes on it. You know the tricks, right?" Irina confirmed. "Use it so you're not loitering when you need to get inside somewhere. Call your family. Call me, if you want. My other number's in there, okay?"

"Yeah."

"Listen." Irina waited until Lucy looked up. "Do whatever you have to not to be anywhere near this library on Sunday, okay? Promise me."

Lucy squinted at Irina.

"There's going to be a police raid, and people get shot in those things. So stay away from here on Sunday, okay? It's how you can thank me for the shoes."

Lucy nodded carefully. "Okay," she said.

"Okay." Irina pushed her feet into Lucy's crumbling shoes and hurried after Sam and Frio, who were already headed for the door.

SEPTEMBER, 1857

"AN UNEXPECTED EVENT IN THE GARDEN, CARTER . . ."

September 24, 1857
Lawrence, Kansas Territory

Dear Miss Voight:

Just received yours of the 2nd inst. and was gratified to hear that events in the Territory continue to occupy the attention of the North. The bundle of newspapers was also very welcome. I do believe that, for the most part, the violence is finished here—having learned that they cannot overwhelm us, or frighten us, our enemies on the other side of the border seem to be concentrating all of their hopes on the convention taking place in Lecompton.

It is kind of you to ask after my health, which I am pleased to say is as satisfactory as a man my age can ask. I was fortunate when I settled here to be in better circumstances than most, and was able to secure lodging that is dry in the rain and warm in the winter. This has done much to keep me in good health, and I only wish I could say the same for many others here who suffer horribly from the cold.

Let me say categorically that you need have no fear of any wavering of commitment on the part of the Free State Party.

Between our work here, and yours there, I am certain we will achieve our goal, and see Kansas a free State. After that, I can only hope you're wrong, and that a gradual and peaceful extinction of slavery will follow.

As a last note, Captain John Brown of Osawatomie, of whom I've written before as the architect of the murder of several unarmed settlers (as well, to be sure, as the commander of a stunning victory), has vanished, and I worry that he might be involved in a mischief that will hurt our cause. If you learn anything of his doings, please inform me as soon as possible.

I hope you remain in good health. Until I hear from you again, I remain, dear lady,

Yours Very Sincerely,
Carter

TWELVE

Not So Much Inclined to Listen

Ren didn't like swimming in it, but she appreciated the smart design of their pool. It was small, but long and shallow, so it used less water, allowed for at least partial lap swimming, and fit neatly into their narrow but deep suburban lot. And Phil had loved it. No. Phil loved it. Still. Or again, maybe.

Ren shook the question off and glanced at Jane, standing poolside next to her, alternately looking from the phone in her hand to Oskar slicing through the water. "He swims laps like he's going somewhere," Jane mused.

"He does everything like he's going somewhere."

Jane nodded, and Ren watched Jane watch the water ripple over Oskar's rippling, and admired her calm. Maybe Ren should stick with yoga.

Jane crouched to fold the wide cuffs of her sweatpants out of Oskar over-splash range, and Ren noticed for the first time that Jane had on different clothes. Sam must have brought her a change when he came to the yoga studio to drive their car home so Jane could bring Ren's car back here. "Don't worry," Jane said, standing. "Sam will want this."

"Jane, if we spike Phil's stub into him—your husband will basically be gone. You know that, right?" Ren couldn't tell whether Jane's offer of her husband as Phil's Second was selfless sacrifice or easy out.

Jane rocked contemplatively onto the balls of her feet and back onto her heels. "That won't be such a new thing."

Ren waited.

"He's pretty much gone already." Jane looked at her toes in the puddling water. "Not physically—although he's home a lot less than he used to be too—but he's stopped seeing me. Even when I'm right across from him. He doesn't hear me when I talk. It's like there's this giant thing right behind me and all his focus, all his looking-at and listening-to and thinking-about gets sucked right past me into it."

"Is he maybe seeing someone else?"

"Shit," Jane said. "I wish." She shook her head impatiently. "He's not *seeing* anything. Not a person or a thing or a project. I know what Sam's like when he has one of those. He's good then. When he was trying to get Southside signed up to be in the model UN program, it was all he could talk about. It made him angry, but he likes being angry. He was happy angry. That's how he was when I met him—all outrage and ready to fight." Jane's eyes drifted to Oskar roiling the pool. "It was so sexy," she said.

"Passion is," Ren agreed.

Jane's smile blended wistful with lustful. "So what happened?" Ren asked Jane.

"We fucked rapturously for weekends of course." Jane grinned, then went back to watching Oskar. "After he moved into my place, I transferred to Howestine because the district doesn't like couples working at the same school. Sam thought I was wasting my abilities up there on kids whose parents gave a shit. I have—Sam thinks I have—some kind of magic, that the kids at Southside needed more."

"So why didn't he transfer?"

"He didn't want that either. Wouldn't even listen to the idea." Jane dragged one of the rickety loungers into the shade. "It was our first fight. Our only one, really. We just have it once a week. Sam can be . . ." She looked for the word.

"Stubborn?" Ren pulled another chaise up beside her. This was what she'd been taking yoga to learn: who Sam was and what was going on with the kids at his school, but her heart wasn't in the meddle anymore. She just wanted to help her friend.

"It's more than stubborn." Jane yanked her cuffs up over her knees and stretched pale shins into the sunlight. "Stubborn won't change. Sam won't change *and* he has to change you." She regarded the shreds of her pedicure. "He's gotten so tied up in not changing that it's changed him."

"Taking Phil's stub would be a pretty big change."

"Yeah, but different. It would be like—" Jane waved her hand, impatient.

"A ladder from the ceiling?" Ren suggested.

"You mean like attic stairs?" Jane frowned.

"Taking Phil's stub would be a way for Sam to get out of the bad place he's in without having to walk through any of the doors he's slammed shut."

"Yeah." Jane sat back against the ropey plastic slats of the lounge chair and closed her eyes. "It's an exit without leaving."

Ren almost said, "Without leaving anything but you," but stopped herself. It seemed like such a Celeste thing to say, even if Jane didn't have Ren's abandonment issues. In Jane's compact shoulders and back, Ren could read the weight of Sam's unhappiness and the magnitude of its impact on their marriage, but nothing in Jane's delicate hands or jaw suggested she was approaching the kind of life-pivot losing a husband felt like to Ren.

Oskar sprang out of the pool and shook himself. Ren waved, but Jane stayed motionless. Not even breathing.

Oskar picked up a towel that looked too small against his torso and dried himself. "Do we know how long Sam's going to be?"

Ren shook her head.

Oskar unlatched the fence to let Susi onto the patio. "He can be in here as long as no one's swimming, right?"

Ren nodded. Susi loved to jump in the pool, but nothing she and Phil had tried could teach the dog to climb the stairs out, and the poor thing had almost drowned twice. If no one was in the pool to remind him it was fun, Susi remembered it was scary and didn't throw himself into the water. Oskar opened the gate, and Susi came skittering around the wet periphery to Ren. Oskar whistled and called, but Susi, very much Phil's dog, wouldn't go to him, and since Jane was keeping her eyes abstemiously closed, Oskar went inside. Susi stuffed himself under Ren's chair, bulging the plastic beneath Ren's calves and grunting. Jane let out a long yogic breath; she was meditating, something she needed more than further conversation, so Ren closed her own eyes. She felt like she had first-date jitters. Sam could arrive any moment.

Ren still had no access to her most recent four hundred years, so she reached further back for memories that felt the way she did now. She was fourteen and her cheeks were striped with burning cold where her tears streaked them. She wouldn't unclasp her hands to wipe her face because she must pray with her hands folded, but she swayed on her stiff knees. "Make me an instrument of your will, oh Lord," she prayed. Her two sisters had both enjoyed their arranged marriages, but she could not. "Make me an obedient and willing instrument." The sob in her throat stuck on the thick shame that she was not willing, that she would not for all the world match herself to so great misfortune. She had been happy in her condition of a single life. "But who am I, oh Lord, sinful dust and ashes, in disputing Thy pleasure? Thy will be done in me and by me in all things."

But not this. Not this miserable encumbered estate of the married.

"Lord my God, let me not be rebellious before Thee, nor add sin to my iniquities."

What had she done in displeasing this great and dreadful God?

Ren opened her eyes and called Susi, who licked her face, smelling like warm sweaters and faith. "What do you think?" Ren asked the sunny fur. "Is it better to bend my will to my beliefs, or the other way around?"

Susi barked and battered his tail into Jane.

"You're fucked either way." Jane stretched her arms over her head with a luxurious yawn. "As long as your morality runs counter to your nature, you're just fucked." She rolled off the chair into downward dog, the back of her legs scored with red imprints from the crappy patio furniture. "I don't get why there has to be all this striving and anxiety. Do whatever gives you pleasure as long as it doesn't cause anyone else pain." She straightened into a graceful warrior pose. "What would feel good now?"

"Having Phil back."

"Then why do you look so constipated?"

Susi bumped Ren's hand with his snout. "Because I can't have what I want."

"Then wanting Phil back isn't what feels good now, is it?" Jane put out her hands to help Ren up. "What would feel good now?"

"Running away? Starting over?" Ren looked up at Jane. "Getting drunk?" She put her hands in Jane's and drew her knees up, straddling the chair in an awkward squat. Jane levered her to standing. "Figuring out what he needs to come back?"

"Really?" Jane held Ren's hands, looking at her.

"I honestly don't know," Ren said.

"Continued indecision and doubt? That feel good?"

"Definitely not."

"Reckless stabs in the dark?"

"Okay, okay," Ren said. "I get it. I'll make an educated guess on the best path and get to work."

Jane followed her into the living room where Oskar and Jimmy were working and grazing. "I think you may not quite be getting the 'feel good' part of this, Ren."

Ren shrugged. "I'm not sure the rigor of being happy is any easier than that of being good."

"For the love of God, Ren!" Oskar looked up from his laptop. "Ever the doubting Incrementalist."

Jimmy opened his eyes, his face wet as Lusanne's had been the morning of her wedding. "I've found the memory for this afternoon," he said. Ren sat down next to him and let his arm cloak her.

"What do you think, Oskar?" Jane's playful tone didn't match the tension in her spine. "How do you know what's right to do?"

Oskar twisted himself in Phil's chair to glare at Ren. "Of course it's right to spike Phil into Jane's husband—what's his name, Sam?—if he ever gets here. What possible, rational objection could you have?"

"Can there be objections that aren't rational, but are still valid?" Jane hadn't sat down.

Oskar unfolded his long body from Phil's chair and, with a courtly flourish he must have tapped his first Second's pre-spike memory to render, offered it to Jane. "There can be objections—irrational, emotional, spiritual, and mystical—made." He proffered the curl of aristocrat's fingertips to her, drew her to him, past him, and into the La-Z-Boy. "They just don't matter. What matters—"

"What matters," interrupted Jimmy with all the gravity of the group's moral core. "Is lunch."

Here's what I was thinking in the moment: I was thinking I should write a self-help book. It would be the most useful and the shortest self-help book ever written. It'd go like this: "Every self-improvement program makes you concentrate on yourself, and the more you do that, the more self-involved you get, and the more self-involved you get, the more you need improvement. So get out of your god damned head for once, and look around. Read a newspaper. Learn what's happening in the world. Get involved in it. Stop wasting your time with self-improvement."

I was thinking that's what Incrementalists do: we look at what's going on around us, and we try to make it better. Sure, I think a lot of what we do is a waste of time, and lot of them think I'm not incremental enough, but fine. We argue about it. But every one of us is trying. We all want to see things improve. We all want to leave the world better than we found it. And that doesn't get done by gazing into your own navel and going, "Oh, how am I to become a better person?" and sure as hell not by going, "How am I to become happier?" It gets done by looking hard at what is all around you, forcing yourself to see what is actually there, and asking, "What would make this better, and how can I help?"

I was thinking, was that so hard?

I was thinking how Phil made me crazy, with his smugness and superiority. You can see it, can't you? In the way he thought he could meddle a true-believer like Brown into a more moderate, incremental agenda? I was thinking I had certainly wanted to strangle Irina more times than I could count, and at that point I didn't yet know that she'd been countermeddling, working with the corrupt and ruthless cop Jack Harris to get Phil arrested in order to force Ren to integrate with the rest of us and to unify popular opposition to the police. I was thinking Matsu, with his platitudes of mystical bullshit, could just go fuck himself. I was thinking that even Jimmy, whom I love, had annoyed me at times with his unwillingness to listen to anything beyond his inner voice. I was thinking Ren made no sense. She was a morass of contradictions: looking inward and outward, sensual and rational, self-effacing and stiff-necked with pride. I was thinking about Ramon, who had always frustrated me the most. Ramon, with his sharp, clear, luminous mind, that he put rigid borders around and wouldn't let himself think beyond their edges. I was thinking so, of course, Ramon was on his way to Tucson too.

But I was also thinking that these were the people I worked with. They were my tribe. And they were, all of them, trying to accomplish something, and that made me proud to be one of them.

I was thinking about the people throughout Arizona being harassed, arrested, beaten, deported, and killed because their skin was too brown and their wallets too empty. I was thinking Occupy Wall Street was listed as a domestic terrorist organization, while the Maricopa County Sheriff's Office wasn't. And I couldn't stop thinking of Phil—of arrogant, supercilious Phil. Always so ready to knock down everyone else's arguments without having any proposals of his own. Always with the smirk underlying his rhetorical questions. God, Phil pissed me off.

I was thinking Phil had been murdered and Jimmy was right, murder had a price. I just didn't know how I'd gotten assigned to help Irina of all people determine who would pay for Phil's death and how.

I was thinking Phil was in stub, and we needed him back. Ren was in tatters, and we needed her whole.

That's what I was thinking. Here's what happened:

—Oskar

"How did you enjoy lunch?" Jimmy asked Oskar.

"Fine," Oskar said, and hoped no one would ask what he'd eaten. Nobody was looking at him. "What?" he said.

"Nothing," said Jimmy, passing him a napkin. "Dry your eyes."

★ ★ ★

"Irina!" Jimmy kissed both Irina's cheeks and his fingertips, appraising her recent Second's young body. "Beautiful, as always," he proclaimed. And the thing about Jimmy was, he meant it. Even in last night's makeup, and with a nasty bruise coming up, to Jimmy, she was always beautiful; all women were, and most men.

He embraced her, and Irina, barefoot and stinking of beer, turned her good cheek to his chest and let his exquisite cologne and love envelop her. Jimmy weighed a bit—okay, maybe twice—what he should, but he was fat for the same reason he was consistently the best lover Irina had had over a series of lifetimes, and he wrapped her in his appreciation and the smell of expensive history.

The last time Irina had seen Jimmy, she'd been closer to seventy than sixty, and thin as a mummy, but he'd wallowed in her like Anthony Bourdain tucks into offal. It had been the best her old body had felt in years, even with Celeste whispering in her head the whole time that her tits looked like spoiled fruit.

Jimmy stroked her swollen jaw. "You've been fighting again."

"And you've been crying," she said.

"I'll bet I shouldn't see the other guy."

"I don't know why not." Irina winked and ushered the other guys inside. "Jimmy, meet Sam and Frio."

Jimmy shook hands like he hugged, and even the wary Frio smiled returning Jimmy's ritual clasp and pump. Frio had a nice smile, if a little crooked. Irina hadn't seen it before, but she knew Ren would like it, which pleased her.

"I thought you might be Matsu," Jimmy said.

"God, he's flying in too?" Irina followed Jimmy into the kitchen.

"*He* was invited." Oskar stood next to the stove, tear-stained and baffled. He had a dishrag in one hand, the other on the fridge door, and Irina thought he should cry more. It made his nose run and gave him an ugly, pink, duck lip—swollen and distended, vulnerable. Kissable.

Okay, maybe not.

"What are you cooking up, Oskar?" Irina stepped around him and went straight for the freezer to get ice for her jaw.

"I don't know."

"We all made sandwiches for lunch," Ren suggested.

"Make mine roast beef and swiss on rye?" Irina gave Oskar an encouraging pat on the tush, breezing by. "Sam, Frio, you hungry?"

"No." Frio spoke for them both.

Sam seemed to be trying to telepathically communicate with Jane, who was as intently watching her coffee mug. Frio watched Oskar.

Ren stood up, and honestly, Irina knew the girl was grieving and all, but that didn't mean she couldn't still blow-dry her hair. She looked like a drowned kitten.

"Hi," Ren said to Sam more than Frio, "I'm Ren."

Ren wasn't just makeup-less, she was pale too; frightened, not just sad. With both Oskar and Jimmy in tears, Irina could see how Ren might be starting to doubt the assurances everyone had given her that they'd get Phil back. But they would. Irina had brought home the perfect recruit. She felt like a cat with a fresh kill for the doormat. Two, in fact.

This is what I like about Irina. She'd cowboyed off on her own to the Southside to discover who killed Phil, but when she saw a chance to help a homeless woman, she took it, and when she spotted a potential Second for Phil, she acted on that as well. This is what I despise about Irina.

—Oskar

Irina put an encouraging arm around Sam. "I know you and Jane have a lot to talk over," she prompted. "Why don't you two go out on Ren's lovely back patio and chat?"

Jane looked up, and the pivot markers Irina had been watching in Sam finally registered in his wife. Irina wondered whether Jane had really not known what her husband was going through. It didn't matter. He'd resolved to tell her. They walked outside together, the space between their shoulders the exact width of a broken heart.

Frio started to follow them, but Irina touched his wrist. "They need to be alone," she told Sam's keen, young second-in-command. "You can still see them from here." She offered him a seat at the kitchen table. "Jimmy, Ren," Irina said, waiting until Oskar looked up from the fridge, and trying not to beam. "Oskar, I'd like you to meet Frio, Phil's new Second."

Of course everyone started talking at once: Jimmy and Ren with Earnest Explaining Things faces, Oskar full of outrage, certain Irina had overstepped and didn't understand.

Well seriously, can you blame me?

—O

But Frio was all Oskar's favorite things: poor, undereducated, a racial minority, and Oskar couldn't take his eyes off him, even as he scolded Irina.

She settled herself in to wait beside the taut, handsome young man sitting across the table from Ren, because really, Ren was who Irina had picked him for. Irina had never meant for Ren to hurt this much. Phil's arrest would have been hard on her, sure, but an acceptable suffering when balanced against the gains Irina had calculated would accrue to Ren, the group, and the world. Also, Irina owed Ren a good turn or two for what happened in Vegas, and for the way Ren had forgiven her. It had to be hard to be an Incrementalist with an incomplete memory. It certainly had to suck to fear your great-aunt had tricked your fiancé into loving you.

"Has Irina explained this to you?" Jimmy resumed his seat at the head of the kitchen table as the generalized hubbub settled down.

"Explained what?" Frio was tight as a trigger finger.

"What we are, what she's recruiting you for?"

"I'm no recruit."

"Ex-military?" Oskar came in from the kitchen on fighter's feet.

"No."

"Don't bullshit me."

"Don't fuck with me."

"Oh sit down, Oskar," Irina said. "Frio was Tucson PD for five years. You're seeing SWAT training."

"How do you know that?" Frio demanded without letting Oskar out of view.

Irina ignored him, talking to Oskar. "Have a seat, dear. Notice I said *was* a cop. A year ago, he shot a kid, left the force, and joined Sam's army."

"Wait," Ren said. "Sam has an army?"

"How the fuck do you know *that*?" Frio turned in his seat to face Irina.

She gave him a flippant shrug. "Sam told me all about the Hourlies," she lied, delighted to have her theory confirmed. "As for you, that wasn't too hard to figure out. You're name's Frio? Spanish for cold? Obviously a code name or nickname, maybe. But for what? Something that sounds like it. Iro? That's common enough."

"Don't call me that."

Irina ignored him and explained to Ren: "Iro is short for Porfirio. I did a little grazing. The Tucson Police Department has five Porfirios, but SWAT only two, one of whom quit recently. I read your resignation letter, Porfirio."

He looked like he might punch her, same as Santi had. "Frio," he said.

"Irina." Jimmy intervened. "Maybe you should explain about Sam's army."

"Please do." Oskar finally sat down.

Irina hated the way Jimmy appointed himself Voice of Reason when Ramon wasn't around, but if he could direct Oskar to pay attention to her instead of measuring dicks with Frio, she'd let Jimmy do his thing.

Irina looked around the table. Ren had her feet tucked up under her in that casual, graceful way that always made Phil sappy. Jimmy's shoulders shifted as he patted her leg under the table.

"Irina?"

Irina smiled at Oskar, whose tiny mind she was about to blow. He had one eye on her and one on Frio, like he was trying to decide which of them was more of a threat. *It's me, Oskar, my love,* she thought. *It's always me.*

Irina may be dangerous, but it's never for the reasons she thinks.

—O

"Sam Kelly," Irina began in her best schoolmarm, "teaches civics at Southside High."

"We know that," Oskar growled. "We were—"

"Oskar," Ren said. "Please do shut up."

*　　*　　*

It was the moment, Kate thought, when Sage came in to gripe that she was hungry, and Daniel had grinned at how Kate said, "Rats!" that she had recognized the problem. But maybe then she had only been frustrated at having forgotten it was her night to cook, and it wasn't until Daniel buttered a slice of bread, folded it in half, and presented it to Sage as a Butter Sandwich Deluxe that she'd seen it. Either way, by the time she put Daniel to work getting drinks and dumping applesauce into bowls while she got the lasagna out of the box and into the microwave, Kate knew she had a problem.

Daniel was funny with the kids, and called Legal One "sir" until they begged him not to. Or maybe that was it? The way he sirred her husband, like they were all so much older than he was. Kate sighed. She had known he was young—technically too young—but that was overlookable, right? And only six years younger than Ren. The critical thing was to get Phil back. And that Ren would have no trouble loving Dan.

After dinner, Legal took the kids upstairs to bed, and Daniel stacked their empty ice cream bowls into his. He looked around the dining room, at the ketchupped plastic army men, the dropped napkins, and piles of Apples to Apples cards. He gave a low whistle that made Kate laugh. "Goodness," she said. "Nobody ever told you family life was tidy, did they?"

"I don't guess anyone ever did." Daniel carried the bowls into the kitchen, but couldn't find a clear place to set them.

"Leave it," Kate told him. "Wrecker will clean up when he gets off the phone."

"Legal and Wrecker?" Daniel came back to the dining room and deposited the bowls back on the table.

"Short for The Homewrecker and The Legal One." Kate opened the liquor cabinet and studied her options.

"But he didn't."

"Cordial? Brandy?"

"No, thank you."

"Who didn't what?" Kate poured herself a generous snifter of B&B.

"He didn't wreck your home."

"No, the kids did that." Kate waved at the mess, but Daniel barely smiled at her joke. And she thought it'd been a pretty good one.

"No," Daniel said. "Your family is exquisite."

"Exquisite?" Kate couldn't laugh at him; he was too sincere. And honestly, pretty darn exquisite himself—almost too good-looking. And too young. "Meh," she said. "They were both named Allen, what was I going to do?"

"You're amazing—wife, mother, doctor—I mean, damn. And good at it all."

Kate downed her B&B. "I'm not a great wife," she said. "I'm a good lover and a good mom, and that combination has a lot of overlap with wife, but that's all." Daniel's admiration suitably squelched, Kate poured herself another snifter. "Come on," she told him. "Let's go back to the den and finish our chat."

DECEMBER, 1857

"I CAN KNOCK YOU OUT AGAIN, CARTER."

December was cold, but the Eldridge had a fire going, and we were warm enough with all the bodies packed together. It also smelled more like a stable than a hotel, but never mind that. I sat in the back and listened.

There was a sense of history like I hadn't felt since the War for Independence—a feeling that big events were astir in the room, and that everyone knew it. It was heady, intoxicating. And speaking of intoxicating, there wasn't as much liquor in evidence as I'd have thought there would be.

It was a surprisingly good debate. It was as if everyone's priority was solving the problem—deciding how to handle the Lecompton Constitution—instead of showing off how smart they were. That doesn't happen often.

In the end, the idea of holding our own constitutional convention won out, and we decided to meet on Christmas Eve in Leavenworth. The question came up about whether we could get the word out in time, but we all agreed we could. Then we gave three cheers for the Topeka Constitution and three groans for President Buchanan and the meeting broke up.

Brown wasn't there, though I knew he'd returned to Kansas last month. I dropped comments, asked questions, listened, and was able to learn that he was recruiting, although exactly for what no one could or would tell me. It didn't make me any less worried.

I went back to my snug little Kansas and Nebraska Cottages house, got a fire going, and closed my eyes. I imagined the smell of cherry blossoms and the taste of chive, and looked around my villa. It was warmer than the house, even with the fire going.

I opened up the circular stairway and went down into the perpetual nothing where everything exists. There should be letters to New England, and if that's where he was, letters back to Kansas as well.

I passed a Cypress tree impossibly growing in the desert, and a bushel of wheat, and blacksmith's tongs sitting next to a new windmill.

There had to be something here. There had to be. You can't communicate without leaving traces, and you can't leave traces without there being at least a good chance of them winding up in the Garden.

I plucked a single red rose, inhaled it, and there was a group that called itself the Secret Six. I didn't know who they were or what they wanted to do, but it sounded ominous. I inhaled more deeply and got names: Higginson, Sanborn, Stearns. There were some indications that even Frederick Douglass might be involved, although I couldn't tell for sure. All of them, in any case, were dedicated Abolitionists, and all of them had, at one time or another, expressed impatience with peaceful solutions.

I dropped the rose and continued.

I found a set of glazed ceramic bowls, nice enough that I wanted to bring them up to the Villa. I held them and studied the deep, subtle swirls of purple and inky-blue, and—

". . . 194 carbines, with plenty of ball and shot . . . 1000 superior Pikes as a cheap but effectual weapon to place in the hands of entirely unskilful & unpracticed men. . . ."

A thousand pikes? A *thousand*?

I found the order for the pikes, and followed it to Brown's military adviser, "Col. F." It turned out to be Oskar's old acquaintance, Forbes, from Italy. I stopped to write a note to Oskar, asking for information and switches for Forbes, and tacked the note to a wheel of the rusty cannon that marks my Garden's border with his.

Then I opened my eyes. The fire was nearly out, and I was shivering, and tired. My heart thumped, as I suddenly feared my old body would give out before I had time to stop him.

I didn't know where, and I didn't know when, but I knew what: Old Brown was planning to go into the South and, single-handedly, ignite a slave revolt.

THIRTEEN

‿Эⵎ

Nothing Anyone Said Would
Stop Either Faction

This is where it all started to go badly wrong. This is where you might have made a difference, if you'd been watching. The spiral Ren made in her Garden, trying to bring Phil back, was running the show, and none of us knew it. How could we all have overlooked what we know about rushing recruits? How could anyone have considered Frio?

—Oskar

"Sam Kelly," Irina repeated herself, just to get under Oskar's skin a little, "teaches civics at Southside High." She surveyed the table again, but she had them all. Jimmy, Ren, Frio, even Oskar were giving her their complete and, if not friendly, at least concentrated attention. Good. She was looking forward to sharing her hard-won knowledge. They'd all be pleased.

"Last year," Irina informed her audience, "with both skinheads and undocumented kids in his classroom, Sam Kelly introduced Viktor Frankl to his students during his block on the Second World War. He wanted to teach them about Frankl's 'last human freedom' but one girl threw it back in his face. Maybe, like Frankl had said about the concentration camp guards, the one thing Arizona police and ICE—that's Immigration and

Customs Enforcement, Jimmy—couldn't take away from her was her ability to choose how she responded to them, but what freedom did the little brother she was half-raising have? Was he even human if he was too little to choose anything but terror every night his papa came home late?"

Oskar swore in a low undertone.

"Yeah," Irina agreed. "So a classmate takes this info and reports the girl's papa, and both her parents get deported, and Sam feels responsible. He's had enough. He suggests to this girl that the kid who turned her dad in is mighty proud of his connections, bragging about his daddy, the deputized citizen. Maybe this kid might impress the pretty girls by bringing something caliber-licious to school and proving he's as dangerous as he says."

Jimmy nodded. "So she does and he does and Sam does a locker check. . . ."

Irina dismissed Jimmy's dated guess with a wave. "The school has metal detectors."

Oskar barked one of his derisive laughs that apportioned equal scorn for bone-headed kids and idiot security.

"Did Jane know?" Ren asked, her voice very quiet.

Irina ignored her. "Anyway, another one of Sam's students does weekend yard work for one of the ICE agents," she continued. "Now Sam has his address and can maybe create a little interference with the cell service at his house. He misses some calls. Develops unusually leaky tires. Some other kids devise a social security number sharing scheme for the kids who want to work and the skinheads who don't. They call themselves Hourlies, cause that's how they get paid, and they're not the Minutemen. It's all very subtle, small-time stuff, until Sam meets Frio here."

Frio was the still of panthers, watching either Oskar or Sam behind him on the patio, and irritating Irina because she couldn't tell which.

"Frio, the cop," Oskar clarified.

"Frio, the ex-SWAT sniper," Irina corrected.

Oskar's aversion to the police was fighting hard with his curiosity. Irina did him a mercy and explained. "Sixteen-year-old kid flunks a test, comes home from school strung out, ends up with Daddy's pistol in his bedroom screaming he's going to off himself."

"Mom calls 911?" Jimmy guessed, anguish in his rich voice.

"And the cops deploy the SWAT team because they can. Because they have to take every chance they get to justify the expense of having one."

"Frio, what happened?" Jimmy could meddle with just the tone of his voice.

Frio looked at his hands on the table, long black lashes soft against the hard adobe brown of his cheeks. "They sent a shrink in," he said. "Our orders were to just watch the kid. Then he put his fist through a window. The team leader called it, and we fired." He looked straight at Oskar. "My lieutenant had been through the Jose Guerena mess and didn't want to hear anything from me about how it went down. Nothing in his world was ever gonna be more fucked up than that."

"So you quit?"

"Yeah."

"You didn't just transfer out of SWAT?" Oskar's smile was predatory and sly. He was starting to see the possibilities. "Still in touch with any of those boys?"

"Some of them."

"And you joined up with Sam and the Hourlies?"

"Yeah."

"That's not just desertion, that's defection."

"Or conversion," Irina suggested.

"What did the cops know?" Oskar asked.

"They knew someone was fucking with them," Frio said. "They didn't much like it."

Irina smirked at the understatement. It had been driving Jack nuts.

"They've been keeping it out of the local press, but someone made a Twitter feed and a Tumblr page, so word's getting out, even with the media guys toeing the line."

Irina nodded, proud of Menzie's work.

"What are they doing about it?" Jimmy asked.

"Pima County has thrown about everything at it," Frio said. "But last intel I got, they don't even have a working theory on who we are. First they went after BAN, then they thought it was the DREAMers, so they put those kids in Eloy, but nothing changed. They've put four different profilers on it trying to figure out who's leading or planning things, but Sam's kept them running blind."

"Why here?" said Oskar. "Isn't Maricopa County much worse?"

Frio just looked at him.

"Oh," said Oskar. "There too, huh? And no one suspects the connection. Sam's better at this than I'd have thought."

Irina nodded. Sam had fooled her too. She had thought it was Phil.

"He's white," said Frio. "Cops look right past him."

"And then here comes Phil." Jimmy shook his jowls. "Discreetly nosing around, just learning the territory."

"He kept coming to the library," Frio agreed.

"None too subtle," Oskar said.

"He had no reason to be," Irina reminded him. "He didn't know it was guerrilla territory or he would have found a way to help out. And nobody on either side was writing much down, everything's been done in person or on throwaway cell phones, so there wasn't much to learn by grazing. I looked."

Frio nodded. "It's something I brought with me from the force," he told them. "My lieutenant was rabid about it. Nothing gets written down. No e-mail, not even notebooks. Said his boss taught him you can't trail a man who makes no footprints."

"Good man," said Irina, thinking of her obedient assistant police chief. "Belief in privacy is a bourgeois luxury these days."

"But Phil left footprints." Ren's voice was tiny.

"Yeah."

"And the police followed them?"

Frio nodded.

"Did the police kill Phil?" Ren's eyes connected with Frio's over the table. "Did someone decide he was the one doing what the Hourlies were doing and pick him off?"

Frio looked away from Ren.

"Frio, did a police sniper shoot Phil?"

Frio looked back up. "My professional opinion?"

Ren nodded, but just barely.

"Yes, ma'am."

Irina saw all the air go out of Ren.

"Alex, our intel guy in Russia, suggested as much," Oskar said. "But we had no notion why."

It was on Irina's lips to argue, to say that was impossible. Jack would have told her if Phil's death had been a police job. Hell, he would have been proud to tell her, but it was a mercy for Ren to have someone to blame, so Irina kept quiet.

Then she remembered Jack talking to her breasts. Had he lied to her? Irina stiffened her spine and sniffed. It would only make it easier on her to turn Jack over to Menzie, which she had to do anyway now to let the Hourlies know he was coming. Still, Irina was finding it hard not to feel bitter.

"So, Ren," she said. "What do you think of Frio?"

Ren pinked up and watched her tea like a mirror. "He's qualified."

"For what?" Frio was used to people sizing him up, but Ren's quick glance made him squirmy.

"I was engaged to Phil," Ren said.

"Yeah," Frio said. "We know."

Ren waited, but Frio didn't offer anything else and she plunged ahead. "Phil was working to change the 'show us your papers' law."

"And we'd like you to consider taking up his work," Jimmy added.

"It won't work," Frio told Jimmy. "Cops love that law, especially in Maricopa County."

"You could maybe convince them not to." Ren managed a shaky smile. "Change some minds on the force?"

"People don't change their minds," Frio said. "They will kill you for trying, and they'll die before they let you."

"You changed yours."

"I—" He stopped.

Oskar opened his mouth, but Jimmy did something under the table—stepped on his foot or put a hand on his leg—and for once, Oskar took the cue.

Frio shifted in his chair for the first time. "Yeah," he said.

"Minds are the only thing worth changing," Ren said.

Oskar opened his mouth again, and again Jimmy stopped him. Irina thought it must have taken hand and foot.

"But you're right." Ren leaned forward in her chair, closer to Frio. "You can't convince a person with facts and proof. Belief is a choice. And people make choices emotionally, then explain them rationally afterward. But Phil really could change people's minds," Ren told Frio. "Not a hundred and eighty degrees, not all the time, but he could be very convincing. He would have made some big changes once he'd learned who needed nudging."

Frio met Ren's eyes. "I'm sorry they shot him."

Irina would swear she heard the spark pop between them.

"Will you help us get him back?" Ren looked at Frio like there was no one else at the table, and Irina was impressed. Ren was recruiting. With no switches and no group consultation.

Frio frowned. "They won't release the body?"

Ren flinched but Frio didn't.

She blinked, and a tear slid out of each eye, but she didn't move to hide it, only steadied herself a moment and dove. "Phil's not entirely dead," she said. "His body is, but the rest of him is stored in something like a back-up drive."

Frio waited.

"And we can reinstall it," she said. "In another body." She met Frio's eyes again.

"And you want me to get you a body?"

It took all Irina's strength not to do her best Mae West with, "No, baby, we want yours."

"Hang on," Oskar said. "Do you believe her?" he asked Frio. "Do you believe what Ren has said about Phil being not all dead?"

Frio was slow to shift his attention to Oskar from Ren. "Does it matter?"

"Do you believe there's some 'rest of him' once a body is dead?" Oskar persisted.

"I don't believe in anything where belief is one of the requirements."

"That's not what I'm asking."

"I don't give a shit what you're asking."

"You should."

"Don't see why."

"You could die," Ren said, and Oskar had enough sense to shut up and let her keep Frio's attention. "I mean your body wouldn't," she clarified, "but the rest of you might."

"Not your memories," Jimmy said. "Phil would know everything you do about the department and their tactics. He'd have your training and the memory of all your experiences."

"You want to put Phil in me?" Frio's incredulity was the only thing keeping his rage at bay.

"So he could pursue your work," Ren said.

"*I'm* pursuing my work."

"You'd do it better as him," Jimmy said softly.

"And you'd be married to Ren," Irina noted.

"That's not a condition." Oskar scowled at her.

Frio never looked away from Ren. "It's not a problem."

"Nor an incentive," Ren said.

"Don't decide now." Jimmy leaned back and smoothed the expensive silk of his shirt. "Take some time, Frio. Give it some thought. Maybe consider letting us show you some of what's involved."

"No." Frio stood up. "No way. If your man had the kind of power you say, and he wasn't doing every fucking thing to stop what's happening, I don't want to be him."

Oskar beamed.

"It's more complicated than it sounds," Jimmy said.

"That's what cowards say."

"He was changing minds," Ren said.

"Who cares? He wasn't involved with the law or the rules of engagement or the way families get ripped up or how many people die in the desert."

"I'd like you to meet him." Ren checked the clock on her phone and stood. "It's almost time," she told Jimmy. "We're holding a sort of funeral for him," she told Frio. "But he'll be there, or an experience of his will be. Will you come with us?"

"Where?"

Ren actually laughed at that. "Just the living room, actually," she said.

"I'm going to take a shower first," Irina announced, feeling like it was all going well enough for her to leave. "I want out of my bum costume." She stood up just as Jane and Sam walked back into the kitchen arm in arm.

⋆　　⋆　　⋆

Kate followed Daniel back through the house, past Wrecker's office, where he was still on the phone with his sister, getting another update on his mom. He blew her a kiss as they walked by, and she and Daniel both waved back. In the den, Daniel took the same chair he'd occupied all day, but Kate was feeling antsy, and perched on a sofa arm.

"Sure you don't want something to drink?" she asked.

"Are you in love with both of them?" Daniel rubbed a hand over the top of his head where his hair used to be before the fire.

"Yes," Kate said.

"I always thought when you fell in love with someone it wiped out your love for anyone else."

"Did you stop loving your brother when you fell in love with Amelia?"

Daniel left his hand on his head, revealing the paler skin on the inside of his arm. "No," he said, stroking his palm over his scalp's new growth. "But I mean romantic love. Being in love."

"Falling in love and being in love are entirely different things," Kate said. "You probably can't *fall* in love with two people at once, but you sure can *be* in love with a whole bunch of them, all at the same time. I don't think I ever loved Allen more than when I was falling in love with Wrecker."

"Because he understood about you wanting the other guy?"

"Even before that, when I was first falling in love, and hadn't said anything to him yet. I loved him more. It was like I just had more love in me—more for the new crush, more for the old love."

Daniel nodded and sat forward, twining his strong, slender fingers loosely. "Did you try to stop yourself?"

"From falling in love? Why? It felt wonderful!" It had felt—in fact—a lot like now. "Anyway," she said, "I've never known that to work well, deciding with your brain to feel something with your heart. Much easier the other way around."

❦

Daniel nodded slowly. "It's easier to justify what you want than to want what's just?"

"Of course."

"But isn't that the whole point?" His hands flew apart and he sank back in the chair. "Isn't the essence of morality putting desires under the rule of the mind?"

"To what purpose?" Kate asked. "Just to enslave them?"

"Well, no." Daniel frowned and Kate wished she could let him off the hook. "I don't mean choosing your head over your heart for its own sake. But if my heart or"—his eyes squeezed closed—"or some other part of me wants something my head knows is wrong . . ." He trailed off.

They weren't talking about Kate's marriage anymore. His eyes met hers, searching.

"Just because you want something doesn't mean it's wrong," she said.

"But sometimes it is." He pressed the back of his head into the chair back, tipping his chin up. "Sometimes I want things that are wrong for me to want."

"Maybe." Kate stood up. "But how do you ever know that what you think is right actually is right and not just your mind providing rationalization for what you're feeling?"

"Some things feel right."

Kate sat down next to Daniel.

"And sometimes you can't tell." He didn't move. "Sometimes you know what you want in some abstract, ideal way. You want justice and compassion. You want true love, and a sense of purpose. You want to serve something larger than yourself and to know you're making a difference, doing the right thing."

He nodded.

"I can give you half of that," Kate said.

"I want it." His eyes, passionate and quick, met Kate's. "All my life I've wanted that—wanted to *do* something."

"I know."

"But I never knew what." All the tension went out of Daniel, and he gave Kate a cockeyed grin. "I could have walked the fuck into Mordor, but I never found a ring."

He closed his eyes, resting against the wing of the chair, his beautiful face turned slightly away as it had been the first time she had seen it pillowed on a hospital bed. Kate had gone into his room knowing he was too young, but hadn't realized he was also too handsome until he had smiled at her like she was pretty, and not a middle-aged woman with two kids and no time to work out. Kate was thick in the wrong places and she didn't take the time she could with things like makeup and clothes and it had been a long time since a young man had looked at her like he saw her, and she knew enough about love to know that few things were as attractive as being found attractive.

Kate took the wedding rings off her finger, and put them in his hand. "Have two," she said.

Daniel stared at Kate's rings in his open palm. She'd had Legal's resized after her first pregnancy, but you couldn't see the mend. Daniel dipped his pinky finger into them.

"You said it's a kind of test of wills."

"That's right."

"Kate, I can't imagine anyone who could move me when I decide to stand, or stand against me when I decide to push."

"I know." Kate patted his knee, settling her comfortable, middle-aged hips into her comfortable, mid-century cushions. Daniel stirred her rings in his hand with one finger and looked up at her sideways from under fierce brows. Pain etched his lips, the bottom one delicious, even twisted in decision. Too young, too beautiful, and too strong. Kate would need to let him go.

Daniel lifted his hand into the space between them, and Kate's rings slid down to the second knuckle of his scarred pinky finger. Kate thought about burn recovery—debridement, excision—excruciating and famously resistant to pain meds. Poor love. A dimple hewed his cheek and exposed what he'd just said, what Kate had known since the butter sandwich, but tried not to believe.

Kate pulled her rings off Dan's curled finger.

"I want this," he said, and because Kate couldn't say she didn't want it too, she leaned in and kissed him.

His lips were delicate but insistent, and his tongue slid currents of wanting, years into her. "I meant the other thing," he said.

"I know," she told him. But she would deny him both. Daniel was everything Ren needed, and exactly what the Incrementalists did not. Phil's Second had to shade. Kate would dust Phil now and after write the forum, withdrawing her recruit.

★   ★   ★

Irina really wanted a shower, but she didn't like the look of Sam's shoulders coming in from Ren's patio. Or the proud tears shining in Jane's eyes.

"He'll do it," Jane said.

Ren was already in the living room, waiting for them to come and dust Phil, but Frio shared Irina's instincts. Everything in him got shorter and denser. "Do what?" he asked Sam.

"I'll explain later." Sam's smile was weary. "Come on, Frio, I'll drive you home."

"Do what?" Frio repeated. "Be Phil?"

"They told you?" Sam turned to Jane.

"Irina recruited Frio," Jimmy explained. "But he's not interested."

"Fuck you." Frio squared off on Sam.

"Frio," Sam almost pleaded.

"It's time," Ren called from the living room, and Irina had to admire her dogged focus on dusting Phil despite more present and pressing concerns.

"Fuck you," Frio said again. "You're not going to let them turn you into Phil. I'm doing it." He glared at Jimmy, then Oskar, then back at Sam. "They already asked me."

"Frio." Jane let go of Sam's hand.

"See?" Frio glared at Sam, pointing to Jane. "You're married. And you're the one—" He stopped. "If you want Phil back, I'll fucking be Phil. I'm not letting you die."

Irina found Frio's loyalty touching and hoped they'd all drop the Sam nonsense and go with her recruit. He was much better for Ren.

"Jimmy." Ren was in the doorway, her face terrifying. "It's time."

177

"Yes of course."

"Ren?" Jane left Sam and went to Ren.

"It's time for Phil's dust ritual." Ren's voice had the control of a high-rope walker. She looked at Frio. "Everyone grazes—relives—one of Phil's memories at the same time as a way of honoring him before he's spiked into . . ." She faltered. "His new Second. That doesn't have to happen right away," she added, recovering her poise. "But the dust ritual happens now."

"Sure," Jane said.

"Dust rituals are the only time all of us are in the Garden at the same time, doing the same thing," Jimmy explained to Sam. "We really can't be late."

"Is it still okay for me to come?" Jane asked.

"Of course." Ren looked from Jane to Sam, then followed the line of Sam's eyes back to Frio. "Irina, would you take Jane?"

"I—" Irina began, but Ren rolled right over her.

"Oskar can take Frio. Jimmy, take Sam. I'm going now." Ren walked into the living room, sat down on the sofa, and closed her eyes.

Jane stepped close to Irina. "I'm ready."

Jane smelled like Dove soap and the swimming pool, and Irina gave a suspicious sniff. "You know how we do this?" she asked.

"Oskar showed me last night."

"Did he now?" Irina's clumped makeup and beer-stiff clothes bothered her more now she was standing close to Jane's clean, soft sweatpants and fresh, noticeably untear-marked face, but she couldn't refuse Ren, and she couldn't miss the dust ritual.

Jimmy put his hand on Sam's shoulder. "Close your eyes," he said gently.

"Um, Jimmy?" Oskar said as Irina put her fingers to Jane's temples. "Maybe you should take Frio."

DECEMBER, 1857

"CELESTE INHABITED YOUR BODY. . . ."

She stood in my doorway, impossible and inexplicable, like a hot August wind sweeping through the snow-covered fields in the middle of a February blizzard. I knew who she was at once, though I hadn't seen her in thirty years, and never in this Second. I knew, yet I asked.

"Celeste?"

Her smile grew, removing any last doubts I might have had. She came in without the invitation I was too amazed to give. She was beautiful in the way Americans imagine French women are: blond curls, including one that rested against her cheek like an exotic jewel; shining violet eyes; a small and delicate mouth in a triangular face.

"Dear Carter," she said from a swirl of white fur coat and blue flounced skirts. "As much as I would love to see you close your mouth before it becomes home to one of your horrid local insects, I must insist that, first, you close the door, which is not only permitting, but even, it seems, encouraging both snow and cold into your otherwise snug if woefully rustic cottage, after which you may serve me well-meant but inadequate refreshment."

I shut the door, filled the teakettle, and set it over the fire. When I turned around, she had seated herself, upright and proper, on one of the two chairs that I now saw as terribly shabby. "It is good to see you,

Celeste." I sat in the other chair, across from her at what I used for a kitchen table.

"Why, thank you, Carter!" Her smile was dazzling in every sense of the word. I hadn't seen such perfect teeth in five years.

"I like your new Second. Recent?"

"A month. The recruit was found—"

"In Boston," I said. "I remember now. I've been a little out of touch, I'm afraid. You were in stub for most of a year."

"You forgot me so quickly, Carter?" She mock frowned.

"It's been— I've been busy. And worried. To what do I owe the pleasure, Celeste? I hope it is merely to visit me."

"It is," she said. "This is my first Second on this side of the Atlantic; how could I not visit my darling man as soon as possible? Though I was hoping you were younger. You need a new Second, dear Methuselah."

"This one still has life, Celeste, and you know how I feel about stubbing ourselves for convenience."

"Only in extreme cases, you say. But is my presence not an extreme case?" The fire gave a quick flare, which made it seem for a moment as if Celeste's smile was literally brightening up the room.

I made her tea, and we drank it, then I took her to town and bought her dinner at the Free State Hotel, now rebuilt by Colonel Eldridge: oysters, roast ham with champagne sauce, corn bread with plum preserves, and a St. Estephe claret. After dinner, we had a J.D. & M. Williams port, and she finally admitted that there was at least some civilization in Kansas.

We drank our port, and she said, "So, who is this John Brown with whom you are so obsessed?"

"A violent Abolitionist," I said. "With a plan."

"What plan?"

"To start a slave uprising somewhere south of Mason-Dixon. I haven't been able to get all the det—"

"My god!" she said, staring. "That would be horrible!"

"I know."

"The slaughter!"

"I'm thinking more of what it will do to the cause."

"The cause?"

"Abolition."

"I'm thinking of all of those families who will be massacred if he succeeds. Can he succeed?"

"I doubt it," I said. "But I could be wrong."

"What are you doing to stop it?"

"I'm at a loss, Celeste. I tried to meddle with him, and got nowhere."

"Maybe I should try." She smiled. "There are methods at my disposal that are not at yours."

I snorted. "Look into his character, Celeste. The row of plants next to the bookshelf in my atrium. Tell me if you think he can be seduced."

She closed her eyes, then opened them again. "I take your meaning," she said. "A Bible-thumper who actually means it."

I nodded. "I've been trying to come up with something," I said. "But—"

"He has to be stopped," said Celeste.

"I know, but—"

"But if you can't meddle with him, are we helpless? With all we know? It's too terrible! To be useless, impotent. One madman with the capacity to do such grave harm to so many, and all of us—you, even—utterly powerless to stop him. Is there nothing we can do!"

"Not nothing, I suppose. I could always shoot him before he ever got to working his plan."

"Then that's what you must do," she told me.

FOURTEEN

Look into His Character, Celeste.

During Phil's dust ritual, I had felt Irina's presence, and Felicia's, and Vivien's most clearly as they had all relived the seed Jimmy had selected. Of them, I thought Vivien had been most moved, and tried hardest to hide it. I had a theory that he had had kind of a thing for Phil for a while, but refused to demean himself by competing with Celeste; or didn't want to get involved with someone so obviously broken; or time and place and circumstance were never right. Or I could just be wrong. I consider that possibility more than people give me credit for. Case in point: What to do with what I'd come to understand during the dust ritual? Should I seed it?

Whatever Irina might have believed at the time, I am not heartless, and there was simply no point in causing Ren needless pain. But facts, as Lenin said, are stubborn things. Facts don't go away because you don't like them. Facts are the foundation of conclusions, and at a time like this, the conclusions we drew would have a profound effect on our choices, and, in turn, on our future, and thus on the future of the nemones. The stakes were immense, so I decided that I, at least, would begin by facing facts.

—Oskar

As the seed Jimmy had selected had played out, Oskar had found his attention focused, above all, on Celeste, as she watched Phil, and on the emotions she couldn't entirely conceal in her face and her body language. The fact was there was no understanding Phil without understanding Celeste. In the four hundred years she had been in the group, she and Phil defined each other—their opposition, their unity. The dialectic of the Incrementalists played itself out in their stormy, emotional, and sometimes even rational battles. All that the Incrementalists were or hoped to be, from the Revolutions of '48, to the American Civil War, to the disaster of Cambodia, to their failures in Palestine, traced back to Celeste and Phil, Phil and Celeste—Phil wanting to make things better, Celeste desperate not to make things worse. Now it was Ren and Phil, Phil and Ren, and the Incrementalists were at a pivot once again; and Phil was in stub. And Ren? Ren was uncertain. Something Celeste had never been.

In 1977, Celeste had been frightened that, as a result of what Phil was saying, the group might again plunge into water so deep they could drown, and even more frightened that she had no power to stop them. She was furious that Phil had such unshakable influence over the group, despite his doubts, and that she had so little despite her conviction.

And under it all, still and nevertheless, Celeste was proud of Phil. She was proud of how deeply he got involved, of how much he let our work hurt him—let her hurt him—and proud of how badly he wanted to be good.

That was what left the scars.

When Phil came out of stub, the scars would still be there, and the entire group, but especially Ren, would have to deal with that. But would it make it any easier for Ren to know Celeste's pride wasn't that of accomplishment or ownership, but of conviction?

Oskar didn't know.

In the end, I seeded my insights, but I didn't put a pointer to the seed on the board. I include it here, not to prove I was right about Ren having to deal with the scars Phil carried, although I was, but to show how I had allowed my concern for her to make me timid. It was unlike me not to call what I had noticed to the attention of others, and it was a mistake.

—O

* ⋆ ⋆

Ren opened her eyes and closed them again like 1977 might still be right behind her eyelids. It wasn't, but 2014 still didn't feel quite real either, so she kept her eyes shut and listened to the room. Oskar's chair groaned as he stretched. Jane whispered something under her breath. Jimmy sighed and yawned. Ren peeked to see who Jane was talking to, and realized she was praying. Sam made fidgeting, throat-clearing noises, and Irina stood up. "I'm going to shower," she announced and walked out.

Ren wondered what the hell had happened to Irina's shoes.

Ren tried stretching and yawning, but it didn't help, and she wasn't going to pray. "There's a really lovely Mexican place not too far from here," she said. "It's where we were going to have the rehearsal dinner." She unfolded her legs and put her feet flat on the floor. "If anyone's hungry."

Of course everyone was hungry, but Jimmy offered to pick up the check if they would agree, instead, to accompany him to his hotel. "I haven't checked in yet, but I peeked at their menu online before I reserved my room, and I'm desperate to try the tamales," he explained.

"What's it on the way to?" Oskar's grin was bait.

Jimmy didn't take it. "It's downtown," he said. "I'll text you the address."

"That's okay." Oskar unfolded himself from Phil's chair and extended a hand to help Jimmy up. "I'll let you chauffeur me."

Jimmy hoisted himself to standing and caught Oskar in a one-armed embrace. "Gladly, my friend. Perhaps I'll even drive you by El Tiradito on the way. It's the grave of a man who died for love."

Oskar groaned. "I'll take my rental."

"The only Catholic shrine to a sinner buried on unconsecrated ground," Jimmy coaxed.

Frio said something in Spanish, and Sam stood, stationing himself by Jane. "We should be going," he said.

"Why?" Oskar's eyes searched Jane's. "Do you know where there are better tamales?"

Jane didn't say anything, but she didn't look away from Oskar's gaze.

Sam put a hand on his wife's shoulder. "I understand why you have to get Phil back," Sam told Oskar, voice steady, but holding on to Jane with umbilical intensity. "I'm ready to do whatever you need to make that happen."

"And I'll do whatever it takes to stop you." Frio was standing close to Ren by the front door and she had no idea how he'd gotten there or when, but found she rather liked it.

"Come to dinner, then." Jimmy's cordial smile took in every wary, worried, tense, and frightened person in the room. "And we'll talk through it all over tamales. An empty stomach makes a selfish mind. Ren, why don't you ride with Sam and Jane? I'll tell Irina where we're going and leave a message for Matsu. I'm staying at the Hotel Congress, do you know where that is?"

Ren didn't answer right away, imagining herself in the backseat of Jane's car with Frio. It wasn't unpleasant. She'd liked watching how he didn't let Oskar bully him or Irina seduce him. She liked his loyalty to Sam.

Jane put her hand over Sam's where it rested on her shoulder, and stood up. "We'll have to swing by our house first so I can change clothes."

Ren shrugged. "I'll go with Jimmy and Oskar, then. I need to eat."

"Are you okay?" Jane asked.

"Yeah," Ren said. "I think so. I'm probably just hungry."

"We'll see you there, then." Oskar angled himself between Frio, Sam, and Jane like a farm dog working sheep, and closed the door behind them. He came to stand over Ren, where she sat on the sofa. "Do you need other clothes?"

"I don't think so."

"Of course she doesn't. She looks lovely." Jimmy returned from Irina's shower with damp trouser cuffs, re-buttoning his sleeves. "Irina won't be joining us for dinner. She has prior plans."

"Perhaps I should stay and accompany her," Oskar said.

Jimmy held out his hands to Ren. She stood up cautiously, but didn't get dizzy. Jimmy held on to one hand, but Oskar reached between them, took Ren by the shoulders, and folded her against his chest. She was still irritated with him, but his large, tender fingers stroked her hair, and he soothed her head down onto his shoulder, his breath matching hers. Ren closed her eyes, and inside that soft darkness, the ache and howl in her chest swelled and thinned. Jimmy opened one arm, and Oskar settled Ren's body between his and Jimmy's, wrapping their backs and coiling his fingers over Ren's wrist. Cocooned inside their gathered strength and comfort, nothing eased or released in Ren, but nothing else broke. If they could all ever agree on what and how, they could do anything. "Come to dinner, *mon ami*," Jimmy told Oskar. "We need each other now."

Ren nodded in agreement against Oskar's chest, and felt the muscles harden under her cheek.

"Work will wait," Jimmy said.

Oskar's sob was almost a bark, and if Ren hadn't felt his arms and chest trembling around her, she might have thought he'd just coughed. Jimmy whacked his back with an open palm and their little knot came apart with Jimmy's battle call of "Tamales, ho!" and Oskar's quickly-turned-away face.

They collected bags and shoes and piled into Jimmy's rented SUV under cover of banter about Oskar's need for speed and Jimmy's tendency to take the more scenic surface streets. Oskar grumbled about having been made to wait at the beginning of the dust ritual, although Ren hadn't minded. She had used the time to warn Jane about the way it felt to relive another person's memory, how you don't fall into it, it's more like coming into a dream, you don't notice the transition, you just are. They hadn't waited long, but until every Incrementalist was in the Garden, the seeds of the stubbed were inert; they could be grazed, but not experienced.

It seemed like a design flaw to Ren, to have all of them offline at the same time, but she guessed it was good for group cohesion. Living another person's memory—actually experiencing a part of their life as they had—created something beyond empathy. Irina's dust ritual had certainly been part of why Ren could forgive her for the poisoned tea. She wondered how many of Phil's memories Irina had relived in the seven hundred years they'd dusted each other. The ritual made them all a part of each other the way each of them had a Garden that was part of the Garden, the way her grief was theirs too, and she was grateful for it.

★   ★   ★

Takamatsu rang the doorbell and waited.

"Well, Matsu," said Irina, opening the door. "How are you? The last time I saw you, you were kicking the shit out of my arm."

"The last time I saw you, you were Celeste," he said.

"Her actions, my arm." Irina stepped away from the front door to let him into the house.

"Where are the others?"

"Where would you expect?" she said, going back into the kitchen where a length of dried bamboo was smoking in a saucer.

"Eating," he said, surveying Ren and Phil's kitchen. "Somewhere nice. Jimmy's paying."

"There, you see? You don't need anyone to answer questions for you." Irina flipped her hair upside down, steeping it in the sweet smoke.

"You're preparing switches," he said.

"Your powers of observation are astounding."

"Switches for—?"

"Meddlework," she snapped.

"Are you angry with me, Irina?"

She considered him from behind her veil of hair. "I don't think so," she said. "But I have someplace to be. Were you on the plane during the dust ritual?"

He nodded.

"You must be exhausted." Irina straightened, pinned up her hair, and opened the sliding glass door. "Get some rest. You have the house to yourself, a big, empty couch, and a dog to keep you company."

Takamatsu let the dog in from the porch, and it sniffed his hand in an information-gathering way Takamatsu respected. He scratched behind the beast's ears as a sort of apology that he was not Phil. "How long ago did they leave?" he asked.

187

"Maybe half an hour. They were going to leave you a note, but Oskar said you'd be hours."

"I made a connection I hadn't counted on."

"Lovely. Now, if you'll excuse me—"

"What doesn't fit, Irina?"

Irina stopped with her hand reaching for the doorknob. "Pardon?"

"There's something that's threatening us, Irina. What is it?"

"You'd know that better than—"

"No, I mean for you. For what you're working on. There's something—someone—you're afraid of. Afraid of for all of us, but I can't see what it is."

She hesitated. "I know you can't. You'll have to trust me. I'm already late. We'll talk later."

"You know," Takamatsu said, "we're on the same side, Irina. We all want the same things. We shouldn't be fighting each other."

"I know," she said, and for an instant their eyes met. "But this isn't about Phil," she said. "It's about Ren. It's always been about Ren." And she was out the door, leaving Takamatsu frowning and wondering.

I now understand why Irina couldn't tell any of us what was going on. Things had run off the rails for her, and she was trying to put them right, knowing we'd all be furious with her for what she'd been attempting, and for how it had gone wrong. Her most recent Second died in disgrace, after all, and the group's good opinion means a great deal to her. Which I don't understand. Still, I can't help thinking if I'd been helping her, maybe things might not have gotten bad as they did. It would have been hard for them to go worse. Especially for Frio.

—O

DECEMBER, 1857

"Is he with her? Is she trapping him?"

Celeste took a room at the Free State, but we spent the days together, Celeste questioning me about when it was right to kill someone. The argument got heated, cooled off, got heated again, and sometimes wandered in and out of our history together and the Incrementalists' mission, but kept returning to the same place and devouring itself like the Ouroboros.

ME: I'm not a killer.

HER: I know, but that doesn't mean you can't do what's needed.

ME: If we find ourselves planning to kill someone who wants to make things better, Celeste, something is wrong with either our goals or our methods.

HER: When our goal is the saving of hundreds of innocent lives, surely our method must be any possible one.

ME (AFTER SOME THOUGHT): I can't answer your argument. But I won't kill a man who is trying to do good.

HER: Even when you know the outcome of his involvement, no matter his intention, will be fatal for many?

ME: We can never know the outcome. We, ourselves, have sometimes made things worse, have we not? How can I kill someone who is trying to end slavery, however much I might abhor his methods?

HER: How can you fail to stop someone who is going to incite the wide-spread murder of innocents?

ME: For the love of—! I told you, Celeste. I can't do it. If you're that certain, then *you* get involved. I won't try to stop you.

HER: You cannot do yourself what you know needs to be done, but you will allow it of me? Your argument is not that we do not kill, but that you cannot? Because you must keep your hands clean, let mine be fouled?

ME: I cannot do it. If you're so certain you're right, then take what action you choose.

HER: And you'll sit in your cottage and knit? You won't stop him. You won't stop me. Your moral conviction prevents you from involving yourself at all. But sins of omission are damnable all the same.

ME: (staring at the floor obstinately silent)

HER: And what will you tell yourself as the death toll climbs? "At least my hands are clean?" You'd suffer lifetimes of shame, and bear forever the guilty burden of the deaths you could have prevented rather than endure the momentary discomfort of looking into a moral man's eyes and pulling the trigger for the good of something greater? We live too long to suffer thus. It is one man's life. Ended but a little early. They will hang him. You would only carry out the law's sentence in advance, and save so many lives.

ME: You're right. We have lived long. And one thing we've learned is, if we find ourselves planning to kill a good man, something is wrong either with our methods or our goals.

Et cetera, et cetera.

It took days, but she finally saw she wouldn't be able to convince me, and resolved to leave. We sat in my cottage and drank coffee and she gave me a Frishmuth Brothers cigar as an apology. It was the sort of cigar Henry's—my Second's—father used to smoke. She put her hand on my leg and said, "I do respect your convictions, you know."

I nodded and let the smoke roll around in my mouth. I didn't care for it all that much, but the memories were nice. Then I looked at it, frowned, looked at Celeste, and said, "Are you—?"

She laughed. "No, dear James Tilly. Just offering an apology."

"All right." I blew smoke out into the cabin. "I accept."

"What do you think will happen?"

"With Brown?" I sighed. "I don't know. Either way it works out, there will be killing."

"And the Abolition movement?"

"He'll set it back. Maybe fifty years, maybe more."

She nodded and smiled at me, a little wistful. I covered her hand with mine, remembering when we were together in London, how she'd looked at me, and Lattimer's old heart gave a thump in my chest.

She spoke softly, almost inaudibly. "All those people," she said. There were tears in her eyes.

She left that evening, catching a ride to the ferry with one of Cody's sons.

I lay down for a few hour's sleep, and my pillow smelled like her hair. As soon as the sun rose, I picked up my carbine, binoculars, and plenty of jerky. Then I bundled up against the winter and started off toward Osawatomie to shoot John Brown.

FIFTEEN

All the Bodies Packed Together

Ren marveled at Jimmy's orchestration of their late-night dinner under the Cup Café's striped awning outside his hotel. He ordered a bottle of wine, choreographed the combining of tables, and explained to the staff that their party might be joined by three to five more people, but that all charges, plus a twenty-five percent gratuity for everyone involved including busboys and kitchen staff, were to be billed to his room. Satisfied it was arranged, Jimmy squeezed past Oskar to sit between him and the café wall. Oskar frowned at the empty chair across from him beside Ren, but she had dropped her shoulder bag on it, and sat with her napkin unfolded in her lap and her feet tucked under the chair like her nana had taught her ladies ought to sit.

Her nana would have loved The Hotel Congress with its abrupt art deco angles in muted southwestern shades. Nana would have appreciated the kitsch and the authenticity of it, the shimmering tile and neon lettering, and the chandelier made of wine bottles. She would not have appreciated the floor tiled with pennies. Money was for saving and sometimes spending. It was not for decorating or folding into bow ties. Ren waited for Jimmy to get comfortable before asking the question she'd been formulating while he drove and argued with Oskar and his phone's GPS.

"I know we check people out before we spike them." She eyeballed

Oskar before turning to Jimmy. "But Frio volunteered, so we don't need to gather switches to recruit him, and he's been working with Sam for months, so we know he's altruistic. What else do we need to do before we can spike Phil's stub into him?"

"Who decided Frio gets Phil's stub?" Oskar didn't rocket forward in his chair, but his fingers curled around its arms like tree roots. "You might remember, Ren, what happened the last time someone spiked a stub into an insufficiently vetted recruit."

Ren didn't wince, and she didn't drop his eyes. "No, Oskar, I've forgotten," she said, perhaps a little tartly. "Can you remind me please, ye great bastion of collective memory, when that last occurred?"

"Where is that wine?" Jimmy looked over his shoulder, jostling Oskar with his elbow as he twisted.

Oskar leaned in toward Ren. "When Phil spiked Celeste—"

"I'm sorry," Ren said. "Who's Celeste?"

Jimmy's face, whipping back to face her, made Ren instantly regret she'd let Oskar pique her. "No, Jimmy." She reached across the table for his hand. "I was teasing Oskar. I remember everything. Or as much as I ever have anyway. I'm sorry, that wasn't funny."

"No," Jimmy said. "It wasn't." He looked frayed, and Ren felt worse for having frightened him. "And I agree with Oskar, as much as it pains me to say so."

Oskar smiled wryly and sat back. "Always happy to cause you pain."

Jimmy ignored him. "I think it's too soon to rule out Sam."

"That's not what I said," Oskar said.

"Well thank god for small mercies." Ren unballed her napkin and smoothed it again.

"What I said," Oskar over-enunciated, reproaching Ren for having cut him off. "Is that we haven't decided on Frio. He's a candidate. As Sam is a candidate. Kate's recruiting too, so whoever she's identified is also a candidate, and I'll bet that's what Irina is up to right now too, working on yet another candidate."

"Why would you think that?" Ren asked him.

"Have you ever known Irina to pass up a meal when Jimmy was buying?"

"No." Ren clarified, "I meant why would she be working on another recruit? She seemed pretty keen on Frio."

"She knew I wouldn't be."

"Why not?"

"He's military."

"He's law enforcement, Oskar."

"That's worse, if anything. Not that there's much difference these days."

"Ex-law enforcement."

"That doesn't matter, I'm not talking job description, I'm talking personality."

"Oh thank god," Jimmy said as a slender sylph of a waitress materialized at Oskar's side. Ren realized that Kendra, the waitress from The Palms, wouldn't know that Phil was dead, and that stupid thought threatened to drive her to tears again. She focused on the wine bottle. The waitress turned it label-out, and presented it to Jimmy first, who nodded, then to Oskar, who also nodded.

"Would you also," said Oskar, "show it to the lady?"

"Of course." The waitress turned the bottle to Ren.

Ren loved product packaging, and would deliberately pay more for soap with a beautiful label or tea bags in an unusual canister to reward the manufacturer, but the wine label was all words, and Ren knew nothing about wine. And Oskar knew that. The waitress caught her not reading it and winked at the childish rebellion. Ren figured the girl was maybe nineteen, and the care she'd taken with her liquid eyeliner and subtly graduated earrings suggested she liked waiting tables here, where customers tipped well and were usually polite.

Polite but so unpredictable. Ren read the irritation in the slight nose twitch under the wink. One table wanted to go ladies first, the next one didn't like it when she looked from wife to wife. The table after that just went in a circle. If she gave the bill to the man when the woman was buying, she'd get the Feminist Frown. If she gave the check to the woman, the man didn't tip. Usually she'd put it in the center of the table and let them fight over it, but not this table. She'd put it smack in front of Oskar for sure. Or she'd try, but Jimmy would get it first.

"Looks great to me," Ren told her, and the waitress opened a little knife and slit the foil from the bottle like it was Oskar's neck.

She poured the sample for Jimmy, offering wordlessly to do the same for Oskar or Ren.

Ren shook her head.

"No thank you," Oskar said, a chord in his voice Ren knew she'd heard before, but couldn't place. Oskar thanked the waitress again when she filled his glass.

"Goodness, Oskar," Ren said when the girl left. "So polite."

"She's making maybe four dollars an hour plus tips. She doesn't need me getting in her face."

"And you think I do?" Ren sipped without tasting. "I make enough money that it's okay to be an asshole to me? Is there a bracket system—assholery relative to income?"

"Ren," Jimmy said.

"What do we need to do before we can spike Phil into Frio?" Ren repeated.

"Ren." Oskar didn't sound angry or even impatient. "Frio may not be the best choice."

"I'm okay with the good-enough choice if it gets Phil back tomorrow."

"We all miss him," Jimmy said.

"We more than miss him. We need him," Ren insisted. "What's wrong with Frio? It will really be Phil, just Frio's body." She turned to Oskar. "Weren't you telling me just the other day that bodies aren't what matter?"

"Bodies aren't all that matter," Oskar said. "But they matter. High levels of endogenous testosterone are strongly correlated with dominance-seeking behavior. In adolescent males of lower social and economic status, high testosterone levels manifest in physical violence and crime. Guess who joins the army?"

"He was a cop."

"He was a SWAT cop. What's wrong with Sam?"

"He's too . . ." Ren couldn't put it into words. Sam's willingness to step aside and let Phil's memories and personality replace his reminded her somehow of her mother. Ren had been the only kid in high school without a midnight curfew because her mom was too tired to wait up for her and enforce one. Ren was always in before twelve. Her mother's exhaustion had more power over her than any other parents' punishment. "Yesterday we decided it was important to keep the fallout of Phil's death from landing on Sam and Jane, right?"

Jimmy and Oskar nodded.

"Letting Sam take Phil's stub would be the opposite of that," Ren said, not looking at either man. "We call ourselves Incrementalists, but maybe it's less a name and more of a warning. Maybe it's how we remind ourselves to move slowly because there's something not the least incremental about every one of us. There's something reckless about us, or we never would have taken the spike. Even me, and I had to be meddled into taking it. But I'm impatient. Like all of us. I suck at acceptance and I do stupid, impatient, irritated things to fix other things. It's the only trait, actually, that we all share, the readiness to gamble our life for a chance to make things even just a little bit better in the world. We can't—we just aren't capable, none of us—of standing still. We aren't hopeless and we aren't helpless. We don't despair and we don't quit. Ever. Not even when we die. We come back."

Jimmy put his emptied glass on the table and looked so deeply into her that Ren was pretty sure he could see her lunch. He didn't smile.

"Sam taking the spike would be a suicide," Ren said at last. "He's a disappointed idealist who lost his faith in change and love. We don't take advantage of that. We fix it."

"Very well." Jimmy's gaze shifted to over Ren's shoulder, and he raised an arm to beckon. "Why don't you see what you can do?"

*   *   *

The dress Irina had borrowed from Ren's closet was snug across the bust—Ren was almost flat-chested, poor dear—but it was short and Menzie was a legs man, so Irina figured she was going to be just fine. She was meeting him at Revolutionary Grounds—a bit on the nose, sure, but the coffee was good and what could she say, the walls were the right red. Against them, if Irina added a little yellow somewhere, she'd be Kumul colors, and Menzie loved his national team.

Irina passed a truck on the right and darted in front of a minivan, fast and agile in her new Second's body and zippy sports car. It had been a gift from Vanessa's dad, and Irina was trying to maintain the relationship between them, but he kept asking her what had changed, and of course she couldn't tell him the truth. It made Irina sad.

Irina twitched the hem up higher as she swept down the entrance ramp to I-10 admiring the warm brown of her thighs. Between the varicose veins, age spots, and the psoriasis around her last Second's knees, she hadn't gone bare-legged in twenty years. They'd hurt too, those knees, and been a bit knobby to boot. Irina sighed. It really had been time for a new body when Phil shot her, but she'd earned every scar and wrinkle on the old one, and been proud to wear them. Her new body felt story-less in contrast.

She had to brake hard and swerve around one of those absurd Porsche SUVs—sports parenting!—but got off the shoulder in front of it easily, still making good time. She'd still been very new to that old body back in 1977, the most recent stub-and-Second among them, and Phil's dust ritual had shown it to her as Phil had seen it—a little gawky and too thin, with some of Lacey's mannerisms still mixed in with Irina's own, letting Celeste bait her.

Her exit was coming, but the right lane was still boggy with the leavings of rush hour traffic. Feeling fast and agile, Irina swung out wide left, then back across them all to the off-ramp. It was snug, and some idiot honked, but she made it.

In 1977, Celeste and Phil had been living together in that little Pittsburgh apartment with its pumpkin- and avocado-colored kitchen, and a slow awareness was waking up in the US about what was happening in Democratic Kampuchea. The article in *Reader's Digest* had helped. Phil was meddling with a congressman from New York, but it was going slowly, as things with Phil always did.

Why had Jimmy chosen a memory from that period—the most painful one in recent lives—to reexperience as they dusted Phil? Irina had been in stub when Sophal died, but she'd grazed every one of the memories Sophal had seeded, scratching the characters into her skin with a fingernail. Irina remembered Sophal's forced march out of her beautiful city with the blood-soaked body of her son—ten years old and on fire with fever—strapped to her body with yards of yellow fabric. She walked with his foot in her hand for hours before she put it down and left it.

Irina parked on Fifth, under a metal awning, and took the darkest sidewalk, almost wanting someone to hassle her.

★　　★　　★

Ren watched Frio, Jane, and Sam thread their way toward her, Oskar and Jimmy, Jane waving, Sam watching her, and Frio watching him. Jane sat beside Oskar, and Ren took her bag from the chair she'd been saving for Frio. He sat next to her, across from Oskar, with Sam on his other side, facing his wife.

"You made excellent time." Jimmy reached across Oskar to pour wine into Jane's glass. "It took us nearly as long to park as it took you to go home, change, and get here."

"We found a spot just across the street," Sam said, handing his glass gratefully to Jimmy. "Jane has great parking karma."

Oskar snorted and Jane looked over the rim of her glass at him. "I'm guessing you don't?"

"That's not a thing."

"Clearly not for you. Maybe the universe is trying to tell you something."

Ren knew Jane was teasing, but Oskar did an actual double take. "The universe can't talk."

Jane laughed like bright gravel, and she leaned in to bump her shoulder playfully to Oskar's. "No, of course not. Not in words."

Oskar shook his blond head. "Not in anything. Not in words or omens or parking spots. The universe has no agency. There is no vast, inchoate intelligence 'out there' struggling to communicate with us through our automobiles. You postulate nature endowed with consciousness, yet everything humanity has ever accomplished has been through increased knowledge and understanding of the objective processes of nature that deny the existence of any such. Including the history of the belief in nature endowed with consciousness. As a pagan, you ought to understand better than most the contradiction between the historical presence of gods in every facet of nature, and where you've ended up today, with, 'I think there's something, sort of.' That process itself—understanding the history of religion, of human thought—is part of the natural world, and subject to scientific analysis."

"I'm not a pagan, I'm a witch." The laughter was stripped from Jane's voice leaving something made of ancient standing stones. "I don't care about what god or gods have made. I care about what we make—about how I can learn to use my power to create and alter my reality. I look into the world and see an elegant web of finely tuned, infinite possibility. But if you want to see a soul-less, purpose-less chaotic tangle, you can certainly build your own nest and sit in it."

"You deliberately choose delusion over truth?"

"No, I chose my delusion over yours."

Oskar scowled, and Jane turned to the waitress, who'd kept her distance during Oskar's monologue. "I'll have the tamales, please, as they come so highly recommended." She winked at Jimmy, who blew her a kiss from his fingertips. "They are good, right?" she asked the waitress, who nodded and gave Jane the first real smile Ren had seen from the girl all night.

Jimmy ordered more wine, Oskar announced he was switching to beer, and the rest of the table put in their orders while he fumed. When the waitress left, Oskar leaned back in his chair to address Jane, and Ren had a sudden hunger for popcorn, followed by a sudden pang of missing Phil. He'd taught her to enjoy Oskar. But Jimmy cut Oskar off before he could get past his first salvo, which promised to be either a contrast of reason and intuition or a quote from Einstein about eternal mystery. "Excuse me," Jimmy said, "but I believe that I have some facility with both reason and intuition."

Jane leaned forward to look across Oskar to Jimmy. "I believe you do," she said.

Oskar said nothing so Ren asked him. "And Jimmy, what do you believe?"

"I believe Oskar would never attack someone's belief system over a lighthearted remark about parking."

Jane sat back in her chair as if to get enough distance to have a good, hard look at Oskar. He didn't move, his face rigorously blank. "Okay," she said and didn't look at anyone else. "And?"

Ren heard a strange, hard note in Jimmy's usually warm voice: "Oskar is acting out because he misses Phil. He feels an urgency he doesn't understand to settle the question of Phil's Second—I feel it too, and understand it not at all—but I am accustomed to waiting. Whereas for Oskar, circumstance has enforced patience on a man of action. He's frustrated. He's frightened. We all are, and this dinner reminds us too much of one we had with Phil in Las Vegas once, except tonight is pivoted one hundred and eighty degrees."

Ren closed her eyes.

"Ren, at least, can acknowledge that. But Oskar would first have to admit the power his emotions have over him, and he can't, so he's fighting it in Jane."

"As Ren once remarked," said Oskar coldly, "I'm right here."

"We both are," Jane said, and she looked at Sam, whose shoulders seemed ready to snap from the intensity of the focus he'd been directing at his wife.

"It's getting to all of us," Jimmy said after a moment. "We're all wound up, spiraling in. If it weren't getting to me, I wouldn't have just done that to Oskar."

Sam poured more wine into Jane's glass. Jane looked at the lot of them—again—like they were crazy. And Ren thought maybe they were. Maybe being a witch was the sanest thing any one of them sitting there was. Something passed between Jimmy and Oskar, but Ren couldn't quite read the nuance.

"Oskar," said Jimmy brightly. "Oskar, have you made the funeral arrangements yet?"

"For Phil," Oskar said, like he'd had to think through the other options: Jane couldn't kill him, he wouldn't eat her alive. "For Chuck," he corrected himself.

"Yes," Jimmy agreed affably. "For Chuck." He looked at Ren in both challenge and support. "What we do next, before we spike Phil into anyone, is grieve Chuck."

"Oh," Ren said, but it sounded different.

"I spoke to his brother and his dad," Oskar said. "They understand that we won't have his ashes yet. People are flying in. I've let the poker room manager at The Palms know, and some local people here. We still need to reserve a place to hold the memorial, but I wanted to consult with Ren before I booked it."

He looked at Ren, and nothing in his eyes said anything about it being just a body.

DECEMBER, 1857

Slavery was legal in every nation on earth.

I might have felt different if I'd thought Brown's plans could work. But I'd been there, I'd traveled through the slave states. The slaves weren't ready to rise, particularly at the call of a white man they didn't know or trust. I remembered Nat Turner. I remembered Irina's seeds from Haiti.

No, it was an adventure and, worse, an adventure that would unify the South against Abolition, and kill Northern sympathy. Like I'd told Celeste, we might be set back fifty years, or a hundred, just by that one act.

He had to be stopped.

I had tried meddling with him, I'd tried sending desperate messages to our New England people to meddle with his collaborators. Nothing. I considered exposing his plan and trying to stop it that way, but I didn't have enough details to make the exposure believable; all I'd accomplish would be to destroy his supporters, including, quite possibly, Frederick Douglass himself.

The Adair cottage was a long way away, and the Sharp's in my mittened hand grew heavier as I made my way thitherward, as if it, too, were reluctant. It was a model 1853 Percussion Carbine, with the pellet primer system and the slanting breech. It had a hinged sight, brass plate, iron bindings. I'd never been enamored of firearms the way some people are, but it was a beautiful piece of work—an efficient and deadly tool. Though shorter than the full rifle, a skilled marksman could reliably hit a small target from a hundred yards. I'd need to be much closer. Close enough to see Brown's face, with its prominent forehead and sharp nose and firm mouth. I'd have to be close enough to see the look of shock on his face when the bullet struck him. And the blood. I might not get more than one shot, so I'd have to shoot him in the head. There would be a great deal of blood.

And then?

Then I'd wait. I wouldn't try to get away. They'd probably hang me, and that was fine. Either I'd come back out of stub, or I wouldn't. At that moment, I didn't much care.

SIXTEEN

Well-Meant But Inadequate Refreshment

Irina checked the yellow silk flower in her hair and the crucifix at her throat as she walked. She pulled her pair of cute-nerd glasses out of her bag and yanked open the door to Revolutionary Grounds.

"Vee!" From a back table, Menzie, shaved bald and squatly muscular, raised a paw in greeting.

Irina waved back, mimed coffee drinking, and got in line. She'd forgotten he called her Vanessa. When they'd first met, she had used her Second's name to make a connection between her Chinese last name and his Papua New Guinean one. She ordered a drink, also a piece of cake, but only because Menzie had a sandwich, and checked to make sure her actors were in place.

She'd called in two anonymous tips and a personal favor, and ta-da—there he was, two tables in front of Menzie, looking alert, but playing it cool—one of Tucson PD's finest. And wearing tactical black instead of police blue. Perfect. Also, Amber, the waitress Irina had hired to flirt with the cop, was wearing the Sun Devils jersey Irina had dropped off for her on her way to Ren's. Amber wasn't due to make her first approach for another fifteen minutes, but she spotted Irina, waved and winked. Irina returned the greeting with her best "Grad Student Conducting A Psychology Experiment" smile and wished she'd thought to grab a clipboard

from Phil's jumbled prop closet. Still, everything looked in order, especially considering how little time she'd had to set it up. She wove her way
through the tables to Menzie's.

"I still miss your dreads." She dragged the empty chair across from
Menzie closer to him and sat down.

He grinned but shrugged her hand off his shoulder. "You sound like
my mama. She's stopped calling me Beautiful Boy. About time," he grumbled, but his face softened.

"You're still beautiful," Irina told him, even though it wasn't quite
true. Menzie's head was almost perfectly spherical, and without the gorgeous, fat dreads he'd worn through college, he looked like a face reflected
in a doorknob. His baldness exaggerated the upswept slant of his eyes and
the width of his cheekbones. But he'd traded beauty for something fiercer,
and Irina liked it. Menzie dragged a messenger bag from the floor onto
his lap, extracted a folder, and slid it to her.

"How you spoil me!" Irina took the file with a wink Menzie didn't
return.

"Open it." Menzie looked from the folder to Irina, and she hesitated,
letting his anticipation heighten his attention. She touched the cross at
her throat absently—it was almost identical to the one he wore—and tilted
her head to put the yellow flower directly in front of the red wall. His eyes
darted back to the folder.

That was a very bad sign. If they were still working toward the same
goals, their commonalities should increase Menzie's sense of belonging
and inclusion, rewarding him with a warm oxytocin wash of bonded-ness
and confidence. Irina pointedly looked from him over her shoulder at the
Tucson police officer, hoping definition by contrast might work where
inclusion had failed her.

"What are these?" She looked up from the photos. "They look like
something from the set of that *Avengers* movie."

"I know, right? Only it's *Star Trek*, not *The Avengers*." Menzie's grin
split his round head like a PacMan mouth.

"What does it have to do with us?"

"Everything. US General Keith Alexander is watching you from his
Information Dominance Center, in Fort Belvoir, Virginia, courtesy of a

set designer hired out of Hollywood. This guy actually spent public money to build a replica captain's chair smack in the middle of NSA headquarters so he can sit there just like Jean-Luc Picard, only without the tea or humanity. Spy on civilians? Make it so!"

Irina wrapped her anxiety-chilled fingers around her mug and gave Menzie her best playful smile. "I'll see your Picard spymaster and raise you a Vader-enabled predator drone."

"Border Control has had drones for ages."

"Not Vehicle and Dismount Exploitation Radar ones."

"Nobody cares."

"You care." Irina kept her voice low, trying for sultry. If Menzie thought she was arguing, he'd set his teeth and never go back to the important work she needed him for. His tenacity was part of his strength, but if Irina couldn't leverage his righteous anger to direct it, he'd go with the outrageous story rather than the insidious one. "You care that city police departments are turning into standing armies. You care that they're walling us in—literally with a fourteen-foot-tall metal fence, and figuratively a one-hundred-mile wide 'constitution-free' zone around the whole damn Land of the Free—borders and coasts."

Menzie pulled the photos of Fort Belvoir from her hands and stared at them. "I'm running these."

"I think you should. They're sensational, just go all the way with it."

"What do you mean?"

She had him. Menzie believed in serious journalism, not sensationalism. He went the distance, he didn't stop shy. "Arizona gets plenty of NSA money," Irina suggested. "Dig. Connect the dots. Bring it back home."

Menzie shoved his rugby player's body back in the little wooden chair so hard Irina thought it might splinter.

"It'd be more work, I know." Irina gave him a moment to feel challenged and equal to it. "But I can help you. It's time to go public with the local insurgency story."

Wrong word. She saw it in the softening of his nasal-labial folds. Menzie wanted to be national.

"You have incredible depth and detail to support a nationwide trend that spans from the heartland to the beltway," she said. "Use these incredible pictures to highlight how insanely off the rails the war on drugs and terrorism has run. The generals are insane and the foot soldiers are brutes. And now here, in our own town, the police have assassinated a civilian. And I'm not talking Kennedys and MLK, or even the US citizen the president authorized the CIA to hunt down, target, and kill in Yemen. This guy's name wasn't Anwar, it was Chuck."

Under an African nose, Menzie's island lips curled in disgust. "Think I don't know that happens? I've never smoked a joint. I didn't drink til I was twenty-one, and I still don't get drunk. I'm flawless, and I'm no pussy, but I have to have a 'yes sir!' plan because those fuckers who are supposed to protect and serve us? They're out to make my ass obey, and it's even worse in Phoenix. You think I don't want to grab this state by the scruff of its neck and rub its nose in the shit it took all over me?"

"I know." Irina wanted to touch him, and not just to meddle him back in her direction, but to comfort him too. She knew what it cost him to admit he was afraid. Instead, she shifted back from him to make sure he had a clear view of Amber as she made her first approach. *Look Menzie, see the enemy get the girl.*

"Vee, I know we're living in a police state," he said, eyes focusing over Irina's shoulder, but sounding tired rather than enraged. "We're training paramilitary police units with tanks and drones and AK-47s. I've been running those stories since I was in college. The one-hundred-and-seven-year-old guy the snipers shot. The SWAT operation that killed the dude in the apartment downstairs. It happens every god damn day. And everybody nods and agrees it's terrible. No, not terrible . . ."

Derision savaged Menzie's face as he combed his memory for the word he wanted. "Everyone agrees it's *outrageous*. And they're all justly outraged. They've seen the pictures of the cops pepper-spraying Occupy kids sitting on the ground. They know. Our government has declared its right to eavesdrop on any of us without a warrant and to kidnap, torture, and kill us on the President's declaration. And the people know that too. But what are they going to do?" He closed the file. "Nothing. What am I going to do?" Menzie pointed the folder at Irina. "This is one man. The head of the fucking NSA. I can take him down. More people have been killed by cops since nine-eleven than died in the towers, but there's no way we'll ever tease the military and the police apart again. I can't win that."

"You know," Irina said again, her voice as gentle and comforting as her rising panic would allow. "You probably can't win that war." But god, she needed him fighting it. At least for one more battle. Irina took a slow breath and unknotted her hair, shaking the saksak-cooking-over-the-fire-in-bamboo smell out of it. "But is that what you want, Menzie? You want to win?"

He looked up at her, and Irina pushed a piece of hair behind the ear with the flower to draw his eye. *See the Kumal colors.*

"This isn't a game," Irina whispered. "You're a warrior."

He looked away from her, but sat so still that Irina pressed it. "You fight the battle that's right, not because you can win." She jabbed a thumb over her shoulder. Amber was due to visit the cop again soon. "That's what they do." Irina leaned closer, fingers on her crucifix again. "That's the point of overwhelming force, isn't it?"

He nodded, ever so slightly.

"That's not who you are," she said.

Menzie looked at her and Irina wanted to kiss him, he was so brave and troubled. But not yet.

"Link the stories. Get Alexander and Harris both recalled."

"It'll never happen." Menzie's stubborn shoulders sagged.

"It might," Irina whispered. Menzie was too young and strong to be defeated. "Keep the pressure up, maybe he'll do something stupid."

"He does something stupid every day. His constituents are good with that."

"A wider audience won't be."

"Maybe not. But what would they do about it? What could I even ask them to do? Stop the drug war? Vanessa, I'm brown. They'll call me a stoner and write off the whole thing." He scooped the folder off the table and shook it at her. "This will be great. We'll point and laugh and embarrass the fuck out of the head of the NSA, Mr. 'Collect-it-All' himself, for wanting to cosplay Picard."

"And he'll step down early."

"Maybe so."

"It won't change anything on the ground."

"I know." He looked at Irina again, but his eyes were locked up tight as a SWAT tank. "Only widespread involvement can do that."

"Menzie—"

"And this isn't something individual citizens can fight."

"We can support the ones who fight in our name."

"I can't write an exposé with 'donate to the ACLU' as its action item, Vee. I'd sound like an ad."

"Menzie." Irina put her hand on his muscular forearm, but Menzie stood up.

"Fuck it," he said. "I'm done with Arizona." Menzie was out the door before Amber even made it back to the cop. Before Irina could tell him about the SWAT raid coming up at the library.

The expansion of surveillance and militarization of enforcement was the most critical pivot Irina had ever seen, and one only the Incrementalists might tip the right direction, and only if they were unified. Phil's death had brought Ren out from his shadow, forcing her to act or break, as Irina had hoped Phil's arrest would do. But it hadn't brought them all together. And it hadn't galvanized the populace.

Irina forced herself to watch Amber's performance as if she were taking research notes, but she was nearly gagging on tears. She needed male hands and someone's complete attention. She called Jimmy, but he didn't answer his phone. Menzie had been her lover, off and on, for almost a year while Irina had learned his secrets and read his e-mail, but he'd walked out of the coffee shop like he didn't owe her a damn thing.

Irina made a phone call, and had the little shit arrested.

*   *   *

Back at Ren and Phil's, Oskar sat alone and watched the empty pool. Inside, Ren was already asleep. Jimmy was at his hotel, Sam and Jane had gone home, either taking Frio with them or dropping him off somewhere. Irina was off somewhere doing something. Ramon was due to arrive tomorrow morning, which left—

The door opened. Oskar looked back as Matsu emerged. Oskar made up his mind to ignore any mystical platitudes Matsu might spout—whatever the group needed right now, more conflict between the two of them wasn't it.

Matsu sat next to him. "Ren is in her own bed tonight," he said. "You slept in the chair last night, so you can have the guest room. I'll take the couch."

"All right. Thanks."

"Any progress?"

"On finding Phil's killer? No. I've been grazing. Nothing anywhere. The detectives assigned to it are already working on something else. Frio says it was probably a SWAT marksman, which is possible. But he was shot at close range with a handgun, which isn't the usual SWAT M.O."

"Could that be deliberate? To avoid making it look like what it was?"

Oskar nodded. "Yeah, I thought of that. It's possible."

"How was dinner?"

"Tense."

Matsu was silent for a few minutes. One thing that Oskar did appreciate about him was he never felt the need to fill silences.

"We should probably rest," said Matsu eventually.

"You know," said Oskar. "Finding a recruit for Phil has been taking all of our attention. That's part of why we—I—have been so slow to work out what happened to him."

"Yes," said Matsu.

"But somewhere out there is whoever shot Phil, and until we find out who, it's going to be hard to find out why. And if we don't know why, we have no way of being sure that whoever we recruit isn't just going to be murdered again."

"Yes."

Reluctantly, Oskar asked, "Do you see anything I might be missing?"

"I spoke with Irina briefly tonight."

Oskar remembered Irina's cavalier introduction of Frio as Phil's obvious new Second. He remembered the subtlety of her fingers on his own arm. "Oh?" he asked with careful neutrality.

"She said it was about Ren. That it was always about Ren."

"What does that mean?"

"I don't know. But I think if we can figure that out, we'll have it."

"In that case," said Oskar. "If it's about Ren, then, right now, it's about Irina. Tomorrow I'll find her and ask her some questions. Maybe this time I'll be the one to shoot her in the face."

Matsu said nothing. His silence irritated Oskar. "Is there a pattern there?" he asked at last. "Anything that might help, a piece that stands out?"

Matsu closed his eyes. A minute later he opened them and said, "When I examine the nodes of Phil's death and Irina, I can see a missing set of points. There is some overlap."

Oskar stood up and began pacing. "I should have followed her tonight." He stopped when he saw the stillness of Matsu's jaw. "What else?"

"When I overlay Ren's grid, all I can see at the nexus of Irina and Ren and Phil's death is a vortex, or a tornado."

ABOLITION AND WAR

I'd already decided to find somewhere near the Adair cottage, because it was one of Brown's favorite haunts. I studied the area, working out a place where I could get close enough without him seeing me. There was a long, gentle slope to the east, leading down to a creek bed. It was deep enough that no one could see me, and I could even get a fire going if I were careful to keep it from smoking too much during the day, and to hide the flame at night. I wouldn't be able to see the cottage, of course, but I could hear anyone approaching in plenty of time.

I got the fire going, then waited and shivered.

The next few days were about as unpleasant as any I'd had since the War. Almost as cold, almost as hungry, lonelier, and that had been a younger, hardier Second. And he'd still been too frail to survive the winter.

There was a lot of activity at the cabin, with Adair and his family coming and going. Brown's wife and two of his sons arrived, which gave me hope that the old man himself would be there soon. Every time I heard someone crunching through the snow, I'd creep up like an animal, stick my head out just high enough to see, then slink back down. The effort of moving quietly through the snow was the hardest part. And then, after two days of waiting, when he finally showed up, my heart near leapt from my throat. It was mid-afternoon, and I saw him from a good distance. He was alone, walking toward the cabin with his determined stride.

I lay in the snow, and checked the load in the Sharps. I flipped up the sight and waited. I focused on his head as he came closer, his arms swinging stiffly.

The sky was gray; there was no sun to reflect off the barrel. I cocked the Sharps. It seemed very loud, but Brown didn't react.

Closer, closer. I was hidden behind a mound of snow at the top of the ridge, and he was close enough that I knew I could hit him. My finger curled around the trigger.

SEVENTEEN

A Mischief That Will Hurt Our Cause

Daniel called at 6:00 in the morning, before Kate had even checked the forums to see what everyone had to say about her post announcing she'd given him up as her recruit for Phil's stub.

"Kate, I have to see you."

"No, you really don't, dear," she told him. "Read the research I sent you. Go to PT with Annie. Everything you're feeling will be gone in two days. If it's not, call me then and we'll have coffee."

"No, Kate, really. I need your help."

There, he said it. Like he knew her switches and was willing to use them. Kate was a doctor because she helped people. It was what she did. The fact is, most doctors she knew went into medicine because of a fascination with how people worked, and a calling to make them right not unlike the way an auto mechanic feels about cars—helping people was almost an afterthought. But not for Kate—for her, that's what it was all about, and always had been, before and after the spike that gave her access to the Incrementalists' shared memory of history. Sometimes she thought it had changed her less than it should have.

She told Daniel to meet her in the cafeteria of the hospital where they'd first met, but changed her mind and called him back when she got out of the shower.

"Does your hotel have a restaurant?" she asked him.

"Yeah, but the food's no good."

"How's the coffee?"

"Worse."

"Okay, I'll see you there."

*   *   *

In the crappy hotel room where last night, at the last minute, she had given her name as Vanessa Pulu rather than Surya, Irina stroked the hair back from Frio's broad forehead and fought back an odd, keen sadness. "Are you sure?" she asked a final time.

They had been talking about it since he woke up, a little shaky and pale with the hangover nemones always get the day after being taken into the Garden, but Irina had made up her mind watching him sleep as the morning seeped into the room. Frio wiped his clean hands on the sheets and nodded. "What do I do?" he asked her.

"We go to the Garden. Same as last time."

The last time had been only yesterday, for Phil's dust ritual, but Jimmy had been the one with his fingers on Frio's temple then. Frio got out of bed, pulled on his jeans, and took Irina's waist in one hand. She allowed herself the comfort of wrapping her arms around him a final time. She closed her eyes. Frio put two callused fingers to her temple.

Irina listened for the sound of surf—the purr and smash of waves gathering and breaking, wearing the world into sand, and she felt for the worn-smooth wood under her palm. As the ocean receded, the long staircase of her Garden came out of shadow behind her closed lids. She climbed the creaky stairs up, not to one of the hundreds of claustrophobic hallways this time, only to the center step where she stopped and looked up.

To Frio, Irina knew, it would look like she was having a seizure, the way her eyelids stuttered, but she figured he wasn't watching her face, so it didn't matter.

She steadied herself with one hand on the rickety banister and stretched, reaching up through the skylight, down a hall, past doors closed on whimpers and panting, and onto another landing. Its open

215

window marked the start of Phil's Garden as it was represented in hers, usually as a floaty vista of fat clouds and flittering birds. It was stormy today, but what Irina needed was just outside, planted in the window box.

"We can't be touching now," she told Frio.

He had been so eager, at the hotel half an hour after she'd called him from Revolutionary Grounds, and so adamant that Sam must not be allowed to get Phil's stub. He'd told her everything, unapologetic and brass, but he was frightened now. Irina felt it in the way his fingers tightened on her hip before he let her go. She put her hand through the window and pulled the tiny, single-bullet pistol from the dirt just outside it. Phil's stub was cold and inert, but messy. Irina tried to dust off the brown powder and strange white flakes clinging to it. She wiped it on her skirts, and scented cinnamon. Odd. She tested the pistol's balance and slid her finger into the oval trigger guard. It felt snug and compact in her hand. She curled her finger at the trigger, and put the muzzle square between Frio's dark brows.

He blinked twice, two rapid beats of his lashes, but he didn't flinch. He stared back at her. He had closed his eyes the first time they'd kissed, and mostly watched her breasts as they made love. Near the end, he had bowed his head, like he was praying over her, and he'd come without making a sound.

Now, for the first time, he looked right into her eyes. Irina liked it, but the gun was growing heavy in her hand. The bullet in the cold chamber twitched. It shuddered like a fledgling and, with a strong whiff of blood, broke free of its metal shell. It stretched itself backward into time and forward into Frio, molting flakes of bark. Its leading edge burned ember-bright, and its telescoping growth rings compressed all of who Phil was into a single stake, and the ritual ignited.

Irina never remembered what happened from the moment she shaped the stub until she used it, but hours or minutes later, the bullet was a stake and the stake was a wager. It was a picket. It was a signpost in the ground, and a club in her hand. It was a torch of stolen fire. It was Phil, and Irina drove it into Frio, right between his eyes.

*　　*　　*

I pulled the, no, he pulled the trigger.

He was pointing the rifle at himself. But that was impossible; his arms were too short and the odds were too long. Either he was Captain Brown, or he was—

I was Carter, and I was jumping into the hole left by the bullet.

Carter can't do it. I can't do it. Frio can't shoot. There is too much of the noise of history, of the spiraling Fibonacci pattern of multiplied suffering. He can't do it, but he, I, did, and the carbine, the Sharp's, no, the Sharp's, couldn't take .9 mm bullets, everyone knew that, even Fred.

I can't won't do it, but I do he does.

Some of me fractures, and some of him remains like the afterimage on the retina from cannon fire at night. It smells like cordite and pomander, and I must not he must not go, but staying would be terribly, terribly wrong. Folding a hand has never before required such exertion.

The bullet hits, splinters, misses, and I dissolve.

*　　*　　*

Frio gave a stifled scream like Irina had shot him, then made a worse sound. Irina staggered back, knocking her hip hard against the sharp edge of the cheap dresser. What the fuck? Frio doubled over and clamped his palms to his forehead, growling with the pain. Why wasn't he sleeping? Irina grabbed him by his shoulders and steered him to the bed, pushed him to sit on the edge.

"Frio!" She tried to get him to focus on her. "What's happening? Can you see anything?"

But Frio only rocked himself and groaned. Irina wanted to put her arms around his heaving shoulders, but he needed her to make the pain stop.

"Phil?" she shouted.

Frio convulsed and clawed at his forehead.

Irina grabbed his wrists and tried to pull his hands away. "Stop it!"

He flicked her off him with a cocked elbow.

Irina scrambled back. "Listen to me, you little bitch!" She got right in his face. "I can help you, but you have to stop ripping your fucking face!"

Frio folded in half, forearms on his thighs, rocking himself in agony.

Irina took a step back, panting. She was cold with fear and sweating, and had no idea what was going on. The stub of a dead Incrementalist stays in the Garden, a symbol of their stored memories, the location of their personality and heuristics, until another Incrementalist forms it into a burning brand and introduces it to an open, living mind.

That's what she'd done.

You have to stay stretched between the inner Garden and the outside world for the spiking ritual, and it hurts, but not like Frio was hurting. It was hard, like trying to do big math in your head, or see detail in something too far away, the concentration an almost muscular strain; but Frio was making gagging, gurgling animal sounds. Irina closed her eyes and tried to concentrate. She had to think things through.

To work the ritual, you hold yourself between reality and your metaphor. You introduce the one—and yes, rather forcefully—into the other. The invaded mind overwhelms, goes into shock and passes out. Always.

"Lie down!" Irina told Frio, but she had to tell him twice before he heard her. "Go to sleep."

His body contorted, but didn't lie down, so she tipped him gently onto his side. His groaning went up an octave and broke. Irina wanted to cover her ears to keep out his terrible gasping sobs, but she lifted his legs onto the mattress. His feet grabbled against the bed, circling and flailing like he was trying to crawl away from the pain. Irina understood that. She wanted to run too. Her mind was already way ahead of her, fleeing over explanations, hurling back suggestions. She should call 911. She should graze. She should try to comfort Frio. She should knock him out with a bat.

"It's going to be okay," she told him. "It's just pain. There's nothing actually wrong with you."

But when there's pain, that's all there is.

"Fuck!" she whispered. "Cock-biting, venomous whore to a faggot!"

Frio puked and started choking. Somewhere, as far away across the room as childhood, Irina's cell phone rang.

"Help!" Irina shouted at it. "Fucking help me!"

Frio wouldn't turn his head, and the gurgling noises were just getting wetter. Irina tried to twist his neck around and felt her gorge rise with the stink and the slippery chunks under her fingers trying to clean out his mouth. Irina had fought with too many dying people. She hated it. Life was ugly, but it was ugliest at its edges.

If she left Frio to answer her phone, he'd choke on his vomit and die. If she didn't call for help, they'd exhaust each other until she couldn't do anything for him anymore, and he'd die all the same only having suffered more.

Once he was dead, Phil would be back with his blunt metal nose in the weird-smelling dirt of her window box, and everyone would be livid because they didn't know Frio was actually a part of something bigger. Then they'd go back to fighting about Sam, who Ren didn't like, and whoever it was Kate had found.

Frio was panting. He could no longer make even muffled screams, and Irina's fear was turning into anger, building it up in thin, protective layers. What the fuck was happening to him? And what was up with the dirt in her window box anyway? And why the hell was Frio in so much pain?

He stopped breathing, and Irina's terror came washing back. She was not nearly worn out enough to let him die. She shook him hard. He gave a sob and inhaled.

Irina's Garden was a fucking whorehouse, and nobody knew it. Everyone thought it was an actual garden, but that was just the courtyard out back. Irina listened to the surf, and felt the banister's smooth wood. It took everything she had just to climb the stairs. The echoes of Frio's agony down the too-narrow hall drowned out the sounds of fucking behind the doors. Up the main stairs, always up the sweeping main stairs, down the kitchen curling ones, and out the back door through the flowers to her garden wall. Irina hadn't brought a quill to write with, but the charred wood of Phil's stub was still in her hand.

As their first symbols were millennia ago, as the Garden was first made, Irina scratched carbon over stone. "Help," she scrawled. "I need medical help. The Hilton hotel on Aviation. Room 217. Please."

DECEMBER, 1857

PASSION AND HEARTBREAK

Brown had the same deep-set eyes as Frederick. And as I looked, I saw Fred Brown's eyes in his father's face—kindly and mad. I remembered Fred so well, lying there, at peace from his madness, maybe, but that didn't make it any better. And here was his father, off to destroy the hopes of Abolition, to keep slavery alive for generations, out of the arrogant conviction that he knew what was best. What gave him the right to make that judgment?

The same thing, perhaps, that gave it to me.

I had him dead. I had him cold.

I watched him walk by.

He had almost reached the cabin when his wife came out, followed by two or three sons. I uncocked the Sharp's, put my mittens back on, turned and headed back for Lawrence. I let the fire burn out behind me.

EIGHTEEN

A Man Who Is Determined to Do Good

After a nice breakfast of eggs and chorizo at his hotel, Jimmy arrived at Ren and Phil's to find Ren getting caught up on work e-mail and Oskar soaking in the sun at the little glass patio table and scowling at his laptop as if it knew all the details of Phil's death but was refusing to give them up. Which might, Jimmy reflected, even be true in some sense. Matsu sat in a lounge chair, eyes closed as he and Oskar each pretended the other didn't exist.

"Any luck, Oskar?" Jimmy asked

Oskar shook his head. "I need to talk to Irina. I know she's involved somehow. But I don't have anything concrete to confront her with. I want something. I want a piece." He sighed. "I'm going to graze again."

As Jimmy was getting settled, Matsu pulled off his clothes, and dived naked into the pool. He was no Oskar, but there was nothing wrong with the view, either. Jimmy watched him swimming laps, easy, hardly splashing, then closed his eyes, and drifted off.

When he opened them again, Matt was out of the pool, dressed, and sitting at the patio table. Ren was there, next to Oskar, wearing Phil's ratty old bathrobe, neither of them speaking, an empty coffeepot on the table between them.

Hours must have passed.

"Something is wrong," Jimmy said, and instantly had everyone's attention.

"What?" Oskar sat up straight on full alert.

"I don't know."

"A feeling?" said Matsu.

Jimmy nodded.

"Do you want to graze?" said Oskar.

Jimmy shook his head. "I was just grazing. I went into the Garden while I was napping, and woke up knowing something was wrong. We need to figure out what it is, but I'm too hungry to graze any more right now. Matt, think you might want to?"

Matsu stared at him like Jimmy had just grown tentacles. He noticed Ren and Oskar were looking at him in much the same way. "What is it?" he said.

"You never call Matsu Matt," Oskar said.

"I know. Only Phil does that."

"You just did."

"No, I didn't."

They all nodded.

Jimmy's heart gave a sudden thud. He closed his eyes and entered the Garden again, knowing exactly where to look. It took only seconds.

"Oh, holy shit," he said. "Phil's stub is gone."

"Irina," they all said together. And, "Frio."

*　　*　　*

Ren was on her feet before Jimmy's words had fully sunk in. Phil's stub was gone from the Garden—he was back from the dead! The ritual was exhausting, so he was probably asleep, wherever he was, and he'd have a fierce headache when he woke up, but Ren knew he'd want to wake up next to her. "We have to find them," she told Jimmy. "Would you call Irina? I'm going to put on clothes."

"No, wait." Jimmy shifted his bulk in the sagging plastic chaise. "Something's wrong."

"Hell yes, something's wrong." Oskar's voice was an angry growl.

"Irina knew we weren't agreed on her fucking SWAT cop. Kate had a recruit she was working with. I was clear about my opposition."

"Kate posted late last night that she had released her recruit." Matsu stayed in his chair, legs extended and crossed at the ankles, but nobody would have mistaken his posture for lounging anymore. "And the clarity of your opposition," he continued over Oskar, "was probably why Irina acted preemptively."

"I never should have let her out of my sight."

"Jimmy." Ren tried to keep from shouting. "Would you please call Irina? I want to see Phil."

Jimmy shook his head again. He had one hand raised, listening, and his palm shone paler than the rich brown of his face. "No."

"Matsu," Ren began, but the stillness of Jimmy's lifted hand stopped her. "Jimmy?" Ren was starting to feel afraid. She made herself speak slowly and clearly. "What's wrong? Be specific."

"Not yet," he said, not moving. He was hardly breathing. He brought his raised hand to his forehead and rubbed.

"Jimmy?" His stillness terrified Ren. Unless he was grazing, Jimmy was always in motion. "Jimmy," she whispered, "when you called Matsu Matt, did you feel like yourself? Or was it like Phil talking out of your mouth?"

"Irina's not answering." Oskar dropped his phone onto the table in disgust. "I knew she was up to something."

"Hush," Matsu said, and Oskar didn't bristle, so Ren knew he was frightened too. "Jimmy?"

Jimmy shook his head. "No, Ren. It didn't feel like that."

"Irina is always fucking shoving her way into places she isn't needed." Oskar wheeled into pacing.

"She spiked Phil into Frio," Ren said. "I really want to be there when he wakes up." Jimmy still wasn't moving, and Oskar couldn't hold still. Ren looked to Matsu. "Can you graze for her address while I drive? She has a condo south of town."

"She won't be there," Oskar said. "For this, she'd get a hotel."

"We—" Matsu began, but Jimmy talked over him.

His voice came, husky and distant, from the round hollow of his chest. "They will come to us," he said. "We should stay here. Certainly Phil will come home. Come to Ren."

"He better not bring Irina with him," Oskar said.

Matsu ignored them both, answering Ren. "We need more information. Something may, in truth, be wrong." He glanced at Jimmy and lowered his voice. "We have had almost as many nonstandard as standard transitions from stub-to-Second since yours, Ren."

"What are you saying?" Ren hugged Phil's thin bathrobe tighter around her, trying not to shiver.

"He's saying Irina shoved Phil into that fucking cop like she shoves her way into everything," Oskar said. "And I swear on my expectation of uprising that if she damaged him doing it, I'll stub her myself."

Matsu waited for Oskar to finish, then continued speaking to Ren. "The most logical explanation for Jimmy's sense of foreboding and his"—Matsu hesitated fractionally—"verbal slip is that something went wrong with the spike."

"I will kill her," Oskar said.

"We have to go," Ren said. "Oskar, call Irina again, and if you get her, for god's sake be nice."

"I won't even—"

"Oskar!" Ren shouted. "Find out where Irina is!"

Oskar picked up his phone and jabbed at it.

Ren crouched at Jimmy's elbow trying to see into his eyes. "Jimmy," she said gently, "I need you to stand up. We're going to get in my car and drive toward town."

Jimmy looked haunted.

"Matsu, can you help me, please?" Ren asked.

Oskar pitched his phone back onto the table. "I—" he began.

"Oskar," Ren interrupted, still speaking to Jimmy. "Oskar is going to graze for the hotel Irina checked into while we drive. Jimmy, can you graze for Phil? See if you can find him in the Garden. If something went wrong during the ritual, maybe there's a new stub, or maybe he can talk to us through you like Celeste did with me, you seem to have a connection to him."

Jimmy's dark eyes met Ren's and closed. "Jimmy!" she shouted. "Jimmy! Let's get you in the car first, okay? Matsu?"

Matsu stood, but he didn't come to help Ren hoist Jimmy to his feet. "We have incomplete information. Ren, you are understandably upset, Oskar is irate, and Jimmy is . . . distraught. I'm not sure loading us all into a car and racing downtown is our wisest option."

"I don't give a damn," Ren said. "I'm going. I could use the help, but you and Oskar can come or stay. I'm going."

Matsu turned to Oskar, who stopped his pacing.

"Do you have a better plan?" Oskar demanded.

"I would like to consider more options and—"

"So no," Oskar said. "You don't have a plan. And Jimmy doesn't have a clue. If Ren has both, I say we fall in line." He stalked over to Jimmy and began gentling the big man to his feet.

"I'm driving," Ren said.

"I just said that." Oskar scowled, his arm still around Jimmy's shoulder.

"Yes," Matsu agreed.

"I meant the car."

Matsu nodded. Oskar hefted Jimmy and bent his blond head to Jimmy's dark one, whispering, tender and urgent.

"Matt's right," Jimmy said.

"Phil?" Ren was almost across the deck to him, but Oskar shook his head.

"Something went wrong with the spike, Jimmy?" Matsu clarified.

"Yes." Jimmy shook himself and cleared his throat. His voice was regaining its richness, if not its customary warmth. "I couldn't find another stub for him, but there's a knife in a hay bale smack in the center of my courtyard that I didn't put there."

"Did you graze it?" Oskar straightened.

Jimmy closed a meaty hand over Oskar's aristocratic one where it still rested on his shoulder. "I tried, but it's not really there. I put my hand right through it."

"Interesting," said Matsu.

"Not the word I'd choose," Jimmy said, leaning into Oskar.

"An Arkansas toothpick?" asked Oskar.

"Yes. How did you—"

"Not now."

"I'm going to put on clothes," Ren said. "Matsu, would you try calling Irina again?"

"I should do the same," Matsu said.

"I'll call her." Oskar raised an open palm for his phone. Matsu tossed it to him, and he followed Ren into the house.

"Do you think this is a bad idea?" Ren asked Oskar as they went down the hall to the bedroom.

"No, I'm just not sure it's the best one."

"Okay," she said.

*　　*　　*

Kate found Daniel waiting behind what looked to be a licked-clean breakfast platter. She ordered coffee and assessed the scabbing on the young man's scalp and forearms. A fine stubble of brown already hazed his head; soon it would be long enough to hide the worst of his scars. He smiled at her as she blew on her coffee, but it was a pensive smile—lopsided and too old for his face.

"Thank you for coming," he said.

"What is it you needed, dear?"

Daniel squeezed his eyes closed like Kate had hurt him and took a slow breath. When he opened his eyes again, it was all Kate could do not to look away from the intensity of his gaze. "I want—" he said, but then he had to stop and master himself again.

"I know, darling," Kate told him. "I know you do."

"You kissed me." It was almost an accusation, fierce and sad. "Kate, I could fall in love with you."

"Oh my dear," she said. "I'm already quite thoroughly in love with you."

"Is that why?"

"Why I won't spike Phil into you? No, of course not."

Kate's phone rang in her purse, and Daniel hesitated. "It'll go to voice mail," she told him. "Daniel—"

"Kate, let me finish?"

"Of course."

"I don't want to be a threat to your family."

Kate reached for her coffee to swallow her initial, unkind, "Oh sweetie, my family is so much stronger than that." His concern for her really was darling. "Daniel," she said, "I know you're full of passion and heartbreak, and you're right to respect the damage that the wild emotions driving you can do. And yes, if you yoke two such youthful engines together, you're as likely to tear each other apart as double your speed. But I'm not going anywhere. I'm where I want to be."

"I want to be there with you," he said, although she could barely hear him. "I want to talk with you, learn from you, but that isn't all I want."

"I know," she said. "Some of it's sexual, but most of it's not."

"Yeah."

"You like having my opinions on things," Kate went on, trying to keep her voice light. "You know I can help you find a direction, and maybe some focus. It's not a mother's role, but it's not a girlfriend's either. More of a mentor's. But it's a role that makes you subordinate to me, makes you feel your youth and my age, my experience and your lack of it. I have experience, you have passion. It's not bad to mix them."

"I just can't see a future for us."

"Of course not," she said as kindly as she could. "There isn't one. You want to get married and be a husband and a father some day. I can't help you do that."

"Kate," he said, and the courage and pain in his voice were almost more than its youth could carry.

Kate couldn't bear to hear his voice break. "You young people," she interrupted. "You have such long-range vision that you fall over your shoes." She forced a laugh. "But that's not a bad thing, darling. You need that kind of seeing to look far into the future and find where you want to be. I can tell you what it looks like once you arrive, but not how to get here."

"I can't see either."

"You will," she promised, and her phone rang again. "I'm due in the office," she told Daniel and, since she was already getting up to go, Kate took the call.

And thank god she did. Things could have been much worse if she hadn't.

—*Oskar*

⋆ ⋆ ⋆

Ren pulled on jeans and a cami, stuck her feet into her TOMS, and grabbed her handbag. "Crap." She walked back through the kitchen. "Jane still has my car keys."

"We all have rentals," Oskar said, heading to the bathroom.

"I'll drive Phil's car." Ren opened the drawer where she and Phil both kept their keys, and her whole body tightened. Knowing Jimmy was watching her, she tried not to look more upset than she was. Phil's phone, keys, wallet, and notepad were all inside looking exactly like they always had. She picked up his phone. "That's weird," she said.

"Oh?" Matsu asked.

"Phil missed a call."

"I imagine he missed several."

"Right, I know," Ren said, holding his phone. "He's dead."

"What?" Oskar came back into the room walking too quickly.

"Phil missed a call late last night," Ren repeated.

"And?"

"And he's dead."

"And?" Oskar stood close to where Jimmy sat, sunk into the sofa.

"Who would be calling him?" Ren asked. "Especially that late. Everyone knows he's dead."

"Play the message." Jimmy stood up heavily.

"Hi, Phil?" said a young man's recorded voice from the phone's speaker. "Remember how you said you might be able to help me if I ever needed it? I kinda need it. I've been arrested. I'm at the Pima County jail."

"That's not Frio," Jimmy said.

228

Ren looked at the phone. "Menzie Pulu," she read. "I have no idea who that is."

"Call him back," Oskar suggested. "Maybe he's been released."

"Yeah, I will from the car," Ren said. "Let's go."

They piled in, Matsu in the front beside Ren, Oskar and Jimmy in the back. Ren called Menzie Pulu and left a message saying Phil was unavailable, but she'd try to help. Matsu grazed for Irina's hotel, Oskar and Jimmy just cuddled, best Ren could tell, but maybe the Prius did it to them. Oskar was as large in muscle and bone as Jimmy was in padding and girth. She missed Phil's arms.

"Irina is at the airport Hilton." Matsu focused on typing the address into Google Maps. Ren waited.

"Take I-10 to the Kino Parkway and follow the signs for the airport."

Ren waited.

"I checked her front gate," he said.

"I did too," Jimmy said from the back. "As soon as I realized Phil's stub was gone. I didn't see anything."

"It's quite new, I think," Matsu said. "And fairly desperate."

Ren's fingers went cold on the steering wheel and she accelerated without meaning to.

"Ren," Matsu cautioned.

"I know," she said, lowering her speed, but changing lanes. "What did Irina's message say?"

"That she needed medical help."

"Did she say anything about Phil?"

"No."

"Anything on his villa door?"

Matsu shook his head, and no one said anything else until they pulled into the Hilton parking lot.

"She's in room 217," Matsu said.

They heard the moaning when they reached the door. They knocked, and Oskar would have kicked the door in had Matsu not pulled a blank plastic card from his wallet and pushed it into the reader.

Ren stepped into the room and covered her mouth to keep from screaming. Frio was on the bed, on his back, thrashing and sweat-covered while Irina fought to hold him down. Another woman bent over them both, a hypodermic needle poised over Frio. As they entered, she looked up.

"Who the fuck are you?" Oskar demanded.

"No time now, Oskar. I'm working." She jabbed the needle into Frio's arm.

MAY 1858

BEFORE HENRY'S BODY DIED

May 19, 1858
Trading Post, Kansas Territory

Dear Miss Voight:

I beg your pardon for not having written to you for so long. I plead a long illness, acquired December last when I foolishly exposed myself to the elements. I have made a good recovery, and there is also news.

Of course, as you are aware, we have carried the matter, or, as you called it, the battle: there can no longer be any doubt that Kansas will be admitted to the Union as a Free State. Even the border ruffians understand this, and for the most part, the violence here is at an end. There is still activity by Lane and his Jayhawkers near the Missouri border (though whether to free slaves, ensure Lane becomes Senator, or just for plunder, I cannot say), but even that is diminishing. I have hung my Sharp's over the fireplace, and long may it stay there. I think we can look for a significant increase in immigration over the next year. Dare I hope that you and yours will join us?

As to what you called the war, I fear that will have a great deal to do with stopping Brown. I cannot express how much

I fear damage to our cause if he carries out his plan. It could, and almost certainly will, cost us the sympathy of the entire North, and might prove to be the end of the Republican Party. I am writing today because I have finally gotten definite word of his movements: he has returned to New England. There is little I can do from here, but I know that you are well acquainted with our people there. If there is anything you can do to stop him—

I stuffed the letter into a pocket, put down my pencil, and stood up from the bench on which I'd been writing while enjoying the spring afternoon. "May I be of service to you gentlemen?" I said.

There must have been thirty or forty of them, and they already had a couple of prisoners as well. I recognized the leader as Charles Hamilton, which didn't bode well.

Hamilton didn't seem interested in conversation. They made sure I was unarmed, then tied my hands together in front of me and put me on a horse. One of Hamilton's men rode on either side of me, and refused to answer any of my questions. When I persisted, one of them, a scruffy-bearded man with almost no teeth, put his hand on his Bowie knife, so I stopped asking. We were on the road for several hours, stopping to take more prisoners in tow; most of whom I knew. Eventually there were eleven of us; none of us armed.

They made us dismount, and pushed us into a ravine with the river at our back, and Hamilton coldly ordered them to aim.

At best, I'd be in stub for months, and, even assuming I came back out as me, it might well be too late. Slavery would continue, and I could have stopped it.

There was an argument when one of the ruffians refused to shoot, and for just a moment, I had hope. If I got out of this, I'd go after Brown again. If I had to dog his every step, I'd find out what he was planning, and I would stop it, whatever it took.

Hamilton raged, roared, ordered, and then fired his pistol. I heard a moan, but didn't see who was hit.

I looked down at the hands that had failed to pull the trigger in December. "Useless," I muttered, and the border ruffians opened fire.

NINETEEN
❧

He Had to Be Stopped

Oskar was across the room and at Irina's side before a word was spoken. Behind him, a confused yammer of, "How did *he* get here? She. He." "What's wrong with Phil?" "Tell us what happened from the beginning," and "How could you do this?" broke out, but he focused on restraining Frio enough that the pretty woman with the large hypo could work. She kept her eyes on her patient, a confident look on her face. But when she met Oskar's eyes over Frio's twisting body, Oskar saw she wasn't sure how much it would take to relieve the pain, knock him out, and still leave his cardiovascular system functioning.

"I wish I had some equipment and a trained staff," she said. "For that matter, I wish we could reach a real doctor. Irina's trying to call Kate."

"Ramon?" Oskar hazarded and was rewarded with a curt nod.

"I haven't practiced medicine since the seventies, and even then it was mostly research."

Oskar remembered Ramon saying that his recent path had been medicine, to biology, to chemistry, to physics, "recapitulating the growth of modern science in reverse, at least in some ways."

"She answered," Irina gasped, holding her phone into the space between Ramon and Frio. Ramon took it, and for some time spoke urgently into it, listening and nodding; no one else spoke. Eventually, Ramon switched it to speaker in order to free his hands. He finally said, "Patient is quiet, breathing well, pulse strong at around sixty."

"All right," came from the phone. "That should do. Keep an eye on him, call me back if anything changes." Kate disconnected and Ramon stood up.

"Ramon!" Jimmy wrapped his old friend's new body in a hug. Oskar grinned seeing Ramon's effort to relax and accept it; to bear up under Jimmy being Jimmy. "A good-looking Second." Jimmy beamed, looking Ramon's new body over with overt appreciation. "I knew she was a genius, I hadn't realized she was quite so attractive."

Oskar looked away. He'd been thinking much the same thing, and seen Ramon's momentary flash of annoyance with them both before shrugging it off. Oskar knew it was something Ramon was going to have to get used to, but at least he knew with Jimmy and Oskar it wouldn't affect how they listened to him.

Ren was looking from Frio to Ramon. "What is happening with Phil, Ramon?"

"Nothing," he said. "He rejected the Second, leaving our patient with all the sensations but unable to finish the ritual."

"Rejected the Second?" repeated Jimmy.

"That's my hypothesis."

"Why?" said Ren.

"I didn't know that was possible," said Oskar.

Jimmy answered Oskar. "No, neither did I."

"Ramon," said Ren, with a snap in her voice Oskar had never heard before, and rather liked. "Where is Phil?"

"I don't know," he said.

Irina said, "But why would Phil—"

"Shut up, Irina," Oskar and Ren said together.

"I'll begin at the beginning." Ramon chose his words carefully, and Oskar remembered a story Ramon had told Phil once, of having to defend his thesis, in 1730, before the Dons, all eyes on him, afraid to speak lest he pick the wrong word. "I was in a queue at the airport waiting for a taxi—"

"Ramon," said Ren.

"In a moment, Ren. I was in the queue, and decided to do a quick graze while I waited, hoping to get caught up. None of you has put up pointers to whatever you seeded, so I found Irina's node, checked the circle, and it overlapped with Phil's, so I called Irina, but she didn't answer. I checked her Garden, and saw she'd left a note asking for medical help, so I came directly here already certain something was very wrong."

Jimmy said, "Ramon, what do you mean, something was very wrong?"

"I mean," Ramon said, trying to keep the annoyance out of his voice, "that Phil's stub isn't where it should be, and yet he hasn't been spiked. He's—"

"Alpha-locked?" Ren asked, her voice sufficiently emotional that Oskar wasn't sure if she'd even be able to listen. "Celeste."

Ramon shook his head, appearing to fight impatience. "It is the nature of the Garden that no two of us addresses it the same way. It's frustrating. If you all saw it the way I do, this would be so much easier to explain. It isn't Celeste; the strength of her influence doesn't remotely approach the levels needed to dislocate Phil any more than a candle flame could evaporate the ocean. And I'm certain it isn't an alpha-lock. Phil's stub *is* there, somewhere in the Garden."

"Where?" demanded Ren with a fierce, frightened urgency.

"Exactly," Ramon agreed. "What has happened before when a spiking ritual was interrupted?" Ramon asked Jimmy, because the others were too young, except for Irina, who was too shaken.

"I don't remember," Jimmy said. "It's been so long. Sometimes the stub moves to somewhere along the person's timeline. Sometimes to somewhere along the timeline of the Primary. Sometimes it splinters, and pieces end up distributed along the timeline. You think that's what happened?"

"No, but the same effect."

"Then what—"

"We have to find Phil's stub. If it's in pieces, we need to find all of them or he'll most likely shade. I don't know how to do that, but we have to. In the past, it's been a long painful search. I don't know if we have the time. We have to find a way to find Phil now, and hope he can tell us something useful."

They all looked at Ren.

* * *

Kate listened to Ramon's information and she calculated dosage by weight and age without nearly enough information. Daniel picked up her briefcase and carried it for her as she talked, and Kate realized that he really wasn't giving up. She popped the locks and Daniel slid the minivan door open while she told Ramon what to monitor in his patient. Daniel deposited her bag in back amid the action figures and craft kits, and climbed into the passenger seat next to her. Kate drove badly, trying to coach Ramon through what he needed to do to stabilize someone so ruthlessly sedated.

By the time she pulled into her parking space in the medical complex garage, Kate was rattled too badly to do more than drop her phone onto the box of wet wipes and stare out the windshield.

"Is he going to die?" Daniel's voice was gentle and calm.

"I don't think so."

"Why didn't they call an ambulance?"

"I just hope no one's called the police." Kate shook her head as if she could knock the suffering from her ears like water.

"Are you okay?" Daniel hadn't unbuckled his seat belt, and the shoulder strap spanned his chest like a bandolier. His torso had the brave and untested suppleness of saplings and colts.

"Yes." Kate gave him her best farmwife smile—the one that never works on children, but does wonders for worried moms.

Daniel didn't buy it. "Tell me what happened."

"Irina—she's one of the oldest members of the group—same personality for something like seven hundred years, and I don't even know how many Seconds—er, that means bodies she's inhabited—spiked Phil into an ex-cop in Tucson."

"Phil," Daniel said. "Wasn't he who you were going to use me for?"

Kate nodded. "He's the oldest of us. More than two thousand years. That's why I didn't." Kate took a breath. "We need Phil to come back as Phil. We need the continuity with everything that's happening."

"And you couldn't be sure, if you put him in me, that he'd make it?"

"He'd have good odds. He's in love. But you're so very young," Kate said, feeling every one of her years. "And stronger than you know."

"No," he said. "I know."

Kate nodded. "I'm glad."

"So Irina picked some other body to put Phil into?"

"Right," Kate said. "Frio. And he almost died."

"Wasn't that what you wanted?"

"Not the personality, Daniel. The body."

"That doesn't happen sometimes?"

"No! How could we ever spike anyone if it did? We already ask too much."

"I don't think so."

Kate knew Daniel was trying to comfort her, and she smiled. "I need to go up," she told him. "I hate to keep patients waiting."

Daniel was quiet the way parents get when you give them treatment options for a sick kiddo. "How does it work?" he asked. "When you put one of you into someone else?"

"There's a ritual," Kate said, more to buy herself some time for resting than anything else. "We have to be able to see the dead Incrementalist's stub for one thing. We turn the stub into a spike—" She hesitated. It seemed cruel to describe the embers and char to a man who'd seen his skin blackened and bleeding. But Daniel wasn't going to have to face it, so Kate told him. "It's like a burning torch, and we introduce it into the recruit's brain through the forehead by force."

"Not really," he said, looking pale.

"No," Kate said, wearily. "Not really."

*　　*　　*

If he were going to make sense of it, Takamatsu was going to have to wait until things became more stable. Yes, it was possible to see patterns in motion, and it was possible to see patterns when they are unclear; but the combination defeated him.

"Here's how I see it," he said, description as preamble to understanding. "Phil's stub is somewhere along the Who of his Primary, in one or several pieces, distributed or concentrated. It could be anywhere and anywhen in the last two thousand years, possibly the last forty thousand. The only good news is that recent is somewhat more likely." Ren was frowning her alert dragon's frown of complete concentration. "You, Ren, are the best choice to search for him, both because of your connection to him, and because of your work last year going into our prehistory."

Jimmy put his arms around Ren, but she shrugged him away. "Tell me what to do," she said.

Ramon, still bent over Frio said, "Use your connection to Phil to search for his stub."

Ren nodded, tearless and grave. "I'm not letting Phil shade," she said. "No way in hell." She closed her eyes to graze.

That Ren did not realize yet the futility of the task Ramon had set her was, he knew, its only utility. But before he had time to examine this, Oskar rounded on Irina. "I demand to know," he said, "why you gave Phil's stub to Frio. Without vetting him adequately. Without anyone's review. Without anyone's consent."

"Especially now," Takamatsu agreed. "That was extraordinarily, uncharacteristically careless, Irina."

Irina's face was burning. "I vetted him more thoroughly than you know."

Oskar nearly exploded. "Fucking someone can't tell you everything about him."

"It can tell me quite a lot, Oskar."

Takamatsu noted the forced calm of Irina's voice held low. He watched her pulse throb in her throat.

"What do you want to know?" she asked.

Oskar didn't put a hand on Irina, but he didn't move back. "Why you spiked Frio."

"He was the right choice."

"Obviously not." Oskar flung an angry arm in the direction of Frio's body, wrecked on the bed. "It almost killed him."

"He could have helped us make things better."

Oskar started to say something, but Takamatsu didn't give him the chance. "How would an ex-SWAT cop have helped us do that, Irina?"

Irina sat back down, and Takamatsu saw how close to complete disintegration she was. She was carrying more weight in secrets and fear than she had the strength to bear.

"You have no idea how bad things are getting." Irina's voice broke. She was telling the truth. "The Phoenix police are an army. They just are. They wear commando uniforms, carry military-grade weapons, operate tanks, Humvees, and drones. They train and think like soldiers. Nominally soldiers in the war on drugs or terror or illegal immigration, but you know what happens when the differences between the army and police get fuzzy. We all know where this goes. And how it ends."

"You're in Arizona because this is where it is at its worst?" Takamatsu asked.

Irina's nod was part shrug.

"I still don't see how having an ex-cop as Phil's Second would be useful," Oskar said.

"He's not an ex-cop."

"What do you mean?"

Takamatsu waited. He could see Irina had nothing left to lie with.

"He's undercover," Irina said. "Still. The resignation was a sham. I didn't know until last night."

Oskar went pale, even for him. "And you spiked Phil into him anyway? Jesus Christ, Irina."

"It's why I spiked him," Irina said. "Phil has a protective soul, and that's exactly what the police are supposed to be. In Frio's body, he could have worked from inside the force to change the culture. He's as brave as Snowden or Manning, and would be as well-positioned to show the country what's really going on in their local precincts."

"No wonder Phil rejected the Second." Oskar sat heavily on the bed's edge.

"Is there any chance Frio was wearing a wire?" Takamatsu asked.

Irina gave him a look. "I frisked him pretty thoroughly."

"If he was working undercover," Takamatsu said, "he'll be expected to make regular touch points. The first time he misses one, if he hasn't already, they will send people for him. We should assume they can track his car. If it's parked outside, we should prepare for company."

"Ramon?" Oskar looked over to him. "Can we move him?"

"No."

Oskar's fists clenched, then relaxed. "All right," he said. "Irina, let's go—"

"No chance in hell," she said. "I'm staying right here."

"Are you afraid to even talk to me?"

"I'm not going to let you—"

"No!" said Jimmy. "Stop it, both of you. Leave, or be quiet."

"Goddammit!" Oskar raged, but he walked over to the window and stared out it, then he turned to Irina again, who was, probably unconsciously, standing behind Jimmy. Takamatsu heard a sharp intake of breath from Ramon, which was what passed for swearing for him, and thought he was about to intervene with Oskar. "He's already waking up," Ramon said, his lips pressed together, his eyes focused on the bed.

Frio's eyes fluttered open. His face was white, and he seemed to be breathing hard.

Ramon went over to the side table and started digging through his kit, and Takamatsu could almost feel the pattern recentering.

Frio looked around at the room, at each of them, and he said, "I don't—what happened? Was I shot? Where is Brown? My head—"

Irina walked over to him and even Oskar didn't stop her. "Frio?" she said. "Are you all right?"

Grouped around the bed, Irina, Ramon, and Jimmy reminded Takamatsu of the Pittsburgh apartment Jimmy had showed them in Phil's dust ritual, the same three all watching Phil with the same intensity. The same three, plus Celeste where now there was Ren. The pattern similar but not the same.

Frio shook his head. "Do I know you, miss?" he asked Irina.

Irina was lonely now, as she had been then, but with a new kind of pride. Takamatsu watched her. It reminded him of Celeste's pride in what she and Phil had endured at each other's hands, in how she had changed him, and how much he had not changed her.

"My name is Carter," Frio said. "What happened to me?"

It was one of the best questions Takamatsu had ever heard.

★　　★　　★

Kate hauled herself to standing. Daniel got out of the minivan, yanked open the back door, and retrieved her bag. "You told me yesterday that married people flirt for different reasons than single people." Daniel put Kate's bag on the ground by her feet. "That for you, it's not the opening gambit of a long game."

Kate nodded.

Daniel put his hands on either side of her face, and bent down to her mouth. His lips were sincere as his eyes, and more convincing, and they stirred more than embers in Kate. She didn't even kiss him back, just let his lips paint ambition and will and passion over hers in delicious, consuming currents. He kissed youth into her with a thoroughness and patience that wasn't young at all.

"Go to work now," he said.

Kate nodded, her face still cradled in Daniel's damaged hands. She wasn't tired anymore.

"Kate," he said. "You said you need Phil back."

"Yeah," she said, surprised by the bubble of tears in her throat. "We really do."

"You should use my body."

"We couldn't be sure—"

"What if you could?"

Kate closed her eyes.

"I won't fight him." Daniel's mouth was so close to Kate's she could feel the breath of his words on her lips. "If that's what you and your people need."

Kate might live through a hundred Seconds and she'd never forget Daniel's eyes when he made her that promise. *If that's what you and your people need,* he'd said. She wanted to hoard him for pleasure and protect herself from grief. This game won nothing she wanted, and staked everything she feared.

It would do all kinds of harm.

"Okay," Kate said, knowing she would never give Dan to the Incrementalists. "Come upstairs with me." And she kissed him again, just like Judas.

*   *   *

Ren opened her eyes. Oskar, Matsu, Ramon, Jimmy, and Irina were all keenly focused on Frio, but the voice that had brought Ren back from the Garden didn't belong to any of them. Not even to Frio.

Ren stood up with great care. "Phil?"

"I'm Carter, miss." Frio frowned kindly at Ren and all the heat flushed out of her. She knelt or fell beside the bed.

"Carter!" Jimmy said, low and under his breath, as if trying to convince himself. He opened his mouth to say something to Ren, then closed it again and shook his head.

"What's going on?" Ren fought to speak coherently, to line up her thoughts like toy soldiers. "Why doesn't he know me? Who's Carter? Oskar, who's Carter?"

Oskar's answer was low, almost a monotone. "The name Phil used until about a hundred and fifty years ago," he said.

Ren looked from Oskar back to Frio. "Phil, it's Ren. Can you remember?"

Ramon spoke slowly and clearly, his voice as calm as it always was. "There must be some of the stub here, if he thinks he's Carter. But perhaps not all." His brows were drawn together.

"Why would that happen?" Ren was on her feet, spinning to glare at Irina, and dizzy from it. "What the fuck did you do?"

Frio said, "I don't—" then he broke off, biting his lip. He looked at Ren. "You're one of us, aren't you?" Before she could answer, he said, "God! My head! Does anyone have morphine? Or, Christ, ether?"

"Yes." Ren sat on the bed. "I'm one of you. I'm yours. I'm—"

Oskar was still speaking to Irina. "Ren wants to know what you did."

Ren turned her head to Oskar long enough to say, "Shut up," then returned her attention to Frio.

Ramon spoke to Frio, his tone precise as it had been before, and, weirdly, sounding perfectly natural coming from the throat of this woman he now inhabited. "I can knock you out again, Carter," he said. "Until your head feels better."

"No!" Ren couldn't lose him again. Not yet.

Frio looked at her, his expression more eloquent than words could have been. Then he said, "Was I just spiked again? I remember being shot. Did something go wrong with the spike?"

"You could say that," said Oskar dryly.

"What if we lose him again?" Ren asked Ramon. She turned back to Frio. "Phil, can you hang on? I'll get you some water. Advil?" She knew she was being selfish, clinging, but she couldn't help herself.

Frio ignored her and looked over at Oskar, and for just an instant, Ren saw a glimpse of the Phil she loved. "You?" he said.

"I'm Oskar."

Phil laughed. "Nice Second, you toad. I suppose you have to beat the girls off with a stick. Oh, god, my head hurts. Why are you calling me Phil?"

"It's what you've been calling yourself lately," said Ramon.

"You changed it," said Jimmy. "Another form of Cartophilus. I'm Jimmy."

"I should have guessed," said Frio, and laughed again, then winced, then groaned. Ren saw the ebb and flow of the pain as it swept through him, and she knew the worst of it must be such that he was hard-pressed not to scream. Her hands argued with themselves needing to touch him, not willing to hurt him. She looked at Jimmy. "I don't know how to look for him in the Garden. Do you know dates? When did he change names?"

"I don't remember. Mid nineteenth century, in general. Maybe around 1855 or '60."

"What the hell is going on?" Carter or Frio, not Phil, asked, fear mixing into his pain.

"It doesn't matter," Ren whispered, bending over him. "We'll figure it out. It's . . . some time has passed. You've had Seconds you aren't remembering right now." Frio's eyes closed and Ren turned to Ramon. "Why would he not remember them? Is it like what happened with me when I forgot Celeste? Is the rest of him loose in the Garden like she was? Jesus. Is he with her? Is she trapping him there?"

"Stop it, Ren." Ramon crouched next to her, glaring into her eyes.

Irina whispered, "Blood and pomander."

"I just—" Ren clawed back to calm. "Okay," she told Ramon.

He nodded and reached past her to put a hand on Frio's shoulder. "There has been an unexpected event in the Garden, Carter, which we are working to correct."

Frio's eyes opened. "You must be Ramon. You look lovely, Ramon, but you're dressed like a whore."

Ren laughed—probably a little too much. She looked past Ramon to Irina. "Don't you move."

Irina had been inching toward the door. She shrugged and stood still.

"Irina?" said Frio. "Well, hello there. Where is Celeste? My head. God. Am I in a brothel? You're all dressed like—Christ, my head."

Ren worked on swallowing.

"Ask Oskar," Irina said.

Oskar opened his mouth.

"Is Oskar my titan?" Frio asked. "Why don't I remember this Second? Who was he? Or she?" He put a hand on his chest. "He."

"It doesn't matter," said Ren. "We'll figure it out. Right, Ramon? You have a theory? Where's the rest of him?"

"Ramon, please," said Frio, his voice dropping to a desperate whisper. "Do you have ether? Anything? Please."

"I'll get the Advil," said Ren, standing.

Ramon nodded to Frio. "I'm going to give you another shot, see if I can help you sleep for a while. You should still be out."

Ren started to argue, but stopped herself. She nodded.

Ramon came to stand next to the bed, a hypo in his hand. "When you wake up, we'll see if we can solve this. With luck, you'll have nothing more than the usual headache."

"Is it safe to give him that much?" Ren asked.

"I don't know," Ramon told her.

"Please," said Frio, and Ren just gave up and let herself cry.

Matsu walked over, nodded to Frio, and said, "My name is Takamatsu. We haven't met. I can help."

"Takamatsu?" said Frio. "From the Japans?"

Matsu nodded, and then he put a hand up under Frio's jawline and sent him to sleep.

TWENTY

Closer, Closer

Something about how Ren stood up from the edge of Frio's bed, the discipline of her rigid, straight spine contrasting with the tears running hugger-mugger down her face, nearly broke Irina. She felt terrible for Ren, whose pain set an uncomfortable prickle of guilt along the soles of Irina's feet. She had never meant for it to go so hard for Ren. Phil's stub and Second should have been a test to prove Ren's strength, not a trial too much for even Irina to bear. Everything was fucked.

But it wasn't her fault. Irina was certain of that now.

I'm still not.

—Oskar

Irina had been ruthlessly honest with herself about her motivations. Yes, her reasons for calling Frio last night might be, if not suspect, perhaps not pure, after Menzie had blown her off, and Jimmy didn't answer his phone, and Oskar—well Oskar wouldn't get a second chance to turn her down.

Heh!

—O

But since then, after the sex, Irina had been selfless pragmatism incarnate. Frio was the Incrementalists' best hope, and the ideal recruit for Phil's stub. Nothing in America needed meddling with more than the police. Laws are how free people agree to organize and govern themselves. The mere availability of martial strength to law's enforcers means the people no longer agree, or are not still free. Surely they'd learned that much from Cambodia.

She's right about that.

—O

And Frio was the perfect vehicle for that work —practically a golden unicorn. He and Ren had clearly had some chemistry between them. Also, he was an idealistic, altruistic, fully informed and well-connected policeman. That the combination was an inherent contradiction, and that Frio had realized it and sacrificed his livelihood on those grounds, proved he met the Incrementalist primary criterion.

Horseshit.

—O

Irina was blameless in that regard at least. She scanned the floor for any of her clothes. Frio had thrown himself on the grenade of Phil's stub to save Sam, after all. And no one could have predicted whatever the hell it was that had happened when she'd spiked Phil into him.

"I think it's encouraging that nothing we've seen or heard contradicts Ramon's explanation for the anomalous spike," Matsu said. "And that it's as benign as Phil rejecting the Second. We can take some comfort there."

Ren did not look comforted.

She looked from Matsu to Jimmy to Oskar, and if Irina hadn't been exhausted, bruised by Frio's flailing, and emotionally way overextended, she would have smiled. This was what she'd been hoping for all along: Ren, forced to act without Phil, turning to her fellow Incrementalists for help.

It wasn't worth it. Not everyone has to be as loved by everyone as Irina wants to be.

—O

"Matsu?" Ren asked. She was trusting and being trusted, bonding with her fellow Incrementalists, albeit not yet over the cause of de-escalating the militarization of the police, but still no longer allowing her loss of Celeste's memories to hold her apart. Irina would have been pleased if she could have felt anything at all anymore.

Matsu met Ren's eyes, then Oskar's and Jimmy's, with nary an aphorism between them.

For once.

—O

"Should I go back to looking for Phil's stub?" Ren asked.

Ramon took Frio's wrist and looked at his watch—a man's watch on one of those men's irritating, arm-hair-pinching old metal bands too big for his new woman's wrist—and counted heartbeats or seconds. "It is a nearly impossible thing—find one point in a field of billions."

"Ramon," Matsu began.

"But at least now we have some idea where to look," Ramon added almost as an afterthought. "Mid 1800s. The Second's name was, ah, Jimmy?"

"Henry something," Irina volunteered, happy to know something she could add. "Wouldn't let anyone call him Hank. I was his titan," she explained, but her voice cracked—exhaustion and maybe tears welling up at the edges. She felt Oskar's eyes inventorying her neck and shoulders, arms, hands, and chest. She turned away, pointing her face at the window.

I was looking for pivot markers in Irina, and finding plenty. She was in crisis. I was certain. And I was right.

—O

"You'll look for him too, Jimmy?" Ren asked, her voice gratingly steady by comparison. "I mean, I have all of his switches buried in my mud, but you're better at grazing than I am."

"I'll look too," said Jimmy. "I wish we knew better where in that Second's life to look." Jimmy's voice remained steady, but Irina could hear the effort that took.

"Okay," Ren said. "What do I do when I find it?"

"Seed the location," said Ramon.

"Are you looking too?" Ren asked him, and Irina thought how stabilizing the weight of something important to carry could be. Then she remembered Sophal and her son, and sat down against the air conditioner under the window.

"No," Ramon said. "I'm going to keep an eye on Carter. Er, Phil. Frio."

"Matsu," Ren said. "You'll watch Irina?"

Matsu nodded and Irina looked away before he could catch her eye. Ren closed her eyes to graze, and a phone rang.

"Oh, shit," Ren said, without standing up. "That's Phil's phone again. It's in my bag." She pointed at it on the ground at the foot of Frio's bed. "Can someone answer it? It's probably that Menzie kid calling back."

All the warmth flushed out of Irina. She needed to get off the air conditioner, but didn't trust her legs. And Oskar saw it.

I did. I was willing to let her break; hell, I was willing to push her to breaking, if that was what it took to get answers out of her.

—O

Oskar took Ren's bag, extracted the ringing phone, and checked the caller ID. "Menzie Pulu," he read, and let it go to voice mail.

Fear opened a cold, frictionless space in Irina's head. All the complicated lines of connection and isolation unwove and tangled themselves, and Oskar was standing too close to her, kinetic with anger. "Irina," he said. "Who is Menzie Pulu?"

Matsu, as still as Oskar was restless, looked no less dangerous guarding the door. For a second or two, Irina considered turning and diving through the window, but the glass wouldn't break like it did in the movies and she'd trip over Ramon's medical bag or get tangled in the filmy curtains, anyway. Also, Matsu would catch her before she got fully into motion.

Irina looked back and forth between the two large, beautiful blond men: Oskar pale and feline, Matsu honed to a cold, keen edge. Celeste had titaned them both, selecting beefcake variations on a masculine theme, the vampire and the surfer version of the same beauty. Oskar had been livid for years. Probably still was.

It was a stupid, selfish, Celeste thing to do and someone should have stopped her.

—O

"Irina?" Oskar held Phil's phone in his hand like a knife.

Phil had left Oskar all the seeds of his work on SB 1070 as a knife.

"Ren?" Irina knew that if she dropped his eyes, Oskar would repeat his question, make demands. She didn't want to have to confess her mistakes. But even more she wanted to put them right. She didn't want to have to turn to Oskar for help, but it was exactly what she'd set out to teach Ren. And Ren had never needed the help of her fellow Incrementalists more. "Ren!" Irina repeated. "Oskar knows where Phil's stub is."

I swear I didn't. Not then.

—O

★   ★   ★

Oskar opened his mouth to accuse Irina of keeping secrets *and* telling lies, but—

"Oskar," Irina spoke directly to him—and even without his Incrementalist training, Oskar would have seen the tangle of emotions holding her together and tearing her apart: fear, shame, pride, determination, and, covering it all like a sheet of black ice on a winter highway, unutterable weariness. She spoke through it all, her voice quivering, but steady: "Phil gave you a knife. You seeded it. It was a knife. But the form it took before it became a knife, was—"

"Fire. Like a falling star or firebomb."

"Celeste," Ren whispered. "She tried to set something in my Garden on fire too."

"No," Irina said. "Not Celeste. But one of Phil's memories of her. And Phil turned it into an index for all the information he had collected on SB 1070." Irina pressed Oskar. "Why? Why would he do that? We all know he only loves Ren."

Oskar felt everyone's eyes on him. Ren's gripped his gaze with her own, as if it were the only rope to the only boat in the ocean. "There was a resonance between the SB information and something related to Celeste."

"Yes," said Irina. "With what?"

"I don't know," Oskar said.

You will understand this better now than I did at the time. Remember, Carter's seeds from the 1800s weren't available to me. Or they were, but not as things I'd had any clue I ought to revisit. They weren't collected anywhere yet. So I was just trying desperately to see whether what I'd learned about Celeste in Phil's dust ritual had anything to do with his most recent death, because Irina was right. I don't mind saying it. Irina was right about Phil not loving Celeste. He didn't even grieve her. But her memory could still flame up in his Garden, and in Ren's, and even, apparently, mine. And Irina was right too that I knew more than I realized. I just had to figure out what Celeste and Carter had in common with Ren and Phil, and the work, and the man who had looked at me through Frio's eyes and called me a toad.

—O

"Kansas before the Civil War," Oskar said. "Phil was working for abolition—it meant everything to him. And now he's seeing it all come back around. The Minutemen are the new border ruffians. The laws being passed are again as much about trying to control the skin color of a region as they are about the economy. It isn't slavery, no; but to Phil, I think, it felt like the same thing. The same fight. And the same failure."

"But abolition succeeded," said Ren. "I don't see—"

"No. Phil wasn't just working for abolition, but for abolition without violence, for a peaceful transition from one mindset to another. He was trying to meddle the nation, to change its collective mind. And he failed. I don't think he ever recovered from it. And it was tied to everything for him—to all of the crap between him and Celeste, and to guns, and when you do and don't pull the trigger. It was tied to what it means to be good or to do good, to what it means to be an Incrementalist, and to what happens when you're not the shooter, but the shot."

"Oskar," said Jimmy, his voice as strong as hope and as determined as insurrection, "Where is he now?"

"Where he failed. Kansas, sometime between when he didn't pull the trigger in December of 1857, and May of 1858, when someone else did. That's as close as I can narrow it. The Second's name was Henry Lattimer."

Oskar turned to Ren.

She nodded. "I'll find him," she said.

Occasionally, I feel a strong sense of acceptance and affirmation, a simple "Yes" in my mind when I consider a given Incrementalist. It's equal parts confidence in them and alignment with me. I call it love. And right in that moment, for the first time, I loved Ren. I loved Jimmy for asking the right question at the right moment. I even loved Irina for showing me I'd forgotten what I knew. But it was Ren, frightened and brave, determined and untried, we sent to collect Phil's distributed stub. I knew where to look, but only she could find him.

—O

I've been interrupting too much. I'll stop.

—O

---

*   *   *

Ren didn't know whether the Garden was made of thought, or by thinking, or simply *was* thought, but it was mental enough to mute the body's howling, and sometimes that was as good as actual quiet. If your brain wasn't too frightened or drunk or damaged to reach the Garden, then your mind, once it was there, was free of its neurochemistry, or alcohol or plaques. The freedom felt a little alien in its distance and sheen; pure thought is a hallucinogen.

Ren's Garden lay at her feet like an etherized patient. She knew something malignant lived below the skin, but not where to put the scalpel in. How could she find Phil in all that wasn't Phil? What do you do when you don't know what to do?

Phil would say you make the next right play, but Ren didn't even know what the game was. Maybe the next right play was to stand up from the cards and go dancing. Knowing the right play depended on knowing the game. But when you play alone, you win *and* you lose—a dialectic. Oskar would be so proud.

Win and lose, first and last, toward and away from, and Phil was always moving forward. So Ren would too. But toward what? Not what scared her, what frightened her away, but toward what attracted her, toward what she loved.

What did she love?

So many things, but they all boiled down to either individuals or ideas—love and imagination. Share your imagination with your lover, and you win.

Play that game.

To get into his Garden, Ren needed a memory of Phil's. She knew he'd seeded escaping Celeste as a gibbeted doll, and although Ren had never grazed the memory, the date was clear in her mind.

I know, I know. I've just promised to be more circumspect in my commentary, and here I am again, but this needs some explaining. Remember at the beginning when Phil was dying and I broke into his Garden? I explained how it worked then, but it's important for you to understand what it meant that Ren was doing the same thing here. That Phil had enough purchase in Frio's brain to call himself Carter, told us his mind had access to his model, his Garden, which would have been impossible if he were fully in stub. So we knew he wasn't anymore. But he wasn't fully in Frio either. Which was a big part of what made all of this so frightening to us, and so dangerous for Phil. And Ren.

—O

Ren conjured the screens and filtered everything else away. She unstrung Raggedy Ann, and the doll burst in clouds of white cotton batting that blew and jettied and became whitewashed walls, stretched and crouched low to form the domed cellar ceiling in the belly of Celeste's garden. Ren knew how it felt to have a full linen shirtsleeve pinned to the wall by a glittering arrow, and she forced the room to smell not of roots, but of salt air. She made the taste in Phil's mouth into root beer, not tears, blending her sense triggers with his to get into his Garden.

She hung on as the ocean pinkened into cherry blossoms, and the root beer washed into chives, until she stood at the back gate of a Roman merchant's villa.

"Phil!" Ren shouted across his garden. "Phil, I need your help!"

Phil's Garden was cluttered with seeds, and Ren wandered it calling for him like they'd had to look for Nana before they hired someone to watch her.

Nana had lost her memory, then herself, so when Ren learned Incrementalists could permanently preserve memories in their collective, distributed imagination, she'd taken the spike, Celeste's stub, and become one of them. But she'd lost Celeste. Ironic, she knew.

As a result, Ren had spent her time as an Incrementalist trying to understand how the Garden worked, how it collected, searched, and shared information, so if there was one thing she knew for sure, it was how to locate and trigger emotional memories in the man she loved. She would create a switch for finding Phil.

Or better, for making Phil find her.

Smells were the best, but impossible now. Music was a very close second.

"When Johnny comes marching home again, hoorah, hoorah!" Ren sang as loudly as she could. It sounded awful, but that wasn't the point. She walked through the back door of Phil's villa, singing.

"We'll give him a hearty welcome then, hoorah, hoorah!" Ren didn't know whether the song had been written before Henry Lattimer died, but she didn't think that mattered either.

Marching home mattered.

Ren walked down the long, dark central corridor to the atrium where a shallow pool of water shone beneath an opening in the roof.

"The men will cheer and the boys will shout," Ren sang, thinking about Oskar and Jimmy and Ramon and Matsu waiting back in the hotel room for Phil.

"The ladies they will all turn out . . ." Ren sat on the pool's raised edge and looked up at the sky and back to where the water in the impluvium had sunk deeper than a grave.

The next line came out tear-choked and whispered. "And we'll all feel gay when—"

Ren stopped. The flicker in the pool wasn't the sun, the moon, or the stars reflecting. It was movement.

"When Johnny comes marching home."

Ren reached into the water, and felt it draining out the bottom through a hole, small as a bullet, large as a hurricane's eye. Ren wanted to stopper the vortex, but she closed her fingers over the emptiness at the heart of the spiral, and retracted her hand, dripping and on fire.

She opened her eyes, shivering with cold in the overcrowded hotel room. "Phil found me."

Matsu turned to her from where he stood between Oskar and Irina.

"I've got Phil's stub in my—around my hand," Ren said.

"Jesus, Ren!" Oskar whispered. "Seed it."

"Yeah." Ren closed her eyes and took the burn out of the fire.

What Ren didn't know, or hadn't remembered yet, was that tune had other lyrics from another time that meant even more to Phil:

"Mighty the engine, vast the field | From coast to coast | The skill of our hands, the wealth they yield | Is all Earth's boast | For ours are the hands on those machines | Just think for a minute of what that means. | And the time has come when we'll not be fooled anymore"

—*Oskar*

TWENTY-ONE

Halfway Out of His Head.
Sometimes More than Halfway

Irina fully believed herself to be as rational as Matsu and as tenacious as Oskar, but she wasn't at her best, and she knew it. She was frayed by what she'd been through with Frio, spun thin with exhaustion and grief, and more scared than she'd been since the night she had waited with a loaded gun for Phil in a Vegas hotel room, and ended up dead on the carpet. Irina looked from Jimmy to Frio—or Phil—or Carter. Whatever Matsu had done had put him into a deep sleep. Thank Christ.

"The police," Matsu reminded them all, "are liable to arrive at any moment."

"I know," Jimmy said. "We need to decide—"

"There's nothing to decide," said Irina. "We need to leave before they get here."

"How do we get Frio out?" Jimmy asked.

"We don't," Irina told him. "For now, his friends can have him. He knows how to get in touch with us."

Oskar bared his teeth. "Oh, that's just fine. And then the police will be looking for us—"

"For what?" said Irina. "Driving an invisible stake into the forehead of an undercover agent? I'd love to see the complaint."

"She has a point," said Matsu, bless his rational heart, or lack of one.

"What about Ren?" said Oskar.

"If she's not done reseeding Phil's stub—and how long can that take?—we either wake her up or carry her."

Oskar's eyes narrowed. "You have this all worked out, don't you, Irina? And what happens next?"

"I believe we're scheduled to attend a funeral."

"He's coming around again," said Ramon, still positioned next to Frio. "I won't leave him if he's in pain."

"He's a cop," said Oskar.

Ramon gave Oskar a look; the blond man shrugged.

"Ramon—" said Irina.

Jimmy stopped her, looking at Ramon. "You're wasting breath."

Ramon took Frio's pulse, and made a grunt that sounded odd coming from his new and very female throat.

Frio opened his eyes.

"Phil?" Jimmy whispered.

Phil nodded. "I'm going," he said. "I shot me."

His eyes closed again and he was out.

"Jesus Christ," said Oskar.

Jimmy turned to the room. "Let's get out of here," he said.

Ramon topped off Frio's sedation and collected his vials, the used hypos and their lids, even the discarded cotton balls. Oskar swooped Ren up in his arms.

"Get dressed, Irina." Jimmy's voice was kind but uncompromising. If Jimmy wasn't willing to accord her the dignity of digging through the trashed bedding for her clothes after everyone else left, Irina knew it wasn't going to happen. She retrieved Ren's gray dress from the wad of sheets, swept her phone into her handbag, and retreated to the bathroom.

★　　★　　★

Each night, in her undoctorly neat block printing, Kate wrote "Sleep," on her to-do list so that every morning could begin with a sense of accomplishment. She kept herself busy—idle hands and the devil and all that, of course—besides, she just liked it, the bustle and productivity. She made sure her office, and both clinics where she donated time, whistled about like windmills in a spring breeze. There were protocols and appointments, set times budgeted per patient with minutes allocated between to dictate notes. But today Kate felt like a bird in the blades. She couldn't shake the agony of Ramon's patient she hadn't been able to see or touch. And she couldn't forget Daniel's sincerity and kiss—not with the young man puppying behind her, anyway.

All morning Kate let Daniel shadow her at the free specialty clinic for children and adolescents with diabetes, and she let the kids stare at his scars the way only children will. Kate introduced him to her young patients and their parents as, "her friend Daniel."

"What happened to your face?" the kids would say, and their moms would shush them, smack their legs sometimes, but after the first couple, Daniel got good at it.

"I was in a fire," he told kids. "Do you know what to do if there's a fire where you live?" And they'd talk about fire safety and not to hide from the men in the masks and suits. Kate guessed at least half the parents they saw that morning would put new batteries in smoke detectors before they went to bed, and half the kids would be drawing pictures of what firemen looked like in full gear.

"You're good with kids," she told Daniel as he followed her back to her office at lunchtime.

"Every kid we saw today would have been The Fat Kid when I was in school."

"Yup," Kate said. "That's the high fructose corn syrup. HFCS's poisonous, totally unregulated, and more addictive than cocaine. Our entire food supply is adulterated, but of course it's the most vulnerable—the poor and young—that get sick first. That's always the case, but here it's particularly pronounced since they put HFCS in almost all cheap food. You have to pay to avoid it."

He looked at her with his gentle, poet's eyes over the wrapper of his sandwich. "You wouldn't have shown me all that if you weren't thinking about letting me help."

Kate shrugged. "I could maybe use an assistant."

"In your anti-sugar crusade?"

"I'm not anti-sugar," Kate said. "Sugar, in moderation, is perfectly fine. Makes life worth living, even. The problem with HFCS is that it's engineered to be so addictive no one can use it moderately. Certainly not kids."

"So you're offering me an apple?"

"What, like Eve?"

"Like any good mom. You said, 'no dessert for you!' but I wouldn't give in, I wanted a cookie, so you're giving me fruit."

"Daniel."

"Kate, I want to make a difference for these kids. I do."

"I'm sure you've already—"

He took her hands. "But I don't really know anything about it. I'd be nothing more than a warm body as your assistant. But with Ren and Phil, my being just a warm body is exactly what you need. You told me what's at stake, that he's the oldest, that nobody can even imagine what it'd be like without him."

But at the word "imagine" something occurred to Kate. Daniel, the love, had such an imagination. He probably saw what Incrementalists did as exciting and heroic all the time. "Let me show you what it looks like," she said.

Kate settled Daniel's lithe body against her side in a gesture uncomfortably reminiscent of shouldering a toddler, and closed her eyes. Daniel, not yet an old hand at following her into the Garden, shuddered in a way altogether reminiscent of something else, and Kate smiled through the cloggy mustiness and itch of her sense triggers.

"Come with me." She waved him up her cobbled pathway, through the den, past the craft room, and out to the back porch. She rolled out her rolly bin of mosaic tiles, and glanced across the labeled lids of repurposed baby food jars. Ramon's peculiar labeling required more patience than Kate often had, so she didn't tend to graze his memories much. But for dissuading Daniel, there could be none better. She pulled out the 1.199, 32.2217.110.9264, 07.24.2013 jar and held it up to Daniel.

"What's this?" he asked, holding out his hand. Kate dumped the shimmery gray tile into his palm.

"A recent memory of Ren and Phil as seeded by Ramon, who went to visit them when they were moving into their new house."

Kate shook the same tile from the same jar into her own hand and walked over to the tray of wet cement that waited, as it always did, on the deep window ledge of the screened porch. "Put it anywhere," she told Daniel, and watched as he selected a place in the rather chaotic mosaic and pressed Ramon's memory into the wet cement, then she did the same.

"Wow," Daniel said, opening his eyes half an hour later. "Ren's really . . . esoteric."

"Yeah," Kate agreed. "She spent almost two whole days in the Garden just trying to figure it out."

"But she didn't really. In the end." Daniel's sandwich had vanished in two enormous bites.

"It's often that way," Kate said.

Daniel nodded, eyeing her sandwich. "She and Phil are really in love, though."

"Yes," Kate agreed. "They really are. She's going to have a hard time adjusting to any new Second."

"What was the thing in September that Phil was worried about?"

Kate gave Daniel what was left of her sandwich and tore into the chips. "The Incrementalists tried to open up our world to the rest of the world. It kinda put Phil in the spotlight. He was nervous."

"But?"

"But almost no one noticed. We're a little too subtle for our own good sometimes, maybe. A little too incremental. But all the clues are still out there, and the website. You could follow them, if you wanted. You could be involved that way. Deputized."

Daniel nodded. "Maybe," he said. "I'm going to go now, okay?"

Kate knew her smile was indulgent, the kind you give when you say the baby can stay up late, but she couldn't quite turn it into a happy one. She had offered him a candy and taken it away when he reached out his hand. She had to let him go. She just didn't want to. "Okay," she said, and ate both the Pop-Tarts in the foil packet, HFCS be hanged.

*   *   *

Irina washed her face in the sink, pulled off Frio's too-starched shirt, and got her emergency panties out of her purse. She checked her phone. It was dangerously low on battery. She'd missed calls from Oskar and Ramon, as well as one from her chief, and two from unidentified numbers, but nothing from Lucy or Menzie, which meant she could go bail him out and hope he'd learned his lesson.

But it was almost noon. Her chief and his wife would walk out the church doors in thirteen minutes and drive the one mile to Chaffin's Family Diner where they would stay for about an hour and a half. If Irina didn't bump into him there, she'd have no way to see him until Monday, and getting him to call off the Southside mop-up raid wasn't a meddle she could pull off over the phone. Irina swore at the mirror, and tried out some of the hotel's hand lotion as a makeup remover. Jimmy tapped on the thin door. "Iri?"

"Fine!" Irina shouted. "Coming!" The lotion made her eyes sting. She walked back into the room bleary-eyed.

Ren was awake and tucked under the canopy of Oskar's oaken protection. Her delicate brows wrinkled in recognition at her dress on Irina, but she didn't say anything.

Matsu opened the door and looked into the hallway. "Let's go." He stepped back into the room, holding it open. Irina glanced at Frio, inert on the bed. Despite her bravado, she didn't like leaving him. He'd been a good lover in that self-conscious way the young men these days had of thinking of sex as an arena of potential expertise. Frio had spent time trying to understand What Women Liked, and Irina thought he had genuinely wanted to pleasure her. And he had. It didn't make him a good lover—a skillful pleasurer maybe—but Irina appreciated the intention.

She let Jimmy, Oskar and Ren, then Ramon file out before she got down on her knees to hunt for her shoes. She found one under the bed. Matsu plucked the other from atop the TV, handing it to her without comment. He rechecked the hall, deployed the DO NOT DISTURB sign, and held the door for her, waiting.

Frio's broad, almost hairless chest rose and fell evenly under Ramon's neatly written catalog of what and when and how much he'd administered. The paper was unsigned, of course, and in letters that you'd think came off a laser printer if they hadn't been on a hotel memo pad page. Irina walked past Matsu into the hall and down the fire stairs to the hotel parking lot where Oskar and Jimmy stood flanking Ren—Oskar all bristling protectiveness, and Jimmy radiating sympathy, tears in his eyes, leaning over her. Matsu materialized in the midst of them all, tweaking Oskar's hackles in a way Irina knew she shouldn't enjoy as much as she did. "We must put some distance between ourselves and Frio."

"Yes," Ramon agreed with a brisk nod. "We need to get out of here and prepare for the funeral."

"Ren," Oskar asked. "Do you have family we should meet at the airport too?"

She shook her head. "I told Mom not to come. I couldn't—"

"Go home, Ren," Irina told her. "Take a long shower and get dressed in your good clothes."

Ren looked at her frankly, no suspicion or cunning in her wide-set eyes.

"I've done this before," Irina told her. "And it isn't easy, but Phil is safe now. You found his stub. And being there for Chuck's family is part of how we make up for what we do to people's lives."

"It's true," Oskar said.

"Can you help her?" Irina asked him, a little lead-footed on Oskar's protector switch, but her assistant police chief would be already in his car. "I'll keep out of it," she promised. "I'll go back to my place and get dressed and meet you at the memorial. I just need to borrow someone's phone."

Oskar's blue eyes narrowed, but Matsu held out his phone to Irina. She took it and groped in her bag for car keys.

"I'll come with you," Ramon offered.

"It's okay," Irina said, turning to go. "I'm fine."

She just needed half an hour with her police chief to meddle him into calling off the mop-up raid, but she needed it now. Church was already out and she had to hit a Target for a Sunday dress and pantyhose. She did not want to wait until Monday to find out what her lover Jack Harris had known. Yes, she'd always planned to expose him for his betrayal of public trust and abuse of power, but if it turned out he'd known the Tucson Police Department had a man, Porfirio Martinez, undercover inside the Hourlies, much less that it was he who had shot Phil . . . Well, Irina might appreciate forgiveness, but she was not above blackmail whether or not Menzie intended to deliver on what she could threaten.

⋆   ⋆   ⋆

"Ren!"

The bathroom door bounced off the steam-slick wall, and Ren flinched.

"Oskar? Jesus, don't you ever knock? You're as bad as Irina with the—" she stammered, wondering how see-through the shower curtain was.

"It's gone again."

Ren made a gap between the shower curtain and the wall big enough for her head. "What's gone?"

"Phil's stub."

Ren dropped the curtain and groped for a ledge to sit on. Her knees were going to wash down the drain. "What do you mean?" She steadied her back against the cold tile.

"It's not where you seeded it." Oskar was impatient with explanations. "I was worried it might have slipped again so I checked and it was gone."

A towel, gripped in a broad fist, shoved between the wall and the shower curtain. Ren took it and Oskar reached in the opposite side and turned off the water taps.

"We have two hours before we have to be at the memorial." Oskar dragged back the shower curtain and stopped. Ren saw the raptor blue of his eyes deepen as he took in the fact she hadn't yet wrapped her body with the towel. He didn't move. His eyes slid down her body—throat and breasts and belly—as a pure heat that penetrated and warmed her like the hot shower hadn't. For the first time since Phil died, Ren wasn't cold. Fear and grief and loneliness thawed under Oskar's eyes. She wanted to keep them on her, but wrapped herself up in the sterile terry cloth.

"Matsu has left for the airport." Oskar made no effort to look away from her body. "I haven't told Jimmy."

Oskar held out one hand, palm raised, and Ren imagined the pale wrist lace-cuffed and proffered to hand a lady down from a carriage. Slippery and shaky, she put her palm against his. "Is his Garden still there?" she asked and stepped over the tub side, holding the towel closed.

264

"Phil's? I didn't check."

"That's the first thing. That's how I found him. I just—" The steamy air and fear made her dizzy. Ren sagged, and Oskar's large, cool hands caught her shoulders and held them. "I don't know how much more of this I can do," she said.

"As much as you have to."

Ren nodded and let her forehead fall forward onto Oskar's chest.

He took her hand from her towel, took the towel from her body, and folded her body against his.

"I've never been in stub," Ren said against the dampening fabric of Oskar's shirt. "What is it like?"

"Like death."

"He's not in pain, is he? Or frightened?"

"I don't know." Oskar smoothed Ren's dripping hair against her head. "But I know he loves you, and he doesn't give up."

Ren nodded. "I'll go back to his Garden and find him again."

Oskar opened one hand against the small of Ren's back, and it grounded her.

"But once I do, I'm going to stay in the Garden with his stub until we have a new recruit for him."

"You can't."

Ren's body tensed against Oskar's size and strength as she started to argue.

Oskar stayed motionless and talked over her. "You're exhausted. Besides, Irina's right about the memorial service being one of the things that justifies what we do to the people who loved our Seconds."

A hard bubble of sobs was accreting in Ren's throat. She nodded again and Oskar's hands, spanning both her skull and her back, held her hard against his immobile body. He kissed the top of her head, and whispered into her hair. "You have to be at the memorial in an hour. I still need to shower."

"I'll find Phil's stub again," Ren said. "Tell Matsu, when he's back from the airport, to join me. He can hold the stub while we bury Chuck."

Ren waited for Oskar to agree or argue, but he only shifted her body against his. He drew a slow, open-mouthed breath and held her. Ren matched his next inhalation, his broad muscled chest and her breasts opening into each other. Her body softened and clung to him. Their exhale wasn't quite a sigh; but something stronger and warmer.

"After I shower," Oskar's voice was heavy as steam, "I'll put something on the forum, make sure we have someone to hold the stub after Matsu, and get a line up for after that. Someone will always be watching that stub until we get Phil spiked into a new Second."

"Okay," Ren said.

"Ren . . ." Oskar handed her the towel back and watched as she wrapped it around her body again. "What did Phil's stub look like when you found it in his Garden?"

"Water spiraling a drain."

"Tell Matsu, okay? He wanted to know." When Oskar reached past Ren to open the bathroom door, his lips grazed her cheek. Then he yanked his damp shirt over his head. Shirtless and stunning, he grinned over his sculpted shoulder—strong and warm and ready to fight to the death for Phil if he needed to.

"Me too." Ren nodded to Oskar, shut the door and went to get dressed.

TWENTY-TWO

We Live Too Long

Tucson gave them a bright day that peeked through the stained glass, which Oskar thought Phil would have liked and Chuck wouldn't have noticed. By Oskar's request, there was no music playing at the Avalon Chapel, and the small group was dwarfed by the room, but it somehow produced a sense of intimacy. There were a few bouquets present, one sent by Ren's boss, and another by the poker room manager at The Palms. Oskar tried to remember if he'd ever met the man, but couldn't bring him into focus.

Chuck's mother made Oskar think of Irina's last Second—small and wizened and gray, but she walked strongly, aided only by a single cane, and sat in the front row. Chuck's sister sat next to his mother: tall and broad-shouldered and sturdy-looking. His mother said, "Oskar. I think I remember Charles mentioning you."

"We were good friends."

"You live here?"

"Munich, Germany, but I've been in Milwaukee for the last couple of years doing some work."

I was glad that they didn't ask what work, because I didn't feel like lying to them.

—Oskar

Chuck's sister looked around. "Where's the pastor?"

"In accordance with Chuck's—with Charles's wishes, there isn't one."
His mother said, "But—"

"I'll be conducting the services," Oskar said, putting quiet finality into it.

Chuck's mother opened her mouth to argue, then nodded. She and the sister went off to find Ren, who was standing in front of the stained glass, studying it. Butterflies, Oskar noticed, and moved away to give them space and time. Then Jimmy, Ramon, Irina, and Ren took their places without anyone saying anything. Irina looked awful. Oskar checked the time and moved to the front of the room. He'd had the podium removed, and looking at them in the oversized room suddenly made him feel small.

Hands motionless at your sides, he reminded himself. *It feels awkward, but looks natural. Speak slowly and clearly. Trust your words.*

"I have only a few words," he said. "Chuck didn't want anyone sitting through speeches about him, but hoped that we would meet each other, and informally, perhaps, tell stories about him."

Oskar looked at the small gathering, nodded, and continued.

"Chuck told me he had become somewhat estranged from his family of late," he said, "and I know he regretted that. He was a good man, and a good friend, and I know that his family is a strong part of the man he became."

I hadn't exactly prepared a speech, but I'd given some thought to what I wanted to get across, and as I spoke, I relaxed, like when I'd addressed the gathering during the Spartacist Uprising, not knowing that Luxemburg and Liebknecht were already dead, and the uprising already defeated. Like then, the words came, and I felt the connection with those who were listening. What is that connection that we feel sometimes with strangers and friends? That I feel with you? That I hope you're coming to feel with me, with Ren and Jimmy and Phil and Kate, and maybe even with Irina? I know honesty and its correlate, trust, are part of it. That's why I'm try-

ing so hard to be honest in these pages. And why I'm trusting you to know what to do when they end.

—O

"Chuck spoke to me of his life in Pittsburgh, of the feel of the handlebars on his BMW, of the ballgames he went to with his Uncle Andy. I know that whenever he tasted plum pudding he thought of his mother and his sister, and he'd smile."

There were tears, now, but it didn't feel like meddlework. It felt like that January day in Berlin, full of life and hope and the power of a moment when he felt like he was riding the cyclone, he no longer mattered as a person; only the task mattered.

"And I know the estrangement began with the fire, that it transformed him somehow, that, to you who raised and loved him, he was never the same person afterward. But this is the time to tell you that he never stopped loving you, and if the damage from that fire took something valuable from him, it also gave him things.

"He proved himself a hero that day, and, for the rest of his life, he proved himself a good and loyal friend, with a quick laugh, a calmness that—" Oskar caught himself; he'd almost said, "as Chuck." "A calmness that he hadn't had before.

"And he never stopped being part of his family. Today, Mrs. Purcell, Cindy, and those I haven't yet met, please welcome him back into your family, and your hearts. There is nothing else he would have wanted.

"I will now ask for a moment of silence, as we all consider what he meant to us."

When the moment was over, Oskar walked off the stage without ceremony, knelt in front of the two women, squeezed their hands and kissed their cheeks.

The two Purcell women hugged Oskar, thanked him, then went over to Ren as everyone stood. An erect gray-haired man introduced himself as Andrew, and folded Oskar into a hug. The man next to him startled Oskar with how much he looked like Phil—same tall, thin body, even the same twisted eyebrow. Andrew introduced him as his son, Rick.

❧

Oskar shook hands with them both, glancing at where Ren was talking with Chuck's remaining family. He remembered her body, naked in his arms just hours ago, and the moment of being simply fully present to one another that they had shared, and he was proud to know she was one of them.

There was still so much to do. They needed a new Second for Phil as quickly as they could safely recruit one. And somewhere in the city—maybe still passed out at the Hyatt, maybe back on the job—Frio, the man who had shot Phil, was still alive and still a cop, thinking his badge made him immune to consequences. They would see.

★   ★   ★

Jimmy's rental was already in the drive behind Oskar's and Matsu's, when they pulled up in front of the house. Jane parked on the street and put a hand on Ren's knee. "It was a lovely service, Ren. You did a great job."

"I didn't do much. It was Oskar."

"Well," Jane said, "I'll be back here tomorrow morning at nine thirty to take you to yoga unless you call and give me a very good reason why I shouldn't."

"I can drive myself, you know."

Jane gave an apologetic shrug. "I've been needing an exercise buddy."

"You have not." Ren shot Jane a mock glare, which she returned with steady friendship. "Thank you," Ren said. "Yoga tomorrow would be great."

She got out of Jane's car and walked through the suburban Sunday suppertimes to her own front door. Susi greeted her, tail wagging, then went bounding off, probably on the assumption that Phil must now be around, somewhere. Ren found Oskar sitting in Phil's chair, and tapped his shoulder as she walked by. "Hey Oskar, you're going to love this," she told him.

"Good." Only his potion-blue eyes moved, tracking Ren across the room.

"Oh god, were you grazing? I'm sorry." Ren put her bag down. The house was quiet despite the three cars in the drive, and at least as many men somewhere inside it.

"What am I going to love?"

"I think you were right about Jane," Ren said. "We could maybe re-cruit her as Phil's Second."

"Ren!" Jimmy came in from the kitchen. He put a glass of wine in Ren's hand, held her by the shoulders, and looked hard into her eyes. "Good," he said and kissed her warmly on the mouth. "Did you get enough to eat at the memorial?"

"Yeah," Ren said, tasting the wine. "Does Matsu still have Phil's stub?"

"Yes. He's a shaman," Jimmy reassured her. "Oskar, wine?" Jimmy looked around Ren to the immobile Teuton on the sofa. "*Mon Dieu,* what a face!"

"Ren thinks perhaps we might recruit Jane for Phil's stub," Oskar said.

"But you . . . But she . . ." Jimmy turned from Oskar's face to Ren. "I'll get the bottle."

Oskar stood up and twisted his back, stretching. "If Sam is right about her, the work Jane is already doing may be too important for us to take her away from it. Nothing mitigates the most pernicious long-term effects of poverty as dramatically as even a single responsive, attentive adult in a child's life. If Jane is able to make her students feel loved the way Sam reports, then she's doing something Phil can't." Oskar bent over and pressed his palms to the floor. "Do you know who Irina's date was at the memorial?"

Ren laughed. "He wasn't her date. That was Menzie, the guy who called Phil's cell last night for help. She went by the courthouse and paid his bail."

Oskar reseated himself, taking Phil's chair, waving Ren to the sofa opposite. "Did you like how he looked?"

"Oh." Ren sat. "You mean would I like him as Phil?"

"Who *now*?" Jimmy was back with wine.

"Menzie," Ren said a little hollowly.

"You had more chemistry with Frio." Jimmy went back to the kitchen.

"Right, and look how that worked out." Ren's fingertips went cold on her glass.

"But you like Jane?" Jimmy came in with a tray of cheeses and crack-ers salvaged from the memorial.

"Yeah," Ren said, remembering the dark eyes in the idling car, their steadiness and care.

"Could you love her?" Jimmy asked.

Ren nodded.

"Could you make love with her?" Oskar asked.

Ren looked at him. "Yeah," she said again. "If she were Phil."

Oskar grunted, the tenderness or fragility gone from his voice. "I'm going back to the Garden."

"What? No!" Ren said. "I need you here."

Oskar closed his eyes.

"Oskar, we need to get Phil spiked into a new Second tonight," Ren insisted. "His stub is way too unstable and we can't ask Matsu or anyone else to stay in the Garden holding on to it."

"So recruit someone," Oskar said evenly.

"We need to decide who."

"So decide."

"That's what I'm doing!"

"No." Oskar opened his eyes. "What you are doing is arguing with me about whether or not I should go back to the Garden and graze. I'm going. You figure this out. Or you and Jimmy or whoever else you want to consult, but I am going back to the Garden to find out whether or not, while we were burying Chuck and consoling his family and attending the reception, the police managed to collect Frio, or whether the housekeeping staff at the Airport Hyatt got a nasty surprise. I'm going to find out what Irina should have seeded days ago about who that fucker really is, and to whom he's actually reporting. He's a hell of a liar. He looked at you and said, 'yes ma'am.' He lies as well as we do. He shot Phil, Ren. He's the guy. That's what Phil meant when he said 'I shot me.'"

"Oh," Ren said. "You're right. Okay."

"Oskar." Jimmy put his wineglass down.

"What?"

The front door clicked, Oskar sprang, and Irina blew in with her arms full of flowers. Susi trotted in, looked at Irina, then at the door.

Oskar bellowed a wordless roar, threw himself back into Phil's chair, and closed his eyes.

★   ★   ★

"No, thank you, Oskar," Irina snapped. "I don't need any help with these."

Jimmy stood, but Irina toed the front door closed and marched across the living room to deposit the flowers on Ren's mantel. "From the memorial," she announced, looking pointedly at Ren.

Jimmy handed Irina the wineglass he'd filled for Oskar. "Ren is considering Jane for Phil's Second," Jimmy told Irina, settling himself on the sofa next to Ren. "Oskar is grazing for news on your friend Frio."

"Aren't you all industrious?" Irina threw her shoulder bag onto the kitchen counter, and collapsed next to Jimmy on the sofa. "I thought you'd still be somber and quiet after the memorial, but spit-spot back to work is it?"

Jimmy kissed her on the top of her head. "Fuck off, Irina."

She sagged against his shoulder. She's been just as busy. Busier. But she couldn't share her stories. She couldn't even seed them. Assistant Police Chief Jack Harris hadn't, in fact, known Frio shot Phil. Irina was glad to hear it, but not that Jack now suspected his man had "gone native." Frio, it seemed, had taken personal time last night and disabled his car's GPS tracking. He hadn't reported in since.

Irina had wangled a solemn oath from her Old Silver to call off the raid on the Hourlies by playing the spooky primitive. It was all very well for educated white ladies like Jane to dabble in superstition and talk about magic, but when a brown woman did it, it was scary. Jack had promised to keep all the SWAT forces in tonight lest Irina's dreams of the wealthy's food poisoned by the poor who cook it prove prophetic. She had tasted his mouth for toxins and told him a memory, true in its details, if neither time nor place, of a one-armed dark-skinned houngan, and how it felt to burn to death.

She shuddered against Jimmy's silken shoulder. "Where's Matsu?" she asked.

"Phil's stub is unstable enough that we're keeping someone in the Garden all the time just to hold on to it," Jimmy explained.

Irina nodded. "Where are Sam and Jane?"

"Jane drove me home," Ren said. "She was at the memorial."

"Yes. Without Sam."

"Yes. Irina. Look, we have to settle on a new Second for Phil, and I feel—"

"Ren, Sam has been running an underground resistance group that's been fucking with everything the immigration and border control cops do, particularly in Maricopa County. They call themselves the Hourlies, and target the private militia most, the wingnuts and the racists, but he's managed to put a crimp in the pleats of the local police too."

"I know, Irina, but right now—"

"But right now, the police think he's dead."

"Sam?"

"The police had noticed Phil. They were watching him. Probably electronically. Possibly here." She jabbed her finger at the sofa to indicate Ren's home. Ren shivered. "The Tucson police," Irina enunciated carefully, "thought Phil was the ringleader of the Hourlies."

"I know." Ren swallowed hard. "They had their undercover man shoot him."

"No," Irina said. "That's just it. They have no idea who shot Phil."

"Frio did," Jimmy said. "Phil said so."

"Right," Irina agreed. "But he didn't do it on orders from the Tucson PD."

"I don't get it," Ren said.

"Have a drink, Ren, you sound like shit."

"Iri," Jimmy chided.

Ren waved his objections aside and took a good gulp. "Go on," she told Irina.

"The police think Phil was the mastermind behind all the sabotage and confusion that Sam's been causing," Irina explained. "They think this because Frio, in his role as undercover agent, had been sending them surveillance pictures of Phil. Even though Frio knew Phil had nothing to do with the Hourlies. He duped the cops who, for the moment anyway, still believe the ringleader of their most closely guarded secret and humiliating defeats was shot by people inside a rival organization, probably the Minutemen. Possibly the skinheads. They, of course, don't so much care who killed Phil. They care"—Irina raised her glass to Ren, toasting—

"that the Hourlies have been completely dormant since his death." She downed her wine with a flourish.

"Frio was an undercover Tucson cop," Ren said, putting the pieces together. "And he shot Phil, but didn't tell anyone at Tucson PD?"

"Exactly."

"He shot Phil either acting on his own, or for some other agency?"

"So it would seem."

"Irina," Jimmy asked quietly, refilling her glass. "How do you know all this?"

"Menzie, whom I hope everyone got a chance to meet today," Irina said, acknowledging Jimmy's re-pour with an imperious nod, "is an investigative reporter. He, it turns out, has been working on a story about the increased militarization of Arizona police departments. Very interesting, no? And then, just last night, he was arrested for driving while brown. As a result, he's highly motivated just now to break a really big story about our local PD." Irina beamed and took a sip. "This really is a lovely wine. Your choice, Jimmy?"

"But of course," he said with an outrageous French wink.

"So—" Irina pulled her pumps off and pushed them under the coffee table. "Now we spike Phil into Sam, and let him keep running the Hourlies, but maybe a little more quietly, and we take everything Phil knows about Frio, having shared his head for a while, and we give it to Menzie for a complete exposé."

"Spike Phil into Sam?" Ren repeated.

"We don't know how much visibility Phil will have had into Frio's memories," Jimmy said.

Irina stood up and put her hands on her hips. "Well?"

"What?" Ren said.

"Fine, I'll get it." Irina rolled her eyes dramatically and walked behind Ren's chair to the front door.

Only then did Ren realize someone had been knocking. Susi was up, looking hopeful, but he never barked at the door.

Irina yanked the door open and shifted her weight into her hip. "Hello?"

"Hi," said a young man's voice. "I'm Daniel Whitman."

Jimmy got to his feet slowly. "Kate's recruit? From Pennsylvania?"

"Yeah."

"When did—"

"I just got off the plane."

"Well," Irina said. "You'd better come in."

*   *   *

If you grip a thing too tightly, Takamatsu knew, it will slip away from you and may be gone forever. Sometimes that was a vague koan-like notion to inspire thought; sometimes it was merely practical instruction. Sometimes it fell in between.

Phil's stub remained before Takamatsu's eyes in the form Ren had discovered it in his Garden, the same one she had created in the mud of her Garden to hasten his return—a spiral that was not a form or a direction, but movement: a verb, not a noun. Takamatsu could hold it, this not-thing, as long as he neither looked away, nor right at it. It was a balancing act, but he had good balance. He had good balance because he was aware of his body, of his center of gravity, of which muscles he kept tense, and which relaxed. These were things that did not exactly translate in the Garden, but neither were they entirely unrelated to what the imagination did in the dense nothingness, in the emptiness that was full.

Phil's stub was the taste of saffron, half a clamshell, the howl of the wind down the passes of Yonaha-dake, the touch of silk on Takamatsu's forehead. All of those, and more, changing from one to the other, independent, yet connected.

He could not find the pattern, because there was none. There could be no pattern, because Phil's stub was both in the Garden and in Frio, and even in Jimmy, maybe in others as well; there and not there; bouncing randomly among the dream-lives of 203 very individual individuals.

Takamatsu could hold it, he could keep it from being lost, he could follow it—for a while. How long a while?

Not as long as he needed to, he knew that much at least.

Ramon once told a joke about a mathematician catching a lion by building a cage with himself inside and the lion outside and then performing an inversion. No one but Ramon knew enough mathematics to think

it funny, but yet, on some level, all the Incrementalists understood. None
of them, however, had ever considered it practical advice.

But in the Garden, the imaginary is real, the mundane is numinous,
and the spiritual is prosaic.

In a fight, you know that the time to act has come when you discover
you have acted. Takamatsu Toshitsugu discovered he had acted.

I should have been with him. He shouldn't have faced this alone,
but I was focused on Frio and action and answers.

—O

---

*   *   *

Jimmy glanced up as Irina stepped back to let Daniel Whitman into Phil's
house, and, looking at him, Jimmy suddenly remembered Phil in 1994.
He'd looked a lot like Daniel Whitman: tall, wide across the shoulders,
narrow at the hips.

Ramon walked in from the hall, headed briskly to answer the door,
and Ren glanced from Daniel to him a little wildly. "Oh hello, Ramon. I
didn't know you were here," she said.

"I brought him back with me." Jimmy heaved himself to standing.

"I was napping," Ramon explained to Ren. "Hello," he said to Daniel.

"You were napping?" said Irina, an hysterical edge to her voice, and
Jimmy considered how exhausted she must be. But when she spoke again,
it was in her honey-silk voice. "Ramon, meet Daniel Whitman. Daniel,"
she added, "shut the door." Then she sat down, and Jimmy saw that she'd
just realized she wasn't going to convince Ren to pick Sam. Not over Kate's
young Daniel Whitman anyway.

"Ramon?" Daniel repeated, but he had enough poise to shake the
delicate, red-tipped hand extended to him.

"You can call me Sarah, if you're more comfortable with that," Ramon offered.

"It's good to meet you, Ramon." Daniel closed the door and his eyes
shifted from Ramon to Irina to Ren. "You're Ren."

"Yeah," she said. "This is Jimmy and that's Oskar."

Daniel walked across the rug like he was counting the steps between Ren and the door, and Jimmy tried to imagine what he was seeing. Ren, at that moment, looked older than she was, certainly older than he was, but pretty still, in that clean-living, fresh-faced honest way of hers that Jimmy and Phil both adored.

Ren started to offer Daniel her hand to shake, but dropped it under the force of his obviously rehearsed, "Hi, I'm Daniel Whitman. Kate recruited me for Phil's stub, but she changed her mind. I know I'm young, and I know I'm willful, but I want to do this for you. For Phil." He cleared his throat and pressed on. "Kate told me about you and how much Phil loved you. Loves you. She showed me your memory of finding him again after you grazed too far back in time. I want to—" He faltered, his script failing him. "I've never—"

"Daniel!" interrupted Irina, now using her gracious hostess voice. "You must have traveled all day. I'm sure you're tired." She shot Ramon a wicked glance but he wasn't paying attention. "Come into the kitchen with me and I'll fix you something nice." Irina stood, and it looked to Jimmy like it was an effort for her to do so. "Are you hungry? I'm sure you need a drink!"

"I'm good, thanks," Daniel said.

"Have a seat." Ren offered him her chair. "Let Irina bring you a beer." Ren smiled at Irina.

Irina looked like she wanted to spit. "He's not thirsty. He just said so."

"Actually, Tucson is pretty hot—" Daniel started.

"Kate changed her mind about you," said Irina. "She doesn't think you're a good recruit."

"I'll check." Jimmy started to graze, but Ramon had his phone out of his pocket, so Jimmy waited.

"Oh, Christ's boiled bottom!" Irina exclaimed, and held out her hand for the phone. Ramon ignored her and turned toward the kitchen. "Kate, please give a call when you get this message. There's a young man here who says he's Daniel Whitman."

"Tell her I'm sorry," Daniel called after Ramon, who didn't look back.

"You said you wanted a beer," Irina reminded him.

"I—"

"Irina." Jimmy opened his eyes, looking a warning at her.

"Jimmy." Irina turned to him as if expecting him to move. He waited, watching her, thinking she looked old again.

Ramon came back in with two opened beer bottles and a glass. "I left a message for Kate," Ramon said. "I'd like to hear back from her before we proceed. She recruited him, she may want to titan."

"I can do it," Ren said.

Jimmy watched Irina watching Ren, whose eyes hadn't left Daniel since he introduced himself. "You want to take him to bed and try him out first, Ren?" Irina got up from the coffee table and flopped onto the sofa.

Daniel looked up from pouring his beer into the glass. "Fuck off, Irina."

Ren laughed, and when Daniel finished his pour, she reached out a hand to him. He stood and took it and came around the coffee table to sit next to her. Ren turned to Jimmy. "I don't think I can do the ritual though."

"Want me to?" Irina said, but Ren just ignored her.

"I'd be delighted," Jimmy said.

Daniel and Ren sat on the sofa holding hands like kids on prom night.

"Shouldn't we even discuss this?" Irina asked.

"Jimmy." Oskar's voice rasped raw. They all turned to look at him, but he stayed limp, the back of his head fallen onto the chair, his face slack.

"What is it?" Jimmy was on his feet instantly, one hand on each arm of Oskar's chair, bending down to him. "Oskar?"

"Phil's gone."

"Not again!" Ren took her hand out of Daniel's. "No," she said from behind both her palms.

"Oskar!" Jimmy cupped Oskar's face in his hands, pushing Oskar's blond hair back from his forehead, rubbing his perfect, pale cheekbones with the dark pads of his thumbs. But he felt it too, sapping him, an abrupt unwinding, like a popped torsion spring.

"Matsu is dead." Oskar's eyes washed almost black with fear. Jimmy's feet suddenly went cold.

"Matsu?" Ren stood, jumped the coffee table, and was down the hall before any of the rest of them had absorbed the information. Jimmy turned and followed.

"Matsu," Irina whispered.

They'd left him alone. For hours now, Matsu had been in Ren and Phil's bedroom holding on to Phil's stub. If he'd stroked out like Frio, he'd done it alone with no one to help him.

"Shit!" Ramon said behind Irina as they ran down the hall after Ren.

Ren threw open the bedroom door, flipped on the light and pulled up short. Matsu's body lay motionless in the dead center of their bed.

They all stopped still. Jimmy saw Ren take a shuddering breath. She crept toward Matsu's body. He opened his eyes.

Daniel made the noise anyone would at seeing a corpse sit up in bed, but Ren stood as still as Matsu should be. Irina started to say something snotty to Oskar, but Ren flew over the foot of the bed and onto Matsu. His arms went around her. "Phil!" Ren said, in a single sob.

Matsu raised his head from Ren's neck and looked up at the cluster of gaping faces in his bedroom door. "Oskar, Jimmy, Irina, Ray, New Guy," he said with a grin and a wild, cocked eyebrow. "Isn't anyone going to ask 'how's the head?'"

TWENTY-THREE

✦

Turned and Headed Back

Phil felt himself grin. Everyone except Ren started speaking at once, questions full of "How—?" But he was more interested in "who," and with trying to understand why, of all the fifty-some times he'd been through the process, this was the first time he'd ever found himself instantly and fully present, with no trace of whoever had last held his new consciousness.

So he kissed Ren, hard, to kiss away her grief and fear and frustration at everyone around her, and she kissed him back, full of relief and promises and questions, and their lips said, "You went away," and their mouths said, "I came back," and there were things that would need saying, in words and in touches, but they promised they'd say them.

Everyone ignored them, their voices like the buzzing of flies outside the window. Phil was interested in what they were saying, but he was much more interested in holding Ren, so when the kiss ended with a mutual sigh, they squeezed each other, and held each other while the rest of them yammered. Phil rested his cheek on top of Ren's head and watched the faces around them: Irina looked torn between confused and furious; Jimmy just stared, shaking his head back and forth; Ray was wearing his Intense Look—like Phil was a problem he was going to solve whatever it took; Oskar's mouth opened and closed, providing a sort of visual counterpoint to Jimmy; and the new guy, like Phil, looked from one to the other uncomfortably, as if waiting for someone to tell him he wasn't supposed to be here.

"Phil," said Ren against his neck. Not a question, a ratification.

"Yeah," he said, and held her, soaked in the spicy scent of her hair. After a while he asked, "How long was I away?" But Ren didn't hear him over the barrage of questions landing like German 88s all around them.

Eventually people stopped talking, and Phil opened his eyes, about to repeat his question, but Ray said, "Phil, we need to figure out how this happened."

"How what happened?" Phil said.

"Matsu."

"Matt? Where is he?"

"Phil, he spiked you into himself."

"Huh? That's impossible."

They all shook their heads.

Phil tried to get up to look in the mirror, but Ren wasn't letting go. "It's true," she said.

He stared at the ceiling. "That's . . . how? Jimmy, could you—"

Jimmy's eyes were already closed. Irina started to say something, but Oskar said, "Wait."

Jimmy's eyes opened. "Yes, it's happened before; maybe half a dozen times in the last forty thousand years. We've had Incrementalists spike themselves into another; the whole ritual takes place in the Garden, and— how *is* your head, Phil?"

Phil blinked. "Actually, it's fine. No pain at all."

"Yeah," said Jimmy, nodding at Ray, whose eyes were wide and gleaming. Whatever else was or wasn't going to happen, Phil knew Ray, at least, was delighted.

Ren kissed Phil's neck. "I can't believe you're back," she whispered, and Phil just squeezed her.

"It's kind of unreal to me, too," he said. "Matt. Jesus."

"Now we'll need to find a recruit for Matsu," said Oskar.

"There's no rush," said Irina. "Not like with Phil's stub going all wonky and us ready to take just anyone."

"I'm right here," said the new guy.

Irina laughed. "No, Kate ruled you out, and Ren won't overrule her now she's got Phil in blond beefcake."

"Irina," said Ren. "Don't drink any tea."

For once, Irina didn't have a reply.

Phil looked at her—at Irina—and tried to imagine what she'd gone through to leave her looking so haggard. His stub-and-Seconds had never been that hard on her before. He could have grazed for it, if she'd seeded anything, but holding Ren seemed like a better idea. "Who are you?" he asked the new guy,

"Daniel," he said. "I'm a friend of—I know Kate."

"Kate? How did Kate get involved in this? No, don't tell me. I'll need it all in order, and I don't want it now. For now, what are we doing about Frio?"

"He shot you," said Oskar.

"Yeah."

"The cops blamed unnamed vigilantes and closed the case."

"I'm not surprised," Phil said.

"Are you hungry?" Ren asked him.

"No," Phil said. "If being hungry means either of us has to move, I'm not hungry."

Oskar's eyes had never left Phil. "What do you mean, you're not surprised?"

"Frio wasn't acting under police orders when he shot me."

"How do you know?"

"I was spiked into him, Oskar, you don't think I was able to pick up anything? Oh, and, speaking of, who had the bright idea to—oh." Phil looked at Irina. She met his eyes. "Irina," he said. "What's your game this time?"

"Making the world better," she said. "You should try it."

Phil felt rather than saw Oskar suddenly go on full alert. He started to say something, but Jimmy cut him off. "Not now," he said. "I think the first thing to deal with is Matsu. I'll titan." He looked at Daniel, who looked back at him; Phil tried to read the expression on Daniel's face. It reminded him of how Colonel Walcutt looked right before they went into a fight: determined, a little rigid, like he wasn't going to acknowledge, even to himself, whatever fear or nervousness he felt.

"Dan's a good recruit," Phil said.

"Seriously?" said Irina. "What's the rush?"

"Irina, you just spit in my face," Phil said.

She didn't apologize, but she stood up and backed off. "Kate had reservations about him, and we still have a truly excellent choice in Sam."

"Irina," said Jimmy quietly.

"I just want to make sure the recruit we pick is vetted. Is that unreasonable?"

"Like Frio was," Phil asked. "The way you spiked me into the guy who shot me?"

"I didn't know that!" Irina suddenly reminded Phil of an attack dog just waiting for the word to go for someone's throat. She played at being all about sex and sensuality; even to herself, and it let even those who knew her well forget how strong she was, how determined she could be, and how she really, honestly, was an Incrementalist in every way that counted. They might forget what mattered to her, because sometimes she did. They remembered that she could be ruthless, but forgot what she was ruthless for.

Phil said, "I don't know what you're doing this time, Irina, but if you need my help—"

Daniel said, "Can someone explain—?"

"No," said two or three people all at once; Phil thought he was one of them.

Irina said, "Look—"

"Oh, we're looking," said Oskar.

"Not now though," Phil said. "Now I'm hungry."

He stood up and reached for Ren's hand.

★ ★ ★

"There's deli meat and bread for sandwiches," Irina told the new Phil-in-Matsu. "And I picked up a couple pounds of chopped beef BBQ."

Honestly, if she weren't around they'd all starve at the first sign of crisis. No one else thought to go shopping.

"Is there still some of my pasta sauce in the freezer?" Phil moved less gracefully than Matsu in the same body, or his foot was asleep. Irina thought the overall effect was a little weird, but Ren couldn't stop looking at him.

"Yeah," Ren said, and climbed after Phil. They walked, holding hands, through the clot of Incrementalists at the foot of their bed. They all crowded in, resurrection band style, a ragged parade down the hallway behind them. Irina thought it would be weird for Ren—liking Matsu, loving Phil, to have the two combined all of a sudden. Phil stopped and offered his hand to the dog, who sniffed it and lost interest. Phil gave a twisted Phil-smirk—odd in Matsu's face—and continued to the kitchen.

The situation would be even weirder for Oskar, loving Phil as he did and loathing Matsu. Irina fought the urge to turn around and look at him. He'd done such a good job officiating Chuck's memorial—compassionate, articulate, a charismatic speaker who knew he was good at what he was doing and enjoyed it, but only because it served the people who needed it. He was a good man, and a tolerable Incrementalist. Just not as smart as Phil who, with his, "if you need my help," had disarmed her more than all Oskar's glower and demands. But Irina didn't need his help. It was all solved, at least for the night: Phil was back, Ren was happy, Menzie was at work on his article, and the SWAT team was staying home.

Irina needed to sit down. With nothing left to do, she had nothing left. She leaned against the hallway wall while Phil surveyed his kitchen like a traveler returned to his harem. He opened the freezer, extracted a frozen concubine of Tupperware, and stuck it in the microwave. This house didn't have the handy bar and barstools that his Vegas kitchen had, and the table was too separate from the workspace for easy conversation, so while Ren moved around Phil in the kitchen, the rest of them stayed clumped between the counter and the table.

Ramon hovered as close to Phil as he could without getting in the way or being pressed into service. He held his slim body motionless on its funeral high heels, but Irina could almost hear him vibrating. "What's the first thing you remember after dying?" he asked Phil. "Oskar reported you gave him a dagger as an index of those seeds you'd been making but not pointing to on the forum. They all pertained to your work on the immigration legislation. Do you remember that?"

"What was up with that, anyway?" Irina asked. "Why so violent? Why so secretive?"

"Irina," Oskar's bass rumble spoke right into Irina's ear. "You have exactly no space to question violence or secret-keeping right now."

Irina hadn't meant it as an accusation. She was only pointing out patterns, but Oskar was right. The anger in his voice unnerved her, but his absolute and uncharacteristic control of it was interesting. An innervating cascade of anxiety, exhaustion, and loneliness made her want to just lean back into him, to rest against his chest and righteous rage. Irina needed arms around her, and Oskar's were lovely.

But he kept on talking. Oskar always kept talking, rattling on to Jimmy and everyone else about Matsu. Irina wobbled into a kitchen chair and watched Oskar's lithe shoulders under the soft black of his shirt until she felt Jimmy watching her watching them. Irina met his eyes, but he didn't smile.

"Christ's tiny testicles, Oskar, what's the fucking hurry?" she finally snapped. "Trying to set a new stub-to-Second record for Matsu? Why? It's not like you're his biggest fan."

"The way Matsu transitioned into stub without his body's death might conceivably transfer the instability of Phil's stub to his," Ramon theorized.

And Ren suggested, "Gratitude, maybe?" She turned to Irina, drying her hands on a kitchen towel. "Some people feel that. It was a pretty extraordinary sacrifice he made for Phil."

"We don't know it was a sacrifice at all," Irina countered. "Phil could have gone all Celeste on Matsu, for what we know. Hell, for all Phil knows. She shared a consciousness with me, if you remember, and I wasn't in the Garden holding on to her stub. Shit, it's possible Matsu's still in there with Phil. Remember Ethan and Qing?" Irina grinned. "How do you feel about threesomes, Ren?"

"I've shot you before, Irina." Phil didn't look up from his work.

"Oh, that's very nice," Irina said, too tired to resist the bait. "Threaten my life. We're not supposed to be the killers, Phil, or the assholes who use violence and threats of violence to win. We're the ones who nudge things a little, feed the good wolf. You remember—incrementally?"

"I'm sorry," said Oskar, unattractively nasal with scorn. "How is having someone arrested not using the threat of violence, if not the actual fact of it, Irina?"

"It worked," was all the comeback she could muster. She was exhausted. "Menzie's helping me make things better in ways and on a scale that may eventually surprise you all." Irina turned from Phil, with Matsu's surfer-boy hair falling into his ancient eyes, to Jimmy, whose moral depth had drowned even his utter sensuality. She scrubbed at her eyes to hide the tears, and came away with mascara on her fingers, goddamn it.

"Irina," Phil said, and the doorbell rang.

"Would someone turn off the fucking bat signal, please?" Irina snapped. "This is getting ridiculous."

"Hello?" a woman's voice called over the sound of the front door opening. "Ren? Anyone home?"

"We're in the kitchen," Ren answered. "Come on in, Jane."

Oskar turned, a little eagerly it seemed to Irina, and stepped aside to make room for Jane in the archway between the living room and kitchen, but Jane had stopped halfway across the living room floor. Oskar opened his mouth and shut it again upon seeing her face.

"I think the cops know it was Sam." Jane choked on a sob, her shoulders shaking. "They've called out the SWAT team."

All Irina's peevishness at Daniel's sabotage of her plans washed away in the face of a much more terrible betrayal. She struggled not to sob.

★   ★   ★

Phil looked up from the pasta sauce. "Jane?" he said. She nodded. Phil turned to Ren. "Jane Astarte. Her husband is . . . ?"

"Yeah."

"Oh." Phil coughed and looked around. "Can someone bring me up to speed?"

Ray frowned and said, "Don't you have Matsu's memories?"

Phil hesitated. "No," he said. "I don't. Does that—"

"It's fine," said Jimmy. "That's another side effect of—"

"What happened?" Oskar abandoned his Irina-watch to wrap Jane in his arms. She tensed at first, then relaxed into him.

"I dropped Ren off here, drove home, stopped at the stop sign to turn onto my street, and had to wait while two SWAT trucks and three cop cars went by."

Irina started to stand, but Ramon seated himself next to her, leaning to whisper in her ear. Phil had never seen Irina so close to a total melt-down. Unless she was faking it. He watched. No, she wasn't faking it.

"Did you try calling Sam?" Jimmy asked Jane.

"It went straight to voice mail."

"We should get Jim—" Phil stopped, because Jimmy was already settled on a kitchen chair across the table from Irina and Ramon, his eyes closed.

"And you're sure they were going to your house?" Oskar asked.

The look Jane gave him actually silenced Oskar. Phil made a mental note.

"No indications that he's been killed or arrested," said Jimmy. "We're going to assume he's alive, and wasn't at the house when SWAT arrived."

"Then where is he? Why is his phone off?"

Ramon let go of Irina's elbow and took Jane by the shoulders. "That may be my doing. I warned him that we had reason to believe the police were listening to Phil's calls, which meant they'd be watching Sam's now that he'd been to Phil's house, and those of anyone he called. It's quite likely he simply turned his phone off."

Jane looked as inclined to sit down as to burst into flames, but she allowed Ramon to tow her into the living room. Phil followed, and Ren came with him, leaving Irina, Dan, and Jimmy in the kitchen.

"Jane—" Ramon perched on the coffee table in front of her, his slender back to Oskar. "If you have information that could help us understand the situation"—he was watching Jane's face intently for clues—"no matter how personal"—Jane's lips tightened—"or illegal . . ." Ramon course-corrected fluidly. "None of us are interested in the letter of the law. We want to help. We may be the only ones who can."

"I know," she said. "It's why I came back here."

★   ★   ★

Keeping an eye on the action in the living room, Irina went to the bag she'd left on the counter, her mind a jumbled snarl. Daniel and Jimmy were the only ones left in the kitchen, and Jimmy was grazing. Irina found the new phone she'd bought at Target along with the Sunday dress and pantyhose, and slid it free.

Jack had lied to her. Betrayed her.

Phil's pasta water was boiling, and the sauce he'd defrosted hiccupped in its pan. Mechanically, Irina turned down the heat and threw a box of penne in while she texted Menzie. If Jack was going to ignore his promise, she was going to make the dream of devastation and ruin she'd made up to get him to cancel the raid come true. She grazed briefly for Jane and Sam's street address, and was tempted to stay swaddled in the Garden's emotional distance but forced herself back. She opened her eyes to find Jimmy's on her.

"What you doing, my love?" he murmured, immobile in his chair.

"You must be starving." Irina gave him her best slow smile. "And I know Phil was famished. I'm just finishing what he started in here."

"No really, Irina," Jimmy said, his voice firm enough now to draw Daniel's attention. "What are you doing?"

"Puttanesca, I believe," she said, turning her back to him. She keyed Sam's address into the text window with Menzie and hit SEND.

"Let me see." Jimmy held out a fleshy palm.

Irina tipped the sauce pot toward Jimmy, wafting rosemary and peppers in his direction.

"Your phone, my love. Give it to me."

Irina tossed her phone at him, maybe just a little harder than necessary. Daniel snatched it out of the air and handed it to Jimmy. Irina resisted the urge to stick out her tongue at the pretty young thing as she brushed by him into the living room.

Phil had wedged himself onto the sofa next to Ren, who had the entire length of her side nestled up against him, despite holding one of Jane's hands. Ramon stood with his back to the fireplace, between Jane and

Oskar. Oskar held on to the arms of Phil's chair like they were Fact and Reason respectively.

"You all can do whatever you want," Irina announced to the room, "but unless someone's going to get ugly and violent about it all, I'm leaving."

"She's messaged Menzie with Sam and Jane's home address," Jimmy tattled from the kitchen. "She told him about the SWAT team."

"Phil!" Irina shouted over the din of everyone being surprised and outraged. "How long were you in Matsu's body before we found you?"

The question made everyone quiet and Phil thoughtful. "I'm not sure," he said. "A while. I was in my Garden and . . ."

"Why, Irina?" Oskar asked, every gorgeous muscle of him making it clear that her freedom to leave in the next few minutes depended entirely on her answer.

"Because, Dr. Watson," she said, "I figure that Phil's stub getting spiked into Matsu probably changed things for Frio, and he's still the person who shot Phil. I want to know where he is."

Oskar's sensuous lips went rigid.

"Frio?" Jane asked. "Sam's Frio? From the library?"

"He's a cop," said Ren and Oskar together.

Jane opened her mouth to argue.

"No," Ren said. "Still. Undercover."

Irina had her hand on the doorknob.

"Where are you going?" Ramon asked her.

"The Crazy Horse Saloon."

"Why?" Jimmy was standing in the kitchen archway.

"Because I could use a cocktail," she said. "Daniel, be a love and drain the penne. Jimmy, can I have my phone back, please?"

His hollow eyes held no love or even trust for her, but he tossed the phone. It hurt Irina to see him so beleaguered. "Get some of Phil's pasta in you," she told him, and left.

In the driveway, she stopped and counted a slow ten to see who would follow, but she didn't do any addition. That was Phil's game; this was hers.

*   *   *

Phil saw that more than anger haunted Oskar's shoulders, watching Irina's car pull away, but couldn't tell what. He said, "Oskar—"

"You don't think someone should be keeping an eye on her?"

When Phil didn't answer, Oskar snagged the Prius keys and left.

"Pasta a la Phil!" Jimmy announced, emerging from the kitchen with two steaming plates of pasta and a dish towel neatly folded over his shoulder.

He handed Phil a plate, snapped the dish towel in the air and spread it over Phil's lap. "Welcome back," he said, and kissed the top of Phil's head. Addressing himself to Daniel and Jane, he said, "Phil and I have the Garden shakes, so you really must forgive us," and settled himself in Phil's chair. "I'm not sure what's about to happen, but I know we'll need to be at our best for it, and at present my best is at least several thousand calories away." Jimmy whipped another dish towel from his back pocket, tucked it into the neck of his well-tailored shirt, and spread the cloth like a picnic blanket over the lawn of his chest. "There's more in the kitchen if anyone else is hungry."

"I could eat," Daniel said, almost as a question. "It was a long trip."

"Bring Jane a plate?" Ramon suggested, and when Jane met Daniel's eyes and nodded, he ducked into the kitchen.

"Good kid," observed Jimmy around a mouthful. "So, you asked to be caught up," he said to Phil. "Here's the situation as I see it. The police believe you—Chuck—were the head of the Hourlies, the group Sam runs out of the high school Ren was investigating for all the student gun busts. Frio knew Sam ran the Hourlies, not you, but he identified you to the local PD as their ringleader. Then he shot you, either acting on orders from someone other than his immediate superiors, or on his own initiative. We don't know why.

"Irina recruited him for your Second thinking he'd resigned from the force and, to be fair, he's a very convincing liar. We all thought the same. I grazed his record too. But obviously you knew he was the man who pulled the trigger and shot you, and you rejected him as your Second.

Things got very unstable and we lost track of Frio trying to keep track of you. But Irina's right. The settling of your stub probably stabilized Frio, and we still don't know where he is—mentally or physically. Irina clearly thinks someone at the Crazy Horse will know how to find him, so she, and now Oskar, are headed there."

"Um," Phil said cleverly. He was relieved that this Second didn't hate what he knew how to cook, but what he really wanted to do was carry Ren off to the bedroom and get started catching up, not to mention taking Matsu's body for a test-spin. It certainly was in good shape. Phil hadn't been on the inside of this sort of muscle tone in centuries, if ever. But there were things that wouldn't wait. "Do we know anything about the place?"

"The Crazy Horse?" Jimmy asked. "Let me see."

He closed his eyes and a minute later, opened them, looking under-nourished again. "Christ," he said. "Irina and Oskar are walking into a shit-storm."

"What sort of shit-storm, Jimmy?" said Ren. "Be precise."

"The Crazy Horse is on the same corner where Phil was killed, and there is a lot of documentation that links illegal gun sales to it. And other things. It's a place where . . ." He hesitated. "It's dangerous."

"We can't lose anyone else," said Ren. "Not even Irina."

"Ren—" Phil put his hand on her knee, but she shook her head.

"You said our work was almost never dangerous, remember? But in the three years I've known you, you and Irina and Ramon have all died, and now Matsu needs a new Second too."

"My death," Ramon interrupted, "was not—"

"Not my point," Ren told him. "Phil was shot. Irina was shot. And now she and Oskar are walking into a situation that Jimmy—Jimmy!—just referred to as 'a shit-storm,' so maybe you're okay with all these deaths and stubs and spikes, but I'm not."

"Neither are we, Ren," Ramon said. "The world is in flux."

"I know," Ren said. "But why is it changing us, instead of us changing it?"

"Where is Sam!" Jane was on the edge of hysteria.

Jimmy blinked. "Oh, I'm sorry. Sam left a handwritten note for someone called Santi at the library, signing it 'Kelly.' He's at the Crazy Horse Saloon."

"The shit-storm one?" Jane was on her feet. "Why aren't we going there already?"

"Because," said Ren, her voice even, "we don't know what would help, and what would make things worse. If we go in there and take a wrong step, we could lose Sam, and Irina, and Oskar."

"But we have to do something!" Jane glared at Phil like she had a thundercloud for a hat.

Ren looked lightning straight back. "We *are* doing something." Ren put an arm around Jane. "This is what we do. I know it's frustrating, but it helps."

Still holding Jane, Ren took her phone from her jeans pocket and made a call. Phil watched her. This was a different Ren, a new Ren.

"Oskar," she said. "Are you in the bar, yet? Good. No, no. You're just where you should be. I—Oskar, shut up for a moment, please? Now, do you think you can go in there and manage to keep anyone from shooting anyone for an hour? We're on our way to you. Yes, an hour. I know it's a long time to . . . yeah, that's right. Okay, see you soon."

She disconnected. "All right," she said. "Jimmy, can you gather all the switches you can find for Sam? I've collected some, and Phil has too, but you're faster than both of us, and you'll find things we missed."

Jimmy nodded. "I can do that."

"Ramon," Ren continued, "can you explain meddling and switches to Daniel?"

"Of course."

Ren sat back down next to him and Phil put an arm around her narrow, strong shoulders. He liked this Ren. Maybe more, if that was possible. "What do you need me to do?" he said into her hair.

"You?" She put the tip of her index finger to a spot on his face between the edge of his mouth and his cheek, and the wistful squint of her eyes made Phil's heart flutter. Then she smiled. "You finish your pasta."

TWENTY-FOUR

No Sun to Reflect Off the Barrel

No carnival of police lights greeted Irina as she turned onto Valencia, and the streets weren't dark enough to hide black-painted vans, so no matter what was happening at Sam's house, and whether Frio or Jack was to blame for it, no one had sent anything this way yet. Still, it wasn't confidence as much as a kind of panic-fed hope that propelled Irina through the door of the Crazy Horse and halfway to where Santi of the strong left hook was standing. No longer slouched on a barstool, he was coiled, almost crouched next to it. Irina rubbed what remained of the bruise he had left on her jaw.

And that's where the obviousness that Santi would know where either Frio or Sam was, and could be convinced to abandon his post before the SWAT team came here next, vanished. It left Irina like Wile E. Coyote, who can run fifty feet out from a cliff on thin air, until he looks at the camera. Irina stopped walking. Santi didn't relax, but at least he kept that one hand behind his back instead of bringing the pistol out. Because of course he had a pistol in the waistband of his jeans. Irina put a hand out for the bar, reached for a stool.

Santi came over to her, standing too close. His hand—his gun hand, gunless—was on Irina's arm, above the elbow, barrel-hard and bullet-cold.

He smelled of beer and itchy anxiety. He was going to tell Irina to fuck off. Everyone was always telling her that.

Irina sat down. She needed a drink. "The SWAT team is at Sam Kelly's house," she said, but she kept her voice low.

"Fuck." Santi pulled the one vowel into four, and sat beside her.

"We need to warn him."

Santi shook his head and patted the bar the way you tap your leg to make a dog come. The perfectly rectangular man behind it cocked his chin, and Santi held up two fingers, like Winnie's V-for-victory, only with the thumb facing in at his chest.

"Do you know where Sam is?" Irina whispered.

Santi gave her the "damn, you're stupid, bitch" look, but he didn't say anything.

The bartender put two cans of beer in front of them.

"Glass of Jack?" Irina asked, and he turned his back without answering.

Santi drank his beer and Irina watched the brick-shaped barman to see if he maybe didn't understand English or didn't think ladies should drink liquor, but he pulled a bottle down from the wall and poured.

"Fuck," Santi said again, shaking his head. "We saw the SWAT call-up code on the scanner." He shrugged his arms onto the bar. "They don't give target location over the air." His elbows held up his shoulders. He was exhausted too. She hadn't noticed it before. Sloppy, Irina.

"So Sam told you I was one of the good guys?" Irina didn't look at Santi. They both watched their beers, but she felt him nod. She poured the first third of her beer down her throat. It wasn't terrible, certainly not American, and so cold the can burned her hand. The bartender put her whiskey down and, on some invisible signal from Santi, ambled away.

"You always watch the scanners?" she asked.

Santi drank beer.

Okay. Too direct.

"Aren't all the police frequencies out here trunked?"

Santi grunted, but with less pointed derision. "Yeah."

Irina waited.

"*Tucson Sentinel* has a web page of 'em, but most you can't hear. We got the raw transmit frequency coming straight outta one of the SWAT trucks. Don't tell us much."

But it'd be enough to give them some warning if TPD headed their way. Irina finished the beer, pushed the can back, and pulled the glass to her. She would have told the bartender ice, if he had asked, but she was glad for the relative warmth. "You don't know where Sam is." Irina worked to keep the question out of her voice, but didn't quite pull it off. Santi's grunt was un-nuanced and starting to lose its charm.

"And you haven't seen Frio all day," she tried again.

"What do you know about that?"

Irina knew a lot, but she wasn't telling. She shrugged. Santi was too loyal to believe her word if she spoke against his friend, but she could feel his questions burning him. Frio had been expected and his absence noticed. Irina gave Santi a suggestive smile. "He was with me."

Santi's new grunt suggested admiration.

Irina put her empty glass down. Santi didn't know where Sam or Frio were and he had the scanner to give him and the Hourlies enough warning to get away. Irina finished off the Jack and stood.

But Santi's hand was at the small of his back again, his weariness gone. The two guys in the back were on their feet, and behind them, Irina caught a flick of red—an Angry Birds T-shirt. The little kid from the bodega, the older one who'd bought Oreos and cat food, was back there too. Santi looked past Irina, reached for her wrist and pulled her next to him. She turned around.

"Irina," Oskar said, walking into the Crazy Horse like it made sense for a six-foot-tall blond of aristocratic bearing to stop in there for beer. Irina thought his weird Oskar-sense seemed to take in the rectangle-man behind the bar, Santi, the two kids in the back, probably even the Oreo kid without ever looking anywhere but at her. He wore his wariness like a cowl.

It was sweet of him, really. Oskar, of all people, to come after her. But his power, obvious in everything from his complexion and height, to his good shoes and the way he kept walking toward her, was all wrong for Irina's operation. "Fuck off, Oskar," she suggested.

Santi stepped around her. "Who're you?" he asked Oskar.

"A friend of Sam's." Oskar's focus slid from Irina's face to Santi's. For a hothead, Oskar moved with the eerie deliberation of a bomb squad.

"Oskar," Irina said in a bright smile, "meet Santi, Sam's best lieutenant." The compliment worked; Santi straightened fractionally. It was too much to hope her gambit would bring his hand out to shake. "Santi, this is Oskar." Irina wished she could explain Oskar as "my jealous boyfriend" with maybe a guilty giggle, and get him out of there, but she'd just blown that by flaunting her night with Frio. "I was just leaving," Irina said, reaching into her bag to pay for the drinks.

"Not quite yet." Oskar was picking up exactly zero of Irina's cues. Or ignoring them. He probably couldn't even see the guy behind him—Irina had just noticed him herself—the blocky bartender, circling around the other side. From behind Oskar, he gestured at the Oreo kid to get out, leave through the back door.

Irina did not want to get shot again. Not for fucking Oskar. But there she was, putting her body up against his in a hug, betting Santi wouldn't shoot her just to drop Oskar. Not yet anyway. Not unless Oskar started talking. Everyone wants to shoot Oskar when he starts talking.

"I'd like to see Sam Kelly, please," Oskar told Santi over Irina's shoulder.

"Everyone would like to see Sam," Irina said brightly. "Let's go," she hissed in Oskar's ear.

"How you know Kelly?" Santi asked Oskar, so on alert Irina expected lights to start flashing. Surely Oskar was reading the flexion in Santi's biceps as the slipping of pistol from pants.

"Santi doesn't know where Sam is," Irina told Oskar, turning to face Santi, pushing Oskar backward with her ass.

"Sam's here, in this bar," Oskar said. "Jimmy told Ren."

"Obviously not." Irina tried to catch Santi's eyes, but he was looking over her shoulder at Oskar. Who was not fucking moving, no matter how Irina shoved at him. The bartender wouldn't shoot them from behind without some sign from Santi. If Irina read it fast enough, maybe she could drag Oskar down in time.

"Santi—" Oskar was using his reasonable voice. "It's Santi, right?" Oskar shifted Irina from in front of him to beside him, her back to the bar.

"Yeah," Santi said, like he was deciding whether to hate Oskar for his size and beauty, or for his arrogance and stupidity.

"You know Frio, right?" Oskar did something with his shoulders, and sat on a barstool. He looked calm, not meek, not even humble, but somehow, Santi was ready to listen.

"Yeah," Santi said.

Oskar could not go there. He was a stranger—a gorgeous, white, rich, tall stranger—coming into their bar to call out one of their own as the worst kind of wicked. As a traitor. They would shoot him and Irina both.

"Oskar," she began, but he just kept going, like a bulldozer, like a SWAT tank.

"Frio's smart, right?" Oskar asked, but he didn't wait for Santi to answer. He rolled on like caissons, like Throwbots. "He's tactical," Oskar said. "And he's a stone-cold fucking killer if he needs to be." Oskar didn't add "right" again, but he waited a second, his eyes on Santi's. Santi was with him. Irina was too. But where the fuck was he going? "If you were Frio," Oskar went on, "and you wanted to hide Sam, if Sam was in real trouble, where would you take him?"

Santi hunkered down, shifting from *Ready* to *Set*. "Why?" he asked Oskar.

Sweet suckling Satan, Santi knew the answer. If Jimmy was right, and he almost always was, if Sam was actually here, Santi had just figured out where; Irina saw it in the way the pinky and ring finger of his right hand curled. Had Oskar noticed?

No. Oskar was watching for something else, reading Santi's face for what his "why" meant. Was it "why does Oskar want to know" or "why would Frio be hiding Sam"? And Irina knew Oskar was right to study it. Determining which question Santi was asking and answering it right would make the difference between getting shot, and getting the truth out of Santi.

Irina really did not want to get shot.

Also, she didn't want Oskar getting shot. He had come after her. He was here, taking risks with her, because maybe, after all, Oskar trusted her the way Phil did. Maybe more than any other Incrementalist, Oskar understood there was only this one world they all had to keep coming back to. And it was only each other left here waiting. That was why Irina had taken the spike all those hundreds of years ago. That was why she joined up with all this madness in the first place—to be a part of something forever. To have people, the same people, with her. She'd lost so many.

The Incrementalists were hers and she was theirs and she stood by them. You stand by your people. That's what you do. Even if they're wrong. Celeste had been wrong—hell, Celeste had been crazy and mean *and* wrong—and Irina had stood by her. Irina had let fucking Phil fucking shoot her rather than betray Celeste's plan to them. And Santi, she recognized, would shoot them all before he gave up Sam. That was the wildness burning in his teeth. Loyalty. Same as her.

"Don't tell us," Irina said. "Send someone to ask Sam if he wants to see us. We'll wait."

Santi's steady glare flickered. Irina pushed it. "Or we can leave," she promised. "Oskar and I will walk out the door right now if you tell us. But I think Sam would want to know we're here." Irina almost had him. "Oskar and I want to do whatever Sam wants us to."

"She's right," Oskar said, and Irina wanted to hug him.

"We work for Sam too," she said.

Santi spoke over his shoulder in a patter of staccato Spanish, and Irina saw the red of the Angry Birds move from one side of the back hall to the other—out of the bathroom and into some other shadow. She waited, listening to the trudge of the kid's big sneakers on the stairs, only a couple of steps, fading into the quiet of distance.

Irina waited, hearing only silence from below, then the flat snap of gunfire.

★　★　★

While Jimmy grazed and Phil ate, Ren tried to be as much of a comfort to Jane as Jane had been in the hospital waiting room, with about as much success. So when Jimmy opened his eyes and announced he'd seeded Sam's switches as a set of halberds in his armory, Ren suggested he enlist Jane in the work of cooking up switches while she and Phil grazed. Having something to do for Sam would help Jane, even if it didn't do a thing for Sam. Jimmy would warm up with someone to radiate upon and Jane could certainly use the affection.

Ren closed her eyes, and from the gooey vastness of her Garden, filtered away everything that wasn't Jimmy in Tucson today. His armory blossomed around her in the exuberant fronds and stalks of a Cotswold cottage garden. Ren strolled moss-grouted cobbles through sunbeams bright with dew and the whir of bees to a bushy stand of pure white foxgloves. She put her face close to the topmost bloom and sniffed. The scent was springtime and powdered honey, but didn't tell her anything. She sniffed again, and breathed in hot chocolate steam through a nose still frozen from the ski slopes. The switch wasn't quite the smell but the sensation—the enveloping, slightly intrusive warmth, sweet and stinging. Sam's switch for "home."

She saw the pastel clouds and sky on the cover of Frankl's book as the mingled blue and white of longing.

She tasted hubris in warm *sake* mugs, Sam drinking too much "tea" before his first sushi dinner, and ending up flushed and giddy when he had wanted to be impressive on his first date with Jane.

Line-dried beach towels smelling of sun and ocean prickled Ren's cheek with independence. She heard friendship as a twenty-sided die on a vinyl tabletop. The intimate press of Jane's spine against Sam's side as he lay on his back was a switch for something deeper than joy or peace. Ren recognized the sensation although she and Phil slept spooned on their sides, or back against back. If that switch ever shorted out in them like it had in Jane and Sam, Ren thought she'd probably be as willing as Sam was to take a new spike and leave the burnt circuit of love behind. Jesus. And Jane had volunteered him.

Ren didn't even try to keep the tears from running down her cheeks. Sam might make a better Incrementalist than she was. He'd been willing to give up on love and home in the name of justice and rebellion, and Ren wasn't even sure she'd taken the spike out of altruism. Sam thought the Hourlies had cost him Jane's love, but Ren knew it hadn't. Jane loved Sam enough to make the same sacrifice. But that was a countermeddle—trying to make things better by making them worse. They could do more good together. Ren might have become an Incrementalist out of some selfish,

Celeste-programmed desire to love Phil, but the world was better—albeit just incrementally—with their love in it.

Ren opened her eyes. Phil wasn't in the living room with her anymore, but she could see him and Jimmy with Jane and Daniel in the kitchen. Susi, now resting comfortably on Ren's feet, was also watching Phil. "What music did Sam listen to?" Jimmy was asking Jane. "Were there particular songs he associated with certain times or feelings? Did he have a road trip mix or one for working out?"

"He has playlists on his phone," Jane said.

"That won't help," Jimmy explained. "He won't have written the song titles. God, but I miss the cassette tape. Daniel, don't forget to keep those tissues directly in the smoke."

"Got it!" Daniel's cheerful voice sounded achingly young.

Phil chuckled and the sound, so very much Phil, felt warmer than matzo balls to Ren. She stood up.

"What?" Daniel asked Phil.

"The irony, is all. For the first time in, I don't know, fifty years? we could really use Matt. And he just arranged for himself not to be here."

"I—" Daniel, still catching the smell of marijuana in a Kleenex, cleared his throat. "I could—" he said, and Ren found she couldn't blame Kate for thinking he would have made a good Second for Phil. They had the same, long-boned grace of horses—no, colts. She smiled at him as she walked into the kitchen.

"It doesn't work like that," Phil told Daniel. "I am me again right away, more or less, in Matsu's body because Matsu was an Incrementalist, right?" He looked at Jimmy, who nodded.

"Has anyone started on the hot chocolate?" Ren asked. "I thought I'd use the Starbucks cup you made for that health care meddlework," she told Phil. It was an elegant bit of engineering that concealed a chemical heating pad in the cup and had a small atomizer nozzle in the lid, with an air bladder glued into the hollow at the bottom.

"But we do need Matsu back," Ramon said from the table where he was alphabetizing Phil's Tupperware of perfume samples. "He is our pattern shaman. And I'm worried the way he went into stub may make his less stable. I'd like to get him spiked into a new Second quickly. And no matter what Irina says—and I do think she makes some excellent points—we really can't spike Matsu into Sam's body. He's in poor physical condition and well past the age—"

Jane glared at him over the table. "You can't have him." A slow wave went through her rigid body and she softened. "I changed my mind, I guess," she said, mostly to Ren.

Phil caught Ren's eye, but she shrugged. She hadn't done anything to meddle Jane into fierceness for Sam. The danger he was in had made her that way. Ren understood the feeling.

"I meant no offense," Ramon said. "Matsu is a fighter, which is another reason why we could use him right now, but even if we started the ritual this minute, he couldn't get to the bar in time to do any good."

"Is there anything I can do that would help?" Daniel stood rigid as a tent pole.

Jimmy turned to him with a grunt that was half laugh. "Well, if seeing how the sausage gets made hasn't dissuaded you—"

"No," Daniel said. "It's even cooler than Kate made it sound."

"I'll call Kate again," Ramon said, and stepped onto the patio with his phone.

★　　★　　★

Sunday nights were always a bit of a panic at Kate's house—she knew they shouldn't be, but there you are—so when the phone rang at almost midnight, and a young woman identified herself as Ramon, it took Kate a minute to make sense of it all, even though she'd talked to Ramon in his new Second just that morning.

"How's our patient?" she asked.

"Patient?" Ramon repeated, which made Kate feel better about her own confusion. "Oh, Frio, yes. He's fine, I think. Or he should be, physically."

"You know it's almost midnight here, right?" Kate asked, hoping this wasn't another medical emergency. Homewrecker's sister had called half an hour ago, and he was upstairs packing for the drive back to Maine, back to his mom's bedside. Kate hadn't even needed to suggest it this time. Now he understood.

"Yes, I know," Ramon said. "I'm sorry. I wouldn't call if it weren't important."

"I know that about you." Kate poured herself half a glass of B&B one-handed, missing the kind of heavy, curly-corded phones you could hold between your ear and shoulder. "What can I do?"

"We have had some unusual developments here." Ramon cleared his new throat like his old one, and it sounded weird. "Phil's stub is now in Matsu, and Matsu is in stub."

"Holy cow," Kate said. She'd been headed upstairs, but turned right back around. "Good gracious. Okay, how did that happen? How's Phil?"

"He seems fine."

"Thank god." Kate topped off her snifter. "Tell him I said, 'How's the head?'"

"Yes, of course. Kate, Matsu's transition into stub absent the physical death of his Second raises some concerns about how fully integrated Phil can be while Matsu remains in stub."

"Really?" Kate said, stopping halfway up the stairs again. Wrecker was packing in the bedroom; she'd be in his way, and he in hers. "You're worried about that?" she asked Ramon. "You? With your purely computational theory of mind?"

"We have all agreed it would be best to have Matsu back as quickly as possible, and since Daniel's here and willing, I—"

"Wait. What?" Kate sat down on the steps. "Daniel's in Tucson? With Ren?"

"Yes."

"When did he . . . How . . . That little bugger." Kate sat down on the step. "He got their address from the memory I was trying to bore him with."

"Kate?"

"So he's there. And Phil doesn't need a Second. Matsu does. So you're phoning because you want to spike Matsu into Dan?"

"That's right."

"Tonight? With no dust ritual for Matsu, and not even a post to the forum."

"We feel the circumstances warrant—"

Kate's mind spun. Daniel was too young, and Matsu needed an athlete's body. Daniel might have permanent nerve damage in his right leg from the fire. He needed several more grafts, and Matsu won't thank anyone for signing him up for that. But—

Kate didn't have two husbands because she was greedy. She wasn't hoarding men, she just . . . she had liked having Daniel around.

"Kate?" Wrecker stood in the doorway to the den with his leather overnight bag and a face like a sinkhole. "Mom died."

Kate had just a tiny moment of not wanting to put the phone down.

"I have to go," she told Ramon. "Do what you need to."

TWENTY-FIVE

Alter the Entire Political Landscape

Oskar had promised Ren nobody would get shot. Now he was running toward the sound of gunfire, down the back stairs of the Crazy Horse Saloon. The stairs weren't entirely happy with his weight, but they held, and Oskar descended into a basement that was moldy and sweaty, full of pallets loaded with liquor boxes. Frio sat, leaning against a stack of Canadian Club, holding his leg, a 9 mm in his hand. There was a pool of blood beneath him, and blood on his other hand where he held the leg. Sam faced him, standing three feet away, slightly hunched over, arms a little in front of him, eyes wide. They both turned as Oskar and Irina came down the stairs, and Frio pointed the pistol at Oskar one-handed, but kept his finger off the trigger. Oskar stopped, trapping Irina behind him.

"You have to help him!" Sam stammered, looking from Oskar to Irina. "It's my fault." Sam staggered and sat down. "It's my fault again."

"Where's your weapon, Sam?" Irina's voice was shockingly calm for someone whose most recent Second had been shot to death.

"He didn't shoot me." Frio kept the pistol steady. "It's just a ricochet."

"So it's not bleeding?"

"It was my fault," Sam said again.

Oskar found self-flagellation repulsive. He turned back to Frio. "You were aiming for Sam?"

"If I'd been aiming, he'd be dead."

Oskar remembered the grouping—three shots directly through the heart from behind. Frio wasn't bragging.

I know Phil recorded feeling the first one in the back of his neck, but that isn't where they hit. I can't explain it.

—Oskar

"Frio, baby." Irina pitched her voice somewhere between Mae West and Cleopatra. "Let us help you?"

Frio grunted and lowered the piece. Irina slithered around Oskar to kneel at Frio's side.

"Any danger that cops will respond to a 'shots fired' call and complicate things?" Oskar came the rest of the way down the stairs.

Frio shook his head. "Not down here," he said. "They want us killing our own."

"Except you're one of theirs." Irina kept her voice gentle. It was almost a question.

Frio closed his eyes. "Not for a long time I'm not."

"Friday wasn't exactly ancient history."

Frio raised his eyebrows without opening his eyes. "Feels like it."

Irina managed a chuckle. It was gruff, but better than Oskar could have done. She was a calculating and manipulative player, but she was good at her game.

"I hear that," Irina said. "Time to put the gun down, Frio."

"Ah hell no," Frio said, but he thumbed the safety back on. "Power is power, Irina. I'll set my gun down when you put your credit cards and education on the floor." He stuck the gun into the waistband of his jeans, grimacing with the pain it caused him. "But I'll put mine where you can't see it, which is more than you'll do for me."

★   ★   ★

Phil ignored remarks about how disorganized his closet full of switch-making materials was. He didn't ignore Ren, working next to him, feeling close and distant, happy and pensive, and above all, as frustrated as he was that there was no time for just them—for welcome back, for touching and talking and being. She was worried about something, and there was no time to reassure her, or to consider if her worry was justified.

"I've spoken with Kate." Ramon's voice was expressionless. "Shall Daniel and I leave you to work?"

Only Daniel missed what he meant. "What? No. I like seeing how it all gets done." Then he went quiet. Then pale. He understood. "Matsu's stub."

Phil caught Daniel's eye and nodded to him. He had the look Phil had seen all around him before the second assault on Vicksburg from those who were determined to go forward and didn't expect to return alive. It brought him back; there was a coldness, and a distance. It wasn't like watching yourself act, it was more like a heightened consciousness of everything else—every breath, the complex action of mouth and throat when you swallow, even the movement of your eyes. It's all realer than real; the moments of courage, if there were any, came before or after.

Daniel returned Phil's nod, and followed Ramon into the guest room.

Jimmy was ready first, and Phil could feel his impatience in his stillness; Jimmy was never impatient. Phil frowned. Since when had he been so conscious of people's feelings? What was—

No. Not now. Now, focus on Sam.

For a rushed bit of half-assed meddlework, Phil was pleased to have found a couple of switches he could use for his part. He had no idea about everyone else, and couldn't afford the attention. *You have one job, Phil; let them worry about their pieces.*

They were ready. Jimmy drove, Jane in the front seat next to him, and Phil paid no attention to the route they took, and didn't remember the drive.

Ren turned to him, and Phil saw the way her eyes corrected for his new, larger body. They refocused affection and distance. "Phil?" she said in a way that was both a request and a promise.

"Yeah?"

"What happened while you were in stub?"

"Nothing. Nothing ever happens while we're in stub."

"Okay. Then what happened when you were Henry Lattimer? Or when Henry became Carter, I guess. Oskar said it resonated with now."

That Second's life had ended over a hundred and fifty years ago, but felt closer to Phil than Chuck's. "Quite a lot," he said. "Now that you mention it."

"I need to know." Ren's voice was gentle but keen.

"Okay." He took her hand. "Where should I start?"

"I think that is actually the question, isn't it?" Ren said, looking at their interwoven fingers. "Where does it start?"

Not an easy question, that. Phil considered. "I suppose," he finally said, "it starts in Illinois."

"Illinois?"

"Yeah. In 1856."

★   ★   ★

Kate rolled out of bed, climbed into her warm, quilted bathrobe and zipped it up under her chin. Her left slipper was somewhere under the bed, or buried in the heap of dirty clothes, or out on its own hunting other rabbits, so Kate pulled on socks instead, and padded downstairs, leaving Wrecker sleeping. She didn't peek in on the girls, and she didn't turn on the lights in the kitchen.

Kate Donnally was a nationally recognized specialist in pediatric endocrinology. She ran a thriving private practice, and donated her time and expertise in two inner-city clinics. She had published in *The Lancet,* and served as children's health adviser to the Governor of Pennsylvania, but a sink full of unwashed dishes could still make her feel like she'd flunked adulthood. She considered throwing herself into cleaning the kitchen but navigated it in the dark instead, and dug her emergency pint of Ben & Jerry's out of the econo bag of frozen green beans.

She'd been prickly since her call with Ramon, restless with the same kind of manic, quick-burn, quick-crash energy you get from high fructose corn syrup. HFCS and sleep deprivation both fuel rash decisions, promote poor emotional control, and contribute to risk-taking behavior. Kate was safer with ice cream. Besides, physical activity increases wakefulness, and she did want to sleep eventually. She had to work in the morning.

Kate settled with her laptop on the sofa in the den, but there wasn't much news on the forum, and an idea had lodged in the back of her mind like food between teeth. Ramon was in such a rush to get his Matsu stub spiked into her Daniel that he wouldn't wait for her to get there. He wouldn't even hold a dust ritual.

Kate wasn't sure whether her sudden, late-night decision to schedule an impromptu one herself was reckless defiance or outraged propriety. Either way, she knew it excited her, and focused her fidgets. Kate posted to the forum that she would hold a dust ritual for Matsu in the privacy of her own Garden in fifteen minutes, and that anyone who wanted to was welcome to come by for tea. Then she ate up most of her ice cream, and closed her eyes.

When Wrecker had spiked the stub of Lady Maud Pelham-Gambirnet into Kate's sturdy Midwestern mid-twenties body, she had opened her eyes to the obligatory deafening headache, and the apparently nonstandard certainty that she, Kate Donnally, wasn't going anywhere. They had made love then, for the first time, Wrecker and Kate, in the whoosh of memories from Lady Maud's seventy years, and ever since, every time she tried to remember something from Maud's lifetime, Kate got a little turned on. Even now, annoyed and overtired, the excitement of a mouth not her husband's, and the memory of bespoke Chanel gave Kate a shiver.

Still, she'd always felt a touch guilty too, about Maud shading, even though Wrecker must have told her a zillion times that Maud was tired and jaded and not particularly keen for "another time about on this mad carousel," and so Kate had given Maud's memories a special spot in her Garden.

The pox itch and dog smell faded as she hurried through the sitting room into the crafts area. It was so organized! When everything in Kate's life, and certainly everything in her Pennsylvania house was always a bit of a jumble, the craft room of her Garden was all tidy drawers and orderly bins. Sometimes, she would just wander around it opening things and marveling how every last little thing had its own place. And it stayed there. Life without kids, maybe.

But tonight, Kate was on a mission. Lady Maud had met Matsu only once, in Hawaii in 1983, when she was fifty and newly divorced. He was a consulting martial arts expert to a film being shot in the "jungle." They had set up a meeting as Incrementalists always will when they have a chance to see someone's new Second, but they had bonded more as foreigners—he from Japan, she born in South Rhodesia—than as immortal do-gooders. They had gotten on so well! And yes, Lady Maud would confess it, Duckie, she had quite enjoyed the second glances sliding their way, peeking at the older, wealthy white British lady dining with the young, lithe, muscular Asian man, so that yes, she had maybe had the tiniest tad too much to drink. They had arranged a second meeting; Lady Maud had something private to ask Matsu.

It was that second meeting—a Baccarat crystal champagne coupe taken from the glass-fronted china cabinet that held all Maud's seeds—that Kate retrieved and placed as a WORLD'S BEST MOM mug onto the tea table in the sitting room of her Garden. Maud had seeded it for safekeeping, not putting a pointer to it on her stable door, so Kate knew it was a memory no one else would have seen. Nor likely would anyone now, what with the late hour and the short notice. Which suited Kate just fine, if she were really to tell the truth.

Kate opened her eyes, checked the time, and wondered whether anyone would show up to help her dust Matsu, even with so little notice, even though he was probably already on his way back out of stub, but she didn't care. She loved. She picked chocolate-covered bits out of the ice cream and didn't check the boards again. At quarter to one in the morning, she closed her eyes, and drank up Maud's secret seed.

★   ★   ★

As Jimmy drove, Ren navigated back to the cottage flower beds that were Jimmy's Garden as represented in hers while Phil collected his seeds from Illinois. Jimmy had added the fresh blades of Frio's seeds to his castle armory, which sprouted by Sam's white foxgloves as three new red-tinged flower spikes. She twisted a bloom from the closest spray and caught a whiff of something wrong. The smell got stronger as she broke off more of the trumpet-shaped flowers until the stalk was stripped to raw green. The blooms overfilled Ren's hands, spilling onto curled fern heads, and the stink of industrial disinfectant burned her eyes. The chemical smell only mostly masked urine and cheap hamburger meat, and Ren knew what confidence smelled like to Frio.

New buds sprang from the stalk, stoppering the smell. Grateful, Ren reached for the next, but saw something shimmering in the empty space between the flower and stem. As she fleeced more flowers, the void shivered darker, more vivid, into an opaque and brilliant fuchsia. To Frio, this was the color of rage—the deep purple-pink of his mother's blouse the last time he'd seen her. His anger was vibrant and material, tinged with sensuality and despair, a wicked butterfly that stayed, wings pulsing, even when the flowers regrew and the shimmer faded.

A springtime sun shone a lazy peach yellow, but Ren had only ten minutes to graze, and she had only two of Frio's switches, and nothing at all of what Phil had seeded about Illinois in the 1850s. Her Garden was maddeningly slow, and she needed more than just ways of triggering feelings in Sam and Frio. She needed context and understanding. She needed empathy. Frio still didn't make sense to her.

She followed the anger plant down to its roots and stuck her fingers in cool, wet dirt, so different from the ground in Tucson or in Phoenix. This was soil that wanted things to grow, that nourished and fostered, that had water to spare. Careful not to break any of the muddy tendrils, Ren got her fingers around the top of the foxglove's root ball.

Frio had grown up in jail, juvie, a concrete box of echoing metal and shouted commands.

His father died overseas in uniform—not military: private contractor.

His mom had been deported. She was illegal. Back to Guatemala. You break the rules, you get caught, your kid suffers. Rage.

Stripping flowers from another stalk, Ren tasted Good & Plenty candy in the big boxes from the movie theater. Frio had paid for himself and watched *Batman Begins* alone. Licorice was the taste of pride, but he only ate the white ones.

"Jimmy," she said. "We need to stop at a convenience store. We need licorice."

"All right," he said.

"Good catch," said Phil after a pause long enough for him to have checked his Garden. "I'll run in and get it. You keep grazing."

When Ren opened her eyes, Phil, next to her in the backseat, in Matsu's powerful warrior's body, closed a silent hand over hers. "About fifteen minutes," he said.

Ren nodded and closed her eyes. "Phil," she said to her Garden with her mind's mouth. "Today, here."

And there they were, the memories Phil had seeded as flowerpots—everything he thought she should know about where he'd been while his stub was lost in the Garden—in her hands as a convoluted corkscrew of braided wool.

She unwound the coil and knew Phil believed he'd fucked up in Kansas.

"Ren," Phil said. "We're here."

"Okay." Ren wove her fingers into the tangle, and felt it loop and twist. "Just a second." There was no time to pick apart all the knots or map them, to tease open thread from yarn, it would have to be enough to hold them all and love him, every snarl and involution.

The car door opened and Ren opened her eyes knowing Phil had been wrong about Brown and the South. Wrong about Abolition and war. And being wrong made you afraid to do things; he'd said as much about Cambodia, about the scars and doubt. He'd had to accept it. But Celeste had meddled him into attempting something he couldn't accept, into being something his nature had revolted against. And he still didn't know whether his courage had failed or his character hadn't.

Ren would have to find a way to make that better.

"I'm ready," she said, getting out of the car.

"Okay." Phil took her hand and strode toward the dingy bar on Matsu's long legs. "What do we do now?" he asked her.

"Now," Ren said, "we do what we do. And it fixes everything."

TWENTY-SIX

Bigger Thoughts, Bigger Plans

Phil felt like they were in act three of an action movie, where all the tough guys walk into the bad guys' stronghold to kick ass. Unfortunately, the only one of them capable of kicking anything tougher than an empty Coke can was in stub. He checked again for his switches, suddenly afraid he'd forgotten them. He always had that moment. But then, showing up ready to do the meddlework and realizing the things you need are still sitting next to the kitchen sink only has to happen a couple of times to make you want to be sure not to do it again.

Jimmy was the first one through the door, then Jane, then Phil, then Ren. Back in the day, pirates used to wear a patch over one eye, so they could swap it to the other eye when going belowdecks, thus saving time for vision to adjust. Or, at least, that's what Phil had been told; he was never a pirate. The point is, he wished he'd had one as he stepped into that bar; it was awfully damned dark.

There was no sign of Irina or Oskar; Jimmy went up to the fat man behind the bar and they had a quiet conversation. It went on for a while, but Phil knew Jimmy; in the three steps up to the bar, he'd had time to graze, and that was all he needed, because he was Jimmy.

The bartender gestured with his head toward the back, Jimmy nodded, and went that way. Phil and Ren followed. The sign on the door said EMPLOYEES ONLY, which Phil liked, because it didn't say Team Members. It was unlocked, and opened to a landing with a mop and a bucket and cleaning supplies, and a stairway down. The stairs were wood and didn't look all that stable. The light was no better than in the bar, but at least they could see. Jimmy hesitated at the top of the stairs, then shrugged and went down.

They found everyone in the basement. Irina squatted next to Frio, pressing a spot high on his left leg. There was a lot of blood, and Frio didn't look happy. Oskar stood next to them. A little apart was Sam, sitting on the floor, sobbing into his hands. As Phil and the gang came down the stairs, Sam looked up and said, "Jane?" putting a whole universe of hope and hopelessness into the word.

"Hey there," Phil said. "We're the cavalry. Who needs rescuing?"

Frio grimaced. "Who the fuck are you?"

"My name is Phil. Last time we met, you shot me three times. How do you do?"

"Yeah, sorry."

"What happened? Sam put it together? Figured out you were a cop?" Phil asked him.

Frio nodded. "He tried to hit me, I pulled on him. He hit me again, and my gun went off. I caught a ricochet."

Jane had her arms around Sam, who was pretty much breaking down. Oskar stood watching and not moving. Irina was concentrating on keeping pressure on Frio's leg.

"So," Phil said. "Want me to take a look at your leg?"

Frio shrugged, and Phil, walking up to him as if there were no gun within reach of his hand, couldn't help thinking how pissed off Matt would be if he got this beautiful body killed in less than a day.

★   ★   ★

Watching Phil come down the basement stairs in Matsu's body reminded Irina of her late-1980s' attempt to learn Italian by watching overdubbed American movies. It was Phil, same as it had been Alec Baldwin, but

Matsu's beauty was as out of place as the deeper, embellished Italian coming out of Baldwin's mouth had been. Phil squatted in front of Frio, hands relaxed. He didn't spare a glance for her, kneeling on the cold concrete, or for Oskar, glowering over them all.

Frio didn't move, but something about him contracted and braced. Irina imagined an invisible carapace clicking into place over his body as Jimmy ushered Ren around them to Sam and Jane.

"You're a law-and-order man," Phil remarked, and waited for Frio's nod. He nodded himself. "Why'd you shoot me?"

"I shot Chuck Purcell."

"Come on, Frio. You've had all this explained to you," said Phil. His fingers were cold on Irina's hand, but she let him move it to peer at Frio's injury. "You didn't have orders to kill me. Why'd you do it?"

"To keep TPD off Sam."

Phil frowned, puzzled. "How does that work?"

Frio snorted a laugh. "It didn't."

"No," Phil agreed. "Seems SWAT's over at Sam's house now."

Frio shrugged, and Irina decided he already knew about the raid and felt as betrayed by it as she did. Interesting. She wondered why.

"What you told my friends about the Jose Guerena raid and the kid with the bad test grade, that was all true," Phil said, and Irina could hear the anger under his Good Guy Meddlework voice. "You'll have to get that stitched." He returned Irina's hand with a glance that told her to keep the pressure up. "But you managed to miss any of the dangerous bits." Irina wondered how much he'd armed himself with—switches and background on the man who'd shot him. Phil settled himself on the ground and went on, conversationally. "You're no fan of the cops. Not anymore. You tried to quit, but your boss had gotten his tires slashed the morning you went in with your resignation letter, hadn't he?"

Frio grunted, letting his eyes slide closed, but not relaxing at all. His cheekbones, always hard and prominent, stuck out harshly from his gaunt face, and Irina wondered how long it'd been since he'd eaten. Or since she had.

"That pissed you off," Phil continued. "SWAT might be fucked, but that doesn't mean gangbangers and junkies should be allowed to do what they want. You went undercover to catch the little shits who'd been nipping at the heels of Arizona lawmen for way too long. Then what happened?"

Frio's eyes flicked open and searched, landing on Sam's face where he sat with Jane, Ren, and Jimmy.

Phil caught it. "Then you met Sam."

Frio locked his gaze onto Phil's face and Irina could see him wondering how much Phil knew, and how much he was just feeling his way. He knew Phil had been in his head. Irina watched, trying to puzzle out the same thing. If what Phil said next was wrong, he'd never get Frio back. And they needed him back. Irina and Oskar exchanged a "here's hoping" look over Phil and Frio's heads.

"I knew a guy once," Phil said, crossing his legs. "Fellow named John Brown."

★   ★   ★

Ren had followed Jimmy and Phil down the stair into the tiny, dank storage cellar to find Frio looking like he'd just sat wherever he'd been standing. Irina knelt next to him, pale and haggard, holding Oskar's shirt to Frio's bleeding leg. Oskar stood over them both with a predatory closeness. Jailor or bodyguard, he was ready to kill Irina, or to die for her, Ren couldn't tell which. Probably both.

"Want me to take a look at your leg?" Phil had asked Frio, and she and Jimmy had gone to talk to Sam and Jane.

"Sam, my friend!" Jimmy clapped a hand to Sam's neck in a manly cuff, and Ren pulled her eyes away from Phil. Jimmy gave Sam one of his brilliant, white-toothed smiles that made the rubies in his ears wink blood bright, even in the dim light. "So, Frio was still a cop after all. Undercover. How did you work it out?"

Jane had her arms around Sam, her chin resting on his head, and his hands, clutching her arm, were the only sign he had given that he knew anyone else was there. He looked at Jimmy with haunted eyes. "You knew?"

"No, no. Not until Phil spent some time in his head, and came back and told us. When did you?"

Sam wiped his face with one hand, and took a long, shuddering breath. "I work at the library during the summer," he said.

Jimmy nodded encouragingly, radiating approval of libraries, and work, and summertime.

"There's a room there, an old community room, where the Hourlies meet. I was there today and Frio came in. I couldn't get him to make sense." Sam scrubbed at his nose with the knuckle of his thumb. "He looked like he'd been in a fight," Sam went on, "but he sounded like a Harry Potter story. Fire-eaters and ruffians, saying he had to talk to me in private. I told him no one but our people ever came in there, but that wasn't good enough for him. We had to get out of the library. 'Just til I get it figured' he kept saying." Sam heaved a dark sigh. "So I came here with him. Why wouldn't I? He was my friend. One of my successes." He snorted. "Hell, maybe my only success. I left a note for Santi, in case he came in early, and—"

Jimmy cut him off. "Once you were in the bar, did Frio tell you everything?"

Sam laughed too loudly and without humor. "He didn't tell me anything. But when he started unpacking shortwave radio gear and MREs from a Canadian Club box, I figured it out. I'm not such an idiot that I don't know a bug-out bag when I see one."

"And?"

"He wouldn't let me leave. I knew he wouldn't shoot me. Even when he pulled on me, telling me to back off, to have a seat. Then little kid feet were coming down the stairs, and all I could think was to get the gun away from Frio. It went off."

Sam took a shuddering breath, but he was involved enough in the narrative thread to keep at least some fraction of his analytical mind tethered, which was what Jimmy was working for. Planning is a leash on despair. You just have to collar it first.

"Go on," Jimmy prompted.

"I thought Frio had shot Manuel." Sam's voice was flat. "It would have been my fault. But Frio was bleeding and the kid was still standing there, shaking, staring at me. I don't know him, really. I'd just seen him around. Frio told him to leave, and he took off, and all I could think was how every good thing I've ever tried to do has always had some kind of terrible backlash. This was just one more colossal fuckup with me at the center of it."

"That's not true." Jane put her hand on Sam's arm.

"Isn't it?" Sam's voice was acid cold. Ren would hate it if Phil ever talked to her that way. "Name one wholly good thing I ever did."

"You married me?"

"And I did such a super job as your husband that you're ready to trade me in—to donate my body to these people." He jerked his thumb toward Phil and Irina, still sitting on the ground by Frio.

Phil had Matsu's athletic legs folded in Phil's long-shanked X shape, crossed at the ankles, knees in the circle of his arms. He was telling a story, if he were sitting like that, and a flood of relief tumbled over Ren that Phil had Matsu's body, not Sam's. Phil would have been as allergic to Sam's helpless despair as he'd been to his own blood on Frio's hands.

"Fellow named John Brown," Ren heard him say.

*　　*　　*

"Who?" Frio sat with his back against the filthy wall, legs sprawled in front of him, Irina's hand keeping pressure on his bleeding leg. Phil couldn't really mirror someone in that position. He didn't even try, just stayed sitting near him, making sure their eyes were at a level.

"Anti-slavery crusader, killed some folk, tried to incite a slave revolt, got hanged. I knew his son, Fred, better, but yeah, I knew Captain Brown, too. Tried to meddle with him." A chuckle came up from somewhere and Phil let it escape and do its work. "Failed utterly," he said. "But I tried."

Phil's next move was to reach into his back pocket and turn on the iPhone; but just as he was about to, he remembered Frio was a cop; seeing Phil reach for his back pocket would put him on alert, and give him all sorts of brain chemicals Phil didn't need him to have. Dammit, that's the sort of thing he would have thought of if they had had time to plan this properly. Maybe later he could hit the switch; for now he needed to move on.

"Anyway, yeah, Frederick Brown. Fred. Believed in what his father was doing, you know? I mean, believed that slavery was wrong, and that it would take violence to end it."

"Right on both counts," said Frio. "Is there a point here?"

"He was with his father at Dutch Henry's Crossing."

"Don't know that place."

"Pottawatomie Creek. Where they murdered a bunch of pro-slavery settlers."

Nothing from Frio.

"Fred couldn't take it. I mean, he was in favor, but not cut out to pull the trigger. Or swing the sword, in this case. It just wasn't in his character to kill."

"Yeah," said Frio. "Some people are like that."

"And these were, well, it wasn't like a fight, where things happen, and you're so busy trying to stay alive that you don't put it together until after. It was—"

"You've been there?"

"Yeah, I've been just about everywhere. Anyway, it drove poor Fred right off his rocker. People would see him wandering around, or running nowhere in particular, talking about how they'd never done the killings, or the killings were justified, or talking to the air. Just, you know, nuts."

Frio nodded. "Believed in the ideal, couldn't live in the reality."

"You've been there?"

Frio focused on Phil, his eyes narrowing.

"You shot me to protect Sam from the cops, while you were a cop," Phil said.

Frio looked at him, and Phil could see him weighing, deciding how much to tell. "Want a drink? I have a flask of whiskey," Phil said, and reached for his back pocket.

"No, thanks."

Phil flipped on the iPhone. It was so low he could barely hear it, and he doubted Frio was even aware of it, but Enrico Caruso's "Serenata" came on nevertheless, and he'd managed to turn it on without making Frio jumpy. In any case, the desert lavender cologne he was wearing would certainly be in the air by now.

So, yeah, Frio. Remember those times you and your friend Pete would sneak off to that empty lot filled with desert lavender? And remember afternoons with your mother's father, his scratchy old opera records going in the background? Remember how that felt? Well, no; it isn't what you're thinking about. But it's there, Frio. Good memories. From back before everything was so complicated. Back to when your mama used to say your legs were too short to get you where you wanted to go fast enough, when your papa's friends would call you Cerveza Floja *because of how you choked and coughed the first time you talked them into letting you have a sip of beer. I'm here, and I signify those memories. Trust me. Trust me.*

"You weren't under orders," Phil said. "You made the call to shoot me."

Nothing.

"Not an easy choice to make. You must have thought you were pulling the trigger for a pretty good reason," Phil went on.

Frio met Phil's eyes.

"Either the cops or the Hourlies had something big planned." Phil kept the question out of his voice.

"SWAT raid on the library. Tonight."

"And you thought Sam wouldn't get out of it alive."

"He might have," said Frio. "He's white."

"That was part of why you like him, isn't it? It made the whole organization safer. But that wasn't all, was it? You wanted to save him because you like him, and respect what he's doing. But it isn't just him. He's a symbol; it's everything he stands for."

Frio didn't answer.

Phil was silent a moment for the Caruso, the cologne. He helped himself to some licorice candy. Frio, almost unconsciously, did the same.

"You know damn well what they're doing in Maricopa County is wrong. And how much better is it here? It's a long way from what it should be, and you want to change it. You want to make it better."

"You don't fucking know—" Frio's forearm twitched, and the gun nestled into his palm, natural as silverware.

"Of course I know what you want," Phil said. "You want to be good. It's all you've ever wanted. Ever since your mama told you, 'I love you, Iro, be good,' when the ICE cops took her away."

Frio hissed, somewhere between shock and fury. Not the best place for the Focus to be, or anyone with a gun in his hand, but Phil might be able to use it, if Oskar would just keep his mouth shut. He looked to be grazing. Phil worked fast.

"It's why jail felt like freedom to you," he told Frio. "Jail taught you how to be good. The COs gave you the recipe, and didn't you follow it! You were so good you got out early and joined the good guys. Be a cop. Catch a robber.

"But the good guys turned out to be assholes. Cruel and arrogant, and mean as any kid you ever knew in the barrio. Then you found Sam, and he was good. A truly good man, with all the happiness and peace that accompanies virtue. But he had no chance. So you set yourself to protecting him. Because that's what cops do, right? Protect and serve?"

Oskar opened his eyes, but Frio transferred the gun to his left hand, and pressed his right hard against his bleeding thigh. Phil took that as a sign that he could continue without getting Matsu's body stubbed the same day he'd been spiked into it.

"You know the state doesn't get to sacrifice its citizens for its own security—not even for theirs." Phil talked to keep Oskar from helping. "Before that happens, the state should fall. The state, particularly this state, is corrupt and *should* fall. But you knew Sam and his tiny rebellions weren't going to topple it. Or even rock the boat. The masses aren't ready to rise, and the state has tanks and drones. Hell, so do the county and the town, even a few school districts, for the love of God.

"How did we let that happen? Who cares. It's too late. We have to accept it as reality. You knew that. You knew revolt would be suicide or martyrdom, and you weren't going to let Sam die."

How about that? Phil makes a long, impassioned, moralizing speech, and I agree with it. Most of it. I don't agree that it's too late, and I certainly don't think revolution is off the agenda, but he was still basically right, and that certainly wasn't the time to argue about the rest of it.

—*Oskar*

"So you shot me," said Phil. "Then what?"

"Sam gave up."

"And that kept him safe," Phil agreed. "But it didn't solve your problem." Phil waited for Frio to acknowledge how futile killing him had been, but Frio didn't move. "Then what?" Phil prompted.

"Then Irina found him," Oskar said.

Phil waited, letting the rest of it sort itself out. "Irina offered you a way to do more than the Hourlies could: take my stub and keep your job. Sam would go back to teaching, inspiring kids, giving them the revolutionary ideals you didn't have growing up. And you could involve yourself on their behalf from behind the scenes. Illegally serving and protecting the people whose rights are being destroyed by our new laws. It was a good plan."

"And it almost fucking killed me."

"Yeah," Phil said. "Me too.

Frio met Phil's eyes and Phil saw something break in him, just a little. "Then what happened, Frio?"

"You left me there like that. Maybe dead, maybe not."

Irina let out a ragged sob.

"That's true," Phil said.

"And when I didn't turn up for work, my boss searched my place."

"What did they find?"

"Hell if I know, but it was enough to send SWAT to Sam's." Frio sagged.

"Just what you'd killed me to prevent," Phil observed.

"Fuck you."

Phil looked from Frio to Oskar to Irina. "No," he said "Fuck them. We'll help."

★   ★   ★

"Sam?" Ren said gently, picking up the Starbucks cup. "Jane didn't try to trade you in. She thinks there's something in you that, in the right circumstance, could be heroic. She didn't want to be in the way."

"Jane?" The weight of hope in Sam's voice almost broke it. "Is that true?"

Ren shifted on the uncomfortable pallet with a cough that masked the sound of her thumb mashing into the bottom of the cup, atomizing heated cocoa steam.

"That's who you were when you met me," Jane said.

"I was an idealist when we met," Sam corrected her, but he took a deep breath, and sniffed.

"I know," Jane whispered. "It was pretty sexy."

"Embittered realist not so much?"

Jane shook her head and pushed the tears away.

"You don't love me anymore." Sam wasn't asking and Jane didn't answer. "I failed at everything I tried. It changed me."

Jane let go of Sam and wrapped her arms around herself.

Sam didn't look at her. "I got angry," he explained to Ren.

"Yeah," Ren agreed. "If only you could have accepted that high school kids were getting married just to stay in the country. If you could have made peace with people afraid to go to the doctor when they get sick, living like slaves in the land of the free, maybe if you hadn't tried to help them, they wouldn't be in jail, some of them, or deported. Maybe it would have been better just to say 'that's the way things are' and to leave them. It would certainly have been easier." Ren gave a dry cough and Jimmy handed her the sake-laced water.

Ren took a drink, and offered the bottle to Sam who took a long pull on the taste of misplaced pride.

"Maybe those kids would have been happier with no one taking risks for them," Ren said. "I don't think, if we asked them, that they'd say that, but you may know better."

Sam swallowed. "Maybe not," he said.

"Maybe Jane was right?"

"I don't know." Sam sounded hollow.

"You don't have to know," Jane said. "You have to hope."

"How can I?"

"Because things are getting better," Ren told him. "Over all. World-wide."

Sam opened his mouth, but Jane talked over him. "Sam won't believe that, Ren. He has no faith."

"I don't either," Ren said. "But I have history." She pushed the rigged coffee cup and water bottle out of her way and pinned Sam the Civics teacher with a stern eye. "Sam, when Celeste, my last Second, was re-cruited, judicial torture was legal and well-attended as sport. England had over two hundred capital crimes including defaulting on a loan and cutting down a tree. Slavery was legal in every nation on earth. Every one. Do you know how many places it's legal now? None. Do you know why? Because people's minds changed. They stopped accepting it."

Ren held up her hand to stop Sam's objections. "You'll say that our own country still tortures and executes, that human trafficking still ex-ists, and I'll say you're right. We're not done. But I have been flogged for kissing. I have been executed by impalement. I have been a slave.

"So yeah, you fucked things up. We do it all the time. It doesn't matter. What matters is you learn and you do better next time. And I do not care how trite that sounds. It is simple, pure, practical truth. Because people see what you do. People like Frio. And then they try too. And maybe they win where you lost. Maybe they fail too, but Sam, these little victories or failures, they aren't what make history. Or heroes."

"She's right, you know," Jane said, unwrapping her arms, but still not touching her husband. "Ren's right about Frio seeing what you do. He quit the police force because he wasn't going to keep being used by men who wanted other men dead, but couldn't bring themselves to be killers out of some kind of easy idealism and blind loyalty," Jane said.

"Almost quit."

"You changed him. He murdered Phil out of doubt-riddled realism and open-eyed loyalty."

"I can't feel good about that, Jane."

"But you know what?" Ren said, the idea surprising her. "I'm starting to." She looked across the basement again at Phil, who still looked like Matsu.

Phil said, "Revolt would be suicide or martyrdom, and you weren't going to let Sam die."

Phil's still-great timing made Ren smile. Jane's eyes followed hers.

"Frio loves you," Jane told her husband.

Sam couldn't ask whether Jane did too.

"And he shot Phil because that's what love does," Jane said. "It gets involved."

"You want me involved in this mess?"

"It's who you are."

"Yeah." Sam gulped down a sob and bundled Jane into his arms, holding her hard against him.

Ren looked over them to Jimmy, who made a quintessentially French *who knows?* shrug, and shifted to sit closer to her, his back against the metal shelving. "You remember Celeste's flogging?"

Ren frowned. "Yeah."

They both watched Jane's spine. It wasn't softening.

"Celeste's memories have been coming back to me all night, as a kind of background noise, ever since Phil's stub got distributed across Henry Lattimer's lifetime and he collected or recollected it to find me."

"You feel like holding a slalom gate to the snow," he told her. "The moment I let go, you spring back from me."

"I want to go home."

"Me too." Sam pulled her closer. "But the SWAT cops aren't going to just give up and go away."

"I know," Jane said, but she didn't relax against him. "I just need some time to work it all out in my head."

"Work it out with me."

"I don't know if I can," she said.

"Tell me what it's been like for you. Talk to me, Jane."

She pulled away again, and Sam let her go.

"I had left you." Jane took a shaky breath.

Ren didn't want to be listening, but the moment was too fragile to withstand any outside movement. Ren closed her eyes and wished she prayed. She remembered being left.

"I mean, we both knew we were in trouble," Jane said. "But I didn't realize until tonight that I was already done."

"But you said—" Sam stopped himself.

"I know," Jane said. "And I meant it. I do love you. Still. I didn't know that until tonight either."

Ren knew Sam would have said anything to get Jane to clarify right then whether she loved him or was leaving him, and have it come down on the right side. But he had asked for her experience, and he had the wisdom to wait for it. "Go on," he whispered.

"Just give me some time."

"Why?" Sam asked.

Jane looked straight at her husband for the first time Ren could remember. It made her breath catch in her chest. "Because I need it," Jane snapped.

"Why?"

"I don't know, to figure things out." Jane fidgeted like all of her clothes itched.

"What things?" Sam asked.

"Stop it!" Jane jumped to her feet.

"What things?"

"God damn it, Sam! Messy, awful, ugly things, okay?" Jane was angry, but her eyes shone huge and brilliant, not narrowed with bitterness. "Things I don't understand. Things that scare me and make my body feel too small for me."

Sam climbed to his feet without his wife's grace. If he touched her, Ren knew Jane would pull away, but she was shaking. "Things I could learn to help with?" Sam asked her.

Jane looked right at her husband, and she wasn't angry or frightened or crying anymore. She was challenging him.

"I love you," Sam said. "If 'messy, awful, and ugly' is part of your power, I'm not looking away."

Jane's eyes narrowed, summing him up, weighing what it meant to let him in.

"Unless you mean like literally ugly and stuff, because, dude . . ." It was maybe a risky joke, but he made it for the right reason.

"Well," Jane said, and she laughed.

"Okay." Sam put his arms around his wife again, and she leaned into him.

TWENTY-SEVEN

To Kill a Good Man

Kate liked having a den in the Garden she could invite people to drop by and not need to run around collecting peanut butter jars and hamster balls first. Felicia was waiting for her in an overstuffed armchair by the fireplace. "How lovely of you to do this for Matsu, Kate," she said with a smile.

"How lovely of you to come." Kate settled herself onto the sofa across from Felicia, arranging her body roughly the way it was back in Pennsylvania. "Do you think we should wait for anyone else?"

Felicia's pretty smile dimmed a bit. "Kate, you know we aren't going to get everyone."

"Of course I do," Kate said. "I'm sorry," she amended. "That sounded snippy. I didn't mean it to. It's been a blister of a day."

"Oh, Kate, it's fine."

"And you're right. We aren't going to get everyone, so there's really no point waiting, is there? Latecomers can join just as easily."

Felicia's smile picked back up, and they both reached for the mug. They laughed a little at the synchronicity, but with the way the Garden was, they could both pick up the mug and hold it in their hands, and it was still on the table. Felicia raised hers in a little toast. Kate did the same, and they drank the memory.

Here and there—Kate was herself, and she was Maud, fifty years old again, and greeting Matsu in the block-long, red-carpeted lobby of The Royal Hawaiian. It wasn't the immersion it would have been if they'd all been there, but she remembered; it came back. She was Kate, with Felicia next to her, and there was John from California, and now there was Gaston, who had been Matsu's titan last time.

I chose not to include the seed Kate played for Matsu's dust ritual because it doesn't matter for what I'm trying to show you, and because it might embarrass Kate. But I did promise complete transparency, so if you're curious, and if, by the end, you understand what I hope you will about us, you can find it. The pointer is Takamatsu_Royal Hawaiian.

—Oskar

As Kate replayed the memory, she knew why she had picked this seed: because Incrementalists don't only meddle with the world. Sometimes they fix each other, and sometimes healing hurts, as painful as recovering from third-degree burns.

It was hard to take that pain, and harder to inflict it.

But Matsu never flinched.

The seed ended, and Kate knew Wrecker was going to need her too much tomorrow to stay up grazing just for fun. Kate made a mental note to ask whether to call him Allen around his family. Then she wrote a note to Daniel on a golden Tahitian saltwater pearl and filed it in a jar. It said, "I know it's common to under-rate heroism in these times, but I have no doubt it's what you are. I was trying to preserve that, to keep you unchanged and untested, but you were right not to accept my protection. You made the decisions you had to to make things better, never mind the pain felt or inflicted. I'll do the same. I promise."

★   ★   ★

Frio needed medical attention, but taking him to any hospital in the state would call down a rain of brimstone and shrapnel on them all, so Irina was just waiting to see whether he'd take Phil up on his offer to fuck the police with their help when Jane popped to her feet on the other side of the basement, shouting, "Stop it!"

Frio tensed. Irina put a hand on his shoulder reflexively, and he didn't shrug it off.

"We really can," she told him softly. "Fuck them, or convince them, or change their minds. Your call. But you know it's time—past time—to get involved. The civilian police force in this state is already an army."

"So what were you doing, Irina?" Oskar squatted by Frio's other shoulder, his whisper erotic in its intimacy. "What were you doing to make that worse?"

Irina looked from Oskar to Frio to Phil, who was watching her from under Matsu's blond surfer hair, then back to Oskar. She sat down on her ass. "I've been building connections with an assistant police chief named Jack Harris."

"There it is. That's the countermeddle." Oskar didn't crow with satisfaction. He just looked sad, and it twisted Irina's heart almost in half.

Frio gave a dry laugh. "It'd be a tall order to make Harris worse. He's about as bad as they come."

"Really?" Oskar asked.

"Not really," Irina said.

"Frio?" Oskar was trying for poised but looked all pounce.

Frio didn't notice. "Harris has been working with the militia groups, shooting at Mexican nationals in the desert, deputizing skinheads, destroying water stations." Frio stretched out his leg and massaged it gingerly, but Irina kept the pressure steady, and after a minute, he left it alone. "The Minutemen are organized more like us now, like the Hourlies, in small cells. They're keeping a lower profile, but they're more radicalized than ever. And more people are dying as a result, especially in places like Gila Bend, where they're scaring off not just humanitarians, but law enforcement too."

"Irina?" Oskar asked, like he was handing around a serving tray.

"Not Jack," she said. "He was on the radio just last Saturday saying how lucky the militia were that his men were all too well-trained to return fire, because their shots don't miss."

Frio gave a lopsided rogue's smile. "Yup. Somehow those boys got their wires crossed out in the desert in the dark. A couple of armored-up border-watch fellas and a couple of camo-wearing deputies each thought they'd collared some smugglers. Who knows how that could have happened? But the Silver Ranger's been helping out the Nativists for at least a year."

Irina felt all the color and most of the control fall from her face. Her eyes darted to Oskar's and knew that he'd seen.

"Ol' Silver figures the feds are the biggest threat to the country, controlled by leftists, legalizing gay marriage, giving amnesty to illegals, and that the highest legitimate law enforcement official in the land is the county sheriff. So he's the one with the rightful authority, and duty, to protect citizens from any unlawful incursions by the feds." Frio shrugged. "Harris figures he's building the army that will set our nation free from federal tyranny sure as the original patriots threw off the yoke of monarchy. He says the next Concord, the next 'shot heard round the world' is going to be fired on an IRS agent by a Pima County lawman."

"That was you, wasn't it Irina?" Oskar's voice was a soft, seductive whisper against Irina's ragged cheek. "I'll bet you put *The Naked Capitalist* right in his hand. You said we had no idea how bad things are here, how much of a police state Arizona already is. This is how you knew? And you were making it worse?"

"Nobody cared," Irina whispered. "Everyone just accepted the small-town SWAT teams, the military tech, the impunity from oversight."

"So you thought you'd create another Ruby Ridge? Another Waco? The problem with the people isn't that police haven't killed enough of them. It's that they don't yet know what they can do."

The sob opened under Irina's ribs like a sinkhole. All the pegs popped, and the Irina tent went down in a heap. Without words, or even sorrow, she was just an empty ache. Her elbows dropped onto her knees. Her hands curled at her ears. She rattled with crying.

★   ★   ★

Phil looked between Irina and Oskar, and settled on the latter. "What did you say to her?" he asked.

"I asked if she remembered the Revolution." Oskar stood and walked up the stairs.

Irina's narrow back shuddered like she was being lashed. Phil took over the job of keeping pressure on Frio's gunshot.

Sam, who'd been first holding and then being held by his wife on the other side of the basement, finally looked up. "How's the leg?' he asked across the room.

"Fuck the leg," Frio said. "And fuck you."

"Frio?" Sam stood up, and Phil, who'd been about to say the leg needed medical attention sooner rather than later, said nothing instead.

"No." Frio stopped Sam before he could sit down. "No. You quit. You told me if I knew the 'why' of my life, I'd be able to stand almost any 'how.' You told me between stimulus and response there is a space, and in that space is our power to choose. In our choices lie our growth and our freedom. Then you fucking quit?"

"Frio!" Jane came over looking worried, leaving Ren to help Jimmy to his feet.

Sam didn't move. "That wasn't me, that's Viktor Frankl," he said.

"You told me despair was the only sin."

"That wasn't me either."

"It was me," Jane whispered. She turned to Sam. "You quoted me to Frio?" she asked, and Phil saw something in her settle.

"Yeah," Frio said. "He did. Then he gave up."

"He didn't," Jane said. "Not on you."

"Now this fucker want me to go double agent." Frio jerked a thumb at Phil. "Does he think I'm stupid? Crazy?" Frio scowled at Phil, who tried to keep his face blank. "He say he's not a killer, couldn't pull the trigger, wasn't cut out that way. But me?" Frio's voice dropped to a dangerous whisper. "You think I am? I was a good kid. Nobody's born this way. But we're useful, right, once we're broken, useful to fuckers like you who want bad shit done, but don't want to get broke doing it. You figure I'm a cop, I kill for them. I quit, I come kill for you, what's the difference to Frio the killer? There's a difference."

Irina lifted her head from her arms. "I never wanted anyone killed."

Her tear-wrecked eyes connected with Phil, and looked nearly as mad as Brown's. And as kind. "That's always the worst way."

"Maybe the worst," Sam said, looking away from Frio for the first time. "But the *de facto* last. As long as people, yourselves perhaps excepted—" Sam waved at Irina and Phil. "As long as *most* people have bodies that can die and feel pain, everything comes down to what you're willing to kill or die for. What you'll inflict or withstand pain to do."

"No." Phil shook his head. It had been Brown, not him, who'd said it was better that a score of bad men should be dragged out of bed and murdered than that one man who settled in Kansas to make it a free state should be driven out. "No. It's simpler than that. It's just a matter of how much can we do without hurting people. Hurting in the physical, bleeding, screaming in the ambulance kind of way. That's counter to who we are. We won't do that."

"But I will," Frio said. "So you'll use me—"

"Frio," Phil said, putting warmth and ice into his voice in equal measures. "We do not want you to kill for us. We want you to help prevent them from killing us. That's it. You have knowledge we can use. We—"

"For fuck's sake, Phil," said Irina. "Don't you get it? We're past that. There are tanks in the streets, a wall on the border, mass incarcerations, and killings based on race. But not because they want us to die, Phil. That's incidental to them. They want us to obey.

"And people do. They obey because it's easy." Irina turned to Frio. "They obey because they want to be good."

Phil remembered the fuchsia blouse, the mother, the "I love you," and he checked Frio's shoulders and jaw and recognized his moment. "Think about Santi," he told Frio. "Think about Manuel. Think about how they and the others look at you—one of their own, a kid from the barrio."

Frio clenched his teeth. "What about it?"

"You're Sam to them."

"I—" Frio started, but caught himself. "Yeah, okay," he said. "Fuck the police."

"You're a good man, Frio," Sam said, and Phil had to look away.

Frio's leg really did need immediate attention.

*   *   *

Words came back to Irina in negatives, like film developing: No. Not again. Not like this. Yes, Oskar. Of course she remembered the revolution. In revolutions, people die. People who don't get Seconds. People whose bodies are fragile, and too small to hold everything they are—everything their children and their parents love—and would bargain their own delicate shells to save. There's no market where you make that kind of exchange. And what kind of asshole would you trade with?

Irina opened her eyes and saw Sam watching her. Jane was on the floor next to him doing some kind of irritating bendy thing. Irina had known yogis before South Carolina announced its secession. They'd been stiller.

"Where is everyone?" she asked.

"Ren and Phil are helping Jimmy get Frio into the car so Ramon can stitch up his leg," Sam told her.

"Oskar?"

"I don't know."

Irina closed her eyes again.

They had been going to build a classless society in just four years. Sure, Oskar had said it wouldn't work, and Celeste had said they'd be sorry if they got involved, but people always argue with any big idea. They had gotten rid of money, abolished the free market, and dismantled all the hallmarks of capitalism. They eliminated the rich and powerful, did away with class enemies: capitalists, professionals, intellectuals, police, government employees. It wasn't even a countermeddle. They thought they were making things better.

They weren't.

No private property or religion. No rich, no poor, no exploitation. That was the plan. But nothing ever goes according to plan. Plans are squat, fickle gods whose DIY charms against despair work only on those with even shorter memories.

"America was supposed to be different," she told Sam.

"I know," he said.

"It was founded by dissidents and protesters. Now guess who gets maced and thrown out of public parks? The sanctity of the private home is baked into our earliest laws. Now the government reads our mail and watches us through our own cameras, and we the people, the same damn people, who were going to secure the blessings of liberty for ourselves and our children know about it and just figure it's okay?"

"And you were going to make things bad enough to shake us out of our complacency?" Jane asked, unfolding.

"I didn't think it'd take so much," Irina said.

"What was the plan?" Sam asked. "Once you'd gotten everyone's attention? You knew you couldn't win on the streets."

"No. We'd shift the battlefield before it came to that. Each one of us can hire an army— fund, privately, anonymously, and heavily, a counter-insurgency: EFF, ACLU, SPLC, CPJ. I put all the links on our site."

"But it got away from you?"

Guilt soaked Irina like oil into sand. Guilt for everything she'd done and left undone. "We do what we can," she said. "What kind of asshole would ask any more?"

"But what kind of asshole would do any less, right?" Sam said. "And we all do less than we can every day, don't we? I know I do. Because I doubt and I question. I'm afraid of doing too much. Or being wrong. And that's worse."

Irina wiped tears into her hair. "I thought it was Phil running the Hourlies."

"Me?"

Irina hadn't noticed Ren and Phil coming back down the basement stairs. She nodded.

"And you pushed your police friend to have me arrested?" Phil asked.

Irina nodded.

"Why?" Ren asked.

"Because he's our pivot."

"Why else, Irina?" Ren crouched next to her.

"That's all."

"No, there was something else." Ren peered into Irina's eyes. "It was me," she said.

"You countermeddled Ren?" Phil's voice went hard.

"She got involved," Ren said, like she was reading the answer from Irina's corneas. "Irina knew not having Celeste's memories made me feel apart from the group." Ren was figuring it out, explaining it to Phil, but Irina had no desire to remind them she was right there.

"As long as I had you," Ren told Phil, "it was like we were cocooned in our little nest, just the two of us, with no idea of the whole tree. I didn't understand until I had to let Oskar help me. I mean I really had to. He was the only one who knew where to look for your stub when I had to find it. I had to trust his memory of your past. It changed me."

Phil nodded Matsu's head. "It's as hard to change ourselves as it is to change the world," he said.

"And I needed to change," Ren said. Her eyes cut to Irina's. "You countermeddled me."

It wasn't a question, but Irina nodded.

"Bitch," Ren said, standing. "Thank you."

TWENTY-EIGHT

Bad Coffee to Decent Whiskey

Oskar helped load Frio into Jimmy's car, and stayed in the bar as long as he could after Ren and Phil went back down to the basement because he knew Irina wouldn't want him to see her in pieces. Then he remembered he still had Phil's car keys.

"Well, congratulations, Oskar," Irina said before he was even halfway down the steps. "You have been proven right. I tried countermeddling and it got Phil killed. I tried to fix it, but spiking Phil into Frio nearly killed them both, and led Jack Harris to Sam. Now if Jack tracks either Sam or Frio to us, it may kill all of Salt. I truly fucked things up, and you saw it coming. You must feel very proud."

I didn't. Pride is her department.

—Oskar

Oskar stepped aside to allow Sam and Jane access to the stairs. Ren put a hand on Oskar's arm. "Will you help Irina pull herself together and get upstairs?" she asked.

Oskar did not want to help Irina. He didn't want to take his eyes off her long enough to argue with Ren. He nodded to Ren and asked Irina, "Were you fucking him? The cop. Harris. Not Frio."

I wasn't jealous, I just needed clarification.

—O

"You know, Oskar, the amount of scorn you have for the persuasive power of sexual desire, or genuine affection, or hell, even simple kindness is positively puritanical." Irina, still sitting on the ground, tucked her feet under her body in a delicate curl. Oskar was vaguely aware of Phil and Ren heading upstairs after Sam and Jane.

"Honestly, Oskar. You think nothing of sneaking into a childhood memory to exploit the soft flannel smell of a stuffed bunny, but using mutual adult attraction and its physical expression is beneath you?"

"Emotions aren't currency," Oskar said. "And there's a word for sex offered in trade."

"What is that word, Oskar? Reciprocity? Maybe communication? Sex, the ultimate dialectic?"

"Exploiting sex for something other than mutual pleasure and deepened intimacy is—" Oskar stopped himself. He held out a rigid hand for the purposes of hauling Irina to her feet. "Harris is a bigoted, corrupt, brutal zealot."

"Not all the time. Not to me." Irina took Oskar's hand and stood. She looked pale, but she didn't wobble.

"Mao and Stalin wrote poetry," Oskar observed. "Franco was a wonderful grandfather. Pol Pot was every bit as much loved by his students as Sam is."

Irina's hand went over her mouth, like she could hold the heartbreak in. She shook her head. "The new face of evil isn't the new Pol Pot's, Oskar. It has no face. It's distributed. It's computer code and government agencies."

"Bullshit. Codes are coded and agencies staffed by people."

"By ordinary, fallible, not-heroic people, Oskar."

I'll grant her ordinary and fallible.

—O

"Can you fix Harris?" Oskar asked.

"No." Irina leaned against the basement wall. "I tried. He swore to me he'd called the SWAT raid off, but I think he was using me all along."

Oskar cupped her elbow and turned her to face the stairs. "Can you break him?"

"Yes, but it'd bring the whole burning roof down on Sam."

Oskar and Irina walked the rest of the way to her car in silence.

"Blackmail?" Oskar asked. "He was married."

"I don't have any proof of us." Irina leaned against her car. "A whistleblower on the inside would have power a reporter on the outside doesn't."

"We have other uses for Frio."

"All I need is the threat. I think I can get Jack to take an early retirement with that." Irina shuddered. "It's going to be an awful meddle." She fumbled in her bag for her car keys. "My penance, I guess."

I'm certain there was some way other than a countermeddle to make Ren feel like one of us, and to prove she was already, but in that moment, all I could think was how much courage it must have taken Irina. Pride is only the opposite of courage like wisdom is the opposite of rage. The one may eclipse the other, but it can also call it forth. Irina is proud, but it's the pride of survivors, not victors. It may not be productive, but it's earned. I put my arms around her on the dark street, and I kissed the top of her tangled head.

—O

"You know . . ." Irina turned her tear-stained face to Oskar. "It isn't just meddling. Or transaction. Sometimes it's nothing more than desire."

"I know," he said. "And a point of commonality."

"Oskar," Irina asked, "have you seen much of Tucson? My condo offers an excellent view."

"I'll drive," he said.

Irina reached up and kissed his mouth. "I'll let you," she said.

★   ❋   ★

Phil studied Ren's profile as they climbed up the stairs from the Crazy Horse basement behind Sam and Jane. Ren must have been aware of his eyes on her, but kept hers trained on the exit sign. Sam stopped to talk to one of the guys standing at the bar, and Jane waited with him.

"Do you know that nobody brought chocolate?" Ren told Phil as they stepped outside. "Seriously. When you got killed—doing I had no idea what down here on the Southside—and people started coming to our house, not one of them brought a box of candy. Irina came with groceries. Our friends sent flowers, and man, you should see your Facebook page, but the one thing I really wanted was one of those ridiculous, two-layer boxes with the chart of what's inside, and the chocolates in those individual brown pleated cups like tiny paper bassinets."

"Ren—"

"It's just that I would have liked some chocolate." Ren leaned against the Prius.

"I'm sorry," Phil told her. "I'm sorry I was killed, I'm sorry I didn't tell you what I was doing. I'm sorry we haven't had thirty seconds to talk until now. I'm sorry for, God, I don't even know what I'm sorry for." Phil watched Irina and Oskar come out of the bar. She was crying again, but Oskar didn't seem to be closing in for an immediate kill. "I'm sorry," Phil said again.

"I'm glad you're back," Ren whispered.

"Me too."

"It's weird to look at you, and see Matsu."

"I'll bet," Phil said. "Good-looking bastard, wasn't he?"

"Is it weird for you too?" Ren's voice was small, and she didn't look at him.

Phil reached for her hand. "Yeah," he said.

"It will be even weirder for him." Ren's fingers curled around his.

"Yeah, I can forget what I look like between mirrors, but he'll be looking right at me. It was a hell of a thing he did."

"I think he had to. We were losing you."

"Yeah."

"We can't lose you," she said. "I mean I know I have to, but *we* can't." Ren swallowed hard. "When you died," she said, "there was nothing I could do. I kept wanting to ask you, what do you do when there's nothing you can do?" She looked at him, tears bright on her cheeks. "But you weren't there and I had to do what seemed necessary, even if people didn't agree, and it might not work out."

"That's as good as any answer I've found." Phil raised Matsu's long arm and Ren stepped under it.

"You know what's funny?" she asked, nuzzling into his chest. "I think we fixed Sam. Which was what I was doing at yoga in the first place."

"I'll bet you did more than that," Phil said, and when Ren turned her face up to look at him, he kissed her until Sam and Jane came out of the bar.

Oskar and Irina were still standing by her car, so Phil gave Ren the Prius keys. "I'll go rescue Irina and drop her off at her condo," he said.

Ren nodded and got in the car. Sam and Jane piled into the backseat and Phil turned up the street just as Oskar bent down and kissed the top of Irina's head. Phil got in the Prius.

"Oskar was always more Grant at Appomattox than he'd want to realize."

"You were there?"

It took Phil a moment to realize that it was Sam who had spoken from the backseat. Phil nodded.

I object to this comparison. It was not sentiment, but genuine fellow-feeling for Irina that made me amenable to her offer, and I've had no cause to regret it since. I wanted to hear more of her thesis on what she called evil, and how it was evolving from personal, immediate, and intentional to something distributed—distant, diffuse, and altogether more insidious. And incremental.

—O

"That's . . . wow," Sam said. "Did you meet him?"

"No. But I met John Brown."

"That's incredible. Old John Brown, whose soul is marching on?"

"Yeah." Phil took in a breath and let it out as Ren pulled onto the street. "You know, he's been called both 'America's first domestic terrorist' and 'the man who killed slavery.'"

"Those aren't mutually exclusive," said Sam.

"I tried to meddle with him and I failed." Phil found himself staring at his hands. "And I very nearly shot him."

"Wow," Sam said again. "What happened?"

"I couldn't." Phil's voice sounded like the report of a Sharp's rifle. He felt Ren's hand on his arm. "I was convinced it was the right thing to do, but I couldn't pull the trigger."

Ren navigated around some slow drivers as if she'd planned for them to be there. She always drove as if everyone on the road was part of a design she'd come up with.

"Good," said Sam.

Phil looked up, and saw Sam in the rearview. "Good?"

"Yes."

"I'm not so sure," Phil said. "Brown was trying to make things better. I was too, and it put us at opposite ends of a gun."

Ren pulled into their driveway and parked behind Jimmy's Escalade next to Sam and Jane's Subaru. The front door opened, and Ramon stepped out onto the front stoop, still wearing his funeral skirt and high heels.

"How'd the ritual go?" Ren asked Ramon as they reached the front door. "You must be starving."

"It went well, I think. Nothing anomalous. And yes, I'm very hungry. Tired as well."

"How's Frio?" Sam asked.

"Sewn up and sleeping," Ramon reported.

"And ready to get to work," Jimmy added, greeting them in the living room. "Whiskey? Poire William?" he offered, waving one slender brown bottle and one squat clear one with a narrow neck and full-grown pear in its belly. "I picked up a Lagavulin and a Miclo Carafon yesterday, so Phil could raise a glass at his wake. I'd hate to have it go to waste."

"God, Jimmy," Phil said, stepping out of Jimmy's bustling range. "Were you never Irish? You can't have a wake after the funeral. What would happen if it worked?"

"Reception then," Jimmy said with a bow, displaying the lovely decanter with its prisoner pear floating in the honey-colored brandy. "Or perhaps initiation?" He raised the whiskey to Sam and Jane.

"No," Sam said. "Not for us. We're just staying in the guest room. We can't go home."

Ren came back into the living room from the kitchen, five glasses cloverleaved in her fingers. She caught Phil's eye and he nodded, and he saw her get the same affirmation from Jimmy. "We'll take care of that," she told Sam. She held the glasses out for Jimmy. "How's Matsu?"

"Sleeping." Jimmy poured. "I'll just check on him in a moment, once I've had a nip."

Ren balanced the glasses, her mouth off-center in the way it always was when she was concentrating. She handed him two glasses and smiled, and Phil's heart turned over again.

Ren carried a glass to Jane, and Phil gave one to Sam with a final, niggling clarification. "So you're of the school that thinks Brown's raid helped unify the North more than it worked to piss off the South?"

"Not really," said Sam. "I said good because if you were able to kill someone trying to end slavery, I wouldn't want to have anything to do with you. Or your group. You're not angels sent down to meddle in the affairs of men. You're human; you fuck things up."

"We do."

"Everyone does. That isn't the problem. The problem is *we* forget. You remember."

"Yes, we do," Phil said, trying to keep the bitterness from his voice. Jimmy clapped him on the back, and Phil took a seat on the sofa.

"You did the right thing, Phil," Sam said. "Or you tried to."

"And you think that's enough?" Even in his own ears, Phil sounded like he was arguing. He wasn't. "Do you think just wanting to help is enough, no matter what the results are?"

"Not enough, maybe," said Sam. "But Viktor Frankl said we should all live as if we were living a second time, and had acted wrongly the first."

"I don't think you did." Ren squeezed Phil's hand. "But he's right."

"Yes, Sam," said Jane. "You're right."

And everyone was looking at Sam, whose mouth hung open. "Was he one of you?" he asked Phil. "Frankl?"

"No more than you are," Ren told him. "But no less."

Phil looked at her hand resting over his and, as if his feet had a plan of their own, he stood up and walked out onto the back patio.

Susi was out by the pool. He looked at Phil, then wagged his tail and padded over. Phil knelt next to him, and the dog licked the tears from his face.

⋆　⋆　⋆

Daniel felt a warm washcloth on his forehead, and opened his eyes. "Thank you," he said.

"How's the head?" Ren asked.

Her eyes were kind, and if he'd become Phil, Daniel would have found it easy to love her. He brushed the thought aside. "It hurts," he said. "Like growth and grief and a boot to the eye."

Ren frowned. "Matsu?"

"He's gone," Daniel told her. "I'm sorry, but I'm certain of it. I tried to step aside during the spiking ritual, but I think Kate was holding on to him."

"Why would she do that?" Ren's fingers gripped Daniel's arm and he felt her deliberately release them.

"She didn't do it on purpose; she wanted to honor Matsu. But she never bought into the urgency to get Phil a new Second. She said everyone in Tucson was wound tight as watch springs. She didn't understand the rush."

"None of us did."

"I do now." Daniel gently closed his hand over Ren's fingers twitching on his arm. "It was you, Ren—the spiral you walked in your Garden—it sucked everybody in, or at least everyone you told about it: first Oskar, then Jimmy and Irina. It transferred to them the urgency you felt, even though they didn't understand it."

"That's not really the way the Garden works, Daniel." Fatigue hung heavily over Ren's attempted kindness.

"No, but sometimes it's how change does," he told her. "Even we don't always understand what convinces a person or a people, or how quickly acceptance is created or power lost. But we remember that it can."

Ren's smile was warm and radiant of love. Daniel didn't covet it, but

he could have. He closed his eyes against the fatigue and headache, grop-
ing for words to describe what he was seeing in the Garden, in the group,
and in the world. "It's all part of the pattern," he said.

★   ★   ★

Ren left Daniel sleeping and went outside. The patio decking was still
warm with the day's sun, but the air had cooled off and the sky felt high
and far away. Ren stood at the pool's edge watching Phil swim like the
surfer Matsu's Second had been. She had known when Phil let Susi into
the house that Phil would be in the pool and ready to talk.

He stood up in the water when he saw her.

"Since when do you swim naked?" she asked. "That's not a very Phil
thing to do."

"I know, but look at this body!"

"Yeah," she told him. "I have been."

His grin lacked both mustache and dimple, but Ren liked it.

"Think I'll have to do exercise things to keep it this way?"

"Probably," she said, dragging a chair over to the pool edge. "Maybe
we should just try to enjoy it while it lasts."

Phil snorted and rolled into swimming.

Ren watched the athletic new body, beautiful and shimmering, and
she wrapped her love for Phil, deep and permanent, around it, snug as
the water. "You know," she said as he returned from his second lap, "when
Chuck was dying, I would have done anything to keep you as him."

"Not anything, Ren."

"I don't know." Ren let the heel of one of her funeral pumps slide off
her foot so the shoe dangled from her toes. "I can be philosophical about
suffering until I'm actually in pain, then I just want it to stop. It's why
torture doesn't work."

Phil quirked a damp eyebrow. "Torture?"

"Celeste confessed to things she'd never do to make the flogging stop."
Ren shivered in the warm night, and Phil swam to the pool's edge to be
nearer to her.

"Did you ever wonder why she tried to meddle you into shooting
Brown?" she asked.

"To keep him from inciting revolt among the slaves?"

Ren stood, and stepped out of her shoes.

"To stop him from setting abolition back fifty years?"

Ren dipped one foot into the water.

"To save the lives of innocents who always die in revolutions?"

Ren looked at him steadily from the pool's edge.

Phil considered the hundreds of years he and Celeste had been on opposite sides and argued and loved each other across them.

"Celeste lacked many things," he said, "but conviction was never one of them. It was because she knew how wrong we can get things that she always advocated for inaction. She thought we were too fallible to get involved, that our highest good was to do no harm."

"I know," Ren said.

"Brown was the only time she ever pushed for my involvement, much less for violence."

"I don't think she actually wanted it." Ren pushed her fingers through her spiky hair. "It was a test."

"And I failed."

"No, she wasn't testing you. She was probing to figure out where her limits were. She found she could meddle you into trying, but couldn't convince you to pull the trigger. She had lost the power to change your mind. And by 1856, she knew it."

"And I'm just now figuring it out." Phil let out a low whistle.

Ren cannonballed into the pool.

She came up with her hair matted flat and her funeral dress stuck to her skin. Matsu laughed Phil's laugh. "Okay," he said. "So we've both changed."

"I didn't want to." Ren stood, her back to Phil, and he unzipped her sodden dress. "You died," she said, "and there was nothing I could do. I felt helpless, paralyzed." She turned back to face him.

"Grief can do that to you." Phil didn't meet her eyes. "So can self-doubt and recrimination," he admitted.

"You have," Ren said, "been carrying that on your shoulders for years without knowing it, haven't you?"

Phil nodded.

Ren threw a ball of her dress and panties onto the deck and twisted into swimming. Phil watched her for a lap before he joined her.

"Celeste's power lay in her noninvolvement," Ren said. "It was like her not-doing and not-talking—her absence and secrets—created a void we all acted around. But what if now we start turning counter-wise?"

"She'd hate that."

Ren grinned. "Celeste used the Garden's ability to collect and sift information to control and centralize it. What if we use it to do the opposite—to set it free and distribute it?"

"Like you did with Sam?"

"And you did with Frio."

"And Brown did with the slaves," Phil said.

"We'll ask the nemones to work with us. We'll be their memory and they'll help us change minds and disobey."

"We've tried that before."

"No, last time we told them who we were. This time, it's an invitation." Ren shook water from her hair. "You'll help?"

"You've been doing okay without me."

"No." Ren stood up, and the air chilled her wet skin. "I was just doing. What I did was okay. I wasn't. I was alone. It was just me, next to this big empty nothing the shape and size of where you should be. Then Oskar came, then Matsu and Kate. Then Jimmy, Irina, and Jane. Then Sam, Santi, Frio, Menzie, and Ramon. And it kept circling out until I felt all the Incrementalists here with me. And even further to include anyone who wants to be. It felt big. Spread out. Like I'd stood up and said, 'I am Spartacus,' and then everyone else was standing with me. And they were all me too."

Phil nodded. "Everyone who stood up was Spartacus. But right now, it's just you and me." Phil's hands, under the water, found Ren's wrists, then her waist. "We two." Their bodies, naked and half-submerged, came together at the waterline. Ren's arms opened and Phil's took her in.

"If we got married"—Phil's mouth was warm on Ren's wet cheek—"we'd be a single unit."

Ren watched Phil smooth his wet hair against his scalp and wind it with the same quick twist she'd seen him tie back wigs and braids. "We could do that," she said. "Wind the whole crazy spiral back to one."

"That's where it starts," said Phil.

No. One isn't where it starts. Not with "I"; with "We." Every one of us is born a nemone. We opt in to memory. Do you remember the Rev. Richard Cordley quote Phil insisted I include, the one about angels coming down and common men and women rising to sublime heights of heroism? It's not as rare as angels. It can't be. The enemy is everywhere. In 2014 we stood up and said our names out loud. Stand with us. Take our name.

It will take courage like Irina's and Dan's, and sacrifices like Jane's and Kate's. It will take wanting to be good like Frio and Phil, and real goodness like Jimmy's and Sam's. It will take a willingness to be changed like Ren or Matsu, and conviction like Celeste's or yours and mine.

Get involved. Make things better.

I've taken a big step here, and maybe it's just jumping up and down plus waving. Maybe it covers all the distance from a gunshot to an invitation. And if you accept it, from Look to Be. Yours are the hands on those machines. Think for a minute about what that means.

—Oskar